MESSIAH

Boris Starling has worked as a reporter on the *Sun* and the *Daily Telegraph* and most recently for a company which specialises in kidnap negotiation, confidential investigations and political risk analysis. He was one of the youngest-ever contestants on *Mastermind* in 1996 and went to the semi-finals with his subjects: the novels of Dick Francis and the Tintin books. Boris studied at Cambridge and currently lives in London. *Messiah* is his first novel.

MESSIAH

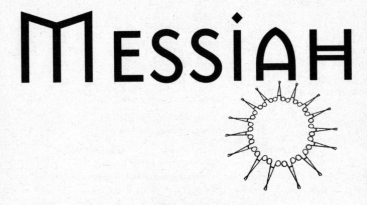

BORIS STARLING

HARPER

Harper
An imprint of HarperCollins*Publishers*
77–85 Fulham Palace Road,
Hammersmith, London W6 8JB

This paperback edition 2007

1

Copyright © Boris Starling 1999

The Author asserts the moral right to
be identified as the author of this work

Lyrics from *Fools Gold* by The Stone Roses reproduced with kind
permission by Zomba Music Publishers Ltd.
All efforts have been made to contact the copyright owners of *The Silence
of the Lambs* by Thomas Harris and *One of Us* by Joan Osborne, and all
claims will be settled in good faith.

A catalogue record for this book
is available from the British Library

ISBN 978 0 00 779130 9

Set in Weiss by
Rowland Phototypesetting Ltd,
Bury St Edmunds, Suffolk

Printed and bound in Great Britain by
Clays Ltd, St Ives plc

To my family, for all their love and support.

And to Iain, without whom this would still be on a slush pile somewhere.

ACKNOWLEDGEMENTS

There are many people whose help has been invaluable in the writing of *Messiah*. I could not have asked for better editors than Nick Sayers and Fiona Stewart, who have offered unfailing encouragement and consistently sound advice.

I am also grateful to everyone at HarperCollins, TalkLoud and PH2, for their infectious excitement and enthusiasm about the project, and to Richard Fenning, who generously allowed me to go part-time at work in order to write *Messiah* in the first place.

In terms of research, it is often said that authors should know doctors and lawyers ahead of the exponents of any other profession. I have been well served in both departments. Professor Anthony Busuttil provided fascinating insights into all kinds of medical matters, while the rest of the Busuttil family steadfastly refused to allow the above conversation to spoil their dinner. My 'expert' team of Godwin Busuttil, Toby Riley-Smith and Rory Unsworth helped me enormously in all matters legal, and at more than reasonable rates (a prawn vindaloo or equivalent each).

Many people read the manuscript at various stages, and made hundreds of helpful (and sometimes unhelpful) comments. They are too numerous to list, but they know who they are, and I am indebted to them all.

Any mistakes in *Messiah* are, of course, my own.

Messiah

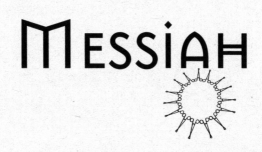

Part One

'HE WHO KEEPS HIS MOUTH AND HIS TONGUE
KEEPS HIMSELF OUT OF TROUBLE'

Proverbs 21:23

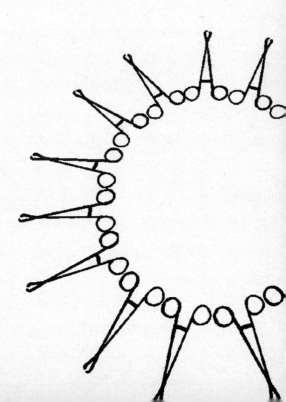

FRIDAY, MAY 1ST 1998

Red sees the corpse's feet as he walks in the door. Two bare feet leading up to bare legs hanging motionless. The line of the first-floor landing prevents him from seeing any more.

He walks through the hall, dodging a thick carrier bag with HARTS THE GROCER printed on it. Red can make out the outline of a packet of croissants and a bottle of orange juice where they press against the plastic.

The carpet is deep green, deeper and darker where a pool of blood has gathered under the corpse's feet. Red walks up the stairs, looking dead ahead. He gets a glimpse of the feet by his head on the fourth step. Five more steps before the stairs turn briefly left and then back on themselves. He won't look at the body until then, until he can see all of it at once.

He talks to himself. Make sure you have it at eye level when you first look.

Up the five steps, eyes quickly shut, turn left, swivel round, eyes open.

Red has a mental image of the body before he opens his eyes. Most hangings look the same: the corpse's eyes wide and bulging, mouth slack, tongue hanging out.

He opens his eyes, looks at the body and knows instantly that something is wrong.

With a prepared image already in his head, it takes Red half a second to work out exactly what is wrong. He goes lightning-fast through a mental checklist:

Eyes wide. Check.

Mouth slack. Check.

Tongue hanging out.

No tongue.

No tongue.

Red looks closer. What was once a mouth is now just a bloody mess, a thick red spilling from the pulp under the cadaver's nose onto his chin and chest then flowing down the centre of his torso and splattering out over his ribs.

So much blood. Looks like pints of it.

The man has had his tongue cut out.

Red runs his hand across his face and shuts his eyes. The image of the tongueless body is seared onto the inside of his eyelids, there for him to see whether he looks or not.

He takes a step to one side and opens his eyes again because he doesn't want to miss anything. A point of light sparks briefly in what's left of the corpse's mouth.

Red peers closer and sees what has caught the light. A piece of metal, wedged hard between the lower teeth and the left cheek. Shiny metal, with a rounded end. Quite small.

A spoon. A teaspoon. Peculiar.

Red has seen other murders where killers have inserted foreign objects such as cutlery into their victims, but almost always into other orifices rather than their mouths. The insertion of foreign objects is designed to be sexually degrading. This doesn't look like a sex attack. It looks like . . .

Well, Red doesn't know *what* it looks like. That's the problem.

Red leans back against the wall and looks at the body again. This time, he starts from the feet and works up.

The hairs on the corpse's legs are matted to the skin by rivulets of blood. The man has been stripped to his underpants – grey Calvins mottled dark brown – and his hands have been tied behind his back. The hanging rope runs taut from the corpse's neck to the banisters above.

Red glances at the man's face and can't even begin to imagine what he would have looked like when he was alive.

He hears movement in one of the upstairs rooms. A uniformed officer comes out onto the landing.

'Not a pretty sight, huh?' The man comes down the stairs and offers his hand. 'DCI Andrews.'

Red doesn't bother to introduce himself.

4

'What have you got?' he asks.

'We're doing fingerprints and forensics right now. The ambulance should be along in a few minutes to pick up the body and take it away for autopsy. We wanted you to look at it first.'

'Any sign of the tongue?'

Andrews shakes his head. 'Uh-uh. Chummy's taken it with him.'

'Too bad.' Red nods at the corpse. 'Who is he?'

'Philip Rhodes. Thirty-two years old. Caterer. Ran his own firm from an old converted fire station down in Greenwich. The firm does mainly big company parties. Five or six full-time employees, others hired from an agency on an as-and-when basis.'

'Who found the body?'

'His fiancée, Alison Bird. Just after seven o'clock this morning. We've taken her round the corner to Heckfield Place.'

'How is she?'

'She was absolutely hysterical when we arrived. There's a WPC doing her best to calm her down right now.'

'What's she doing? Lacing the tea with Valium?'

Andrews laughs. 'Something like that. Couldn't make it taste any worse.'

Red peels himself off the wall. 'I'd like to talk to Alison.'

'You'd be lucky to get a word of sense out of her right now.'

'Then I'll wait until I do.'

'Do you want to see any more here?'

'Not at the moment. But I'll come back later and have a longer look, when it's quieter. Can you make sure the yellow tapes stay up, and keep a constable on the door for at least twenty-four hours?'

Andrews nods. 'Sure.'

Red walks down the stairs and out of the front door, past the constable keeping guard. Half a dozen neighbours are still hanging around. Life and death in a big city. A bit of gossip for the next few days and then quickly forgotten. Red looks at the hangers-on and wonders if any of them even knew Philip Rhodes when he was alive.

He glances down the road and notices that it is almost totally symmetrical. The houses are virtually all painted white or cream, each boasting a three-sided bay window on the ground floor. Only the odd estate agent's sign breaks the uniformity of colour and texture, announcing in red on black or green on white that such-and-such a property is for sale.

A car alarm is blaring a two-tone soundtrack and a huge removal van blocks the road towards its north end. No one takes a blind bit of notice of either.

Red turns back to the young constable on the door.

'Have any press been round yet?'

'No, sir.'

'If they do, make sure that they get nothing. *Nothing*. They can talk to the neighbours all they want, but anything beyond that, refer them to Scotland Yard.'

'Yes, sir.'

Red climbs into the Vauxhall and reverses out onto the Fulham Road, waving his thanks to the taxi driver who lets him into the traffic. A nice cabbie. That *is* a turn-up for the books. Maybe today won't turn out so badly after all.

2

The traffic is gridlocked down to Fulham Broadway and probably beyond. The cars inch forward, brake lights winking angry red in frustration as they ripple down the line like luminous dominoes.

Red curses. It would have been quicker to walk.

He flicks open his mobile and dials the Yard press office. Some of his colleagues leave the media work to others, but Red likes to handle it personally. If there has to be press coverage – and there almost always does, on big murder cases – then he wants to control who says what, where and how they say it. Properly handled, the media can be crucial in helping catch a killer. Left unchecked, they can drive him underground for ever. However much the public has a right to know, that public also includes the one person with the whole story: the killer. Too much information can tell him how close the police are to catching him and prompt him to change his habits and cover his tracks.

Red glances at his watch. Not even half-past eight. Most of the press office staff won't be in yet.

The phone at the other end rings about ten times before a breathless voice cuts in. 'Pressoffice,' it says, running the words together.

'This is Red Metcalfe. Who's that?'

'It's Chloë Courtauld.'

He doesn't recognise the name. Maybe she's the blonde he's seen there a few times over the past couple of months. He knows they've hired someone new. That would explain her being in early – keen to make a good impression. It won't last long.

'Have you got a pen there, Chloë?'

'Yes.'

'Right. There's been a murder down here in Fulham. A guy called Philip Rhodes. A caterer. Lived in Radipole Road. If anyone calls, tell them that the case is being investigated and that burglary is suspected. A simple housebreaking gone wrong. Play it down. Don't sound excited about it. I'll tell you more when I get back to the Yard.'

'How was he killed?'

Red thinks for a second. 'Stall them. Tell them the autopsy's being carried out and we'll only know for certain after that. I'll be back later.'

He ends the call.

The digital readout on the dashboard tells Red that the outside temperature is already nineteen degrees centigrade. The weathermen reckon it'll be up in the high twenties by mid-afternoon. Summer heatwave, come nice and early this year. Fine if you can play Frisbee in the park all day long. Not so good if you're a slightly overweight detective superintendent poking around tongueless corpses.

It takes Red fifteen minutes to travel the quarter mile to the Fulham police station. He turns left into Heckfield Place, dodging an articulated lorry coming out of the Safeway car park at the end of the street, and parks on a double yellow line. He props his POLICE DETECTIVE sign in the windscreen and asks at the front desk for Alison Bird.

'The one whose boyfriend's just been done?' The duty sergeant looks as if this is the most exciting thing to happen all year. 'She's down in 13A. Been there about an hour now, I'd say. All over the shop, she is.' He opens the partition to allow Red through. 'Up the stairs, through the swing doors, second door on your left. Listen for the sound of wailing and teeth gnashing.'

Red finds 13A without trouble and knocks gently on the door. Footsteps inside and then the WPC Andrews mentioned appears. Red can see the back of Alison's head beyond her.

'I'm Red Metcalfe.'

'WPC Lisa Shaw.'

'How's she doing?'

'OK. Coherent, at least. Do you want to talk to her?'

'If she's up to it. How much have you gone through with her?'

'Almost nothing. I've just been comforting her, mainly. I think she's ready to answer questions now. Maybe she'd like to get it over with sooner rather than later.' Shaw opens the door wider. 'Come on in.'

Red walks in and past Alison, who looks up at him.

'Alison Bird? I'm Detective Superintendent Metcalfe. I'm so sorry about Philip.'

Alison nods mutely. Her eyes are stained dark pink from crying.

Red sits down opposite her, giving her a quick once-over as he does so. Blonde hair cut in a bob. The blonde is peroxide: her dark roots show at the scalp. Nose slightly too big for her face. Nice mouth. No make-up, and just as well. The amount she has been crying would have dislodged the toughest mascara.

'I'd like to ask you a few questions. Do you feel well enough to answer them?'

Alison nods again.

'Would you like some tea or coffee before we begin?'

'Tea, please.' Alison's voice comes out croaky from the tears.

Shaw, still standing, says, 'I'll get the tea.' She looks at Red. 'Would you like some too?'

'Coffee for me, please. Milk and one.' Red thinks fleetingly of the day's sacred first cup of coffee, abandoned half-drunk when he got the phone call from Fulham this morning.

This morning. Less than an hour and a half ago, to be precise. It seems like years already.

The door clicks shut as Shaw goes out.

'What do you do, Alison?'

Red feels like he is making small talk at a cocktail party.

'I work for a computer software company. In Reading. I'm going to be late for work.' She says this last sentence as if it has only just occurred to her. Perhaps it has, thinks Red.

'I'm sure they'll understand.'

'I've got a sales meeting at nine-fifteen. I'll never make it by then.'

Your fiancé has been brutally murdered and you worry about being late for work. Not an untypical reaction. Shock, making the voice distant and putting the mind to flight.

'Alison, I just want to ask you a few things. It'll only take a few minutes, OK?'

'Sure.'

'How long have you known Philip?'

Should be 'had', not 'have'. Shit. Alison doesn't seem to notice.

'Five years.'

'And you had been engaged for how long?'

'He proposed to me six weeks ago. March the 15th. The Ides of March. We often joke about it.'

Her turn to mix up the tenses and again she doesn't notice.

'Had you fixed a date for the wedding?'

'Yes. October 17th.'

'Can you tell me how you found him this morning?'

'I went round there early. We had an argument last night. Something trivial about the wedding. He wanted to invite someone I didn't want there.'

An ex-girlfriend, Red thinks, and I bet it wasn't trivial. He motions with his hands for her to go on.

'So I went home –'

'Home? You didn't live together?'

'No. My parents are very strict Catholics. They don't approve of that sort of thing.'

'And home is where?'

'West Kensington. Castletown Road. Not far from here.'

'Yes, I know it. So what time did you go home?'

'About ten-thirty or eleven, I think.'

'And what did you do then?'

'I went to bed, but I couldn't sleep. I was so furious with Philip. Eventually I must have dropped off because I remember waking at about four o'clock this morning and suddenly wanting to go and tell Philip that I was wrong and that he could invite

K . . . this person if he really wanted. It was *his* wedding too, after all. So I went round as early as I dared. I didn't want to wake him up at the crack of dawn and start another row. I bought some breakfast on the way from that all-night grocer opposite the hospital –' the grocery bag on the stairs, thinks Red '– and let myself in.'

'You've got your own key?'

'Yes. Of course.'

'And you unlocked the door?'

'Yes.' Puzzled.

'So the door hadn't been forced open before?'

'Ah.' She sees what he is driving at. 'No.'

'Does anyone else have keys?'

'No.'

'No one? Relatives? Friends? Estate agents? Cleaning ladies?'

'No. Philip had a cleaning lady, but he sacked her last week. He's looking for a new one.'

'And he took the key back off her when he sacked her?'

'Yes.'

'Could she have copied the key?'

'No. It's one of those Banham ones, where you can't have it copied without authorisation.'

'Right. Go on.'

'So I let myself in, and I started to go upstairs and then I saw his feet dangling there, and –'

The door opens behind Red and Shaw comes back in with her fingers curled round three plastic cups. She puts them down on the table.

Alison is mopping at her eyes, using the interruption to compose herself. Red turns to Shaw.

'Could you arrange for a squad car to take Alison back home in about five minutes? And could you ring her employers and tell them she won't be in today?'

'Sure.'

Shaw goes out again, closing the door behind her.

'She's been really nice to me,' said Alison. 'Will she be able to stay with me this morning?'

'I'm sure she will.' Red smiles. 'There's just a few more things. Going back to the moment when you found Philip's body . . . what was the first thing you thought?'

'I thought he'd hanged himself. I thought he'd killed himself because of our argument.'

'Did you think that was likely?'

'What?'

'I mean, was Philip the kind of person who would . . .' he gropes for the right phrase, '. . . who would react in such an . . . um . . . extreme manner?'

Alison winces. 'No, not at all. I mean, he was a stable person. He wasn't perpetually happy or upbeat, but he wasn't a depressive either. He wasn't like *that* at all.'

'But your first reaction was still that he had killed himself?'

'Yes, but I was . . . I was feeling guilty about the argument. I thought it was my fault.'

'So if you'd gone to see him at a time when you *hadn't* argued and found him dead, you wouldn't have thought that he had taken his own life?'

'No. I mean . . . No, definitely not. But that's the first thing you think when you see someone's been hanged, isn't it? That it's suicide. Hanging's not how people kill other people, is it?'

'True.'

'And then I saw the blood and I saw what had been done to him and . . . I don't remember very much after that, I'm afraid.'

'You remember phoning the police?'

'Yes. I remember that because I was looking at the grocery bag while I was phoning them. I must have dropped it on the stairs when I saw Philip and I noticed it while I was telling the police where to come. And I kept thinking . . . I kept thinking, if only I had been there, if only I hadn't gone away, then perhaps we could have fought him off, between the two of us.'

Red leans forward. 'Alison, if you'd been there last night when Philip was killed, the only thing that would have happened to you is that you would now be lying in the morgue alongside him. I'm sorry to be so blunt, but that's the way it is. The argument you had with him effectively saved your life.'

She looks blank. 'Oh.'

'There's just one more question and then we're through. Can you think of anyone who might have wanted to kill Philip?'

'No.' Instant response. 'He was a nice man, a good man. He didn't make enemies. No, I can't think of anyone who would have wanted to kill him.'

Red stands up. 'Alison, you've been terrific. Thank you for being so helpful. We might need to talk to you again. If we do, we'll ring you first to work out a time that's convenient. And if *you* need anything, or if you remember something which you think is important, then please feel free to give me a ring.' He hands her a card and points to the phone numbers. 'That's my number at the Yard and that's my mobile.'

He walks her out into the corridor and hands her over to Shaw, who is coming back the other way. Red and Alison shake hands, and he wishes her luck.

Poor girl. Not much fun, seeing your fiancé cut up like that. God knows what she'll be like in a few hours' time when the impact of what's happened really hits her.

Out in front of the police station now and Red's mobile is chirping. He pulls it from his jacket pocket, tugging hard as it catches in the lining, and opens it.

'Metcalfe.'

'This is Detective Inspector Robert Nixon, Wandsworth. We've got a body that we'd like you to have a look at.'

Red sighs.

'Why me?' Why me, today of all days?

'The victim's been savagely beaten, for a start. And there's a couple of things that look weird.'

'Such as?'

'It's hard to tell, but I think his tongue has been cut out.'

Red stops dead in his tracks. He exhales slowly and makes sure his voice is calm before he answers.

'You're sure?'

'Pretty sure. We haven't got too close, but his mouth is open, there's lots of blood and we can't see a tongue.'

'What's the other?'

'I'm sorry?'

'You said there were a couple of things that look weird. His tongue aside, what's the other thing?'

'There's a spoon in his mouth.'

Red tucks the phone into the crook of his neck and snatches the notebook from his pocket.

'Give me the address.'

'Wandle Road, off Trinity Road. It's the bishop's house.'

'It's *whose?*'

'The Bishop of Wandsworth. He's the one who's been killed.'

And then Red is running for the car.

3

Trinity Road runs straight as an arrow as it bisects south London. From Wandsworth Bridge it seems to stretch into infinity, where ahead of you is tomorrow and behind you is yesterday. It is down this rigid axis of tarmac that Red now drives as if the hounds of hell themselves were clinging to his exhaust pipe.

He swings right into Wandle Road just after the turn-off to Earlsfield. If Radipole Road is an example of perfect urban symmetry, then Wandle Road is quite the opposite. Houses of different styles and different colours jostle each other in line from the pavement, dark red brickwork giving way to light yellow and then onto pale blue. Two white stone lions flank the door of number 26 and arches of overhanging plants radiate from the entrance to number 32. Middle-class suburbia, just like Fulham, places where violent murder simply doesn't happen.

Nixon is waiting outside the bishop's house. Red gets out of the car and walks up to him.

'In here, sir,' says Nixon and leads Red through the hall into the living room.

The body of the Right Reverend James Cunningham, Bishop of Wandsworth, is lying in the centre of the room. Red squats down next to it and Nixon's words about a savage beating sound in his head.

'Savage' doesn't even begin to cover it.

The bishop, naked except for his underpants, has been attacked with unimaginable ferocity. In life, his fat, bloated body would probably have been pasty white, save for the sub-cutaneous eruptions of blood vessels caused by heavy drinking. In death, that very body screams angry colour: red for the blood, dark blue and purple for the bruises, brown for the streaks of shit down the legs. Sporadic patches of white

15

force themselves to the surface through this anarchic riot of hues, as if to prove that there really was once a human being under there.

Cunningham is lying on his side. His left arm has fallen across his face and the bone of the forearm sticks through the flesh where it has been broken by the force of a descending blow. The thin ring of grey hair which stretches from temple to temple around the back of his head is snarled thick with blood.

Blood. So much blood. Just as with Philip. It is everywhere on and around Cunningham: his face, his neck, his shoulders, his front and his back, and in a splattered archipelago on the floor.

Red squints down at Cunningham's face where yellow teeth ring a tongueless mouth. The spoon is clearly visible, wedged less firmly into the cheek than with Philip. Its handle rests lightly on the floor, like a line of saliva between mouth and carpet.

Red hops back onto his feet and turns to Nixon.

'Who was the last person to see him alive?'

'His brother Stephen. They had dinner together last night in a restaurant down the road. Stephen says he dropped James off here at about eleven-thirty and then drove back to his own house in Battersea.'

'Did the bishop live alone?'

'Yup.'

'Ever married?'

'No. Never.'

'Who discovered him?'

Nixon flicks through his notebook. 'A guy called Gerald Glazer. One of the vergers at Wandsworth Cathedral. The bishop was supposed to be conducting a service at seven-thirty this morning. He didn't turn up.'

'Obviously.'

'Er . . . yes. Obviously. After the service, Glazer rang here and got no answer, so he came round. The cathedral's just over there; it's not very far. Glazer knocked on the door, again got no answer, looked through the window and saw the body lying here.'

'Bit excessive of Glazer to have come round, isn't it? If I'd been him, I'd have thought the bishop had simply overslept or was ill.'

'Glazer says Cunningham hadn't missed a service in more than ten years. That's why he thought it was so unusual. Anyway, he might not have bothered if he hadn't been so close by in the first place. It wasn't exactly much of an effort for him.'

'Where's Glazer now?'

'He's at the station.'

'And Cunningham's brother?'

'Also there.'

'Have they made statements?'

'Should have done by now.'

'They weren't too shocked to speak?'

'No.'

Red thinks fleetingly of Alison Bird and wonders what she is feeling right now, back in her house with just Lisa Shaw and her memories of Philip for company.

'I'm off back to the Yard. Can you fax their statements through to me?' He gives Nixon the fax number. 'And I'll be back here later, so make sure this place is sealed off and guarded. Refer all press to Scotland Yard.'

Red turns to leave and then stops.

'By the way,' he says, 'was there any sign of forced entry?'

Nixon shakes his head. 'No. None at all. The lock wasn't broken or tampered with and all the windows were shut.'

Red nods thoughtfully and goes out to his car.

FRIDAY, FEBRUARY 12TH 1982

This is where it all starts. Under the lamppost marked REALITY CHECKPOINT, where Charlotte Logan's body is discovered by one of the university rowers on his way to dawn training at the gym. The bruising round her neck and the way her eyes spring staring wild from her face leave little doubt as to how she has been killed. Charlotte Logan, second-year undergraduate at Clare College reading natural sciences, most of her life ahead of her, is now a half-frozen strangled corpse.

Cambridge CID manages to establish everything apart from the most crucial fact of all: who killed her. They discover that Charlotte was at a house party the night she was killed and that she was seen there as late as quarter to three. No one remembers seeing her leave, let alone recalls if she left with anyone. By that stage of the evening, no one seems to have remembered very much at all.

Charlotte obviously decided to walk back to her college and never made it. She wasn't sexually assaulted and she wasn't robbed. There are no fingerprints round her neck; in the sub-zero temperatures of an East Anglian winter, anyone out in the small hours would be wearing gloves as a matter of course. It is a murder without clues and without apparent motive.

The front gate of Clare College nestles in the lee of King's Chapel at the end of a cul-de-sac. This cul-de-sac is now besieged with TV crews, photographers and reporters, all kept outside the college walls by a succession of unsmiling porters who occasionally leave their posts to escort the more vulnerable students through the gauntlet of microphones and notebooks. The officer in charge of the investigation, DCI Derek Hawkins, appears against the backdrop of brownstone walls and black metal gates three times a day and uses different euphemisms on each occasion to disguise the fact that the police are getting nowhere.

Charlotte's father Richard, who made more than twenty million pounds through the sale of his carpet business last year, offers thirty thousand pounds to anyone who can provide information which leads to an arrest and charge. One of the reporters asks him if he thinks the money can buy back the life of his daughter. No, he replies, but it might buy justice and that would be the next best thing.

It doesn't buy either. As the days haul themselves wearily through the cold, the prospects of finding Charlotte's killer begin to fade like the morning mist on the River Cam. Cambridge works and plays and laughs like it always has – it can't spare more than a short time to grieve with the Logans and with Charlotte's friends.

Red knew Charlotte vaguely, though he's not sure where or how he met her. He was a year above her, in a different college and doing a different degree. He feels sorry for her family and mildly angry at the unknown person who snatched her life away. But her death doesn't exactly turn his existence upside down.

Until a week later, that is, when he discovers who killed her.

5

The faxed copies of the statements made by Stephen Cunningham and Gerald Glazer are already on Red's desk by the time he gets back to the Yard. He skims quickly through them and finds without surprise that they haven't said anything he didn't expect.

For the officers who took their statements, Cunningham's murder is just another incident, now done and dusted. For Stephen Cunningham and Gerald Glazer, it is trauma which will last them a lifetime.

Red stretches his hands behind his head and looks at the walls. His eyes flit over the framed newspaper articles dotted around the office. A large profile from the *Daily Telegraph*, complete with a soft-focus close-up of Red looking brooding, has pride of place behind his desk. Reminders of his successes, the cases he has helped solve, the mild personality cult which so gets up the noses of some of his colleagues.

Nothing about his failures. He keeps those articles stuffed in an anonymous folder in a locked drawer. If you were to ask him where they are, he would feign ignorance, though he knows exactly where he keeps them – he can never forget them. He hoards much of what is written and what is said about him, but he chooses to display only those pieces which puff him up and make him out to be the Bruce Wayne of the Gotham City that is London.

The clock says ten-fifteen in the morning. Three hours since he got up. Two murders in that time. And one thumping headache as a result.

The preliminary autopsy reports on both bodies will be ready by lunch time. Red needs to get a team together by then. This is his baby. Red will ask for, and get, *carte blanche* to do virtually whatever he wants on this case. As long as he keeps getting results, the powers that be will indulge him in his way of doing things.

First things first: the team. He wants to keep it small, but not too small. Two people is too few. That's the way they always do it in the movies, usually with a pair of mismatched cops who grow to respect and like each other by the end of the film, but two straight lines of thinking will never connect, not at both ends. So he needs at least three minds. Three minds make a triangle, neatly joined at the corners. But three is a bad number too. It is uneven and can lead to two-on-one splits and someone feeling marginalised.

So it will have to be four. Four is just right. Him plus three. The question is, which three?

It's not just a case of who is good at their job. Everyone he will consider is good at their job. He takes that as read. Nor is it simply a matter of being able to work well in a team. What Red wants is for the people he chooses to bring different things to the party. It's not much use if everyone turns up with lager when he's asked for white wine, vodka and peach schnapps. He wants people who spark off each other because they think in different ways, so that the whole becomes greater than the sum of the parts.

Red runs his hand through his shock of orange hair, taking a clump from his fringe and twisting it down and round on itself in front of his eyes. He takes his hand away and watches the knotted hair slowly unravel. Then he opens his notebook and writes down six names in alphabetical order.

Adamson, Beauchamp, Clifton, Pritchard, Warren, Wilkinson.

He looks at the names for a few moments, twirling his pen round and round his middle finger.

First cut. He crosses out Adamson and Wilkinson, ticks Beauchamp and Clifton and puts question marks by Warren and Pritchard.

With Adamson and Wilkinson gone, he writes the remaining four names out again. Clifton and Beauchamp come first, then a line, then Warren and Pritchard, the two with question marks.

Clifton and Beauchamp definitely in. Clifton because Red has worked with him for five years now and because he's good – good enough to be Red's successor one day, perhaps. Beauchamp because she's the best woman they have, and Red wants a woman on the case – not to appease the merchants of political correctness, but because going into one of these cases without a female point of view is like having one hand tied behind your back.

Besides, she and Clifton get on well. Too well, for some people. Rumours of an affair have been floating round for a while now. Red's heard the rumours and he thinks they're probably true, though he doesn't particularly care. Clifton's a good-looking bloke, she's a nice-looking girl. They could both do a lot worse for themselves. If they're banging away like rabbits, then good luck to them.

So Clifton and Beauchamp are in, affair or not. Warren and Pritchard are borderline.

He needs just one of them. Tough call.

Pritchard has a lot of potential, but relatively few years under his belt. He's good – enthusiastic, energetic, never seems to get down or lose heart. But maybe he's too like Clifton and Beauchamp, maybe he'll just be doubling up on their strengths and weaknesses.

As for Warren . . . well, he's straight out of the old school: forty-something, hardened on the mean streets of Manchester's housing estates and jaded by too much exposure to crack pushers and teenage joyriders. He can be a joyless so-and-so sometimes, especially when he plays up to the cynical 'I've-seen-it-all' image. And he might not get on well with the other two, not least because he's got ten years on each of them.

Red reaches into his jacket pocket, opens the Marlboro packet in there, takes a cigarette and brings it out. It's a habit he's had for years – taking the cigarette out of the packet while it's still in his pocket. He can't remember where or why he started doing this. Some people accuse him of trying to avoid sharing his snouts, but that's not true. Besides, so few people smoke nowadays. More fool them. Red's seen enough autopsies to know that living in London makes your lungs go black whether you smoke or not.

The flame on his lighter flares large when he flicks the flint. He adjusts the gas until it is back to normal size and lights his cigarette.

Red thinks for ten minutes and it doesn't get any clearer. The only factor he doesn't take into account is their current work schedule. Whoever he chooses will be pulled off everything else with immediate effect. This is going to be their lives until they catch the fucker who cuts out people's tongues for fun.

He'll have to toss a coin.

Red feels in his trouser pocket and pulls out a 50p piece. Pound coins might be heavier but they aren't as wide and so don't fly as well as 50p pieces.

Strictly alphabetical order still. Pritchard heads; Warren tails.

The coin turns over and over in the air.

He catches it in the palm of his right hand, slaps it down onto the back of his left hand and takes his right hand away.

Tails it is.

6

Jez Clifton is sweating heavily as he chains his bike up in the car park underneath Scotland Yard. It is a warm morning and he has cycled hard from Islington.

His rigid cycling shoes clatter on the concrete as he walks to the basement showers. The changing rooms are empty, bar two detectives from the Obscene Publications division who are about to play squash. They look at Jez's orange vest and Union Jack Lycra shorts in mock horror.

'Fucking hell, Clifton,' says one. 'You should be arrested for that. Wearing loud clothes in a built-up area.'

His colleague laughs. Jez smiles and gives him the middle finger.

He peels off his cycling gear and steps into the shower. Even though he is still sweating, Jez runs it as hot as he can stand. Summer and winter alike, his showers have to be steaming. Jez simply can't understand those people who spend the last thirty seconds of any shower under freezing jets of water. He tried that once, and all he can remember is the feeling that his balls had retracted into his abdomen at Mach 1 and were never going to come out again.

Jez soaps the grime of the city off his body. The pollution always feels so much worse in summer, though he remembers reading somewhere that in fact it is higher in winter, when there is no hot air to rise and take the smog with it. Either way, he'd rather be cycling through London in the refreshing crispness of January than the close smoky heat of July.

He turns his head into the spray and pinches his stomach to test for fat. The summer triathlon season is only a few weeks away and Jez wants to be in good shape for the five races he has entered. With the intense narcissism of the athlete, he tenses his body hard and admires what he sees. Not bad. Not bad at all.

Five minutes is up. Jez turns the shower off, dries himself and pulls on one of the shirts hanging neatly inside his locker, yawning as he does so. He was working the four pm to midnight shift yesterday, which is why he is only arriving at the Yard at eleven-thirty, and he still feels sleepy.

Fully dressed now, he takes the lift to the fourth floor. As he walks down the corridor he can hear his phone ringing, one trill at a time. An internal call. They can wait. Callers from inside the building usually hang up after five or six rings if they get no answer. But the phone is still trilling by the time Jez gets to his office. He picks up the receiver without enthusiasm.

'Clifton.'

'Jez, it's Red.'

'Hi. Howy're doing?'

'You can have bad or fucking awful. What do you feel like?'

'I'll take fucking awful. It can't be any worse than what I'm looking at.' Jez flicks disinterestedly through the contents of his in-tray. Internal memos, conference papers, government recommendations. Another yawn.

'A tenner says it is.'

'You're on.'

'My office, now.'

'I'm on my way.'

7

Kate Beauchamp is bored out of her mind. Judging from their body language, most of the other delegates at the conference feel the same way.

She looks at her watch for the umpteenth time this morning. Eleven-twenty. At least an hour until lunch, probably more. To amuse herself, she tilts the face of her watch until she can see the outline of her head reflected in it. She still hasn't got used to her new short haircut. The shoulder-length hair she used to have framed her face and softened her features. Now her ears stick out and she looks about five years older. Her boyfriend David says the new look suits her. She's not so sure.

Kate starts to doodle on her pad. She draws the person sitting diagonally in front of her, working on the half-profile that she can see of him, and gives him a wide open mouth with big exaggerated 'Z' snores coming out of it.

Aren't conferences designed so that the interesting guys speak in the morning? Every conference she's ever been to has followed a strict pattern: best speakers first up, when everyone is still awake and interested. There'll always be a few delegates who leave during lunch, and there is some sort of tacit understanding that the second afternoon speaker will be talking to a room full of sleepers. That is the dead time, once lunch has settled in the stomach and tea is still some way off.

If this is one of the best speakers they've got, then God help the worst. He is talking about psychometric testing in a low monotone and his Dutch accent is so heavy it's largely incomprehensible. He is doing nothing which might grab the audience's attention. He has no visual aids, he doesn't move his hands and he doesn't vary the pitch or pace of his voice. Big hall, little interest.

Kate flicks through the delegate pack until she finds the

speaker's name. Rolf van Heerden. Currently representing the European Union in the Boring Olympics, and competing for a place on the world team to take on Mars in next year's All-Solar System Championships.

Kate's got a lot to do back at the Yard and here she is about to expire with ennui.

One of the conference helpers, a young woman with glasses and a green jacket two sizes too big, comes hurrying into the hall and heads for the stage. Kate watches her. Maybe she has been sent to kill Rolf van Heerden and do them all a favour.

The woman climbs the steps to the stage. Van Heerden, visibly annoyed, pauses in mid-sentence. The woman whispers something in his ear. He says something in return, low and sharp. She replies. He shrugs angrily and takes a step back. A little mime charade.

The woman leans forwards and speaks into the lectern microphone: 'Will Detective Inspector Kate Beauchamp please go to the conference organisers' desk, which is located directly outside this hall? There is an urgent phone call for her.'

Kate is so stupefied that it takes her a second or two to register that the woman is talking about her. Surprised, she stands up, grabs her handbag and edges her way along the row, squeezing past the backs of people's chairs as they pull themselves nearer the tables. A few people look at her curiously, wondering what on earth could be so urgent as to merit interrupting a speaker in mid-talk.

It's something she is wondering too. Bad news? Her mother has been ill recently. She hopes it's not that again.

The woman in the green jacket catches up with Kate at the exit to the hall.

'It's just through here.'

She directs Kate to the organisers' desk and points to a telephone with the receiver lying alongside it. Kate picks it up.

'Kate Beauchamp.'

'Kate, it's Red.'

'Hi.'

'Can you come back to the office?'

'Right now?'

'Yes, this second. It's urgent.'

'OK. I'll be there in two minutes.' She is in the conference centre opposite Westminster Abbey. Scotland Yard is a quick walk down the road.

Kate hangs up and grins. She doesn't have to sit through another forty-five minutes of Rolf van Heerden. Perhaps there is a God after all.

8

Duncan Warren cradles the receiver between his neck and his right shoulder and drums his fingers impatiently. Helen always takes a long time to answer the phone.

Little cow. She's probably keeping him on hold just to annoy him.

He knows he shouldn't let it get to him, but it does. After ten years of divorce, his antipathy towards Helen – and hers towards him – ought to have cooled into studied indifference. But it hasn't. It's still there, as strong and bitter and destructive as ever. When Duncan is spoiling for a fight, he sometimes rings Helen just for the sake of it, because he knows he'll always get a rise out of her. And if that wanker Andy who now lives with her wants to put his oar in, so much the better. At six-two and eighteen stone, Duncan knows he could kick the living crap out of Andy any time he feels like it, even if that eighteen stone is now substantially more fat than muscle.

But right now, he doesn't want to fight with Helen and he doesn't want to beat up Andy. He's got too much work to do. All he wants is to sort the weekend out and get off the phone.

Her voice sounds loud and sudden in his ear.

'Helen Rowntree.'

She took back her maiden name the minute the decree absolute came through.

'Hi. It's Duncan.'

'I know. What do you want?'

And there he is, rising like a fish to it.

'What do you think I want? To sort out arrangements for this weekend.'

'Bloody hell, Duncan. The arrangements are the same as they've always been. You pick Sam up by six tonight and you

29

have him back by six on Sunday evening. And be on time. I'm not hanging around if you're late.'

'Where are you going?'

'Mind your own business.'

He sighs. 'All right. See you at six. How *is* Sam?'

'He's fine.'

'Good. And how are you?'

'What do you care?'

From passionate love comes passionate hate. Duncan can't be bothered, not today.

'I'll see you later.'

Helen hangs up without saying good-bye. Duncan slams the receiver down and swears at the four walls of his office. The phone rings again almost instantly. He snatches it up.

'Yes?'

'Duncan, it's Red.'

'Hello.'

'Can you come to my office, please?'

'Right now?'

'Yes, right now. It's urgent.'

'This had better not involve screwing up my weekend, Red. It's my turn to have Sam.'

'Duncan, just come.'

The phone goes dead. First Helen, now Red. Both hanging up on him without saying good-bye. It must be catching.

THURSDAY, FEBRUARY 18TH 1982

It's not as if Red is expecting it. There is no preamble, no clue that it's on the way. One moment he doesn't know who killed Charlotte Logan, the next moment he does. A split second which tears his life in half.

He is sitting in his brother Eric's room in Trinity. It's late, past midnight. They've been in the college bar and now they're having a nightcap. Red's tired, and he's about to leave. He's tipsy and Eric is drunk, very drunk, not loud sing-song drunk but maudlin philosophical drunk. They're talking about this and that. And suddenly Eric says, 'I killed Charlotte Logan.' Says it with so much desperation in his voice that Red doesn't for a second doubt him, doesn't think it's some kind of sick joke. And even before Red can reply, the dam of Eric's self-control finally breaks and his confession comes flooding over his brother's head.

'I walked home with her from that party. I left just before her, but I stopped for a piss in the street and by the time I finished, she'd caught up with me. We were both shitfaced. We were weaving all over the place, half-walking and half-kissing, and somewhere on Parker's Piece she put her hand down my trousers, and . . .'

He stops dead, as if the memory of the next bit is too painful.

'Go on,' says Red softly. 'I'm listening. I'm not judging you.'

Eric swallows hard and starts speaking again. 'She laughed at me because I didn't have an erection. It was freezing cold, for fuck's sake, and I was legless. Of course I didn't have a fucking erection. But she started laughing

31

and taking the piss. She'd got her hand on my cock, and she said, "If I wanted a cigarette, pencil dick, I'd have asked for one." She kept on and on at me. I thought she was joking at first, but somewhere along the line it turned malicious. So . . . so I hit her.'

'You *hit* her?'

'Yes. Open-handed. More a slap than a hit.'

'And what did she do?'

'She hit me back. Punched me. Quite hard, as it happens.'

'And then?'

'I don't really recall. I remember reaching out for her neck, because she had a scarf on which was undone, and I remember her trying to push my arms away. And the next thing I knew, she was on the ground by the lamppost and my fingers were hurting. From the strain, I guess.'

'Jesus *Christ*, Eric.'

'I didn't know what to do. I knew she was dead. I felt for her pulse, and she didn't have one. Then I legged it. I just scarpered.'

'How the fuck have you kept it quiet so long?'

'God, it's been *awful*, Red. I don't know how I could have done what I did. I've been terrified that someone saw me and will go to the police. Every time someone's knocked on the door this past week, I've been convinced that it's the police come to arrest me. And the worst bit was that I wanted to tell someone. I almost went to the police yesterday, almost went and turned myself in.'

'Why didn't you?'

'Dunno. Lost my nerve, I guess.'

'Thought that if you tried to ignore it, it would go away?'

'Yeah. Yeah, I suppose so.'

Red takes a sip of his whisky and tries to think. Be practical or be conciliatory? He sees Eric's angst, but equally he knows that his brother has killed someone and the very thought of that revolts him. So it's easier for him to be practical, to distance himself from the scale of Eric's deed.

'You have to tell someone, Eric.'

'I *have* told someone. I've told you.'

'No. Someone official. Someone like the police.'

'No. Definitely not.'

'Why not? You almost did yesterday.'

'I know. But I didn't. I'm glad I didn't. I'm so scared by what I've done, Red, you wouldn't believe it. What I've been through in the past week has been punishment enough. I never want to suffer that again, not ever.'

Eric pauses, trying to convince himself of something. Red waits him out.

'Everything will be fine, given time,' Eric says. 'Everything will be normal again.'

Normal again. Not for Charlotte Logan's family it won't. Red gets up.

'Where are you going?' Eric, alarmed.

'Out.'

'*Where?* You're not going to tell anyone, are you?'

Red looks at his brother through weary eyes and avoids the question.

'I'm tired, Eric, and I want to go to bed.'

'You can't tell anyone. You *can't.*'

'Why not?'

'Because I'll get in trouble.'

Trouble. Talk about understatement.

'Eric –'

'Promise you won't tell anyone? *Promise?*'

Red sighs. 'I promise.'

Eric hugs him, an awkward confluence of limbs which Red wants no part of. He allows his hands the merest contact with Eric's shoulder blades and tries not to disentangle himself too obviously or too quickly.

Eric walks over to the turntable in the corner. Red moves towards the door.

'I'm going, Eric.'

'No. Hold on a second.'

'I've already told you that I won't . . .'

Eric takes a record out of its sleeve. 'Just listen to this, Red, and then you can go.'

Red sits heavily back down on the chair, humouring his brother one last time. The speakers crackle as the needle settles on the groove of the record.

String instruments, soft and soothing.

'What is it?'

Eric walks over to the door and turns off the overhead light. The music fills the darkness.

Eric's voice over the strings: 'Handel's *Messiah*. Part Two. The air with contralto. It's called "He Was Despised".'

Red can hear scuffling as Eric lies down on the floor.

'Why are you playing it to me, Eric?'

'It's from Isaiah. Chapter 53, verse 3: "He was despised and rejected by men; a man of sorrows, and acquainted with grief".'

'Eric, why are you playing it to me?'

'I played it when I got back from . . . when I got back that night. I thought it was appropriate. You're my confessor. You should hear it.'

A female voice comes in, floating away on the featherbed of strings. Holding her notes for seconds at a time, clear and unwavering. Despised. Rejected. Words drop into silence and are picked up as they fall by the merest brush of bow across violin.

Red listens to *Messiah* in the darkness for five minutes and then he gets up to leave.

By the door, Eric's chest rises and falls with the rhythm of sleep. His mouth is open and his breath has the pungent tang of whisky. Even in the darkness, Red can see that slumber has softened his brother's face, ironing out the lines of worry and pain.

Red walks over to the bed, takes the duvet off it and lays it over Eric's body. He squats down next to Eric, tucking the duvet in at the sides and around his feet to make sure that Eric is warm.

Promise you won't tell anyone?

I promise.

Red leans forward and kisses Eric on the cheek.

My brother. My baby brother. Forgive me for what I am about to do.

10

The meeting room is cramped, warm and stuffy. Red has tried to get one of the better rooms, but they are all being used. Scotland Yard is crawling with high-powered foreign delegations: one from Interpol, another from Japan and a third from Chile. God only knows what they're all doing.

Red sits at the head of the table. Jez and Kate are to his left, both looking clean and well-scrubbed. Duncan sits to Red's right, wafting tobacco tangs across the room. At the other end of the table is Professor Andreas Lubezski, the Home Office pathologist who examined Philip's body. Behind him, more than forty pictures taken at the two murder scenes are held against a whiteboard by small red magnets, like drops of blood at the corners of the photographs.

They all know Lubezski well and like him. He is a Pole who came to Edinburgh in the 1960s on an exchange scheme from the University of Warsaw and never quite got around to going back home. He was the chief pathologist at Lockerbie, where he went three and a half days without sleep while performing autopsies on more than 200 bodies. Of the thousands of cases he's carried out, it's the only one that he refuses to talk about. In 1992, the University of London offered Lubezski their Professorship of Forensic Medicine and he swapped Edinburgh for the Big Smoke and Celtic criminals for Cockney ones.

Neither Lubezski's penchant for bow ties nor the curious combination of Polish and Scottish inflections in his accent can obscure the fact that he is extraordinarily good at his job. Like Red, he tackles the horrific with the same unruffled equanimity that he brings to reading a book or driving a car. But Red suspects that this equanimity runs through Lubezski like writing runs through a stick of rock, whereas Red knows that in his own case it is barely skin deep.

Lubezski clears his throat. 'I have carried out a preliminary autopsy on the body of Philip Rhodes and I have also spoken to Dr Slattery, who conducted a similar examination of James Cunningham's cadaver.' Lubezski brandishes the piece of paper on which he has made notes of his conversation with Slattery. 'As far as it is possible to tell, both killings are the work of the same man. The signatures common to both bodies – the severed tongue, the spoon, the underpants – suggest as much. And by the phrase "the same man", I mean exactly that. The injuries suffered by James Cunningham in particular are not consistent with a female attacker. Nor are they consistent with the presence of multiple assailants.'

He pushes his chair back and walks over to the photographs on the whiteboard.

'Philip Rhodes was almost certainly killed first, if we use the measure of a drop in body heat of one and a half degrees Fahrenheit for every hour after death at normal room temperature. Philip Rhodes' body was found at around seven o'clock this morning, by which time he had been dead for at least five hours. I would put the envelope of his death at between midnight and two o'clock. James Cunningham was probably killed between three and five o'clock this morning. His body was just slightly fresher when he was found before nine o'clock.'

Red scribbles on the pad in front of him. *Rhodes killed by two o'clock at the latest, Cunningham no earlier than three.* That gives the killer at least an hour to get from Fulham to Wandsworth. Perfectly feasible by any form of transport, particularly at that time of night.

But what about the blood? London is never totally deserted, even in the dead of night. How does he get from one place to another, covered in blood, without being seen?

Lubezski goes on. 'Philip Rhodes was killed by hanging. The force of the drop off the landing broke his neck. James Cunningham, on the other hand, was quite literally beaten to death. He was ultimately killed by repeated blows to the head. Even if his head had been untouched, however, he would have died from the blows to his body within a few hours. Outside of high-impact car crashes, I have rarely seen a body which has suffered such massive internal haemorrhaging as James Cunningham's.'

Lubezski gestures at a selection of photographs depicting Cunningham's body. The same scene viewed from ten different angles, with death freeze-framed in all of them.

'I would suggest that the attacker used some sort of wooden club – perhaps something like a baseball bat. You can't see it too well here, because of all the blood and bruising, but the impact marks showed a clear pattern under autopsy. The marks are quite well-rounded. They form an ellipse with an average diameter of about three or four inches and the wider end of the marks are found towards the centre of the body. This suggests that the weapon was broader at one end, like a baseball bat. And Professor Slattery told me that they found a few fragments of wood embedded in the hair at the back of Cunningham's head.'

'Why do you think it's only one attacker?' asks Jez.

'Because most of the blows were carried out the same way. They were delivered from the same side of the body, at largely similar angles and with similar force. With more than one attacker, you tend to find blows coming from different sides and delivered with different power. In addition, there's no bunching of blows. The attacker very rarely hit Cunningham in the same place twice. Again, if you've got two or more assailants, they often pick an area of the body and rain alternate blows on it, like lumberjacks chopping down a tree. Hence the bunching.'

Red is writing again. *One killer only. Motivation?? Why change method? Why hang one victim and club the other?*

'As for the signature,' says Lubezski, 'we know quite a lot about this already. Firstly, the tongues. Both men's tongues were cut out with what must have been a very sharp knife, perhaps even a scalpel. By the look of it, our man knew what he was doing. He cut under the tongue, down each side in turn and then across the back. Rather like opening one of those suitcases with two zips which meet in the middle. In each case, the frenum – the flap which anchors the tongue to the bottom of the mouth – was sliced through and he severed three major blood carriers, including two arteries. That explains the vast amounts of blood on and around the bodies. The killer must have taken the tongues with him. There's no sign of them anywhere on the bodies or at the murder scenes.'

Red writes single words on the paper in front of him. *Tongues. Sex? Silence? Supergrass. Omerta. Secrecy. Warning???*

Duncan opens his mouth to speak, but Lubezski has anticipated the question.

'The tongues were removed while the men were still alive.'

Jez winces. Lubezski ignores him.

'If they were cut out posthumously, there wouldn't have been all that blood. The patterns of blood on the bodies and in the mouths shows us that the killer severed the arteries while they were still pumping at reasonably high pressure. In fact, the blood came out so powerfully in such a confined space that it tore flaps in the roofs of the victims' mouths.'

'What about the spoons?' asks Duncan.

'The spoons were wedged into the mouths after the tongues were removed. They're silver, not stainless steel. Forensics are working on them as we speak. I've got photographs of them if you want to trace their origin.'

Silver spoons. Obvious symbolism. Born/died with silver spoon in mouth. Resentment of the rich. Check finances.

Red draws an arrow out from the last two words, *check finances*, and then splits the arrow in two, writing *caterer* by one and *bishop* by the other. He adds some more question marks.

'As you know,' says Lubezski, 'both men were found in their underpants and both men had passed stool reflexively sometime during the attacks or in their death throes. And according to SOC, a nightshirt – unbloodied but slightly ripped – was found by the door on the floor of Cunningham's bedroom.'

Red is writing again. *Underpants. Sexual?* He links *sexual* back to the *sex* he wrote while thinking about the severed tongues. *Clothes. What did they sleep in? Pulled from beds? Hours of attack imp. – probably asleep.*

'What about sexual interference?' asks Kate.

'Absolutely none.'

Red looks up. 'None at all?'

'None. No evidence of anal penetration by any foreign object. No semen on the bodies. In fact, we haven't found anything on the bodies at all so far. No semen, no hairs, no saliva, no fingerprints, no fibres, no skin particles. Nothing. Obviously we'll do a full body examination under microscope, inch by inch. That will take a few days and might turn up something. If we *do* get something, we'll send it off for DNA testing. That will take about two weeks.

'But I wouldn't be too hopeful, especially on the fibres front. I often have cases where I can't find any unknown fibres. If the body is disturbed, or if there's a gust of wind – even one caused by something like a door opening – then the fibres get blown off and we might never find them. Remember, too, that both these men were found semi-naked, which also reduces the chance of us finding anything on their bodies. Clothing catches far more pieces of evidence than bare skin does.'

'I suppose there was nothing under the fingernails?' asks Kate. 'They might have caught a bit of the attacker's skin under there if they were trying to defend themselves.'

'Unfortunately, no, they didn't. Not in this case.'

No physical evidence, writes Red. *A pro*.

There is a knock at the door and a young woman peers hesitantly round the corner.

'Detective Superintendent Metcalfe?'

'That's me.'

'I'm Chloë Courtauld, from the press office. We've had tons of calls today and I was wondering if you wanted to do anything about them beyond what you told me this morning.'

Red clicks his tongue in his throat. All his good intentions about handling the media, and events have simply overtaken him. He clean forgot about press statements.

He stands up. 'I'll come with you now, Chloë.' To Lubezski: 'Andreas, thank you so much. You'll let me know the moment you find anything, won't you?'

'Of course.'

Red turns to the others. 'Duncan, you come with me. Kate and Jez, you go back to the victims' houses and see if you can find anything that may help us in all this. Double-check with neighbours, friends, relatives, whoever. I'll see you all back here at –' he thinks for a second, '– half-past nine tomorrow morning.'

'Does that include me?' says Duncan.

Red looks at him like he's an idiot.

'Of course it does.'

'But I've got Sam this weekend.'

'Duncan, I couldn't care if you've got the Pope and Nelson Mandela coming for the weekend. I need you on this.'

'I –'

'Save it. Come on.'

Duncan gets unwillingly to his feet. Red steers Chloë out of the door.

'Who's been calling?'

'Everyone. BBC, ITN, Sky, all the papers. They've been ringing incessantly to see if we know any more than we've told them. They've all got people down at the house in Wandsworth –'

'Wandsworth?'

'Yeah, at the bishop's house.'

'What about the one in Fulham?'

'A couple of people called early this morning, but no one since then. I didn't even know there had been a murder down in Wandsworth until I got the first call about it.' There is mild reproach in her voice.

'I didn't know there'd been one down in Wandsworth when I spoke to you, Chloë. I'm sorry. It completely slipped my mind. So nobody's interested in our Mr Rhodes?'

'They don't seem to be. They all want to know about the bishop.'

Red thinks for a moment. 'Good. Fine. Duncan will go down to Wandsworth and deal with them, and then maybe the fuckers will push off home.'

11

'Good afternoon. I'm Detective Chief Inspector Duncan Warren. I'm sorry to have kept you all waiting so long. I'll make a short statement and then answer any questions you might have.'

Duncan is standing on the pavement outside the bishop's house so the photographers and cameramen can get shots of him framed against the entrance. He looks at the expectant scrum jostling with each other to get a good angle. All told, there must be more than thirty journalists of one sort or another crowded onto the pavement and a line of cars and TV vans are double-parked in the street. Not a good day to be a resident of Wandle Road.

Duncan clears his throat. 'James Cunningham, the Bishop of Wandsworth, was found at around nine o'clock this morning by one of his staff. He had been beaten to death. We suspect that robbery may be involved.'

They are sticking to the line of a simple robbery gone wrong. That's why Duncan is handling the media: Red's face and his distinctive riot of ginger hair are too well known for anyone to give any credence to the robbery angle and, at forty-five, Duncan looks more like the traditionally solid member of Her Majesty's Constabulary than either Jez or Kate. He stands in front of the cameras like a pillar of the law, broad shoulders set back and chest swelling to fill his jacket.

'This cowardly attack on a defenceless old man occurred between three and five o'clock this morning. We would ask any member of the public who saw or heard anything between those times to come forward as soon as possible. Any questions?'

Clamour. A dozen people speaking at once, thrusting microphones and tape recorders into his face. Duncan holds up his massive hands.

'Please, please. One at a time.'

'What was taken from the house?'

Duncan almost says 'nothing', but catches himself just in time.

'At this moment in time, it's hard to tell.' He can do police speak with the best of them, using five words when one will do. 'Bishop Cunningham lived alone and there was no formal inventory of his possessions. We are going through the house as thoroughly as possible with the help of his relatives. You will appreciate that this will take some time, particularly as they are naturally distressed.'

'Do you anticipate an arrest soon?'

'We are confident that we will find whoever did this, yes.'

'What weapon did the attacker use?'

'We think it might have been a wooden instrument, something like a baseball bat.'

'What kind of person are you looking for?'

'A reasonably strong male.'

'That's all?'

'Yes, that's all so far. When we get something, you'll be the first to know.'

There is a brief silence. Duncan seizes the opportunity.

'I hope that's enough for you, ladies and gentlemen. I'm only sorry that we have so little to give you at the moment. We will of course keep you fully informed of any further developments. In the meantime, I would ask you please to leave the residents in peace now. There really is nothing more to see here. Thank you.'

He knows that they won't leave immediately. Hell will freeze over before journalists voluntarily accede to anything other than a direct police order. But Duncan reckons that they will all be gone within the hour when they realise that there really *is* nothing going on down here. Nothing that they're going to know about, anyway. If it was just an ordinary punter who'd been killed, the story would be lucky even to make the local news. But since it's the bishop, there'll be some good old-fashioned Christian outrage in tomorrow's papers – particularly the blacktop tabloids, the *Mail* and the *Express*, bleating what Middle England wants to hear.

Duncan hopes that the story will be a one-day wonder for the media. He knows that it will be a lot more than that for the four members of the team.

12

It is a few minutes before one in the morning. Towards the dead time, when those who aren't asleep are at their slowest.

Red sees no one. He walks down Jesus Lane, past the student houses on the right and the ADC Theatre on the left, big black letters prominent on the theatre's white wall. Past the Rover garage where the road starts its long gentle curve round to the right down towards Jesus College and eventually to Newmarket.

He walks alone, wrapped in the chilly cocoon of the fog. He knows where he is going, and with each stride he puts distance between himself and the man-child who sleeps the sleep of the troubled on the floor back in Trinity.

Promise you won't tell anyone? I promise.

Eric's words, his own reply, chasing each other round his head.

Red is walking past Jesus College. He glances quickly down the Chimney, the long bicycle-studded pathway which leads down to Jesus' main gate. A slab of black where the gate is shut tight. Untold wisdom behind that barrier, and all of it denied to Red, not only because of the ungodly hour, but mainly because he has to make this call on his own.

He is walking one way and his mind is moving the other.

Protection. Silence brings protection.

Shut up about it and no one will ever know. No one except Red and Eric, confidant and perpetrator. Just another brotherly secret and another unsolved murder. Today's news – tomorrow's fish and chips wrapper.

Protection.

Red envisions the alternative: Eric in custody, on trial,

going down, their parents destroyed, absolutely destroyed, unpicking every last stitch of their lives to see where they failed. Their mum trying to ignore the pain by busying herself with her obsessional tidying and their dad looking blankly out of the window at work and blankly into his glass of whisky at home. Their father's tie-making business is going down the pan already; the house is remortgaged and they sold the second car off a week ago. It's touch and go whether he can stop himself from going bankrupt as it is.

A fast track to their father putting a rifle in his mouth and their mother rolling around a padded cell.

Protection.

Red reaches the roundabout at the end of Jesus Lane.

He can't go through with this.

He starts to turn back.

The noise of an engine cuts through the fog. Two spots of light move towards him, from where he has just come, down Jesus Lane and onto the roundabout. The first thing to cross his path since leaving Eric's room.

Red stands on the edge of the pavement so he can see the car as it goes by. A Volvo estate carrying four people, skis on the roof-rack, suitcases and holdalls piled high in the back. The mother, in the front passenger seat, looks at Red as they drive past. He sees her face swivelling away from him, her mouth moving silently behind the glass as she says something to her husband and the slight smile which cracks the driver's lips as he slows down towards the roundabout. Two teenage children are in the back, the boy lolling asleep against the inside of the car door, the girl leaning forward between the two front seats.

The car is past him. Its brakelights flash briefly and then the fog swallows it up as it turns right and disappears.

A family back from holiday.

A family.

Five years down the line and that girl has just been strangled by someone who couldn't get it up through the cold and the booze, who killed her for mocking him. The boy still sleeps against the car door, but where the girl used to lean forward is now nothing, an empty space around which memories chase each other. What if that family lost their daughter? What if that family became like the Logans? Their lives shattered and not even the consolation of knowing the reason why. You lose a child and never find out who did it. Every minute of your life, you know the killer is out there somewhere, unpunished and unavenged. You see people on the streets and you wonder if any of them is the person you're looking for. All you seek is knowledge but even that is denied you.

Like Charlotte Logan's parents, if Red keeps quiet, as he promised Eric. And what if the police catch someone else? Everyone wants someone arrested and charged with Charlotte's murder. What if the police, out of desperation, get the wrong man? Red couldn't stand by, not then, not knowing that an innocent man would suffer for something he hadn't done.

And if another man was caught and charged, and it was only then that Red went to the police and told them the truth, then he would be in trouble. Perverting the course of justice. Aiding and abetting. Accomplice to murder. Random phrases, turning over and over in his mind.

The time of agonising is past. He has no choice. He must do what must be done.

Red crosses the roundabout and heads right. He walks faster now. Left onto Parker Street where bicycles stand unchained outside houses and no one bothers to steal them. Moving past the vast expanse of Parker's Piece, its grass hard with frost, the fog blotting out the lamppost in the middle which last week stood guard over Charlotte Logan's body.

Red pushes open the door of the Parkside police station and walks in. The place smells of disinfectant and a patch of floor by the far wall is wet: a drunk's vomit, swiftly cleared up. The constable in reception looks at Red over the rim of a mug of tea.

'Can I help you, sir?'

'I'd like to see whoever's in charge, please.'

The constable calls something over his shoulder and turns back to Red.

'Won't be a sec.'

Red nods his thanks.

There is a row of hard vinyl chairs. He chooses the one furthest from the patch of disinfectant and stares at the wall opposite. The pale yellow paint swirls in his vision.

Promise you won't tell anyone, Red? Promise promise promise?

A door opens to his left and a tall man with glasses and severely brushed hair appears. One of the shoulder patches on his dark blue jersey is coming off.

'I'm Sergeant Ackerman. How can I help you?'

Red stands up.

'Can we talk inside?'

'Sure.' Ackerman stands aside to let him pass. 'Just through there. First door on the right.'

The constable on reception turns to watch Red as he goes past and raises his eyebrows in question at Ackerman. Ackerman shrugs in return.

First door on the right leads into an interview room, small and spartan. Four chairs, one table, no window. Red wonders what kind of lowlife has passed through here over the years and asks himself if what he is about to do makes him lower than all of them put together.

They sit down. Ackerman looks at Red, waiting for him to start.

Last chance to turn back.

Red takes a deep breath and speaks fast, so he won't lose his nerve halfway through.

'I know who killed Charlotte Logan.'

Ackerman says nothing. His expression of tired expectancy remains fixed. Maybe he gets visits like this every night.

Red goes on.

'He's called Eric Metcalfe and he's a student at Trinity.'

There. Said it.

For the first time in the interview, Ackerman speaks.

'How do you know this?'

Red can see his own head and shoulders reflected in Ackerman's glasses. The lenses stretch his features out, putting his eyes on the sides of his head and making him look like a frog. But even through the distortion he can see the sadness in his face. A profound, inestimable sadness. Grief for the loss of a loved one.

'Eric Metcalfe is my brother.'

13

Susan isn't home when Red gets back. He is quite glad to have the flat to himself and bashes away the pang of guilt for feeling that way. He needs some time to unwind. In fact, he wants to sleep for a year. But he knows he can't, because later tonight he has to do what he hates most: take a walk round the murder scenes, all alone. This is why he has come home so early, to try and get some rest before putting himself through the mangler.

He shuts the front door behind him and goes into the kitchen. Red and Susan live on the top two floors of a three-storey building: kitchen and living-room on the lower floor, bedroom and bathroom above.

Red takes the last remaining can of Heineken from the fridge and goes through the double doors from the kitchen into the living-room, where he slumps onto the sofa. His weight sends the TV remote control skittering off the edge of the cushions and onto the floor. Too tired even to reach down and pick it up, Red sits staring at the black face of the TV.

Two bodies in one night. Quick work.

Red lights a cigarette and sips at the can's cold metal neck, hoping that between them the nicotine and the alcohol will kick-start his exhausted body.

They don't.

Red finishes the Heineken in five or six slugs, drinking it rather than sipping. He pushes himself upright and goes back through the double doors into the kitchen. Maybe food will give him energy. He finds some pasta in the cupboard above the sink and, in the fridge, some vegetables. Red and yellow peppers, avocado and cucumber. They'll do.

Red hears the main entrance door to the block of flats opening. Susan?

The door to the downstairs flat bangs shut. Not Susan. The footsteps must belong to Mehmet Shali, the record producer who lives below them.

He fills a saucepan with water and sets it on to boil. With the sharpest knife he can find, he begins to chop up the vegetables. He'll sprinkle what is left of the French dressing over them, combine it with the pasta, and kid himself that he is vaguely healthy, Marlboros and Heineken notwithstanding.

Red is always resolving to get fit again, to follow Jez's example. He used to be in good shape, back when he was young, but now he's let himself go and there are a hundred and one excuses as to why he can't – won't – try to get it back.

A city's cadence hums softly in Red's kitchen. Then the bassline starts, thumping hard from Shali's stereo through the floor and up Red's legs.

For fuck's sake, thinks Red. Today, of all days, he would like a little peace.

Red and Shali have been fighting a running battle over music levels for around a year now, during which time Red has complained to Shali or the council on at least ten separate occasions. The environmental health officers have been round twice, armed with decibel meters, and have done nothing more than send Shali a couple of warning letters.

Red has tried to sort it out amicably, without pulling rank as a senior policeman, but right now he has had enough. The tiredness clings to him like tentacles. He really can't be bothered with confrontation, but equally he can't be bothered with hour after hour of shuddering bass.

He goes out of his front door, descends the short flight of stairs to Shali's flat and leans on the doorbell. The music continues. Red jabs his finger against the doorbell again, and this time he doesn't let go until he hears an irritable 'All right! All right!' from inside.

Shali opens the door. He is wearing a lime-green silk shirt and a lot of attitude.

'Yeah?'

'Turn the music down.'

No 'please'. No 'would you mind?' A demand, not a request.

Shali's gaze slides from Red's face to his right hand and his eyes widen. Red is still holding the knife he has been using to chop the vegetables. The blade is smeared with avocado pulp.

'You threatening me with a knife, man?'

'Turn the music down.'

Shali runs his hand through the curly black hair perched at the top of his wide forehead.

'Ask nicely, and I'll think about it.'

'TURN THE FUCKING MUSIC DOWN.'

'You know what your problem is, man? You're too uptight. You need to –'

And suddenly Red is on Shali, pinning him against the wall, knife slashing across Shali's throat, Shali's eyes wide and wild with surprise, blood clinging to the avocado smears and spraying in a wide arc into Red's face and the wall behind him as the knife is driven hard through the green silk shirt and into Shali's stomach, plunging again and again and again, the bassline a shuddering soundtrack to the killing and Shali screaming high and loud and the warm goo of his intestines on Red's hands as they slither out of the grinning gash in Shali's stomach . . .

Shali is up against the wall, pinned there by a hand clenched around his neck. Red looks at the hand and from there to the arm and the rolled-up sleeve of a white shirt.

His white shirt. It is his hand holding Shali.

Red asks one more time: 'Turn. The. Fucking. Music. Down.'

Shali twists his head and shouts something into the flat. There must be someone else in there.

The music stops dead.

Silence, except for Shali's ragged breathing. No blood on the knife or the wall. No warm intestines cupped in Red's hand.

Red takes his hand away from around Shali's neck. Shali straightens his collar and goes back into his flat, slamming the door as if to reassert his machismo. Red slumps against the wall and tries to rein in the galloping aftershock.

By the time Red has made it up the stairs and back into his flat, he is shaking badly. The water is boiling, ready for the pasta. He turns the cooker off. He doesn't want to eat now.

He takes a pair of headphones lying on the table and plugs them into his stereo. Large shell-like headphones, fully encasing each ear. He presses the PLAY button on the CD player and lies down on the sofa.

The headphones are like chambers, depriving Red of all senses except sound.

The swelling start to the overture, grave and massive and laden with doom, thunders through his head. Red closes his eyes and lets the music sweep him up. He knows the entire oratorio backwards. He knows everything about it – when the music rises and falls, when the voices sing and when they are quiet, when the wind instruments fly solo and when the strings join in. The knowledge is a comfort to him.

Handel's *Messiah*. The only recording Red possesses.

14

Red flashes his ID at the constable – a different one from yesterday morning – who is guarding the door of Philip Rhodes' house.

'The crime scene's been done and dusted, I presume?'

'Yes, sir. Forensics left a few hours ago. No one's been in here since early evening.'

'Keep it that way. Good work.'

The constable opens the door and Red walks into the house. It is a few minutes after one o'clock in the morning. Saturday is barely an hour old.

Red pushes the front door shut behind him and turns on the light in the hall. Philip's body is gone and the piece of carpet at the bottom of the stairs where his blood pooled has been cut out and taken away for forensic analysis. A square of dirty grey concrete, a cold island in a sea of fluffy green, winks at Red.

He takes a few deep breaths and smooths the hair on his temples with the heels of his hands.

Silence in the house. Just like there would have been twenty-four hours ago, in the precious moments before the killer arrived.

And now Red is going to re-create the interaction between killer and victim. What were the dynamics of the brief and extraordinary relationship which existed between them? Who did what? Who said what?

If Red can re-create that, then he can go some way to finding out what his man is thinking. But he can't do it while half the police scientists in London are crawling all over the place. So he lets them get on with their jobs and, when they are gone, he comes along in the still of the night and does his.

The big hush infects Red like a virus. He looks at his notes for what feels like the hundredth time.

Motivation? Tongues. Check finances. Caterer. Bishop. What did they sleep in? A pro.

Words on a page, mocking him in their nonsense.

Why do you do it, my man? Why do you do what you do?

Red is talking to the killer, but he might equally be talking to himself.

Why do you put yourself up against these people?

He knows the answer.

Because you're good at it. You're better than they are.

Now he is talking to himself.

That's why you catch them. Even now, when you're standing in a strange house and you don't know north from south and the killer's got you all ends up, you're better than him.

Red shoves his notebook back in his pocket and slaps his cheeks.

Let's do it.

15

Philip Rhodes' house is nice enough, but it's hardly a mansion. So why the silver spoon motif, with all the envy and resentment that implies? Maybe Philip has hidden riches somewhere. Somehow Red doubts it.

Red walks slowly round the house, familiarising himself with its layout. On the ground floor are the entrance hall, kitchen and living room. On the first floor are Philip's bedroom, a bathroom and an airing-cupboard. The back door of the kitchen opens out into the garden. Red flicks on a torch and shines it through the glass pane in the door. The beam arcs across a small paved area, a barbecue and a flowerbed against the far fence.

The garden is totally enclosed. There are no passages running down either side of the house. So, if the killer comes through the garden, he would have to get there via someone else's property. Garden-hopping at one in the morning? Unlikely. This is Fulham. Someone's bound to have security lights above their back door.

Red talks to the killer, wills him into his presence. You've killed two people and so far we haven't found a trace of you. You're not going to risk tripping lights and alarms, are you? Besides, the kitchen door is locked and bolted. You don't come in through the garden. You can't. There are no side passages. So you come in from the street.

Red walks back to the front of the house and looks for streetside points of entry. On the ground floor there are only two. The front door, obviously, and the living room window.

He walks upstairs and tries not to think about the body that was hanging there yesterday morning. He turns into Philip's bedroom and walks across to the sash window. Red pulls it up halfway and peers out. He is a good fifteen feet above street level. There are no drainpipes running up the outside of the house. You'd need a ladder to get up here. And if you don't risk garden-hopping, you won't be climbing ladders in full view of the neighbours.

So you come in at ground level, through the front. Front door or living room window?

Red goes back downstairs and into the living room. The window is locked.

Would you really open the window and then relock it? Unlikely. So you come through the front door.

Red examines the inside of the door. Three locks, all fitting the same key, the middle one a deadlock. None has been tampered with or broken. That leaves three possibilities.

One, you pick the locks.

No. Time-consuming and dangerous. Too much chance of being seen or heard.

Two, you have your own key and let yourself in.

But no one has keys except Philip and Alison. And the killer's almost definitely a man.

Which in turn leaves only one possibility.

Philip Rhodes opens the door to you himself.

At one in the morning?

There is a peephole in the door. Red peers through it and sees the constable's back warped absurdly wide in the fish eye.

Philip must look through the peephole first. He surely wouldn't open the door at one in the morning without doing so. And he feels comfortable enough to open the door to you.

Someone Philip knows. Not the gasman. Not the bloke who's come to repair the TV.

If not someone he knows, then someone in trouble.

Or *pretending* to be in trouble.

Who is at the door? Who are you?

Come back to it. Whoever you are, Philip opens the door to you.

Philip's probably wearing his underpants when he comes to the door. He won't come down naked, and it's a warm night, so he won't shrug on a big thick dressing-gown.

Philip's in his underpants and he opens the door.

But you have to go back up the stairs for Philip to be hanged. And you need a plausible reason to make him go back up those stairs. You can't just hang someone against their will. You can't slip a noose on someone's neck and make them jump off a landing. They simply won't do it, not unless you're bludgeoning them into submission. And there were no marks on Philip's body, apart from where his wrists had been bound – and on his neck, obviously. No sign of a struggle.

So Philip doesn't know what's coming.

He goes back up the stairs. You're – where? In front of him? Behind him? Behind him, probably. You get to the landing and jump Philip with the noose. One end tied to the banisters and the other round his neck.

And then you push him off into space. Philip's grabbing at the rope, trying to loosen it from around his neck. But he can't. His hands are tied.

So you must be threatening him with something, if he submits to having his hands tied.

He trusts you enough to open the door. Which means he doesn't know that you have a weapon.

What have you got on you? You've got the rope, and the kni –

Of course. The knife you use to cut his tongue out. You can threaten him with that.

His hands are tied when you push him off the landing.

And when do you cut his tongue out? Before you push him off, or after?

Red walks up the stairs to the landing. He can see the abrasions on the banisters where the rope rubbed against them.

No blood on the landing. The blood is on the floor below. If you cut the tongue out before you push him off, then there would be blood all over the landing. But there's no blood.

So you push Philip off, and then . . . as he's hanging there, gasping for air . . . you lean down, reach into Philip's mouth and slice his tongue clean out.

Red feels himself rushing. He is Philip himself, a body jerking on the end of a rope.

You lean down, until you fill my entire field of vision. Your left arm is wrapped around my neck to hold me still and your right arm is forcing the blade into my mouth.

Lubezski's words: 'The blood came out so powerfully that it tore flaps in the roofs of the victims' mouths.'

Red clamps his hand to his mouth and throws up between his fingers.

16

Red can still taste the vomit in his mouth half an hour later as he walks around James Cunningham's house.

He doesn't want to do this. He wants to cut corners and say that the same thing happened at each location. But he can't say that until he knows for sure. And he can't know for sure unless he puts himself through the wringer again.

He has to treat each killing as an episode in itself. What happened to James Cunningham is related to what happened to Philip Rhodes, but is not a part of it.

Start from the beginning, like before. No way in other than through the front door. No side passages into the garden and no way up to the first floor without assistance. Just as in Radipole Road.

So the basic premise that Cunningham opens the door to the killer holds good.

Someone he knew? How likely is it that he and Philip Rhodes had any mutual friends?

Not likely at all. They were two generations apart, did different things for a living and lived in different parts of the city.

It's four in the morning and the doorbell goes.

Where's James Cunningham? In bed, of course.

Red goes upstairs to the bedroom. Cunningham sleeps – *slept* – in a large double bed. The bedclothes on the left side are rumpled with the sheets partially visible and the pillows dented. The other side of the bed is untouched. No sign of a struggle.

James Cunningham kicks back the bedclothes when he hears the doorbell. He's not dragged out of bed or attacked in this room. So why is his nightshirt found on the bedroom floor? He won't answer the door in his underpants, let alone naked. Does he sleep in his nightshirt *and* his underpants? Unlikely.

Red turns round and walks slowly back down the stairs.

It's four in the morning and the doorbell rings. Cunningham goes downstairs and answers the door. And then what?

And then he's having the shit kicked out of him on the living room floor, that's what. But somewhere along the line, he takes his nightshirt off and put his underpants on.

The images form and re-form in Red's mind. He can feel them crystallising.

Links with Philip.

The underpants. Where does Cunningham keep his underpants?

In the bedroom.

So you force Cunningham upstairs into his bedroom, where you make him put the underpants on and take the night-shirt off.

How do you force him? Easily. You're younger and stronger. And you've got at least two weapons: the club with which you hit him and the knife with which you cut his tongue out.

Red goes back up to the bedroom. He stops just inside the door and looks around.

You're in here, forcing Cunningham to get changed. He goes to the chest of drawers over by the wall and gets a pair of underpants out. Then he puts them on.

Is he naked in front of you?

He won't strip totally unless you make him. He won't want to be naked in front of you. He'll put his pants on under his nightshirt and then take the nightshirt off. And if you do make him strip totally, then why do you let him put his underpants back on before you kill him?

So he's never naked in front of you. Which means you let him have at least some dignity.

Red is standing just inside the bedroom door. If he wills it hard enough, he feels as if he can spring the bishop from his mind and back to life, right here in the room with him.

And you? Where are you during all this?

With a start, Red realises that he is standing exactly where the killer would have been standing.

You follow Cunningham up the stairs, so you enter the

bedroom after him. And you stand right by the door to make sure he doesn't escape. So why take him back downstairs to kill him? Why not just do him here, in the bedroom? Have you left the weapons downstairs? No. You've got them with you, to threaten the bishop if he gets out of line. So there's no point in taking Cunningham back downstairs.

Unless . . .

Lubezski's words run through his head: 'A nightshirt – unbloodied but slightly ripped – was found by the door on the floor of Cunningham's bedroom'.

Slightly ripped.

Red stands stock still at the door of the bedroom and waits for it to come to him.

The bishop's standing there in his underpants and he's holding the nightshirt he's just taken off.

And he *throws* it at you. That's what he does. It hits you full in the face, unsettling you for a second. And in that second, while you're pulling the nightshirt off your face, Cunningham pushes past you.

You pull hard at the nightshirt. That's why it rips. You pull it hard to get it off your face.

And Cunningham is out of the door, but he's old and fat and slow and he's going to get caught.

Red looks around him and sees it almost instantly. A splintering of wood in the door frame, at about shoulder level.

You swing at Cunningham with the baseball bat, but it misses and hits the door frame. You're quick, though. You swing again and this time you hit him. You're still on the first floor, because you hit Cunningham before he has a chance to cry out. He's still got his tongue, because there's not much blood up here.

If you let Cunningham run down the stairs, he's going to be out of the door screaming blue murder. And because he doesn't do that, you must hit him at the top of the stairs. So why take him downstairs? There's plenty of room to kill him up here.

Because . . .

Because you hit Cunningham so hard that he falls down the stairs. That's why. And there's not enough room in the hall to

62

swing a cat, let alone a baseball bat. So you take him into the living room and do him there.

The weapon rising and falling like the last scene of *Apocalypse Now*, with the bishop fat and helpless like Brando on the floor.

When do you cut his tongue out? You do it when he's alive, Lubezski said. But you can't know for sure exactly when Cunningham dies. So you do it early in the beating, when he's still demonstrably alive. And then you really go to town on him.

Sweat prickles on Red's body and not just because it's a warm night.

So now I know how you do it. But I still don't know *why*.

17

Two police cars streak silent flashes of blue through the night.

They come into Trinity Street together, then break left and right like jet fighters. One pulls up outside Whewell's Court and the other stops on the cobblestones which run down to Great Gate.

Vehicle doors open, giving the muted static of restricted radio channels. Men move with purpose; they're going to arrest a killer.

Red gets out of one of the police cars. The policemen, four in all, pull their helmets on. Red points the way.

'Third courtyard, last staircase on the left. Staircase J, room five. It's not locked.'

They nod at him and disappear through the gate.

Red sits on the low wall that runs knee-high outside Trinity and buries his head in his hands. The blue lights on the roofs of the police cars rotate lazily in the fog and their rear lights glow red on the cobblestones.

Colours. Blue for cold. Red for shame and anger and betrayal.

The gate of Whewell's Court opens again.

Eric is in between the policemen, the collar of his old tweed overcoat tucked in on itself, his eyes cast downwards and his mouth slack. The policemen have hold of his arms and Eric bumps slightly against them as they walk to the police cars, as if he is some amiable drunk about to be carted off to Parkside and left in the cells there to sober up. A minor troublemaker, rather than a murderer.

One of the officers pushes Eric's head down as he gets into the back seat of the car nearest the gate and he doesn't resist. The policemen pile in around him, two in the back and one driving, leaving the fourth to drive the other car back to Parkside.

Eric doesn't see his brother sitting on the wall ten yards away because he doesn't look up or around him even once.

Saturday, May 2nd 1998

The morning papers are spread out across the large table in the middle of the newly-commandeered incident room and every single one of them carries a story about Cunningham's murder. The *Sun*, the *Independent* and the *Daily Mail* run the story on the front page and *The Times* and *Daily Telegraph* carry obituaries in addition to the reports on their news pages.

Most of the articles say the same thing: quotes from Duncan, tributes from the Archbishop of Canterbury, comments from neighbours. They have all bought the robbery angle unquestioningly and Philip Rhodes is not mentioned anywhere. A bishop killed is news; a caterer killed is nothing.

Since it's Saturday, they have all come in casual, and since Jez is Jez, he's taken it to extremes. He turns up last, wearing skimpy running shorts and a vest.

'Fwooooooar,' says Kate. 'Fancy a bit of that.'

Jez blows her a kiss. 'Don't touch what you can't afford, love,' he says. 'Besides, you'll never catch me. I'm too quick for you.'

'Been training already?' asks Red.

'Oh yeah. Triathlons wait for no man.'

Duncan glares at Jez. 'You'd be better off getting pissed and getting laid, if you ask me.'

'And you'd be better off not stinking like a brewery, so wind your neck in.'

'Do you get laid, Jez? Or are you so in love with yourself that you never get beyond wanking?'

Red steps in. 'You two. Knock it off.'

Red knows what the problem is. Duncan resents not being able to have Sam this weekend and his anger's made worse by the greasy swells of his hangover. So he wants to lash out at someone. And Jez – bright, young, one of Thatcher's children at heart – is a good target.

Red moves to defuse the tension by getting down to work.

'I suggest we recap what we've found so far and then we can discuss any theories we have as to who and why. Anyone want to start?'

Kate is the first to reply.

'I'll start. Do you want the good news or the bad news?'

Red thinks for a second. 'The bad news.'

'We've got nothing from the scenes of the crimes themselves. Jez and I tracked back across much of the same ground yesterday, just to make sure we hadn't missed anything, and we drew a complete blank. None of the neighbours in either Fulham or Wandsworth saw or heard *anything*, as far as we can make out. If they did, then no one's talking. You know what it's like in cities – everyone just minds their own business. Someone else's problem isn't their problem.'

'What about forensics? Have they turned up anything useful?'

'No. Nothing at all.'

'So what's the good news?'

'A couple of things. First, we've got hold of the firm which made the silver spoons.'

Red raises his eyebrows.

'I *am* impressed.'

'It's an outfit in Sheffield, unsurprisingly. The Rivelin Valley Metalworks. I spoke to their general manager, Malcolm Fremantle, late yesterday afternoon.' She points to some figures on a notepad. 'The spoons come in sets of twelve, solid hallmark silver. They retail for around £250. If you want it cheaper, you can get the same stuff in silver plate for under £80. They're average prices, obviously. What individual retailers charge is up to them. Off the top of his head, Fremantle reckons that they've sold about 6,000 sets since 1989.'

'Why 1989?'

'That's when Rivelin Valley Metalworks took over the factory. They don't keep figures before that. Anyway, Fremantle's going to check what he's got and get back to me first thing on Monday.'

'Have you got a list of the retail outlets which Rivelin Valley supplies?'

'That's another thing he's promised me for Monday. But from the sound of it, they pretty much go nationwide.'

'If they've only sold 6,000 sets in about ten years, though, there can't be that many places to check.'

Kate nods. 'I guess not.'

'And also, at £250, most people buying them will have used credit cards or cheques, not cash. That should make the buyers easier to trace. Anyway . . . what's the other bit of good news?'

'That's also to do with the spoons. The silver spoon symbolism was so obvious that we checked up on the victims' finances. And guess what?'

'What?'

'Philip Rhodes had a substantial private income. We couldn't get too much detail in the short time we had yesterday afternoon, before office hours ran out on us, but we got enough to be going on with.'

She shuffles through a few papers.

'Here. Details of conversation with Philip Rhodes' father at Heckfield Place, timed at five-fifteen yesterday afternoon. He came down to London when he heard about Philip's death. Turns out the family is real old money. The parents live in some castle or other in Warwickshire. And Philip's got a massive trust fund, administered by a firm of City stockbrokers. Trust fund valued in excess of one million pounds.'

'Bloody *hell*. But he lived a pretty normal life in Fulham, didn't he?'

'Apparently he couldn't get his hands on most of the dosh until he was thirty-five. And I got the impression that Philip and his father had had some kind of disagreement over it all.'

'Why's that?'

'Old man Rhodes didn't say as much but, reading between the lines, it seems that he wanted Philip to come and run the estate. It's been in the family for hundreds of years and Philip was an only child. If he didn't take it up, it would pass out of the family when his father dies.'

'And Philip didn't want to play ball?'

'Doesn't seem so. His father kept muttering things about "making a go of his life" and "wanting to stand on his own two feet", as if they were fatal diseases.'

'But the disagreement wasn't serious enough for Philip to be cut out of the inheritance?'

Kate shrugs. 'Presumably not. Anyway, there was nowhere else for the money to go, except charity. No grasping relations or anything. I checked.'

'So that's Rhodes covered. What about Cunningham?'

'Jez looked at that.'

Red turns to him. 'Jez?'

'Yeah. I couldn't get anything substantial on him, but unlike Philip he didn't seem to be especially well-off. The clergy don't exactly get paid a fortune. I got hold of Cunningham's bank manager just before he left yesterday afternoon, though he didn't tell me anything concrete.'

'Did he think you were winding him up?'

'Oh no. He knew I was for real. I made him call me back and go through the Yard switchboard.'

'So what did he say?'

'He didn't give me exact details, but he did say that there weren't any "exorbitant" – his word, not mine – sums of money in Cunningham's account. I spoke to Cunningham's brother as well, who told me largely the same thing.'

Red spreads his palms on the table.

'Do you think it could have been mistaken identity?'

'Who knows? Could be. The whole thing's a mystery. If this guy's got a big thing against rich people, why doesn't he do their houses over while he's at it? It makes no sense. Surely he would be nicking everything in sight? And why isn't he trying the really big houses in Mayfair or Belgravia? Security's not great on some of those places. The two he's done are nothing special, are they?'

No one has an answer.

Red stands up. 'Right. That's the footwork covered.' He goes over to the whiteboard. 'I went back to the houses last night, and did a bit of thinking. The most obvious point is that there are absolutely no signs of forced entry at either location. So I reckon both Cunningham and Rhodes opened the door to their killer.'

Under the harsh white lights of the incident room, Red tells his three team members the results of his guess-work from the night before – how Philip Rhodes didn't know he was going to be hanged and that James Cunningham tried to escape. What he doesn't tell them is that he threw up from the fear of being alone with night perpetual in the houses of the dead.

'My theories are by no means foolproof,' Red concludes. 'But I reckon they're the best we've got, until we find something to the contrary. And I'm sure you've all got a pretty good idea of the kind of person we're dealing with.'

Red picks up a marker pen and draws a stick man on the whiteboard.

'Let's have some ideas.'

'White,' says Jez.

'Huh?' says Kate.

'He's white. The killer is a white man. You know the theory – serial killers rarely stray across racial lines. Whatever colour the victims are, it's more than likely that the killer will be the same.'

Red nods, and writes *white* on the board next to the stick man.

'Under fifty.' Jez again. 'I'd be surprised if anyone much older had the kind of strength that was used to pummel the bishop.'

'Well educated.' Duncan this time. 'Your average labourer isn't going to be carrying silver spoons around with him.'

'Yup,' says Red, writing it all down. 'Keep going. Kate?'

'Familiar with London. This guy must have done some kind of reconnaissance before he struck last night. He isn't some hick from the sticks. He lives in London. Somewhere reasonably central, probably.'

'So we've only got eight million people to sift through,' says Duncan. 'Great.'

'Maybe he has some kind of medical background,' says Jez. 'Lubezski said that those tongues were cut out expertly.'

'Good.' Red writes *medical?* next to the stick man and then turns back to face them.

'Why does he cut out the tongues? And why does he take them?'

'Medical experimentation?' suggests Kate. 'If he's got medical knowledge, then maybe he wants to play around with them.'

'Mmm hmm. That's a possibility.'

'It's quite a Mafia thing to do, isn't it?' asks Duncan. 'You know, against informers and the like. Cut out their tongues because they spoke when they shouldn't have. Do you think either of the victims could have been mixed up in the underworld or something?'

'Those two?' snorts Jez. 'Do me a favour.'

Duncan glares at him and again Red moves in fast.

'We don't know that for sure, Jez. We'll investigate it, like everything else.'

'OK. I'm sorry. But talking of informers, I thought of something along vaguely similar lines last night. What do we use tongues for?'

'Speaking,' says Duncan. 'Like I just said.'

'And what else?'

'Eating,' says Kate. 'Well, tasting, at any rate.'

'Exactly. Eating and speaking. Now, Philip was a caterer and James was a bishop. Philip prepared food – hence the eating – and James preached, hence the speaking. Both used their tongues in the course of their work.'

Red scratches his ear.

'That's an interesting way of looking at it. But virtually everyone uses their tongues in the course of their work.'

'Yes, but some more than others,' says Jez.

Duncan's sarcasm fights its way past his headache. 'So who's on your hit list then, Jez? Bus conductors, double-glazing salesmen, politicians, singers, actors and that bloke down by

Safeways who yells at you to buy the *Evening Standard?* That's a great start.'

'Duncan, you're not being helpful,' says Red.

'Oh, come on, Red. We're fishing in the dark and you *know* it. All this bullshit about motive is ... well, bullshit. It's not going to get us anywhere.'

'So what do you propose we do?'

Duncan leans back in his chair and looks around the room. 'Pray.'

19

They leave Eric in the cells for two hours before questioning him, partly to soften him up and partly to allow DCI Hawkins to come in and handle the interrogation personally.

The interview takes more than an hour and a half and Eric does not cry once. Nor does he scream or shout or smirk or demand to see a lawyer. He doesn't bluster or try to maintain his innocence. Eric answers Hawkins' questions quietly and politely, even if he does spend most of the interview looking at the floor. In fact, he acts more like the survivor of a car crash than the man who until a few hours ago was the city's most wanted criminal. He seems broken.

In spite of himself, Hawkins almost feels sorry for Eric. It is a fleeting emotion which he stamps on hard. But it is definitely there, tugging at his shirt-tails as he gets up from the interview room and walks down the corridor to find a cup of tea and a charge sheet.

At a quarter to nine in the morning, Eric Metcalfe is formally charged with the murder of Charlotte Logan.

20

Interlude

They find nothing. Absolutely nothing.

Jez and Kate check the list of Philip Rhodes' friends and James Cunningham's friends, but no name appears on both lists. They examine everyone who might have come into professional contact with either man and again there is no match. Only in death do the two men have a connection. Why did the killer pick those two, in a city of millions?

Question after question after question and no answers to any of them. The only positive thing they come up with is a nickname for the killer, whom they christen 'Silver Tongue'.

Duncan handles the lists of those who bought the spoons. Of the 6,000 sets sold, fewer than 500 were bought in the Greater London area. They trace and interview every single buyer. Most of them have their sets fully intact. A few say that they have given the sets away as gifts to relatives or friends. These in turn are all checked and found to be bona fide. Two people say that their credit cards were stolen and used to buy the spoons (among other things). The credit card companies confirm this and add that they have reimbursed the victims. Four people say that they lost the sets when their houses were burgled. Police reports and insurance claims verify this. Eleven people bought their sets outside Greater London but then moved into the area. They are all interviewed and cleared.

The psychological profilers come up with little more than Red and his team managed with the stick man on the whiteboard. The FBI's renowned Behavioral Science Unit is too busy to lend any men: it is working flat out on a big case in Gary, Indiana, which has the dubious honour of being not only America's most violent city but also the hometown of the Jackson Five. Officials deny that the two are related. And besides, Silver Tongue has only killed two people so far. According to the FBI, you need five victims to be officially classified as a serial killer.

The media lose interest with predictable rapidity. The follow-up calls slow to a trickle and then dry up altogether barely four days after James Cunningham's body was found. No journalist in the country seems to know that Philip Rhodes even existed, much less care that he was killed.

Red, Jez, Duncan and Kate chase their own tails. They keep looking until they don't know which way is up any more. They go over the same ground time and again, doubling back down alleys they know are dead ends and finding that every new line of enquiry becomes a cul-de-sac almost before they have even started.

And all this time, Red is no nearer to understanding *why*. Two murders in a day and then nothing. Red wonders why Silver Tongue hasn't struck again. Maybe he has been picked up for another unrelated crime and is currently in custody. Maybe he has died or gone abroad. Or maybe he is just there, biding his time, watching and waiting and taunting them with his silence. He hasn't made any effort at communication. No notes or telephone calls or faxes or e-mails. No demands for cryptic messages in the classified advertisement pages or via the teletext services on TV.

Nothing.

Red remembers the case of Colin Ireland, who in 1993 killed five homosexuals before he was caught. Ireland *did* contact the police. He told them that he was going to kill one homosexual a week until he was caught. Red remembers it well. He also remembers the appeal they made to Ireland: 'We need to speak to you. Enough is enough. Enough pain, enough anxiety, enough tragedy. Give yourself up – whatever terms, whatever you dictate, whatever time.'

But they can't make such an appeal, not in this case. Silver Tongue hasn't called, so they can't talk to him directly. And the killings aren't public knowledge, so they can't appeal to him through the media.

No contact. The silence stretches out ahead of them. A week. A fortnight. A month. Two months. The relentless sledgehammer heat continues without a break. Every day, they take their sandwiches to St James' Park and sit under the same tree, turning things over in their heads, and every day they are no closer to finding Silver Tongue when they go home than they were when they arrived at work that morning.

On July 1st they take bets on whether they will get to August 1st – exactly three months after the murders of Philip Rhodes and James Cunningham – without another death. They each put £25 in the pot. Jez and Kate reckon they'll make it unscathed, because they will get a lucky break and nail their man. Duncan hums and haws and then decides to go with them, more because he thinks Silver Tongue has gone to ground than because he thinks they'll catch him.

Only Red says that Silver Tongue will kill again before August.

So Jez, Kate and Duncan stand to make £33.33 each if no one else is killed, and Red stands to take the whole one hundred pounds if someone is. Kate says it is unfair that the three of them will get such a small return on their wager if they win. Red points out that the odds are stacked in their favour – or at least *they* all think so, otherwise they wouldn't have staked their money against him.

Red wins.

SATURDAY, JULY 25TH 1998

James Buxton isn't answering his doorbell.

'I'm *sure* he said twelve-thirty,' says Caroline.

'He may have just popped out to the shops for a sec,' replies Rupert. 'We could always go to the pub and try again in half an hour.'

'No, Rupert. All those pubs down by the river at Putney will be heaving by now. We won't be able to get a seat outside for love nor money and it'll be roasting inside. Anyway, it's *very* unlike James to be late. He'll be here soon.'

'I'll try ringing.' Rupert fishes in his pockets. 'Damn. Forgot my mobile. You haven't got 10p, have you?'

Caroline opens her purse and sifts through the shiny silver pieces. 'No, only 20ps.' She hands him one. 'I think there's a pay phone round the corner. There, just beyond that telephone pole.'

Rupert turns to go and then stops. He peers myopically down the street at a man carrying four bags of what look like heavy shopping, holding them away from his body so that they don't knock against his legs with the motion of his walking.

'That's Nick, isn't it?' he says.

Caroline follows his gaze. 'Yes, I think so.' She raises her voice. 'Nick. Nick!'

Nick Buxton raises the shopping bags in his right hand to waist height in what passes for a wave and quickens his step. When he reaches them, he is out of breath and a trail of sweat drips down from in front of his left ear.

'Bloody hell, I'm out of shape,' he says, leaning down to kiss Caroline on both cheeks. 'Caroline. How lovely to see you.'

He turns to Rupert and pokes his middle finger out from

under the handle of the carrier bags by way of a handshake. 'Rupert, old boy. How the devil are you? And what are you two doing standing out here like a couple of waifs and strays?'

'We're supposed to be having lunch with your brother, but he isn't in,' says Caroline.

'He isn't? I'm sure he said he'd be here. Mind you, I've only just got back from the country.' Nick gestures with his head to the holdall slung over his back. 'Thought I'd pick up the shopping on the way home. Bloody hot, isn't it?'

He off-loads two of the shopping bags onto Rupert and opens the door. The hallway is dark and cool. Rupert and Caroline follow Nick up the stairs to the first-floor flat. Nick puts the shopping bags on the sideboard in the kitchen and wipes his brow.

He calls out for his brother. 'James? James? Rupert and Caroline are here.'

No answer.

Rupert wrinkles his nose as he puts the two shopping bags he was carrying on the kitchen table.

'Funny smell in here.'

Nick, halfway out of the kitchen, looks over his shoulder. 'Probably James. You know what soldiers are like. Bet he hasn't washed in a month.'

They walk into the living room.

And then Caroline is screaming and screaming and there is a thud as Rupert hits the floor in a dead faint. Nick just stands there, and he knows that the image he is seeing will haunt him for ever.

22

Red speaks softly into his dictaphone.

'James Buxton. Caucasian male. Twenty-four years of age. Army officer, Coldstream Guards. Body found shortly before 1300 hours by brother Nicholas and two friends. No sign of forced entry anywhere in flat.'

He moves closer to the body, pressing the dictaphone hard up against his mouth. The black plastic casing brushes his lips as he speaks.

'Cadaver has been decapitated. Head found lying approximately two feet from rest of body. Body stripped to underpants, lying on left side. Hands have been tied behind back.'

He pauses, and adds the unbearable.

'Tongue has been cut out and silver spoon placed in mouth.'

Red looks up over what is left of James Buxton.

'Blood has sprayed across far wall by fireplace. Blood pooled on floor around body.'

He switches off the dictaphone and swivels slowly through a full circle.

It is a nice room, tastefully decorated and furnished. The deep pink wallpaper is studded with antique prints of hunting and fishing and the curtains are tied back by tasselled straps. It looks like an advertisement for Liberty.

Red wanders over to the magazine rack by the TV set and runs his eyes along the row of spines: *Tatler, Harpers & Queen, Horse and Hound, The Field, Top Gear, What Car?* The typical interests of the British landed gentry, he thinks – society balls, killing small animals and driving fast cars.

He pokes around the rest of the flat. James' bedroom is impeccably neat and his bed has not been slept in. Red looks at the photo collages on the walls and finds James' face in most of them. James standing ramrod straight in regimental uniform;

James grinning drunkenly at a black-tie dinner. It is a pleasant and happy face.

And now it is lying on the floor in the next-door room with no tongue.

23

'What happened to Caroline?' asks Nick.

'We got a GP in to authorise sedating her,' says Red. 'You saw how hysterical she was.'

'And Rupert?'

'Shell-shocked. We've got an officer with him now.'

'He fainted when he saw the body, you know.'

'Yes, I know.'

Nick looks out of the window onto the Upper Richmond Road, where the traffic is gridlocked and the exhaust fumes darken the brickwork of Putney police station still further.

If you didn't know, you wouldn't say that Nick and James were brothers. They looked nothing like each other. James had a strong jaw and a crooked nose; Nick's chin seems to disappear seamlessly into his neck. Brother unlike brother. Nick and James. Red and Eric. Red tries not to think about that.

He flicks the lid off his pen. 'Ready?'

Nick turns his head back towards Red, and nods.

'When was the last time you saw James?'

'About two or three weeks ago, I think. When he last came down to London.'

'And you were supposed to meet him in the flat today?'

'Yes, for lunch. I'd been away doing a job in Newmarket, and only got back this morning.'

'What sort of job?'

'I'm a security consultant. We were doing a counter-terrorism audit on a couple of offices up there.'

'And how long had James been in the flat?'

'Oh, only since last night.'

'Do you know what time he got in?'

'Well, I rang him on his mobile at about half-ten and he was in the pub. So any time after that.'

'Which pub was he in?'

'The Star and Garter,' he said. 'It's one of those down by the river.'

'I know it. Who was he with?'

'A couple of friends. I've got their details if you want.'

'Please.'

Nick pulls a diary from his pocket and turns to the address section at the back where he has handwritten a long list of names and phone numbers. He points to two. Red writes them down.

'You don't know if they went on anywhere after the pub?'

'I wouldn't imagine so. Not too late, anyway.'

'They wouldn't have gone to a nightclub?'

'No. James didn't like nightclubs. The only place they might have gone after the pub was to a curry house.'

'And after that, they'd have gone their separate ways?'

'Yes.'

Red does the mental calculations out loud. 'So . . . pub shuts at eleven, twenty minutes drinking-up time, then another hour or so for a curry, a few minutes' walk back to the flat . . . He wouldn't have been home much after one at the very latest.' Half a statement, half a question.

'I guess.'

'Anyway, I can get all that from the people he was with,' Red pauses. 'Nick, the next questions I'm going to ask you may seem a little strange. Please believe me when I tell you that they *are* relevant and that they might be vital in helping catch whoever killed your brother.'

'Sure.'

'Who lived in the flat?'

'James and me.'

'And who owned it?'

'We did, jointly.'

'You shared a mortgage?'

'No, we bought it outright.'

'With what?'

'Money from a trust fund.'

82

'Are your parents rich?'

'That depends on what you mean by "rich".'

Nick is not being confrontational, merely seeking clarification, and Red recognises this.

'OK. In conventional terms, would you say your parents are rich?'

'I guess so.'

'What does your father do?'

'He's a banker.'

'Is he successful?'

'He's a partner in a big City firm. Pretty successful, I would think.'

'Is he a millionaire?'

'Well – on a good day, if his shares go up, then probably.'

'Mmm hmm . . .'

Silver spoon. Silver spoon fits here, like it did with Philip. But not with James Cunningham.

Red steeples his fingers. He lets his mind roam back to what he observed at the Buxtons' flat.

James' body, stripped to his underpants.

James' head, cut clean off.

Pictures of James on the wall, young and friendly and hopeful.

Something about the pictures.

The pictures were arranged in collages and stuck behind glass frames. The kind of collages that people make of themselves and their friends.

Something about the pictures.

Red almost has it. He lets it come to him like he let the image of James Cunningham in his nightshirt come to him, knowing that it will flee if he tries too hard to grab it.

The people in the pictures.

He's got it.

The people in the pictures were almost all men. There must have been about one hundred photos on James' wall and only a fraction had any women in them.

Red looks intently at Nick. He wants to see Nick's reaction to what he says next.

'Nick?'

'Yes?'

'Was James homosexual?'

'No. No, of course not.'

'Not even a little bit?'

'What do you mean, "a little bit"? Either you are or you aren't.'

Or you're bisexual and double your chances of pulling on Saturday nights.

'I mean, had he ever had any homosexual experiences?'

'No.'

'You're sure?'

'Yes.'

'Absolutely positive?'

'Yes!'

Half a shout. Definitely a lie.

'Nick, you're lying. I know you're lying.'

'I'm *not*.'

'You are. You know how I know? Because you haven't asked *me* the most obvious question of all.'

'Which is?'

'*Why?* Why do I think that James was homosexual? If there's no reason to think that he was, then the first thing you'd want to know is how I came to a wrong conclusion.'

'I'm telling you. My brother was straight.'

'Then why are all the photos on his walls of men?'

'I don't know. He had lots of friends.'

'Male friends?'

'Yes.'

'What about girlfriends?'

'Do you mean friends who are girls, or actual girlfriends?'

'Both.'

Nick swallows. His eyes plead with Red not to keep on with this line of questioning.

It's not such a taboo, thinks Red. It's not like I think your brother was a paedophile or a cannibal or anything.

'Nick ... I need to know. You're not betraying James'

memory. If we're going to catch the person who did this, then you have to tell me everything you know, no matter whether you think it's important or not. There's a lot you don't know about this whole thing and there's a lot I can't tell you. But please just trust me.'

Nick looks down, then back at Red and raises his hands in what looks like a gesture of surrender.

'OK. James wasn't very good with girls. I mean, he had the odd fling here and there, but none of them lasted very long. The longest relationship he had was about six weeks, I think. He wasn't very comfortable with girls. Oh, he'd join in all the beery lads' behaviour – you know, whoorrrr, get your tits out, boasting about his conquests, that kind of thing – but his heart wasn't in it. That kind of carry-on really wasn't his bag.'

'But was he homosexual?'

Nick's answer comes circuitously, via the scenic route.

'You've got to remember that James was in the army. That's all he ever wanted to do, be a soldier. He never wanted to be anything else. Not a racing driver or a Test cricketer or anything. Just a soldier. Right from when he was about ten years old, I think. And he wanted it so much – *so* much – that he tried to push all other doubts to the back of his mind.'

'Doubts about what? His sexuality?'

'Yeah. He . . . um . . . experimented at school.' Nick's fingers describe apostrophe marks around the word 'experimented'. 'I don't think it was very serious. I'm sure half his year were up to it. But James was terrified that people would find out, that people in the army would find out.'

'How many people did he experiment with?'

'Oh. Just one.'

'Who was he?'

'Who was who?'

'The person James experimented with.'

'Someone called Justin Rizzo.'

'And what does Justin Rizzo do now?'

'He's dead. He was killed in a car crash in his year off.'

'Oh.'

Red takes a Marlboro out of the packet in his pocket and lights it. He squints at Nick through the smoke.

'So, would it have been that important, if someone had found out about James and Justin?'

'Of course. They'd have thrown him out of the army, wouldn't they? The army's not exactly queueing up to admit gays, is it? Bad for morale and all that. And even if they hadn't thrown him out, they'd have made his life hell. James was a damn fine soldier. He didn't need to take any shit from something that happened years ago.'

'How many people know this?'

'Just me.'

'You're the only one he ever told?'

'Yes.'

'Not your parents?'

'Shit no. Dad would have hit the roof. No, I'm the only one James told. So *please* don't mention this to anyone.'

'Nick, I can't promise you that. It might be crucial.'

'But –'

Red holds up his hand.

'What I *will* promise is that no one will ever know it came from you. I'll pass it off as my own suspicions. We've got enough already to have worked this out off our own backs.'

Nick's eyes widen in murky comprehension.

'You think that the guy who did this was . . . You think it was some sort of gay thing?'

'I don't know. But equally, I don't know that it wasn't.'

24

On the phone to Parkside after breakfast, Red listens to Hawkins sucking his teeth before deciding that Red should break the news about Eric to their parents in person. Informing the next of kin of deaths, accidents or arrests is usually a job for the police, but Hawkins agrees that these are exceptional circumstances.

Red is just about to hang up when he hears Hawkins wish him good luck. He mumbles a surprised and inarticulate thanks and it takes him three attempts to replace the receiver in the cradle.

The fog has cleared as Red walks across Great Court, and in its place has come an unbroken vault of azure sky against which the spires and crenellations of Cambridge's colleges stand in magnificent sharpness. A crisp winter's morning, with cold and sun combining to cleanse the souls of those who go about this day as if it is any other.

For Red, this day is already seven hours old and it will never be like any other.

It takes him fifteen minutes to reach Grange Road where he keeps his battered grey Mini Metro. Students aren't allowed to keep cars at Cambridge without official permission, but Red has ignored this rule since he started his final year last October. He leaves his car on Grange Road because there are no parking restrictions there, and because the only figure of vague authority likely to see him is the groundsman who tends Trinity's playing fields.

It takes Red less than half an hour to get from Cambridge to his parents' home in the village of Much Hadham. He comes down the village high street shortly before ten o'clock, and suddenly he hates this place where he lives. He hates the Middle England smugness that Much Hadham not only embodies but actively embraces: the black-beamed white Tudor houses which dot the roadside, the twee petrol stations which are so small that they seem three-quarter size, the sign which boasts this is HERTFORDSHIRE'S BEST-KEPT VILLAGE. Stinking, selfish, hard Tory lives, secure in their own comfort and oblivious to the rage beyond their well-trimmed lawns.

Red imagines the effect which Eric's arrest will have on the village and his knuckles tighten white on the steering wheel. He pictures the gossip over coffee in the mornings and over evening beer in the pubs: two-faced harpies revelling in the drama and the excitement and the Metcalfes' shame, offering help that they know they will never have to give, confiding to one another that they always knew, *always*, that something was wrong with that boy.

Robert and Margaret Metcalfe live just beyond the village, in the first house after the road sign signalling the resumption of the national speed limit. Red pulls into the drive and almost collides with his father's Rover as it inches out beyond the gate.

His father winds down the window. 'Red! What a surprise. Bloody lucky you didn't hit me there. Are you staying long? I'm in a bit of a hurry, but I'll be back sometime this afternoon.'

Dear Dad. Ever the genial optimist, even though his business is going down the tubes. The four-minute warning could be going off and he'd still be making sure that everyone was fine and dandy for G&Ts. Red leans out of his window.

'Dad, I need to talk to you. You and Mum.'

'Can't it wait? I've got a meeting with my bankers in the City at half-eleven and I'm worried that they're going to foreclose on my debts unless I come up with some good excuses pronto. They've already started muttering about receivership. It really is vital that I get there in time.'

'Dad . . . something's happened.'

The pain must show clearly on Red's face because he sees consternation arch his father's bushy eyebrows.

'What? What's happened?'

'Is Mum inside?'

'Yes. Yes, of course she is. What's happened, Red?'

'I'd rather tell you both together.'

'What is it? Are you OK? Has something happened to Eric?'

'Dad. *Please*.'

Red drives over the gravel, right up to the parking space outside the larder window. His father lets him go first, and then reverses alongside him. They walk into the house in silence.

Red's mother is ironing in front of the TV in the kitchen. She gives a little gasp when she sees her son and steps out from behind the ironing board to embrace him.

'Margaret.' Her husband's voice. 'Red's got some bad news.'

She stops a few feet short of them, looking uncertainly from one to the other.

'What? What's happened?'

Red pulls out a chair from under the kitchen table.

'Sit down, Mum. You too, Dad.'

They sit obediently, like dogs waiting for food.

Red doesn't know what to say, so he just starts at the beginning. He is standing absolutely stock still, so that the only parts of his body moving are his mouth and his eyes. He keeps his hands pressed hard against the fabric of his trouser pockets and he does not sway on his feet.

It takes Red twenty minutes to recount the story in its entirety. The only thing he leaves out is his promise to Eric that he wouldn't tell anybody. Otherwise, he tells them everything – Eric's confession, *Messiah*, the walk to the police station, the arrest, the charge. He doesn't know what to spare them, so he spares them nothing.

Red watches his parents all the way through his mono-logue. He sees his mother's hand go to her heart and stay there, as if her touch is the only thing that keeps it beating. His father, shaking his head slowly from side to side and murmuring, 'My God. My *God*,' under his breath. Tears slide out from under his mother's eyelids and run down her face until she licks them from her lips. Decent people, ordinary people who don't deserve to have their lives shattered in this way.

There is silence when Red finishes, measured in the aeons spanned by the second hand of the wall clock.

'Where did we go wrong?' asks his mother, more to herself than anyone else.

'Mum . . .'

'Never mind that.' His father, trying to be authoritative. 'Never mind where we went wrong. The question is, what can we do now?'

'There's nothing we *can* do, Dad.'

'Nothing? There must be something. We can see Eric, presumably?'

'I don't know. We'll have to check with the police.'

'But he's our *son*,' wails Margaret. 'We have to see him. It's our . . . *right* to see him. Isn't it?'

'Mum.' Red puts his hand on hers.

The scrape of chair leg on linoleum as his father gets up.

'Got to phone the bank. Tell them I can't make it.'

'Robert! Is that all you can think about? You and that bloody bank! Your son's just been –'

Red presses his hand harder down on his mother's.

'Let him go, Mum. Dad's right. He should get that out of the way first.'

Before all this really sinks in, thinks Red, but he doesn't say it.

They watch Robert walk out of the kitchen, his back held straight against the pulverising force of shock, and hear his voice from round the corner as he speaks on the telephone.

'Michael? Robert Metcalfe here . . . Very well, thank you. And yourself? . . . Excellent, excellent . . . Listen, something's come up here . . . No, that's right . . . I'm afraid I won't be able to make it ... Something quite serious ... Can we reschedule when this is all cleared up? ... Yes, that's very kind ... No, not at all ... Thank *you* ... Good-bye.'

Robert comes back into the kitchen. He slumps in his chair and rubs his hand over his eyes, exhausted from keeping up even that most shallow of acts on the telephone.

Red's parents look at him.

'What are we going to do, Red?' asks his father. Not a request for advice. A plea for help.

His mum and dad, shell-shocked beyond the capacity to decide. Red is now the parent to them, protecting them where once they had protected him, making choices as they had for him when he was a child. Red and Eric, both men of action in their own ways, blazing trails and setting off events which rage through the cosy world of Robert and Margaret Metcalfe like a hurricane. Parents dependent upon their elder son, to help them deal with what their younger one has done. Red sees their helplessness and knows that he must not let them down.

'We're going to leave here, right now, and go back to Cambridge. You're going to book into a hotel under false names, and ...'

His father's voice cuts him off.

'Red, I owe the bank thousands of pounds. The house is remortgaged already and I'm about this far away from bankruptcy.' He holds his thumb and middle finger a millimetre apart. 'Where are we going to find the money for a hotel?'

His father's bonhomie is gone now, as the magnitude of what is happening seeps slowly through.

'Dad, we haven't got a choice. The press are going to find out about Eric any minute now and then they'll be down here like a shot. This place will look like Piccadilly Circus by lunch time. You won't be able to blow your nose without them reporting it. You have to leave. *Now*.'

'I'm not going to let some bloody ... *reporters* trample

over this place. I'll stay here. I'm not going to some hotel.'

Robert's token attempt at defiance is pathetic in its futility. Red puts a hand on his father's shoulder.

'It doesn't have to be a smart hotel, Dad. There are plenty of B&Bs around which will be perfectly adequate. You can check into one of those and then we can find out about seeing Eric. But you are not going to stay here. We'll ask the police to come and keep an eye on the house.' He looks at his mother. 'Mum, why don't you go and throw some things in a suitcase?'

She nods vaguely and shuffles out of the room. Father and son sit in the kitchen, listening to the noises from upstairs as she packs.

Ten minutes later they are heading back to Cambridge in the Rover. Red is at the wheel, because right now he doesn't think either of his parents could even make it to the front gate without crashing.

25

Monday, July 27th 1998

'Took his head off with one swipe? Woh woh WOH. Nice shooting, Tex.'

Jez is leafing through the scene-of-crime photos taken in James Buxton's flat. He keeps his knees clamped tight together so that the autopsy report won't slide between them and onto the floor of the car. The warm air from outside blows gusts on Jez's face as Red keeps the Vauxhall at a steady eighty-five. On the opposite carriageway, a four-mile tailback snails towards London.

Lubezski's report says that the killer probably used an actual sword to decapitate James. The line of separation was very sharp and there was no trace of sawing or hacking – which there would have been if the head had not been severed cleanly.

Just one clean swipe and off with his head.

Jez scans the typewritten words. There is little in there that he couldn't have guessed at himself. Tongue cut out and spoon inserted before death. Rub marks on knees suggest that James was kneeling at the moment of decapitation. Time of death estimated at between two and four o'clock in the morning. No signs of forced entry into the flat. No signs of sexual interference.

Jez tucks the photos inside the report and turns to Red.

'Well, Mr Metcalfe, it seems congratulations are in order. You are one hundred pounds richer this morning than you were on Friday.'

Red grimaces.

'It's one hundred pounds I'd rather not have, if you must know.'

'So you're not going to take it?'

Red smiles.

'Now, I didn't say *that*, did I? One hundred pounds is a hundred pounds. And it's especially satisfying to take it off you fuckers. But seriously, I'd willingly give it up – and more – for any hint of a decent clue in this case.'

'And you think going back to see Alison Bird is going to help?'

'I don't know. It's worth a shot, especially in view of what James' brother told me.'

'Which James?'

Red glances sharply across at him.

'Fuck me. I hadn't thought of that. I was talking about James Buxton, but I suppose it could just as well have been James Cunningham. They've both got brothers, haven't they? No, I meant Nick Buxton. Anyway, I tried to get hold of Stephen Cunningham. He's on holiday for two weeks.'

'You think it's something to do with the name James?'

'Could be. But then why was Philip Rhodes killed?'

'Maybe his middle name was James. Can you remember?'

'Not off the top of my head, no, and I haven't got the file with me. We'll ask Alison when we get there.'

Red nods towards the big blue sign on the grass verge. 'This is our junction.' He indicates left and cuts across into the slip lane.

'So what *did* James Buxton's brother tell you?' asks Jez.

'He said that James experimented with homosexuality at school.'

'So?'

'So maybe Lubezski's wrong about this not being a sex case.'

'What, just because one of the victims indulged in a bit of teenage experimentation? Do me a favour. Anyway, none of the bodies have been interfered with.'

'That need not matter. Look at it this way. The underpants bit has always puzzled me. Let's assume that our man is gay, or thinks that he *might* be gay. Either way, he's a bit of a prude and sexually inadequate to boot. He gets off on watching these guys undress in front of him. Maybe he makes them take all their clothes off and parade round before they put their pants back on. Maybe he talks dirty to them. He likes to watch, but he doesn't try anything else. He can't get an erection. He's impotent. He just watches them and then he kills them. Hence the lack of sexual interference.'

'Sounds pretty thin to me.'

'To me too, but we haven't had many better ideas, have we?'

'You still haven't explained how the tongue and the spoon fit in.'

'The spoon I'm stuck for, granted. Philip Rhodes and James Buxton fit the bill on that front, because they both had some sort of private income. But not the bishop. He's never been rich by anyone's standards. So either we assume that the bishop was killed in a case of mistaken identity, or we're barking up the wrong tree. And loath as I am to admit it, I think the latter is true.'

'OK. What about the tongues?'

'If this is some sort of sex thing, then there's any number of reasons why he might take the tongues. If he makes them suck him off or something like that, then he won't want to risk some trace of his semen or skin being left there.'

'But you just said you thought he was impotent.'

'Correct. Which is why I've all but discounted the idea that he makes them do things to him. And anyway, cutting the tongue out wouldn't necessarily destroy evidence left elsewhere in the mouth or in the stomach. So let's rule that out. Look at it from another angle. Tongues are used for kissing. Tongues are a sign of intimacy. You don't kiss prostitutes, do you? You just shove your cock in them and be done with it. But if Silver Tongue thinks that he can get intimate with these people before he kills them, then he might regard the tongue as a symbol of that intimacy. Which means he might take their tongues with him, to keep and look at. And if he's impotent, then tongues represent just about the level of his experience. So it makes sense on that front.'

'What about the bishop?'

'From what I can gather, he was more asexual than anything

else. But gay clergymen are ten a penny. If Silver Tongue *thought* that Cunningham was gay, then that might have been enough.'

Jez thinks of Cunningham, fat and bloated and repulsive in death. 'I don't see how even the most hardcore pervert could have found *him* attractive,' he says.

'Jez, we're talking about a bloke who cuts people's tongues out while they're still alive and shoves spoons in their mouths. He's not exactly short-listed for the Nobel Peace Prize.'

'But why does he change the method of killing, when he keeps other things constant? Why did he hang one and beat another and behead the third? *Why?* It doesn't make sense.'

'I know. I know it doesn't make sense. But I still think the gay angle is worth pursuing.'

'I don't buy it. But you're right on one thing.'

'What's that?'

'We haven't got any better ideas.'

They have made good time. The traffic is usually light coming out of London in the morning rush hour, barring the occasional snarl-up around Heathrow or at the junction where the M4 meets the M25. It has taken them barely forty-five minutes to get from Scotland Yard to the outskirts of Reading.

'So we're going to ask Alison Bird if her late fiancé was gay?' says Jez.

'Yup.'

'Oh, good. She *is* going to be thrilled. What a way to kick off Monday morning. We should have our own TV show. Start the week with Metcalfe and Clifton. Give Richard and Judy a run for their money.'

He pulls out Alison's card from his pocket and reads it out loud.

'SoftCentre. Computer software products.' He snorts. 'SoftCentre. What a dreadful name.' He dials the number on his mobile and scribbles down the directions which the receptionist gives him.

'Well, I don't feel great about barging in on her like this either,' says Red once Jez has hung up.

They lapse into silence and think of what lies ahead. Not only are they going to rake up embers from the past which Alison probably wants dead and buried, but they also know that the office – any office – is the worst place for the police to interview someone. Once the police arrive, you can't move for sly looks and furtive nudges among your colleagues.

Red wanted to interview Alison at home over the weekend, but her flatmate had said that she was away on a business trip all weekend and was going straight to the office from Heathrow on Monday morning. No, she didn't know what flight Alison was coming in on. No, she didn't know exactly where Alison had been either. Somewhere in Scandinavia, she thought, but she couldn't be firmer than that. Was this really the police?

They wanted Kate here too, in case Alison needs handling with kid gloves, but Kate has gone into hospital for a check-up. Women's things, she told them, and they didn't push for more details. She's due back at work this afternoon but, since time is of the essence, they haven't waited for her. Duncan has volunteered to stay and man the phones back at the Yard.

SoftCentre House is a blue glass building in the middle of a business park, all gleaming fountains and shiny cars parked neatly in designated spaces. Red and Jez pick their jackets off the back seat of the Vauxhall and step out into the sun. Another day of mind-numbing heat in store, sapping their energy and frying their brains.

The reception is air-conditioned and pleasantly cool. Red gives their names to the receptionist but doesn't say that they are from the police. He wants to spare Alison that, if possible. Telling the receptionist would be like broadcasting it on Radio 1.

'Is Miss Bird expecting you?'

'No, she isn't.'

The receptionist opens her mouth to say something, but Red cuts her off.

'Just get her, please.'

She hits four digits on a phone and speaks into it.

'Alison? It's Lorraine at reception. A Mr Metcalfe is here to see you.'

Lorraine looks puzzled as she listens to the reply, then turns back to Red.

'Can I ask what it's in connection with?'

Red leans over the reception desk's high counter and grabs the receiver.

'Alison? It's Redfern Metcalfe here. We met in . . . somewhat unfortunate circumstances a few months ago. I wouldn't have come here if it wasn't important . . . Yes, yes, that's exactly it . . . Thank you very much.'

Red hands the phone back to Lorraine.

'She's on her way down,' he says.

Jez laughs at this impromptu role reversal. Lorraine looks even more puzzled than before.

Red and Jez sit on the sofa in reception. Red flicks through the copy of the *Daily Telegraph* provided, while Jez straightens his legs in front of him and massages his hamstrings.

Red looks up.

'Do you ever stop?' he says.

'Stop what?'

'Exercising. Tuning your perfect body.'

Jez smiles and pats Red on the stomach.

'Oh dear, Mr Metcalfe,' he says. 'Very cuddly.'

'I used to be quite an athlete in my youth,' says Red.

'Youth? You're only a few years older than me, mate. Don't give me all this youth crap.'

Alison comes down the stairs. Red is on his feet immediately, shaking her hand firmly.

'Alison. Good to see you again. This is my colleague, Jeremy Clifton.'

He doesn't say 'Detective Inspector', not while Lorraine can hear them.

'What's happened?' asks Alison. 'Have you found the person who killed Philip?'

Lorraine's ears prick up. Red shoots her a sharp look.

'Is there somewhere we could talk in private, Alison?' asks Jez.

Alison crosses over to the reception desk and consults a small book.

'The Blue Room's free,' she says. 'Lorraine, can you book me in there for . . . ?'

'Half an hour,' says Red.

'Sure,' says Lorraine.

They leave her positively itching to find out what's going on.

The Blue Room turns out to be the company boardroom, painted in a shade of light turquoise. They take the three seats around one end of the table, with Alison at the head and the two men either side of her.

'Have you found the killer?' she asks again.

'Not yet, but –'

'So what can I do for you?'

Red phrases it delicately.

'Some new information has come to light.'

'Which is . . . ?'

Jez, abrupt and blunt, takes up the talking.

'Did Philip have any homosexual tendencies?'

Red almost laughs. There is he, trying to put Alison at her ease and soften her up gently, and in comes Jez with all guns blazing. He looks sharply at Jez, who holds up his hand, as if to say, Let me do this my way.

Alison's mouth drops open.

'Did he *what?*'

'Have any homosexual tendencies.'

'That's none of your business.'

It would be easier for her to deny it outright. Red and Jez look at each other.

'With all due respect, Alison,' says Jez, 'it *is* our business.'

'Philip's sexuality was his own concern.'

'And yours too, I would imagine. Did you and Philip have a good sex life?'

'That's none of your business either.'

Red feels guilty about treating Alison like a suspect, but he knows that it might well be the best way to get information out of her. Whatever secrets she has about Philip, she won't want to tell them. So either Jez browbeats the answers out of her, or else he'll make Red seem so reasonable in comparison that Alison will tell *him* anything.

'Alison, *please*.' Red at his most placating. 'Detective Inspector Clifton is asking you these personal questions because we have reason to believe that Philip's killing may be sex-related.'

'Our sex life was fine.'

'How often did you have sex?' Jez again.

'Often enough.'

'How often is often enough?'

'Probably more than you get, Detective Inspector.'

'Did Philip ever ask you to do anything unusual?'

'What's unusual?'

'Did he ever try to sodomise you, for instance?'

She bites her lower lip and flushes deep red.

It is enough. They know.

Jez is about to say something else, but Red flashes a glance which stops him. Jez has gone far enough, and his tactic has worked.

Alison turns to face Red. She will tell him, not Jez.

'OK. Philip was bisexual. He used to play around a lot when he was young. Men and women, straight and kinky. You name it, he did it. When we first started going out, he wanted to tie me up, bugger me, all that kind of stuff. I told him I wasn't having any of it.'

'And then?'

'When he realised that I really meant what I said, he stopped. He said he loved me and that he would do whatever I wanted. He said his life was empty before me. He said I had made him realise that man was meant to lie with woman and not with man. It was some Biblical quote he had found.'

'Biblical? Did he rediscover religion?'

'No. I think he just liked the quote.'

'Was he ever unfaithful to you?'

A quick smear of pain slides across her face.

'Yes.'

'How often?'

'Only once. Once that I know about, that is.'

'When you say once, do you mean one occasion or one person?'

'One person.'

'Was it a one-night stand, or an affair?'

'An affair.'

'And how long did the affair go on?'

This time her voice does not waver.

'A year and a half.'

'What was the other woman's name?'

'It wasn't a woman. It was a man. Someone called Kevan Latimer.'

She watches Red write it down. 'That's Kevan with an "a",' she says.

'Who is this Kevan Latimer?'

'One of Philip's friends. Fancies himself as a bit of a playboy. I think he's a piece of shit.'

'What does he do?'

'God only knows. Claims to be a businessman. He's been in jail, I know that.'

'Do you know where he lives?'

'Somewhere near Paddington. Don't know the exact address. He'll be on your records, though.'

Red thinks for a second.

'Why did their affair end? Was it because you found out about it?'

Alison shakes her head.

'I didn't know anything about it until Philip told me. He only told me once it was all over.'

'Did he say why the affair ended?'

'Yes. He said the sex had gone out of it. Kevan couldn't get it up any more.'

Sexually inadequate. Impotent. Red and Jez look at each other again.

Alison is determined not to cry, just as she was back in May after Philip's death, but now there is no WPC bringing tea and giving her time to compose herself.

Red leans forward.

'Alison, you have no idea how much we appreciate this. Thank you for being so co-operative.'

She nods mutely.

Red fumbles for words. He feels compelled to offer her some comfort.

'It must have been very hard for you.'

Alison swallows.

'I got over it. The bit I found hardest to take was the lying. He told me he didn't fancy men any more, and there he was screwing the arse off one of them behind my back. I wasn't sure if it was better or worse than if it had been another woman. I thought . . . at least he can't make any direct comparisons.' Her insecurity hangs naked in the air. 'I did my best to forget about it. And then . . . and then Philip messed it all up.'

'How?'

'He wanted Kevan to come to the wedding.'

Something trivial about the wedding she had said the first time Red had interviewed her. He wanted to invite someone I didn't want there.

Not an ex-girlfriend, as Red assumed. An ex-*boy*friend. No wonder she flipped.

And yet she went back the next morning to tell Philip that Kevan could come to the wedding after all. She backed down when lots of people would have held their ground. She was either very forgiving or very spineless. Red can't decide which. Either way, she doesn't deserve what has happened to her.

Red and Jez get up to leave. She shakes Red's hand and dabs at her nose to avoid having to shake Jez's hand.

'Can you find your own way out?' she asks.

'Yes. Thank you.'

Jez presses the button for the lift and then remembers something.

'Alison?'

She is halfway down the corridor. She stops and turns round. The hostility towards him blazes in her eyes.

'Yes?'

The lift opens.

'What was Philip's middle name?'

'His middle name? John. Why?'

'Just curious,' says Jez, and thanks the lift doors for closing on him and his lie.

26

Red is sitting at the desk in his room when there is a knock at the door.

He looks at his watch. Twelve-twenty-five. It can't be his parents, because they've been gone less than twenty minutes. Gone to see Eric without him, on Hawkins' advice. Hawkins' discomfort down the phone was clear when he told Red what had happened. Eric, back in his cell after being charged, had suddenly started hammering on the door, yelling that he would snap Red's fucking neck just like he had snapped Charlotte Logan's fucking neck, and four policemen had to subdue Eric and threaten him with sedation before he would shut up. A transformation as sudden as it was drastic, from docile acceptance of his fate to fury against Red for breaking his promise not to tell anyone. So all in all, sir, it's probably best if you stay behind right now. Let your parents come on their own to see Eric. You can see him when he's calmed down.

Nothing for Red to do but agree.

The knock comes a second time, and louder. Red gets up from his desk, goes over to the door and opens it.

The man standing there looks familiar, but Red can't quite place him. Shiny brown hair flecked silver at the temples. Grey suit. Pink-striped shirt with white collar, gold pin through his tie, tassels on his shoes. He is more than six foot tall and broad to match, but somehow he seems bigger still. A man accustomed to authority, to being obeyed rather than having to obey.

'Redfern Metcalfe?' he asks.

'Yes.'

'I'm Richard Logan.'

Richard Logan. Charlotte Logan's father, the carpet magnate.

Recognition flashing through Red's brain. Logan appealing for information on TV after his daughter's murder. Red remembers the silver in Logan's hair and the hardness in his face as he faced the TV cameras, and he remembers the holiday snapshot of daughter nuzzling up to father which some of the newspapers used the next day.

Face to face with the father of the girl his brother has killed, and Red can't think of the first thing to say.

Logan's hand comes towards him. A grey-sleeved arm snaking out to smash Red to the floor in pulverising vengeful rage. Red flinches as the fear clutches tight and sudden in his lungs.

Logan grasps Red's right hand in his own. 'Nice to meet you.'

Red feels the firmness of the grip on his palm. His heart flutters in relief.

'Can I come in?' asks Logan.

'Wha . . . ? Oh, sure. Please.'

Red takes a step back. Logan ducks his head slightly to fit through the door frame.

Red, talking to fill nervous time. 'Can I get you something? Tea? Coffee?'

'I'm fine, thank you.'

'Er . . . would you like a seat?'

Logan walks over to the low armchair by the dormer window. He pauses for a second with his back to Red as he looks out over Great Court, and then turns round and lowers himself into the chair.

Even when sitting, with his backside a foot above the floor and his knees as high as his shoulders, Logan's presence expands effortlessly to fill the room. Red sits on the hard chair by his desk and he can feel the man's power wisp around him like mist.

'This is a nice room you've got here, Redfern. There can't be that many students who get rooms in Great Court.'

'No, there aren't. I was lucky. We get given ballot numbers at the end of our first year, and then they are reversed at the end of our second year. I was in the bottom ten on the first list, so I got virtually first pick when it was switched round. You should have seen the hovel I had in my second year.' Red laughs nervously. Logan smiles, a quick lupine stretching of his lips.

'I heard about your brother,' says Logan, and the smile is wiped clean from his face.

Red swallows, and says nothing.

'Detective Hawkins rang me this morning. He told me that the police have charged your brother with Charlotte's murder.'

'I'm so sorry, Mr Logan.'

'So am I, Redfern. So am I.'

The clock in Great Court strikes the half hour. Ding-dong, ding-dong, with the last clang fading on the air in Red's room. Logan clears his throat.

'Hawkins also told me how the police found Eric.'

'Mr Logan . . . I don't know what to say.'

'You don't have to say anything, Redfern. I came here to thank you.'

'*Thank me?*'

'Yes. For putting my mind at rest. Charlotte's killer has been caught. You don't know how much that means to me.'

'It hasn't brought Charlotte back, though, has it?'

Logan ducks the question.

'You did a very brave thing, Red. That's why I'm especially grateful to you. Turning your own brother in . . . I can think of a lot of people who wouldn't have had the courage to do that.'

To do what? Break your promise? Betray your own blood?

'I didn't really have much of a choice. I just did what anyone else would have done.'

'No, you didn't do what anyone else would have done. You did what almost everyone else *wouldn't* have done. If

I'd been you, and it had been my brother . . . I don't know
if I could have done what you did.'

Red looks at the floor.

'Thank you,' he mumbles, embarrassed by the unexpected
praise.

He feels the smarting of tears behind his eyes. He can
deal with his brother's hatred and his parents' bewilder-
ment, but not with the kindness of a stranger. Red pinches
the water from the corners of his eyes against the sides of
his nose and hopes that he can pass the action off as fatigue
rather than emotion.

Logan's voice cuts through his pain.

'I didn't come here just to thank you, Redfern.'

Red looks up.

'When Charlotte was killed, I offered a reward for anyone
who provided information which led to the killer being
caught. Do you remember?'

Red nods. 'I remember.'

Red knows what's coming. Don't say it. Please don't.

Red can't form the words in time. Logan is speaking,
piling on the guilt without even realising.

'You found the killer, Redfern. The reward's yours by
right, if you want it.'

27

Jez peels the print-out off the printer and whistles.

'Got a bit of form, has our Kevan,' he says. 'Six months inside three years ago for persistent cocaine use. Attempts at rehab said to be patchy. Also petty theft, a couple of convictions for speeding and one charge of indecent exposure. Sounds like an absolute charmer. Businessman, my foot.'

'What address have we got for him?' asks Red.

Jez scans the text. 'Norfolk Square, W2.'

'Bloody hell,' says Red. 'I know Norfolk Square. It's literally across the road from my flat.'

'What charming neighbours you have. Shall we go and pay him a visit?'

'He might not be there – that address may not be current. But there's no harm in trying, is there?'

It takes them fifteen minutes to get from Scotland Yard to Norfolk Square. The house they're looking for is on the south side, but the one-way system means they have to go all the way round the square. Most of the buildings they pass are cheap hotels.

'Jesus Christ,' says Jez. 'Look at this place. Backpackers' paradise. God knows why they bother coming all the way to England if they're going to end up in a shithole like Paddington.'

Red nudges the Vauxhall wide of a man in paint-splattered jeans who is vacuuming out the inside of a white Mercedes estate and follows the road round the square.

'I'll have you know that *chez* Metcalfe is about one hundred yards in that direction,' says Red, pointing past the front of Jez's nose.

'I rest my case. It must be a pretty grotty neighbourhood if they allow the likes of you to live here.'

'And you can fuck off with that. Which house are we looking for?'

Jez peers at the door numbers as they crawl slowly past. 'There. That one up ahead. Dark green door.'

The house in question needs a lick of paint and a good scrub. Triangles of dirt clog the corners of the windows and sickly yellow light filters through the strip of glass above the front door.

There is a parking space two car lengths ahead of them. Red stops just beyond it and reverses in, twisting his head round to check his bearings. Jez glances in the wing mirror.

'What does Kevan Latimer look like?' he says.

'No idea,' replies Red. 'Why do you ask?'

'Because there's a bloke coming out of that house and I want to know if it's him.'

'Well, why don't you ask him?'

Red puts the car into first gear and turns its nose in. Jez opens his door and leans out as far as his seatbelt reel will allow. The man is walking down the steps from the dark green door to the pavement. Medium height, white T-shirt, brown cotton trousers, training shoes.

Jez calls out. 'Kevan Latimer?'

The man stops and looks at him. Jez calls again, 'Are you Kevan Latimer?'

The man looks at him blankly, as if he doesn't speak English. And suddenly he starts running.

'Jesus Christ,' shouts Jez.

He flicks the seatbelt release catch and is out of the car in an instant, the reel rewinding across his body as he moves. Feet splayed outwards and arms pumping as he gains speed from stationary, just like a proper sprinter. Behind him, he hears the car doors slamming as Red follows. But Red is almost forty, and a smoker to boot. He's never going to be able to keep up.

Latimer gets to the end of the square and turns right towards the station. He dodges a taxi and sets off up the middle of the road, against the traffic. Jez is ten yards behind him. The great vault of the station roof looms ahead of them as they run towards Paddington.

Past the rotating postcard stands on one side of the road and Burger King on the other. Across a mini-roundabout and down the wide ramp into the station itself. The taxi drivers coming up the ramp blare angry symphonies on their horns.

Jez can feel the heat building on his face and under his shirt as he runs. Latimer is still ahead of him, and he is quick, but Jez is fitter than him. He *must* be. It is the height of the triathlon season. Give him and Mr Latimer any kind of stamina test and he'll take him to the cleaners.

Latimer comes off the taxi ramp and veers left, across the concourse. Impressions of movement on the concourse's white floor as objects criss-cross in front of them: motorised luggage carts, a stream of people from the train just arrived at platform four. They slice through the motion. Jez is dimly aware of faces turned towards them, old faces with glasses on their eyes and pipes in their mouths. No one moves to help or intercede. They probably think that Jez and Latimer are two friends having a laugh.

Latimer cuts diagonally across the concourse, leaving the octagonal information booth to his left, and then cuts sharp right down a platform. A train painted the green and white of Great Western Railways is just pulling out. Latimer dodges two post office workers pushing a mail trolley. He heads under the big three-sided clock halfway down the platform and suddenly takes a sharp left, through the pillars and onto the feeder road where vehicles drop and pick up passengers. Jez is still following, the gap now five yards and closing.

Paddington Station is set in a dip. Whether Latimer goes left or right, he has to go upwards. He chooses right, and Jez is gaining perceptibly on the climb. They reach the bridge at the top no more than a couple of strides apart. Latimer goes right again, but takes the turn too sharply and stumbles, scraping his hand on the ground as he tries to keep his balance.

It is enough. Jez jumps the last four feet and spreads himself on Latimer's back like a giant spider. Latimer goes down, hitting the ground with elbows first and then his chest. Winded by the fall and by Jez's weight on him, he gasps for air like an asthmatic.

Minimum force. That's what police officers are supposed to use. But exceptions can be made. Jez gets up off Latimer and kicks him hard in the ribs, twice. No air in Latimer's lungs for him to scream with.

A voice behind them.

'Fucking hell.'

It's Red, blowing hard. His face has gone almost as red as his hair.

'You got him.' Pant pant. 'Good lad.' Pant pant. 'Read him his rights.'

Jez cuffs Latimer's hands behind his back.

'Kevan Latimer, I am arresting you on suspicion of murder. You do not need to say anything, but I must warn you that it may harm your defence if you do not mention when questioned something which you later rely on in court. Anything you do say may be given in evidence.'

Latimer twists his head round. The movement crinkles the skin on his neck. He is smiling.

'The pigs. Well, bugger me sideways. I thought you were McAllister's boys come to get your money back.'

28

'So it wasn't him?' asks Kate.

'No. Not even close,' says Red. 'He didn't know what we were talking about. Thought we were the heavies come to reclaim some gambling debts off him, and he kept grinning like an idiot when he found out we weren't. If he wants to get mixed up with loan sharks, that's his problem, but it's not a crime. No, he is Kevan Latimer, but he's not our man, worst luck. We could have done with a break.'

'Couldn't you have done him for resisting arrest?'

'No. We didn't identify ourselves as police officers until the moment Jez got him.'

'And all his alibis check out?'

'Sadly, yes.'

'Let's have a look,' says Duncan.

Red slides Latimer's statement across the table to him. 'They're all kosher,' says Red. 'The night Philip and James Cunningham were done, he was in some rehab clinic down near Hurstpierpoint in Sussex. He was there for almost a month. Checked in April 17th, discharged May 15th. Pretty hopeless case, according to the warden there. I got the impression that he's pretty sick of the sight of Kevan, but he can't really turn him away.'

'Why not?' says Duncan, still studying the statement.

'Because the council pays the fees.'

'And there's no way Kevan could have escaped for the night?'

'No. None at all. The clinic is locked at night and the duty officer ensures that everyone's accounted for. Kevan was registered as present at eleven pm and then again at seven the next morning.'

'He could have got to London and back again in that time.'

'Duncan, he couldn't even have got out of the fucking clinic. And if by some miracle he had, then he couldn't have gone far. The last train to London is at ten-forty-eight, and he hasn't got a car.'

'He could have stolen one.'

'No vehicles were reported stolen that night within three miles of the clinic.'

'An accomplice?'

'Lubezski is adamant that the killings are the work of one man only. You think Kevan Latimer's got a chauffeur who waits quietly outside people's houses for him while he brutally murders the occupants? Get real.'

'What about last Friday?'

'Staying with a friend in Potter's Bar. All night.'

'What kind of friend?'

'A male friend, though I get the impression that he pays for services rendered. The local force checked it out and they're sure that it's kosher too.'

Duncan drops the statements back on the table. 'Doesn't sound watertight to me,' he says.

'Look.' Red is beginning to get exasperated. 'I want Latimer to be Silver Tongue as much as you do. I want it to be him because then we could close the case, and because he's an unpleasant little faggot. But Latimer's not Silver Tongue. He's simply not. He hasn't got the balls to do what Silver Tongue has done. Latimer's a loser. He's not ... *good* enough to be Silver Tongue.'

'"Good enough",' says Duncan, raising his eyebrows. 'That's a bizarre way of putting it.'

Red shrugs.

'You know what I mean, Duncan.'

'No, I don't. "Good enough" implies approval, admiration. Do you admire this guy, Red? Do you like him?'

'Don't start, Duncan. Not here.'

'So what now?' says Kate.

'We're going gay,' says Red.

Duncan looks up sharply.

'You must be joking.'

'Not in the slightest. Two of the three victims had

homosexual tendencies, and the other came from a profession – the clergy – which isn't exactly immune to gay scandal. All of them have been found naked apart from their underpants. It's our best hope so far.'

'If you think that I'm going cruising with the leather and moustache boys . . .'

'Yes, Duncan. That's exactly what you're going to do. When Colin Ireland was on the loose, that's what Jez and I did.'

'Must have been fun for the poofters. Have any luck, Jez?'

Jez looks levelly at Duncan and says nothing.

'Shut up, Duncan,' says Red. 'We went to gay bar after gay bar, talking to people, listening to what they'd seen. And yes, it was strange. I've lived in this city for more than ten years and I didn't know that this whole subculture even existed. I didn't know that in some pubs you could walk into the toilets and find two men having sex under the urinals. I didn't know that gay men advertise their sexual preferences by the colour of the handkerchief in their back pocket.'

'Fat lot of good it did you, in the end.'

'What do you mean?'

'All your trawling around faggot pubs was in vain, wasn't it? Because Ireland came forward in an attempt to eliminate himself from enquiries and you ended up getting him that way. So you needn't have bothered.'

'But we *did* bother. At least we tried. And if we don't try this time, then one day, when this whole thing comes out, we're going to have every gay rights group in the country shouting about how the police don't give a shit about them and how we only go and solve crimes when the victims are pukka white men who bat for the right team.'

Red opens a cardboard folder and pulls out photographs of the dead men. They aren't crime scene photos, but snapshots of the men taken when they were alive. A passport photo of Philip Rhodes, looking serious. One of James Cunningham, relaxed at dinner with a glass of wine in his hand. And the official Sandhurst portrait of James Buxton, beaming with pride in his regimental uniform.

There are four copies of each. Red hands them round like a blackjack dealer.

'There are about 120 gay bars, pubs and clubs in London. I've checked with the gay community liaison people as to where the most promising spots are. We've hit on the West End and Earl's Court as the best places, so that's where we're going to start tonight.'

Red unfolds two photocopied pages from the *A to Z*, with hastily drawn red circles standing out sharply against the patchwork of black and white streets.

'We'll take this in pairs.' He slides one of the pages across to Duncan. 'Duncan, you and Kate have got the West End beat. Go to the places I've marked here. Jez and I will take Earl's Court. I don't have to tell you to do everything you can not to cause wholesale panic. Confine your questions to barmen, doormen, managers and so on – they're the ones who see everyone and everything in their establishments. Just ask if they've seen any of these men. Don't say why you're looking, obviously, and don't go round the general punters either. Keep your eyes and ears open. OK? Stay out as late as you need. See you back here tomorrow morning, ten o'clock sharp.'

Kate turns to Jez.

'You watch yourself out there, young man,' she says, waving a mock admonishing finger in his face. 'Don't go copping off with any of the nasty men you meet.'

'Or what?' says Jez. 'You going to get jealous?'

'Damn right,' says Kate. 'You know I want you all for myself.'

'Well, ditch Mr Dull. Then you might have a chance.'

Kate flushes. 'Fuck off, Jez. Don't talk about him like that. You don't know him.'

'No, but I –'

'You can be a real shit sometimes, you know. Just shut it.'

She gets up to leave. Duncan follows her.

'Oh, and Duncan . . .' says Red, still sitting.

'Yes?'

'Try and blend in.'

29

Lunch time comes and goes without Red even noticing. He holds Logan's business card by the edges and turns it over and over in his hands. The room seems smaller now Logan has gone, as if he has taken more than just his presence with him. All the while Logan's words fizz in Red's mind: 'Think about it, Red. There's no hurry. Call me when you've made up your mind.'

Red is still thinking about it when his parents return.

He knows from the moment they walk in the door that the meeting with Eric has not gone well. The space between the two lines which run down from Margaret's nostrils is stained red where she has been blowing her nose from crying and the knot on Robert's tie is pulled small and tight by his constant tugging. Red puts Logan's card down on his desk and goes over to his parents. He guides his mother to the armchair where Logan was sitting, and lets his father take the small sofa which faces it. Red pulls the hard chair out from behind his desk and puts it next to the sofa, turning the chair round so he can lean forward against its back.

'How was it?' he asks quietly.

His father shrugs. 'As well as can be expected.'

'How's Eric?'

'That policeman – what's his name?'

'Hawkins.'

'Yes, Hawkins. He said that Eric was very quiet this morning.'

'But how is he *now*, Dad?'

'I . . . I don't think he really knows what's going on.'

'Is he still quiet?'

'No. No, he's not.'

'So what did you talk about?'

Robert tugs at his tie again. Margaret examines her nails.

Red knows what they talked about. Him. He sighs.

'What did he say, Dad?'

'Let's not talk about this now, Red.'

'No, Dad. I want to know. What did he say?'

'Red, we'll talk about it later. Your mother and I are very –'

'*DAD!*'

'OK, OK. I'll tell you. Though I should also say that you won't want to hear some of it.'

'Dad, just tell me. I can guess at most of it anyway. Eric blames me for what happened, doesn't he? He wants to break my fucking neck.'

A sharp shocked gasp from his mother. Red ignores her.

'Those were the words he used, weren't they, Dad? "I'd like to break his fucking neck." Weren't they?'

'How do you know?'

'He used them earlier. That's why Hawkins wanted you to go alone.'

'Eric says you promised him that you wouldn't tell anyone, and then as soon as he was asleep you went to the police and told them.'

'Is that true, Red?' asks his mother.

'Yes. I promised him because he wouldn't have let me leave otherwise. What else did he say?'

His father answers. 'He said that, if you had just kept your . . . mouth shut, then we could have worked something out between us.'

'Us?'

'You. Me. Your mother. The family.'

'What does he mean, worked something out? Worked *what* out? He's killed someone. What the hell is there left to work out?'

'I don't know. Something.'

'And what do you think, Dad? Do you think we could

have –' he describes apostrophes with his fingers, '– worked something out?'

'Red . . .'

His father's hesitation is proof enough in itself.

'Do you agree with him, Dad?'

'Does it matter whether I do?'

'Damn right it does. Do you think I was wrong to go to the police?'

'I . . . I think you might have told us first.'

'Why? What good would that have done?'

'We could have got Eric some help, perhaps. We could have controlled what happened to him.'

'*Controlled?* Dad, he killed someone. I know it's hard to take, but it *happened*. Just because you don't like it doesn't mean that it isn't there. Would you rather that I hadn't told you at all? Would you rather that I'd just kept it between Eric and me? Another brotherly secret, like the ones we've kept since we were kids? Then you would never have known anything.'

'It's not about that, Red.'

'Yes, it is, Dad. I'm very sorry that you and Mum have had to find out that Eric is a killer.'

'Was. *Was* a killer.'

'Was. Is. It doesn't really matter, Dad. He still did it. I'm very sorry that Eric is probably going to spend most of his life in jail. And I'm very sorry that you see fit to blame me in some way for what happened. But this is not my fault. I wasn't the one that killed Charlotte Logan. *He* was.'

'No one's blaming you, Red.'

'You could have fooled me.'

'Red, all I'm saying is that there were other options which you could have considered.'

'Dad, I did what I thought was right. My brother did wrong. He deserves to be punished. And at least –'

'"Deserves to be punished"? Since when have you been playing God, Red?'

'– at least this way there's some justice for Charlotte. At least her family will have some peace now.'

'And where does your loyalty lie, Red? With us, or with them?'

Silence, angry and antagonistic. They don't want to believe it of Eric. They don't want to believe that he did what he did. So they shoot the messenger instead.

The challenge to Red's loyalty lingers unanswered.

Margaret speaks now, and her voice is distant.

'Eric wants to know if Logan's been round to give you your reward yet.'

30

You can't see into the Coleherne pub from the outside. The windows are tinted black, the curtains are often drawn and the interior is kept so dimly lit that even a quick glance in as someone enters or leaves doesn't tell you very much. All you can make out is a crepuscular tableau of gentle movement, shapes and forms in hazy outline against the gloom.

The Coleherne is situated on a busy but unexceptional stretch of the Old Brompton Road. The pavement reflects the yellow neon of the mobile phone showroom next door and fruit spills from the boxes outside the all-night grocery across the road. A few metres away, the northbound traffic thunders up the Finborough Road. There is almost nothing to betray the Coleherne's status as one of London's most famous gay pubs.

Nothing, that is, except for the clientele. Stand on the street corner, even for five minutes, and you cannot fail to notice the regulars and casuals of the Earl's Court gay scene. Tight white T-shirts. Jeans rolled up an inch or so above the ankle. Perhaps leather trousers or a leather jacket. A crew cut, almost always. A moustache, sometimes. Young and old, fat and thin, muscular and flabby, they converge on the Coleherne and nearby Brompton's nightclub like moths round a flame.

The Coleherne is the pub where Colin Ireland picked up his five victims in 1993, and it was on the investigation into these killings that Red and Jez first met. All Ireland's victims were tied up in bondage-style rituals before being strangled. As far as most of the police on the case were concerned, the killer was bound to be part of the gay community – a man who moved at ease in those circles and who gained some form of intense sexual gratification through the act of torturing and killing his victims.

But Jez, only twenty-seven at the time and taking part in his first big case, disagreed. He contended that the murderer, far from being a homosexual himself or a 'queer hater' who wanted to take revenge on gays, was a naturally violent person who simply wanted to be known as a serial killer and who picked on homosexuals as an easy target. Therefore, he would pretend to be gay for as long as it took to tie his victims up, and then he could do what he wanted with them. As a result, they were wasting their time looking for a homosexual. What they should be doing was looking for someone who already had some sort of criminal record and who was strong enough to kill the victims in the way he had.

The others on the case scoffed. But Red listened, and remembered. When Ireland was caught, he matched Jez's description down to a tee. And so Red took Jez under his wing, not just because he had been right, but because he hadn't been scared to pitch his case to a crowd of people all much older and more experienced than him.

Now they are back at the Coleherne, but this time the circumstances are different. During the hunt for Ireland, they knew that the killer – then unknown – had been in the pub on those five nights in question, though it was difficult to get a positive ID when three-quarters of the clientele had the same dress sense and haircut.

This time, they've got nothing. Just three photos and the knowledge that at least two of the victims had had some sort of homosexual experience.

Red parks the Vauxhall on Coleherne Road, by the side of the pub.

'Why doesn't Duncan like me?' asks Jez, levering himself out of the car.

Red shrugs.

'I mean, didn't you think about that when you put us on the same team,' continues Jez, 'or is this another Metcalfe special about creative tension and the joys of discord?'

Red smiles thinly.

'You cunning shit,' says Jez.

'Look on the bright side. At least I didn't make you go with him tonight. Imagine what a lovely time you'd have had.'

'I'm sure Kate will thank you for it.'

'Kate can more than handle him, Jez. Anyway, I'm hardly going to put you two together. You'd probably sod off back home and fuck each other's brains out, wouldn't you?'

'Not on duty, boss,' says Jez, warming to the joke. 'Never on duty.'

'Anyway, it's you and me, like it or lump it. Would you like to escort me into this public house?' Red holds out his crooked arm, inviting Jez to take his elbow. Jez laughs.

'Don't be daft. We don't want to blend in too well round here.'

They walk into the pub. The long transition from day to night is finally over, so it is not that much darker inside the Coleherne than it is on the street outside, but it still takes Red and Jez a couple of seconds to see exactly what's what.

A few heads turn to assess them as they stand in the doorway. Red and Jez both know that they don't look like regulars and they don't look like men on the pull. That means they're either tourists who have mistakenly wandered in here, or cops. And tourists don't wear suits.

Neither Red nor Jez has been here since the Ireland case, more than five years previously. Within seconds, the two strongest sensations of that investigation come flooding back: hostility towards their status as policemen and unashamed frankness in eyeing them up.

'Jesus,' says Jez. 'Now I know what it feels like to be a woman.'

'You're so predictable. You said that the last time we were in here. And you're the one who should be worried, lover boy. You're the super-fit triathlete with the wonder body. I'm the fat git with red hair who's the other side of thirty-five. Lucky you didn't come in here wearing all that tight Lycra you normally squeeze into. You'd never have got out with your sphincter intact.'

'In that case, Grandad, can I buy you a drink?'

'I doubt it. You probably look too young to be served.'

Jez chuckles and gives Red the middle finger.

They walk towards the bar, watched all the way. They watch back, their gazes sweeping methodically across the room like the green line on a radar screen. Uncowed, but not aggressive. Just enough to say: we're not here to start something, but we're ready for it if you do.

The hostility they remember well, even though relations between the police and the gay community have improved significantly since the Ireland case, when the police managed to put some of the force's most notorious homophobes on the investigations team and then wondered why they were criticised.

There is a space at the bar big enough for one of them, but not both. Jez goes in there first and subtly elbows the men either side along a few feet so that Red can stand next to him.

The barman wears a denim shirt with paisley patches on the shoulders and speaks with a slight lisp. 'What can I get you, gentlemen?'

'I'd like to speak to the landlord, please,' says Red.

'And I haven't even done anything wrong yet.'

Jez smiles. Red doesn't.

Paisley Patches walks over to another barman, chatting to a couple of drinkers, and taps him on the shoulder.

'Jeff, these two gentlemen would like a word with you.'

Jeff reluctantly peels his massive forearms off the bar and turns to them.

'What can I do for you?'

'I'm Detective Superintendent Metcalfe and this is Detective Inspector Clifton. We'd like to ask you a few questions.'

'About what?'

Edgy and suspicious now. Jez catches the mood first.

'Don't worry,' he says. 'We're not from vice and we're not here to arrest anyone. We'd just like you to look at a few pictures and tell us if you recognise any of the people in them.'

'If you're not from vice, then where *are* you from?'

Red leans forward and there is steel in his voice.

'Sir, you heard what my colleague said. Now, if you would, we'd like you to look at these photos.'

Jeff looks at both Red and Jez, then nods.

Red hands over the photos. There are six in all: Red has added three controls, photos of men now dead who could not in a month of Sundays have been known to anyone in the Coleherne.

Jeff's huge hands scoop up the photos and hold them under the light by the cash till. He flicks through them twice with quick thumbs, rearranges them and hands them back to Red.

'I recognise him.' He points to the picture he has placed on top. 'He's been in here a couple of times.'

Red looks at the photo, and catches his breath in excitement.

The picture Jeff is pointing to is that of James Cunningham, the late Bishop of Wandsworth.

31

They are in the kitchen of the flat above the pub. Red and Jez are drinking mineral water while Jeff waves the bottle of Beck's in his hand to emphasise the points he is making.

'I last saw him in here . . . oh, it must have been six months ago. During the winter, definitely, because he had this great big coat on.'

'How many times had he been in before?' asks Red.

'Just one or two, that I saw. 'Course, he might have come in here on my nights off or before I started working here, about three years ago.'

'And so you'd seen him a maximum of three times in those three years?'

'Yes.'

'You must have seen thousands of people come through here in that time. How come you remember him so clearly?'

They haven't told Jeff what Cunningham's name was, let alone why they're making enquiries about him, and Jeff hasn't asked. He's dealt with the police enough times to know that asking them questions they don't want to answer simply annoys them. They'll tell you what they choose to.

'Because he was old. Older than most of my clientele, that's for sure. And because . . . he never came in with anyone and he never left with anyone.'

'Is that unusual?'

'Reasonably. People either come in here with their boyfriends or they come in here unattached and pick someone up.'

'But surely lots of people come in here looking for a pick-up and don't get lucky?'

'Yes, of course. But the thing with this guy was that he didn't seem to try anything on. With *anybody*. He would just come in, have a couple of drinks, chat to whoever would talk to him and then leave again.'

'Mind you,' says Jez, 'he wasn't exactly love's young dream.'

Jeff shrugs. 'Who cares? People in here go for all sorts.'

'Is there anyone in here tonight who you can remember talking to him?'

'Jesus, now you're asking. Let me think.' Jeff furrows his eyebrows. 'No, not that I can remember. I can think of one, maybe two people who I remember talking to him, but neither of them are in here tonight.'

Red hands him a card.

'When they do come, could you ask them to give us a call?'

'Sure.'

Jeff walks down the stairs with Red and Jez and sees them out of a side door. They are almost at the Vauxhall before either of them speaks.

'So what do you think?' asks Red.

'Uncommitted homosexuals, all three of them. Confused about their sexuality. Maybe Silver Tongue preyed on that. Maybe he wanted them to think that he was gay, or just wanted to scare them. I don't know. I haven't got my head around this at all.'

'Me neither,' says Red. 'He doesn't touch them. He doesn't fuck them or come on them or anything. He doesn't strip them fully naked when he kills them. It's like . . . it's almost like he's as unsure as they are.'

Red reaches in his pocket for the car keys.

'Fuck,' says Jez.

Red looks at him across the roof of the Vauxhall.

'What?'

'I just thought. You remember Emmanuel Spiteri?'

'Ireland's last victim?'

'Yeah.'

'What about him?'

'He was a caterer.'

Red gets it instantly.

'Just like Philip Rhodes.'

126

'Exactly.'

Red finds the keys, turns them in the lock. The central locking disengages with a loud clunk.

'Could be coincidence,' says Red as he slides into the driver's seat.

'And he could be taking up where Ireland left off. Spiteri last, Rhodes first. A seamless join.'

Red starts the engine, checks his wing mirror and pulls out into the road.

'Dear God. Ireland Part 2. That's all we need.'

32

'I hate these kind of places,' says Duncan.

'We haven't even been in yet,' Kate replies.

'Do we need to? Look at it. Some poxy faggot club hidden away in a dingy Soho back street.'

Duncan clears his throat and spits on the ground in disgust. Kate pushes past him and walks through the door into Substation.

'Come on, Duncan,' she says. 'Let's get it over with.'

There are two people on the door: a woman with purple hair and a ring through her nose and a bouncer whose shoulder-length hair is rucked up in waves all the way down the back of his neck. Kate is reaching for her ID when the woman with purple hair says something.

'I'm sorry, sir, but you can't come in.'

Kate is momentarily confused until she realises that Duncan has come in behind her and that the woman is talking to him.

'Why the hell not?' asks Duncan angrily.

'Because you're improperly dressed.'

'But I'm wearing a suit. How can I be –'

'No ties, sir,' says the bouncer.

'So if I take my tie off, that'll be OK?'

'Yes, sir.'

Duncan taps his finger to his head. 'This is crazy.'

The bouncer takes a step towards him. Kate, ID now in her hand and pressed up in the bouncer's face, gets between them.

'Detective Inspector Kate Beauchamp and this is Detective Chief Inspector Duncan Warren.'

The bouncer steps away again.

Kate does the talking, as she and Duncan have agreed. They'll probably get further that way.

'Have you two worked here long?'

'Two months,' says the woman.

'A year,' says the bouncer.

She turns towards the bouncer and reads the name on his lapel badge: Edwin Green.

'And you work here every night, Mr Green?'

'Most nights, yeah.'

'In that case, would you mind looking at these photos for me and telling me if you recognise any of the people in them?'

He takes the photos from her. The three victims, and the three controls.

'Why? What have these guys done?'

'Just look at them, please.'

Green flips through them quickly, too quickly, and shakes his head.

'No. Never seen none of them.'

'Look through them again, please, and pay some fucking attention this time.'

Surprised and chastised, he does what Kate tells him. When he shakes his head this time, she knows that he means it.

Green gives the photos back to Kate, who hands them onto the woman.

'You too, madam.'

Same procedure. Same result.

'Mind if we take a look around?' asks Kate.

Green gestures down the stairs. 'Go ahead.'

Kate and Duncan set off down a short staircase which has seen better days. The music, which until now has been a muffled vibration under their feet, grows louder as they turn the corner of the stairs. There is a TV screen on the wall above their heads and Kate instinctively looks at it as she goes past, expecting it to be a music video or maybe a closed-circuit security camera.

It is neither. What she sees is hardcore gay sex on video.

There are two men, both naked, one behind the other. The one in front has his eyes shut tight and his hands are reaching back to grip his partner's bottom. The one behind is cupping the first man's genitalia in his hands while sodomising him. They move to a frantic rhythm all their own.

'I don't know,' says Duncan, following her gaze. 'There really is something wrong with these people.'

Kate says nothing.

The club itself is hot, dark and loud with drums and synthesiser thumping through the red night sweat. Faces of dancers pause, distorted through the strobe lights. Kate and Duncan stand with their backs to the bar and look round. There are indistinguishable huddles in darkened corners. A couple in white vests and military fatigues are on the edge of the dance floor, looking like twins in reverse negative: one black with hair peroxided silver, the other white with a jet-black crop. Ebony and ivory, with the chords mixed up.

Kate looks all the way around the club and then all the way back, and something strikes her: no one is talking to anyone else.

How depressing. Everyone putting themselves on display like lots at an auction, wanting to be picked up and go home with someone, and for what? Temporary physical gratification, followed by the anguish of a phone that doesn't ring and the fear of the STD clinic. Licentiousness and lust under the streets of London, like a modern-day Sodom and Gomorrah.

Kate wonders whether it would make any difference to her if this was a straight club. What does she object to? The fact that they're gay, or the fact that it's a cattle market? She takes some of the men and puts women's faces on them, and then changes some of those back into men, and looks at it again. It doesn't make any difference whether they're gay or straight – it's still unbearably depressing.

She leans across to Duncan and speaks loudly in his ear, so that he will hear it over the music.

'You don't understand, do you?'

'What?'

'All this.'

'No. Not in the slightest.'

'Nor do I.'

He looks surprised. 'I thought you liked them,' he says.

'Who?'

'Poofs.'

'I've got nothing against them. They don't turn me on, but I don't see why people like you hate them. When I said that I don't understand, I meant that I don't understand why people degrade themselves so much by coming here and putting themselves on show like this. It wouldn't make any difference if they were straight or lesbians or bug-eyed monsters from Mars. It would still be a cattle market.'

Duncan turns his head to her ear.

'Let's go.'

'Why? We haven't even asked around yet.'

'Because I say so. I've had enough.' He heads towards the exit.

Kate's liberal principles don't extend to enjoying being left here by herself and Duncan knows that as well as she does. He's called her bluff and called it right.

There is a crowd of people on the stairs and Kate has to fight her way through them. By the time she makes it out of the main door Duncan is halfway down the street. She runs to catch him up.

'What is *wrong* with you, Duncan?'

He rounds on her, and for the first time she sees how angry he is. Not just about tonight, but about *everything*.

'Listen, Kate. This case has been nothing but trouble from the moment we were drafted onto it. I lost a weekend with my son and set whatever tenuous relations I have with Helen back by about a century. We've been chasing shadows since the start and this is no different. Red's big theories are bullshit, and he knows it. He's clutching at straws. There's absolutely no evidence that Silver Tongue is either a bender or picking on benders. All that stuff about teenage experimentation and being bisexual is nothing. *Nothing*. If we had a half-decent lead on this case, we would have thrown that kind of shit out in a flash. But since we've got nothing, we end up trawling around shitholes like that –' he gestures back at the club, ' – for absolutely no reason whatsoever.'

'But if the connection doesn't lie here, Duncan, then where the hell is it?'

'I don't know. But it will come to us, in time.'

'*Time?* You mean we're supposed to wait around for Silver Tongue to pop off a few more victims before we start getting close to him?'

'No. That's not what we're supposed to do. What we should do is throw out all our preconceptions and start again, right from the beginning. Now I know that line of thinking is not going to make me popular, but it happens to be true. If you and Red and Jez think that we're up against some poncey bender who kills for kicks, then good luck to you. Wherever and whoever Silver Tongue is, he would be wetting his pants if he could hear you now.'

33

It is past two in the morning when Kate gets home. The lights
are off in the flat. When she goes into the bedroom she can
hear David's breathing, deep and regular as he sleeps. She
undresses quickly and silently and climbs into bed alongside
him. He doesn't stir and she is glad.

They've only just moved in together and already she's starting to think that it was a mistake. She should have ended it
when he suggested living together, not gone along with him.
They've had two years together and there's nothing left for her
in their relationship. But she *did* agree with him, because that
was the path of least resistance. And Jez was right when he
called David 'Mr Dull' earlier this evening, because that's what
David's become. Maybe that's what he always was, and Kate
just didn't see it. But that's certainly what he is now. That's
why she was so defensive about it to Jez, because he hit the
nail right on the head.

Kate Beauchamp, who deals with Silver Tongue and all his
horrors every day of the week and yet is too spineless to finish
something she knows she ought to. She doesn't even know if
David thinks they've got a problem, let alone how he's dealing
with it.

But she knows how *she's* dealing with it. She's thinking
about Jez.

She wants Jez, not David, in bed next to her. Jez, with his
athlete's hard body. She wants to kiss around his broad swim-
mer's shoulders and down from there to the washboard lines
which ridge his abdomen, and then she wants to run her hands
down the slabs of muscle which bulge over the top of his
kneecaps when he tenses his legs. She wants to wake up before
he does and look at him while he slumbers, with his hair
sticking up on one side where he has slept on it. She wants

him to make her laugh at home the way he does in the office, when he flirts with her and makes her feel, however briefly, that she is – she could be – the most important thing in his world. She wants to solve this case with him.

Kate is in love and it's not with David.

Two nights ago she dreamt about Jez, so vividly and powerfully that she was convinced David must have known. David was in the dream too, watching TV while she and Jez made love in the bedroom. And when she woke up, she went sprinting into the living room to see if David was still there, as he had been in the dream. Even when she had calmed down, it was all she could do to stop herself confessing everything to him over breakfast.

Lying in bed. Lying to her boyfriend.

And she has no idea if Jez thinks the same way. They're good friends and they flirt like crazy, but he doesn't know – *can't* know – what she really feels about him. They flirt because they can, because she lives with her boyfriend and therefore she's 'safe'. She doesn't know what Jez does with his time, apart from train for his triathlons. She doesn't know if he has a girlfriend. She doesn't even know if he's straight. Maybe he's stayed behind in the gay bars tonight to do some 'research' on his own time. Maybe she's 'safe' not because she's attached but simply because she's female.

About the only thing Kate *does* know is that she has to see Jez at least five days a week and it's breaking her in two.

34

Red hauls himself to his feet and walks over to his desk. He picks up Logan's card and reaches over to hand it to his mother. She looks at it for a few seconds and then puts it on the arm of the chair.

'He came round while you were seeing Eric, Mum.'

'That was quick.'

Red shrugs as he sits back down. 'Suppose so.'

'What did he say?'

'He said the reward was mine. If I wanted it.'

He said he admired my courage and reduced me to tears. That's what he said.

'And what did you say?'

'I told him I'd think about it. It came as a bit of a surprise.'

'So you weren't expecting it?'

'Expecting what?'

'The reward.'

'No, of course not. I'd forgotten that Logan had even offered one.'

'When did you remember?'

'When he mentioned it. I didn't even twig why he'd come round until then.'

'So you had forgotten about it until the moment he offered it to you?'

'Yes.'

'Had you, Red? Had you really?'

And now Red sees what she's driving at.

'I don't believe I'm hearing this.'

'I only ask because Eric –'

'*Eric?* Are you seriously telling me that Eric reckons I went to the police so I would get the reward?'

'He ... er ... yes, that's exactly what he thinks.'

'You tell him that I'll break *his* fucking neck for even *considering* that.'

'Redfern!'

'I swear to God, the first time I thought about the reward was when Logan mentioned it. If Eric seriously thinks that all the time I was listening to his confession I was rubbing my hands in anticipation of getting thirty grand, then ... I don't know what. I don't know what kind of person he thinks I am, to even contemplate that.'

'So why didn't you turn Logan down flat?'

'Because it was a shock to me. I didn't want to do anything hasty.'

'Like going to the police this morning, you mean?'

She believes Eric. She really thinks that Red turned him in to get the money.

Red breathes deeply through his nose, in and out, to stop himself from hitting something.

'Let's get a couple of things straight, Mum. No matter what you might think, I didn't turn Eric in to get the reward. If I had done, then I would have taken the money straight away, wouldn't I?'

'Maybe you have, Red. Maybe you've taken it already and haven't told us.'

'Is that an accusation?'

'It's a possibility. That's all.'

'How many times do I have to tell you? I haven't taken the money. The money didn't enter into my consideration as to whether or not to go to the police. Which, by the way, I believe was the right thing to do. I certainly didn't do it to get the reward. And I also believe that I was right not to give Logan a definite yes or no on the spot. If you – or you, Dad – don't go along with any or all of those statements, then that's tough. We'll just have to agree to differ.'

His mother arches her eyebrows. 'But presumably you *are* going to refuse to take the reward, Red?'

'Probably.'

'Not definitely?'

'No, not definitely. Not if there's something good we can do with it.'

'Like what?'

'I don't know yet. I haven't thought that far ahead. But let *me* ask *you* something, Mum. Why are you so adamant that I shouldn't take the reward? Is it because you still think that I turned Eric in to get the money, or is it because you think we – as Eric's family – shouldn't benefit from someone who has suffered because of what Eric has done?'

She doesn't answer. She doesn't need to. Red knows what she thinks. He knows that it is easier to imagine one of your sons as a money-grubber than to accept the other one as a killer.

Whatever happens after this, he thinks, life will never be the same for any of us.

'What would you do with the money, Red?' she says. 'Would you use it to help defend Eric?'

'No, Mum, of course not. How could I? How could I take Mr Logan's money and use it against him like that? That would be like him footing the lawyers' bill for the man who killed his daughter. That's ridiculous. He can't bankroll Eric like that. Can he?'

Silence.

'Can he?'

It seems so self-evident to Red. He can't work out why his parents don't see it that way too.

Where does your loyalty lie, Red? With us, or with them?

The workings of their minds flash into his brain. He sees it now. This is your chance to redeem yourself, Red. Take Logan's money and put it towards getting Eric the best lawyer he can afford. You were the one who got him there in the first place, and now you can be the one to help get him out. You can do the one thing which will in some way take the sting out of your betrayal. But you refuse point blank. Where does your loyalty lie, Red? With us, or with them?

Red pushes himself away from his chair, moving backwards and upwards.

'Stuff this.'

He stalks towards the door.

'Where are you going, Red?' asks his mother nervously.

'Out. For a walk. Until you two get some sense into your heads.'

He slams the door so hard behind him that little puffs of plaster billow out from above the door frame. The student who lives below opens his door to complain about the noise, sees the look on Red's face as he comes down the stairs, and disappears back inside his room again.

Red has no coat and it is cold outside. He leaves Great Court by the side gate which opens onto Trinity Lane and turns right towards the Backs. If he walks fast enough he should be able to keep warm. His parents' suspicions stick like needles in his skin.

There were other options you might have considered. So you had forgotten about the reward until the moment Logan offered it to you. Had you, Red? Had you *really*?

And still Red, hoping that somehow it will all work out fine, tries to find excuses for them. They're shocked. They don't know how to deal with what's happening to them. They'd stop if they could only hear what they sound like. Had you, Red? Had you really? His mother, twisting everything he said about the reward, not even letting his father get a word in edgeways.

No. That's not right. There have been plenty of opportunities for his father to say something – when Red challenged them to believe him about his decision to go to the police or in the long silence after he told them that he wouldn't put Logan's money towards Eric's legal fees.

But his father has remained quiet. Out of choice, he hasn't said a single word since the reward was first mentioned.

And then Red sees why, and with it he sees a way to get some good out of this godawful mess.

TUESDAY, JULY 28TH 1998

'I *still* don't think it makes any difference,' says Duncan.

Jez spreads his hands out wide.

'Duncan, we've got evidence that all three of the victims had homosexual leanings. We've got evidence that they were all uncommitted and unsure of their sexuality, just like Silver Tongue seems to be. We've got three people who to varying extents led double lives, hiding a part of themselves away from the world. Philip Rhodes had a fiancée but used to screw his boyfriend on the side, James Cunningham – a *bishop* – went to gay bars alone and James Buxton was terrified that he would get thrown out of the army if they found out about some minor dalliance he had in the past. What more do you want?'

'I told Kate last night and I've told you just now: I think we're barking up the wrong tree.'

'*Why?*'

'I don't *know*. I just think it.'

'That's not enough.'

Duncan leans forward, his forefinger jabbing the air towards Jez and Kate.

'Listen, Jez, I've been on the force longer than the two of you put together –'

'I don't really think that's relevant here.'

'– and you know as well as I do that a lot of crimes get solved because someone has a *feeling* about it. A feeling, a hunch, that's all. There's too much here that doesn't add up. I don't know what the connection is, but I *do* know that it's not the one we're currently looking at.'

Red, hitherto a silent mediator, holds up his hand.

'Right. Round the table, quickly. Duncan, if it was purely up to you, what would you do from here?'

'I'd keep looking. I'd go back over what we've already got and see if we've missed something. Look at it from angles we haven't thought of, no matter how stupid they might seem.'

'Jez?'

'I'd make an announcement that a serial killer is on the loose and he seems to be targeting uncommitted homosexuals. Warn the gay community that this is going on, and that they should watch their backs . . . as it were.'

Duncan jumps to his feet in anger. 'Jez, have you any idea what –'

'Sit down, Duncan,' growls Red.

'– kind of panic that would cause?'

'DUNCAN!'

Duncan glares at Jez for a second or two and finds his stare steadily returned. Then he subsides slowly, picking his chair up and dusting the seat before he sits down. Red turns to Kate.

'Kate?'

'I'd keep on the way we are. Perhaps let a couple of responsible gay committees or magazines in on our suspicions, though obviously without telling them too much. But I wouldn't make a public announcement, not at this stage.'

Jez's turn to protest. 'Come on, Kate. If we let the cat out of the bag, it's got to be on our own terms. As soon as this goes beyond the force, it's going to spread like wildfire – and we won't be able to do a thing about it. There'll be rumour and counter-rumour flying around. If we make an announcement, at least we have some hope of controlling what's being said and done.'

Red is nodding.

'Jez is right, Kate,' he says. 'The last thing we want is for this to creep into the public domain from any source other than us. We can't just let a few people in on the secret and expect them to keep quiet. They simply won't. So the question is simple: do we make an announcement, or do we stay silent and keep on plugging away behind the scenes?'

Jez is adamant. 'Make an announcement. Warn people. Get it out in the open.'

'It'll drive Silver Tongue underground,' says Duncan. 'We'll lose him.'

'No, we won't. He'll kill again, or at least he'll try. If we can let people know that they might be in danger, then we may be able to pick him up before he strikes again. If he's seen acting suspiciously, or if he approaches someone he doesn't know, then he may get reported and we'll have him. So far, he's killed everyone who's seen him. The only people who know who he is are in these photos here, and they're all six feet under. What we need is for someone to see him *and* stay alive, so they can tell us what he looks like and who he is. The best way of accomplishing *that* is to forewarn people. It's our best shot.'

'And if we're wrong?' says Duncan.

'What do you mean?'

'No matter how much you want to believe this theory of yours, Jez, you know it's got more holes than a Swiss cheese. Personally, I think you're wrong. But I'm willing to concede that in time you may be proved right. If you are, then *that* is the time when you should go public – when you *know*. There's still too much doubt. What happens if you make this announcement and you're proved to be wrong? What if this gay serial killer theory is all just moonshine? Not only will we have lost all credibility, but we'll also have sent everyone in totally the wrong direction, and we'll have a killer who won't believe his luck. For me, it's too risky.'

The prosecution and the defence, both resting their cases. Red to be the judge. He looks at his hands and thinks about what they have said.

If they make an announcement, they will obviously keep the details of the killings hidden. Nothing about the tongues, the spoons or the underpants will be published. Nor will they reveal that, between the four of them and Lubezski, they refer to the killer as Silver Tongue. This way, they can weed out the hundreds and possibly thousands of crank calls they will receive from people claiming to be the killer. And they *will* get lots of calls on this one. Queer-bashers, pissed students, the sad and lonely – they'll all be reaching for their phones as soon as the story breaks.

What if they *don't* make an announcement, and someone else is killed? A young man home alone one night. Someone like James Buxton, perhaps. The doorbell rings. He goes to answer it. And the next day his body is found, battered or hanged or decapitated or otherwise mutilated. But if that young man had known there was a killer on the loose, would he have opened the door in the first place? Or would he have dialled 999 and maybe helped them catch the killer? One life lost and one killer still free, when Red has the means to prevent both.

Imponderables. So many imponderables.

Red was so sure, the previous night in the Coleherne, that they were onto something. But Duncan has made him think again. He might be a miserable old sod, Duncan, but he's been around longer than all of them, which was half the reason Red wanted him there in the first place. Red is the man who goes swimming with the sharks, but Duncan has seen much more of the pathetic plankton which makes up society's detritus. Duncan wouldn't say what he did without good reason.

You're standing at a crossroads and you don't know which way to go. Do you wait for the direction to become apparent, or do you make a choice and go one way, knowing that every step could be taking you further and further away from where you want to go?

More holes than a Swiss cheese.

Red looks up. Three faces are turned towards him expectantly.

He has the answer.

'We keep a lid on it,' he says. 'For the time being.'

36

Robert Metcalfe is still there when Red returns to his room half an hour later, but Margaret isn't.

'Where's Mum?' asks Red, blowing on hands flushed red with cold.

'Gone back to the hotel. She says she needs to lie down.'

'I think we all do.'

'I guess so.' He pauses. 'Red ... I'm sorry that we argued just now. We shouldn't have had a go at you like that. We just wanted to ...'

'Lash out at someone?'

His father creases a weak smile. 'Yes. Something like that.'

Red shrugs, but he says nothing that might indicate forgiveness.

'Do you want a cup of coffee, Dad?'

'No thanks. Actually, I'm about to push off. I just wanted to catch you before I went.'

'Stay for a bit. I want to talk to you.'

'You do? About what?'

'Let me get the coffee first. Sure you don't want some?'

'Twist my arm. OK then.'

Red busies himself in the small kitchen on the landing outside his room and comes back with two coffees. He hands one to his father and sips gingerly at the other one.

'Tell me about your business, Dad.'

His father looks surprised. 'Why?'

'Just tell me. Then I'll tell you why I ask.'

'OK. What do you want to know?'

'Everything. Why you're in trouble. How much trouble you're in. I know what you do, in general terms, but I don't fully understand the mechanics of it all.'

'Red, I really don't think that –'

'Dad, after the kind of accusations you and Mum have been bandying about, you're not in much of a position to bargain.'

Robert holds up his hands in surrender. 'OK, OK. For a long time I used to get the ties straight from a factory up in Humberside. I would buy them from source and then sell them on to the retailers, taking my share of the profits in the middle. Cheap ties, nothing special, selling by the bucket load in department stores. You with me so far?'

'Yes.'

'Right. About three or four years ago, we started getting real problems with the unions. Work to rule, strikes, picket lines, all that. You name it, we had it. It was especially bad in that dreadful winter of '78–79. You remember? It was the winter that effectively finished Callaghan and the Labour government. It also effectively finished me. I thought it would get better under Thatcher – and it has, to a small degree – but the damage had been done long before that. Even after the Tories came in, production levels were still down, supply was unreliable and all the trouble with the workers meant that I simply wasn't clearing the kind of money I should have been.

'So last year, I jacked my lot in with Humberside and decided to go down an entirely different route. I set up a joint venture with a manufacturer in Italy, just outside Milan. It's a much smaller operation, but also much classier: hand-crafted silk ties, rather than the polyester rubbish I was dealing with before. Of course, the mark-ups are much higher from factory to shop, so what I lose in volume, I get back in the margins. That was the plan, at any rate.'

'What went wrong?'

'There just isn't the demand for expensive ties that I thought there would be. The franchises that *do* cater to the rich are all sewn up – excuse the pun – and I don't seem to be getting anywhere in the market. It may be that I'm looking in the wrong places, or else that I'm in the wrong game altogether.'

'But either way, you're in hock to the bank?'

'Yes.'

'How much do you owe them?'

'It *was* a lot. I've managed to get most of it paid off, by selling the other car and remortgaging the house and getting rid of a few shares, but I still owe them quite a lot.'

'How much, Dad?'

Robert doesn't want to answer. Red stays silent, pushing his father to speak.

His father relents. 'Twenty-two thousand.'

'And how long have the bank given you to find it?'

'A few days. Start of next week. No more.' Robert shakes his head. 'They're pretty fed up, I think.'

'Do you have any idea how you're going to get the money? I heard you talking on the phone this morning about a few proposals you had in mind.'

'Oh. *Those*.' Robert swallows hard. 'Hot air, I'm afraid. I'm clean out of ideas.'

'So you don't know how you're going to find the money?'

'No. Not really.'

'Not really, or no?'

'Jesus *Christ*, Red. No. Categorically no.'

'So what will happen?'

'I'll be placed into receivership and declared bankrupt, I'd imagine.'

'So Richard Logan's thirty grand would come in quite useful?'

Red says it casually, without changing the pitch or timbre of his voice, and it takes a second or two before his father reacts.

'Redfern! I couldn't *possibly* take that money. It would be scandalous.'

'Why?'

'It's blood money, Red. You must be able to see that.'

'Oh yes. *I* can see it. But I doubt your bankers will.'

145

'No. No way. I would rather declare myself bankrupt than use that reward to shore up my business. I won't do it.'

'Come on, Dad. You can't tell me you haven't thought about this already.'

'Of course I haven't.'

'You can't sit there and tell me you weren't thinking it half an hour ago, when Mum was having a go at me about it.'

'No. Absolutely not. How can you suggest such a thing?'

'Because you didn't say anything during that entire part of the argument, that's how. You were so keen to chastise me over going to the police then suddenly the reward comes up and you're quiet as a mouse. I *know* you were thinking it. It was written all over your face.'

'Then why didn't you say so at the time?'

'Because I was so furious with Mum that I didn't see it straight away. I only realised in retrospect, once I was halfway to the Backs. And even if I *had* twigged, I couldn't have suggested it while Mum was here. You saw how she feels about me taking the reward. She'd have thrown a screaming shitfit.'

Robert smiles thinly.

'I wouldn't have put it quite that way, but yes, she probably would have done.'

'That's why I wanted to get you on your own.'

'It makes sense, Red, but it's still . . . *wrong*.'

'Why? We might as well get something positive out of this whole mess. There's no reason why you or Mum – or me, for that matter – should suffer because of what Eric's done. It's not our fault. You should take the money and keep the wolves from the door.'

'What will Logan think?'

'Logan? The man's a multi-millionaire. He'd probably admire your display of initiative. God, Dad, he might even give you a job.'

'Don't joke, Red.'

'I'm sorry. But what do you care what Logan thinks? When

Logan put that money up in the first place, he knew that he would probably have to pay out. It doesn't make any difference to him who the money goes to, just as long as he gets justice for Charlotte. For all he cares, it could have gone to the Ayatollah Khomeini. So what does it matter that we're Eric's family?'

'Our son killed his daughter. That's what matters.'

'No, it doesn't. The only time it would matter would be if we used it to help defend Eric. But we're not going to. You really can't expect Logan to fund the defence of the man who killed his daughter.'

'But you *can* expect him to save the business of the father of the man who killed his daughter?'

'Yes, of course. Why not?'

Robert sighs. 'I just don't like it.'

'I know. Nor do I, much. But it's making the best of a bad situation.'

'What will your mother say?'

'What will she say if you go bankrupt, Dad? What will your bankers say if they find out that you can get the money you need but choose not to?'

'We don't *deserve* this money, Red.'

'And Charlotte didn't *deserve* to be killed. This thing has already ruined the lives of too many people. We might as well salvage something from it.'

Red, playing father to his father once more.

'Take the money, Dad. Just because you don't like doing it doesn't mean it's wrong.'

Robert runs his hands through his hair, ruffling it up with his fingers and then smoothing it down with the heels of his palms.

'OK. Go on, Red. Call Logan and tell him we'll take his reward.'

FRIDAY, AUGUST 7TH 1998

Kate manoeuvres her way deftly through a group of suits by the bar, flops down into the chair opposite Red and puts the drinks down on the table. Pint of lager for him, vodka and tonic for her. A barmaid takes the ashtray from their table and empties it into a plastic box.

Since most of the drinkers are standing on the pavement outside, Red and Kate have the pub almost to themselves. They are sitting in the corner furthest from the door so they can see everyone who comes into the pub. There is a stained dark red carpet underfoot and stale cigarette smoke hangs low over the tables.

Red rubs his hand across his eyes.

'I know how you feel,' says Kate.

He looks at her.

'Pretty shitty week, huh?'

'You can say that again.'

He takes a long draught of the pint glass, already his third of the evening, and feels the alcohol numbing his tired muscles. There is nothing he would like more than drink himself into oblivion. Four or five pints before switching to shorts, so that by closing time his brain is swimming in his skull and his mouth is drying faster than the desert. He'd drink with Kate if she wants to, or by himself if need be, sit by the bar and stare into space as he lets ethanol kill the pain of failure.

Fuck tomorrow's hangover. He needs to get drunk.

They're no closer to finding Silver Tongue now, more than three months into the killings, than they were at the start. Red is working sixteen-hour days, from eight in the morning until past midnight, six or seven days a week, in the hope that piling on the work will somehow give him the breakthrough he craves. It is blind stupidity and deep down he recognises it. He knows that he would be better off doing exactly the opposite. He should go somewhere wild and remote, the west coast of Scotland perhaps, and wait for the fresh air to bring the answers to him.

But it is not enough to be working hard. You have to be *seen* to be working hard. And pushing off to Scotland might smack of dereliction of duty. So Red stays in the dirt and the smog of the city, and every day he pushes himself through the same destructive cycle of adrenaline and fatigue. The mornings he survives through caffeine. Sometimes, late in the afternoon, when he literally cannot drink any more coffee without being sick, he finds an empty office and lies on the floor for half an hour, hovering between wakefulness and sleep in that twilight state where a thin film comes down, hazy and opaque, between him and reality. And in the evenings, while the city comes home from work and then goes out again to play, Red keeps working.

And where has it got him? Nowhere. Absolutely nowhere. The bags under his eyes are like kangaroo pouches and the skin seems to be falling off his face through fatigue.

'You look knackered,' says Kate.

'Feel it, too.'

'No, seriously, Red, you should take some time off. Look at the state of you. I've seen corpses in better shape than you.'

He sticks his tongue out at her. 'At least I've still got this.'

'Don't joke about it, Red.'

'I'm sorry. And you're right about my being knackered. Thank you for your concern.'

'Even though you're not going to do anything about it, because you're a stubborn bastard.'

He blows air out of his cheeks. 'Let's put it this way. I'm not going to do anything about it because I want to catch this fucker more than anything else in the whole world. And right now, he could be under my very nose and I wouldn't even know.'

His stomach bloats with the lager. He should have eaten something before he came out, but he has to go to a dinner party with Susan tonight. If he is going to turn up drunk, he should at least have the decency to still have an appetite when he gets there. Red can taste the beer on his breath as he speaks.

'In all the time I've done this, Kate, all the cases I've worked, I've always had some sort of . . . control, I suppose. Take any case, except this one. However horrible the killings have been, I've always known that we'd catch the perpetrator eventually. It's like hide-and-seek, except we can seek for longer than he can hide. There aren't an infinite number of hiding places. No matter how anonymous or invisible he thinks he is, he's still got to breathe and eat and drink and sleep. He's still got to *exist*. And, over time, he does things that increase his chances of being caught. So we, the police, know that we're going to find him, and therefore *we* have the initiative. We're going to win. It's just a matter of where and when we win.'

'And of how many people get killed in the meantime, before we win.'

'Yes, to a degree. You have to accept that as inevitable, that you won't catch someone first off. But there's two things there. One, the more he kills, the more likely he is to give himself away, leave a clue or a piece of evidence or something. And he *will* give himself away. Look at Colin Ireland. He killed five people and made one mistake. You know what that was?'

'Of course. I've read the case file too. The thumb print on the window grille in Dalston. He went to look at a disturbance in the street outside and left his thumb mark.'

'Exactly. Not even a full print, just a partial one. A tiny tiny mistake, but it was enough.'

'What's the other thing?'

'That no matter how many people he kills, he would always have killed more but for the fact that we catch him. Killers don't stop voluntarily.'

'OK. I'm with you.'

'But this one, Silver Tongue . . . I've just got no fucking idea what he's going to do next. I don't know the first thing about him. He doesn't leave a single clue. Not one. He kills twice in a day and then he goes underground for almost three months. We know that he's strong enough to have battered James Cunningham to death. But we don't know if that strength is big fat bloke strength or small wiry person strength. Physically, we've no idea what he looks like. The only people who've seen him, or even spoken to him, are all dead.

'And as for what he's *thinking* ... Kate, this is the bit I'm supposed to be good at. Getting inside their heads. Feeling what they feel. Even the real wackos. I've interviewed Sutcliffe, I've interviewed Nielsen, I've interviewed Rose West, I know what they're thinking – or as much as they know themselves. I know what makes them tick. I've got a brother doing life, for fuck's sake. There's nothing I see that makes me stop and think, "wow, that's way too fucked up for me". However degenerate or perverted something appears, it's still *understandable*. But when it comes to Silver Tongue ... I still don't know the first thing about what he's thinking. Every time we sit and come up with a theory as to why he does the things he does, there are 101 ways that theory can be shot down in flames. I've never had this before. *Never*.'

'Red, you need to –'

'No, listen to me, Kate.' Slight slur on the 's'. 'Lishen.'

'OK. I'm listening.'

'You know how this feels? You're good at something, you make your name doing something, right? Well, my something is tracking killers. That's what people know me for. That's why I'm famous, that's why there's articles written about me and why the TV people were on the phone today wanting to do a documentary on me. "That's Red Metcalfe. He gets inside killers' heads and reels them in." That's my thing. Are you with me?'

'Yup. So far.'

'Then imagine that one day someone comes along and takes that thing away from you. He walks up to you and picks it out of your hand, just like that. You don't even realise it's gone. All that you're good at, this person steals from you in a flash.

No matter how good you are, *was*, he's better. He's in control. I look left, he goes right. I look right, he goes left. Someone once said that George Best was so tricky he gave his opponents twisted blood. That's how I feel right now. Twisted blood, from chasing shadows. And do you know how much it hurts?'

'Red, we'll find him. I promise you we will.'

'Only if he *lets* us. He's not like the others, Silver Tongue. He's better than us. Don't you see? It's not *our* choice any more. If he wants us to know who he is or where he is, if he wants to stop, then he'll come in. But he won't. He won't stop.'

'Oh, come on, Red. This thing's only been going on for three months. You know that plenty of murder cases go on for a lot longer before they get solved.'

'Yes, but in those three months we've had nothing. After three months, you should have a pretty good idea of what's going on. And we don't. We don't have a single fucking idea.'

'Red, you mustn't let it get to you.'

'But I *do*. That's the point. I can't just go home and forget about it. It's with me all the time. When I go to bed at night, it's there. When I wake up in the morning, it's there. And all through the day, obviously. So my failure –'

'You haven't failed.'

'– my *failure* is not just a reflection of me as a detective. It's a failure of me, Redfern Metcalfe, as a human being.'

'Red, you're being stupid.'

'No, I'm not. Let me tell you something. My best friend at university got a Third in his finals. He worked really hard, he was a bright guy. He was supposed to get a First and he got a Third. He got the second lowest mark in his year. Now, to me, he was still the same bloke as he ever was. He fucked up his exams. So what? It didn't make him a less worthy person. We went to the pub, and I was trying to console him, and he turned to me and said, "You don't understand." "Understand what?" I asked. "Understand that this is about *me*, as a person," he said. "It's not just about me as a brain, my image of myself as an intelligent bloke. It's not about a few dodgy exams. It hits at the very core of me. I've started to doubt my worth as a person. Because I tried my hardest and I came up badly short. That's a basic character flaw." And that's what I feel now, Kate.'

Kate stares into her vodka and tonic. There isn't an awful lot she can say.

'My mate put himself on the line, Kate, and it wasn't enough. It's easy to fail and say that it doesn't matter because you didn't try your hardest. It's much harder to fail and be forced to admit that you have done your best. I'm doing my best right now and I'm failing badly.' Red looks at his watch. 'Shit. I'm going to be late.' He drains the rest of his pint in one go and stands up. 'Kate, I've got to go. Thanks for the drink. And thanks for listening to my rantings as well. Are you and David doing anything nice this weekend?'

'David's playing cricket all weekend. I'm off to stay with a girlfriend in Windsor.'

'Are you going to go and watch Jez on Sunday?'

'Watch him do what?' She says it nonchalantly, as if she doesn't know. As if.

'His triathlon. It's in Windsor.'

'Oh. *That*. Sounds like too much of an early start for me. I think I might be following your lead and getting alarmingly drunk.'

'Good thinking.'

Red picks up his briefcase.

'By the way, is there anything going on between you and Jez?'

She forces herself to look puzzled.

'What on earth makes you say that?'

'Well, you know. Rumour, gossip, that kind of thing. Besides, you seem to like each other.'

'I do. He's a nice bloke.'

'That's not what I mean.'

She laughs. 'I'm a kept woman, Red.'

'And I'm the Queen of Sheba. About the only thing that could keep you would be a ball and chain, my dear.'

Kate finishes her drink and hitches her handbag over her shoulder.

'Come on, Red, you'll be late. Where are you going?'

'Fulham. You?'

'Other way, I'm afraid. Back to the Docklands.'

It is only later, when Red's taxi is halfway down the King's Road, that he realises that Kate didn't give him a straight answer about Jez.

38

'What is *wrong* with you, Red?'

The traffic lights are turning from green to amber and then to red as Susan stamps on the accelerator. Over the junction and flicking through a left-right dogleg with deft touches on the steering wheel. Susan is angry. She only drives fast when she's angry.

'I asked, what is wrong with you?'

The loping New Zealand vowels, another trait exacerbated by her wrath. No chance of a sensible conversation. She's livid, he's drunk. They'll end up shouting at each other. Red doesn't need this. He tries to defuse the situation.

'Just had a hard week, that's all.'

'*You've* had a hard week?' Sarcasm clear in her voice. 'And that gives you the right to turn up to dinner half-cut and start an argument with someone you've never met before?'

This is Susan at her worst. More concerned about the feelings of total strangers than about her husband's imminent disintegration. The storm is coming. Red tries to head it off one last time.

'Susan, I'm sorry. I've been totally wrapped up in this case.'

A quick shift of eyes narrow with rage as she glances across at him.

'I'll say. Coming home past midnight, out the door again before breakfast, not a word to me about it, no telephone calls to say you'll be home late, no effort to put even one evening aside for me –' Red notices the 'me' not 'us', '– no fucking thought for anyone else but yourself. Jesus, Red, we're supposed to be married.'

'I'm *sorry*, Susan.'

'When you *are* home, you still seem miles away. At least we haven't had any mysterious phone calls. Otherwise I'd think you were having an affair.'

That snaps him.

'Christ Almighty, Susan! You want to hear what I've been doing? You want to know what Silver Tongue *does* to people? You want to come down to the Yard and see the pictures of the corpses? Do you? This is the worst fucking case of my life and all you do is moan because I upset some pathetic twat of an accountant over dinner tonight. If you *looked*, if you *listened*, you might have guessed something of what I'm going through.'

He's shouting and she is too now, voices bouncing off the close walls of the car and around their heads.

'So it's *my* fault now, is it? Red, you don't *talk* to me about this case. You *never* talk about it. And then you've got the nerve to turn round and accuse me of not listening. If you want to talk to me, then I'll listen. I don't ask because I presume you don't want to tell me.'

Red slams the lid on his own rage and tries to be reasonable.

'Susan, I'm not asking you to be my counsellor. All I'm asking is that you give me a bit of space until this is over.'

'Over? And when's that going to be?'

'I have no idea.'

'Weeks? Months? Years?'

'I said I don't know.'

'And so you'll have to keep working all the hours that God sends until you catch him? You mean, there's no one else in the *entire* Metropolitan police force that can do the job for you and give you a break just now and then? Or is our killer going to run wild until supersleuth here nails him?'

'Susan, *don't*. Don't mock me. Don't mock what I do.'

'Red, we're *married*.'

'I know.'

'Well, I just hope the wacko is grateful that you think about him a thousand times more than you think about your wife.'

Appealing to his loyalty. Just like Eric had.

'That's not true.'

'Yes, it is. Red, don't take me for granted.'

There's no answer he can give, because he *has* taken her for granted and he knows it. But he isn't going to be able to make her see his point of view, not tonight.

Red falls silent and looks out at the streetlights clicking past the window.

At Shepherd's Bush, Susan joins the elevated carriageway of the A40, sweeping on the curves of the road as it slices through a barren hinterland of urban depression. Grey high-rise blocks with the lit windows like slices of lemon, opening up onto hundreds of shitty lives inside. People crammed in on top of each other, living in a powder keg and giving off sparks.

Red is drunk, and in his head he talks to Silver Tongue.

Do you live one of those shitty lives, my friend? Are you standing at your window right now, watching the traffic roar past? Are we two adversaries peering unknowingly at each other through the night?

Susan cuts across three lanes of traffic to take the slip road off to Paddington.

Do you even know who I am, Silver Tongue? Because I sure as fuck don't know who you are.

They walk into the house in silence. Red checks the answerphone and flicks through the TV channels. By the time he's established that there's nothing worth watching, Susan is in bed with the light turned off.

Red is asleep almost before he hits the pillows and is wide awake before dawn. Alcohol and worry have jerked him back to life and his hangover is beginning to kick in. He looks across at Susan's back, and wonders if the gulf between them has ever been as wide as it is now.

Friday, April 9th 1982

Red presents himself at the main gate of Highpoint prison. The tension puckers in his bowels.

He speaks into an intercom set in the wall to his right.

'My name is Redfern Metcalfe. I've come to visit my brother.'

The intercom buzzes and a small door set in the vast greyness of the main gate clicks open. Red steps through and finds himself face to face with two prison officers.

'If you'd like to come with us, sir.'

They escort him across thirty yards of grass to the reception block. Their faces are grooved with lines from stress and lack of sleep. Red wonders idly if you can tell how long a warder has been in the service simply by the lines on his face, like dating a tree from the rings on its stump.

Red signs himself in at reception, steps through the arch of the metal detector and holds his arms out from his side so that he can be frisked. Another warder leads him down a corridor. They pass through metal gates which stretch from floor to ceiling and the warder makes sure that each gate is locked behind them before they go on. He explains the rules as they go: 'Do not attempt to pass your brother anything at any time during your meeting. There will be two officers in the room with you at all times. They will be there for your own safety and they will not leave on any account. You will have a maximum of half an hour with your brother. When you are asked to leave, you must do so immediately. Is all of this clear?'

Red nods. The back of his neck hurts, just above the top of the spinal column.

The warder leads him into a small, sparse room. Table, chairs, grey-washed walls. Just like the one at the station at Parkside, where he betrayed the brother he has now come to see.

'They'll be along in a few minutes,' says the warder as he leaves the room.

Red sits on the chair furthest from the door so he can see whoever comes in. He reaches round the back of his neck and starts to massage it with his fingers.

It has taken six weeks of persuasion to get Eric to see Red, six weeks during which their parents virtually begged Eric to let Red visit him. And, now Eric has finally agreed, Red isn't even sure if he wants to go through with it. He was arrogant enough to assume that he could talk Eric round to his point of view. Now that the time is on him, the arrogance has osmosed into fear at the prospect of seeing his brother again.

Why did Eric agree in the first place? To shut Mum and Dad up, probably. Agree to one meeting, and make it so unpleasant that they will never ask again.

Please God, let this be all right.

The door swings open, and in walks Eric.

Not all right. Not all right at all.

Sheer blinding hatred spurts from behind Eric's eyes. Eric flicks his arms free of the warders' too-light grip and moves fast across the room, his hands rigid like claws come to tear Red's soul out and his mouth stretched screaming, distorted wide.

'BREAK YOUR FUCKING NECK.'

Movement blurred in criss-cross. Red rolls off his chair, and feels a sharp pain banging through his knee on impact with the floor. The chair rocks on two legs and then over-balances, brushed by Eric's fingers as he plunges past it. The warders are finally on top of Eric, one of them pulling his arm up behind his back in a half-nelson as the other sits on his legs.

Red pushes himself up against the wall, and Eric yells at

him with fury-curdled words from under the warders.

'You fucking cunt you took the money you took Logan's money you fucking Judas I trusted you I told you everything because I trusted you and because I'd *stopped* and then you just fucking go to the police to get the money my fucking *brother* fucking mercenary you've destroyed the family you stupid selfish bastard Mum and Dad come to see me and they don't know me any more I'm some kind of stranger some kind of monster to them it's going to kill them and when it does it'll be because of what *you've* done not me you fucking wanker . . .'

The warder sitting on Eric's legs turns to Red.

'Out. Get out. Bang on the first gate you come to and they'll let you out.'

'I –'

'Just *go*.'

Red scuttles to the door.

He wants to leave without looking back, but he can't. He takes one quick glance over his shoulder to get a final image of Eric, because he knows this is almost certainly the last time he'll ever see him.

Eric's face is red from the anger and the weight of the men on top of him. The vein which runs down the left side of his forehead stands out proudly against his skin and a line of frothy saliva stretches from the corner of his mouth to the floor.

And that is how Red remembers his brother.

Sunday, 9 August 1998

More than two hours of searing pain lie ahead and Jez isn't ready for a minute of it.

His mind is elsewhere, roaming highways of terror and mutilation. He should have pulled out of this triathlon long ago. He hasn't had the time or energy to train properly. An early-morning run here, a late-evening swim there, and of course cycling to work and back each day; but it isn't nearly enough.

But equally he needs this race. *Any* race. He needs to go out and hurt himself. Red and Duncan find their solace in the bottle, Jez in endorphins. This is his release. Exhaust his body and clear his mind.

The Thames is lined filthy with green algae and brown sludge. Jez has never wanted to get in a river less in his life. He wonders briefly how much of it is raw sewage. Might as well have flushed himself down the S-bend of his toilet and got a flying start.

Swimmers line up on the bank like penguins in their wet suits. The silence of focus.

A flurry of dark movement as they are ordered into the river. Most jump in feet first, holding their noses with one hand and their goggles with the other. Jez dives in, flat and skimming like a racer so as not to scrape himself on the bottom. The water under the wet suit against his skin, cold thawing to warm with his body heat. His swimming cap is snug against the tops of his ears and his goggles fit tightly round the back of his head. He runs his fingers along the strap to make sure it isn't twisted.

Muscles weak and fluttery with tension. Bad nerves, too, demanding flight not fight; the kind of nerves which say 'I don't want to be here' rather than the ones which say 'Let's get it on.'

Yellow swimming caps bob like ducks in the murky water. The starter's whistle sounds loud and clear in the morning air and suddenly four score kicking legs make the water choppy and frothing white. This is the worst bit, when you've yet to find your rhythm and you're getting knocked to shit. Impact after impact in the melee. A soft underwater contact of arm on leg, and then pain sharp and numbing as someone's foot hits Jez square in the face. Goggles are knocked sideways and he reaches out with one hand to put them back on straight. Not gone twenty strokes yet.

Get the rhythm.

Right arm over, left arm over, breathe to the right, right arm over, left arm over, breathe to the right. Pain trickles across his shoulders and down his arms. Keep kicking, two-stroke for balance, not six-stroke for a sprinter's speed. Use the wake of the man in front.

They turn under the railway bridge, 750 metres gone and halfway into the swim. The pack bunches as they approach the turn. Jez keeps to the inside, so as to have less far to swim.

The sun is warm on his hands and face as he turns and the light refracts through the spray, catching little droplets of water and turning them red.

Like blood.

Blood on Jez's hands and his face and his wet suit and his feet, spurting from severed arteries in tongueless mouths.

The blood of the dead.

White panic in a sea of red. Jez opens his mouth to breathe when his head is still underwater. The Thames is warm and sweet and sickly in his throat.

Like blood.

And then he is through the turn with the sun behind him. The spray is clear and transparent again. He stops dead and starts to tread water, breathing deep from his diaphragm. Exertion and fear send his heart rate through the roof.

Jesus Christ. Jesus Christ, cool it.

162

He wants to be out of the water and on his bike, where the wind will dry his skin.

Twelve more minutes in the water and then the marshals' hands are under his armpits at the landing stage, pulling him up and out so he doesn't block those behind him. Reaching behind his back as he runs to the transition area, he pulls the big zipper down and peels the top of his wet suit off.

Numbered racks in the transition area are gleaming with shiny bicycle metal. He knows the drill. Wet suit easily off Vaselined legs. Vest on. Wraparounds on. Helmet on. Bike off the rack. Out of the transition area. Onto bike. Feet into shoes clipped to pedals. Tighten shoes. And move.

Out through the Windsor suburbs, past yellow-jacketed marshals keeping the traffic at bay. The twenty-five miles stretch long and lonely in front of him. He does not dare look behind.

The first of the long hills in the emptiness of the countryside, and the start of real pain. Jez changes down two gears and stands up in the saddle, dancing on the pedals to maintain his speed. Stabbing aches as his thighs tighten. His breath is loud in his ears and sweat wets his brow.

Just like when he saw the bodies.

Images dotted in his head, like Lubezski's photos on the whiteboard. Rhodes and Cunningham and Buxton, names on toe-tags in the morgue.

Over the summit of the hill. Jez flicks the bike back into top gear and lies flat against the handlebars, spinning his legs faster and faster until they can no longer keep up with the bike's speed. The tyres hum on the tarmac.

Coming fast up on another cyclist. Jez swings wide to overtake him. The two bikes are side by side for a second or two and the other cyclist looks across. It is Philip Rhodes, his face contorted in agony. Philip Rhodes' head and a cyclist's body.

The man turns away again. The card stuck on his bike says that he is competitor number 273.

Up out of the saddle again as the road switchbacks and climbs, keeping up the speed to flee 273 Rhodes. Jez looks over his shoulder. Number 273 is still there, ten or twelve bike lengths back. Just another competitor, who for a split second was Philip Rhodes.

Jez passes more cyclists and gets passed by a few, and he looks at none of them. He is in his own tunnel, as narrow as his shoulders and as long as the road on which he rides.

The last miles through Windsor Great Park, when the energy reservoir is bare and nothing seems to hurt any more. He wobbles back into the transition area and takes his time putting his running shoes on.

Out on the road and Jez's legs simply don't want to move. All the blood which flowed into his thighs during the cycling is pooling in his calves. Imagine the worst pins and needles sensation, multiply it by ten and add a whole heap of lactic acid. That's close to what it feels like.

He wants to stop and curl up in a heap somewhere. But he must keep going. Get a rhythm.

His shoes slap on the road and under them appear the faces of the dead men. A thirtysomething caterer, a fat bishop and a young soldier. He stamps on them as they alternate beneath his feet. Right, Rhodes. Left, Cunningham. Right, Buxton. Left, Rhodes. Right, Cunningham. Left, Buxton. And back to the beginning. An endless cycle of six.

The heat builds as the clock ticks on. The running course is six miles, three times round a two-mile loop which goes over Windsor Bridge and up into Eton before coming back on itself.

The last few miles jumble in Jez's mind: sweat in his eyes and faces on the road; the crowd shouting at scullers gliding under Windsor Bridge; the distorted voice on the PA squawking that Siân Brice has won the women's race; figures on his watch mocking him for all this pain and not enough pride; running on empty.

The big digital clock above the finish is flashing two hours and ten minutes as Jez comes underneath it. He wobbles over to the railings and throws up pale yellow liquid, hunched double for five minutes, retching air long after he has emptied his stomach.

41

Red sits on the bonnet of his car for several minutes before he feels able to drive. He holds his body rigid, like a cartoon stick man, with his knees locked and his arms held out straight in front of him, to quell the shaking in his limbs. He thinks he's going to shit himself.

The unblinking eye of the car park surveillance camera watches Red as he looks across at the staff estate. It looks like a normal village made up of bunching semi-detached houses with cars out front and a playground where three children are playing football, until Red swivels his vision left and then all he can see is the brooding monstrosity of Highpoint, with its double perimeter fences topped with coils of barbed wire and dotted with alarm klaxons. An island of filth in the middle of the countryside, keeping the evil in and the innocent out.

When Red finally feels he has regained some control over his body, he gets into his car and drives off. He is going back home, to Much Hadham, but first he has to stop off in Cambridge to pick up some books he has left in his room. Term doesn't start for another two weeks and he wants to get some early revision in for his finals.

The road down into Haverhill is deserted. It is the Easter weekend and most people have already returned home or gone away somewhere. Red's car ploughs a lonely furrow along the tarmac which twists through the Suffolk flatlands. An expanse of monotonous green, relieved occasionally by the yellow splash of a rape field.

Break your fucking neck. Break your fucking fucking neck neck.

Red coasts down the long slope into Haverhill, concentrating fiercely on his driving. At the bottom of the hill he turns right, shifting up through the gears and darting glances between all three car mirrors.

You took the money you took Logan's money you fucking Judas.

It is getting dark. Red fumbles for the headlights switch, turning on the windscreen wipers and then the indicators in quick succession before he gets it right third time. He should be able to find every switch in this car blindfold. He must still be shaken up.

Red turns on the radio, flicking aimlessly from channel to channel. Nothing worth listening to. It will have to be silence. Alone with his thoughts. Again. He could do with a change.

His knee still hurts. Eric's contorted face, his saliva dribbling onto the floor, is only one of a thousand images bouncing around in front of his eyes.

He comes over the crest of the hill at Wandlebury and sees the white confetti of the lights in the windows at Addenbrooke's hospital.

Cambridge. Already? Shit.

Red can't remember anything about the last fifteen minutes, from the moment he entered Haverhill. He remembers concentrating hard at the first roundabout and then . . . *nothing*. Like driving drunk, or being abducted by aliens. A section of his life vanished for ever.

He stops at some traffic lights, slaps his face and breathes deeply. It starts to rain. He turns the windscreen wipers on.

Even in town there is very little traffic. He doesn't have to stop once all the way up Hills Road and over the bridge, train station to his right and Regent Street straight ahead, the depressing mile of estate agents and small cafés which could be seamlessly transplanted to any town in the country.

The access restrictions to Market Square mean that Red has to go the long way round to Trinity. He swings right past the bus station and heads towards Parkside, where he started the chain of events which culminated half an hour ago in the welter of his brother's rage.

Red doesn't want to go to Parkside. He sees the left turn into Emmanuel Road late and takes it too sharply. The momentary squeal of the tyres breaks the silence inside the car.

Down Emmanuel Road, towards Jesus roundabout. The familiar route he took to get to Parkside when he went to turn Eric in.

The wipers clunk across his windscreen, smearing the rain splatters over the glass. Looking through their arc, Red remembers the lonely figure trudging through the fog towards the police station on that bitterly cold February morning.

The same route, only in reverse.

He has a sudden choking desire to undo what he has done. An abrupt hope that he can roll back his steps on this road and rewind that long lonely walk so far in time that eventually Charlotte Logan doesn't exist and his little brother has the chance to grow up normal.

He reaches the roundabout. His indicator clicks dappled-orange as he turns left and heads down Jesus Lane. The road is slick and shiny with rain.

The speedometer tells him he is doing fifty-five in a thirty zone. Too fast.

His right foot doesn't want to move across from the accelerator to the brake. He isn't going any faster now, he just isn't slowing down.

There are no other cars on the road. It's not as if he is driving dangerously.

Up ahead, on the pavement opposite the main gate of Jesus College, Red can see a boy beginning to cross the road. He is dressed in tracksuit bottoms and a baggy sweatshirt, and he is juggling a football from one foot to the other as he walks. The rain has flattened his hair against his scalp. He looks sixteen, seventeen perhaps.

The boy is still a long way away. He'll be safely on the other side of the road by the time Red gets there.

Red doesn't slow down.

The boy lets the ball drop to the road and puts his right foot on it to trap it.

The ball is slippery. It shoots out from under the back of the boy's foot and cannons into his other leg, sending him sprawling face first with his arms stretched wide.

The ball bounces gently into the gutter.

The boy is lying in the middle of the road, and now he isn't going to make it across in time.

Red stamps hard on the brakes.

Too hard.

The wheels lock underneath him, and the car begins to aquaplane, sliding across the wet tarmac.

Red remembers what his driving instructor taught him about skids. Whatever your first reaction is, do the opposite. Instead of steering away from the skid, steer into it. Instead of hitting the brakes, hit the accelerator. That way you'll get some grip back. Then – only then – can you correct the skid.

So much for the theory.

Red panics. He flings the steering wheel clockwise, away from the skid, and stamps on the brakes again.

The car is turning on its axis, spinning round on itself like a dog chasing its own tail.

Red stays strapped in his seat while the world whirls around him.

He is going to hit something. The kerb. A wall. A lamppost.

The boy.

The car has gone through a full circle. It is facing forward again.

Red steers with the skid this time, and feels the purchase on the road.

The kid. He can't see the kid. Where's the fucking kid?

Two bumps in quick succession, under the car, jolting

from tyres to pedals and steering wheel, and from there to Red's feet and hands and brain.

Oh God.

Red brakes as hard as he dares. The car judders slightly and then comes to a halt, just where the road starts to curve left up towards the back gate of Trinity.

He looks in his rearview mirror. The boy is still lying in the road. Motionless.

He is lying on his back, not his front, which means that the car must have flipped him over.

Oh God. Oh God oh God oh GOD.

Red should do something. Go back and help the boy, call an ambulance, take him to hospital. Something.

What if the boy is dead?

Doing fifty-five on a wet urban road. Fast, much too fast.

Driving without due care and attention. Reckless driving. Manslaughter. What could he expect for manslaughter? Five years in jail, probably. Seven if he is unlucky.

Both Metcalfe sons in prison. That would be it. That would kill his parents, as sure as if he walked in and shot them himself.

Red is way out of his depth here.

If the boy is dead then he's too late to save him anyway. If the boy is alive, then he'll be found soon enough. It's a main road. There'll be a car along in a minute or two, even on Good Friday.

Which means he has to go.

Now.

Red can't believe he's thinking this.

He looks frantically around him to see if anyone witnessed the accident.

No one in front of him. No one behind him. No one to his left or right.

For the second time in two months, Red prays forgiveness for what he is about to do.

He lets out the clutch and drives towards Trinity.

Monday, August 24th 1998

A sheet of paper with a big heart drawn on it. Lots of little hearts tracing the inside of the big one, some of them drawn so fast that they look like sloping Bs. And inside them, the words, *Love missive to Susan Metcalfe. Kensington Place, 8.30 tonight. A secret admirer.*

Not so secret. Today is Red and Susan's wedding anniversary. Time for a night's truce, to pretend against the evidence that everything is still all right between them.

Red admires his artwork for a second and then feeds the sheet into the fax.

Jez at his shoulder, chuckling softly.

'You soft shit.'

'Sensible shit, I'd say.'

The sheet comes out of the fax, and Red drops it into the shredder.

'I'm off to get a sandwich. Coming?' asks Jez.

'Yeah. Wait a sec. I'll just get some money from my jacket.'

Red goes back over to his desk. His jacket is slung over the back of his chair. He rootles around in the pockets, finds a handful of change and spreads it out in his palm. Pound coins and 20p pieces, mainly. Just over four pounds in total. That should be enough, even at central London prices.

Jez is standing by the doorway.

'Ready?'

'Yes.'

'Let's go. This highly-trained athlete is starving.'

The phone rings. Jez makes a face. Red picks it up.

'Metcalfe.'

Jez can only hear one side of the conversation, but it is enough.

Red crooks the phone between his right ear and his neck and starts writing frantic notes.

'Where . . . Where's that? . . . Yes, I know it . . . And the body's got all the signs . . . It's been *what*? Jesus Christ . . . Yes. Yes. We'll be there in fifteen minutes.'

He puts the phone down and looks at Jez. His face is pale.

'Another one?' asks Jez.

Red doesn't answer. He grabs his jacket and runs for the door.

43

The squad cars get the four of them from Scotland Yard to Wapping in twelve minutes. Duncan wonders why they even bother hurrying. The police surgeon has already pronounced life extinct. It's not going to make the slightest difference to the poor bugger who's dead whether they arrive in minutes or days.

Red and Jez sit in one car, Kate and Duncan in the other. It is the first time they have all been to a crime scene together.

Red reads the street sign as they slam to a halt. Green Bank, E1. To their left is Jackman House, a brown council estate dotted with satellite dishes. Directly opposite is a brand-new housing development with a massive industrial chimney outside. A sign on the wall of the development reads CHIMNEY COURT. HIGH-QUALITY WAREHOUSE APARTMENTS.

Red gets out of the car and walks towards Chimney Court. Jez calls after him.

'Not that one, Red. *This* one. The council estate.'

Red turns in surprise. 'The council estate? Not many silver spoons in there, surely? I'd have thought our man would have picked one of the Yuppies in here.' He gesticulates behind him, towards Chimney Court.

Jez shrugs. 'I know. Doesn't seem to fit, does it?'

They walk through the main arch of Jackman House. There are graffiti on the walls and the misshapen pink of a discarded condom nestles in a drain. Hostile stares too from the residents of a place where the police are seen not as upholders of law and order but as agents of the ruling class.

A policeman in shirtsleeves is standing outside the first entrance beyond the arch. Red feels the sweat prickle under the armpits of his own jacket. The policeman steps away from the entrance.

'Ground floor. Down the end on the right. It's not pretty in there.'

The smell of death seeps out in wisps and tendrils from the open door at the end of the corridor. Then they are inside the tiny hall and the unbearable stench of bodily juices putrefying in the heat hits them like a sledgehammer, smashing up into their nostrils and overwhelming them. There is a flash of light in a room to their left as the scene-of-crime officer takes pictures. Red heads in that direction as Jez, Kate and Duncan fan out behind him.

This is going to be bad. Worse than the others have been. Red can taste it.

A scene-of-crime officer has his back to them when they walk in. He turns his head, but does not move.

'Who is he?' asks Red.

'Someone called Bart Miller, apparently. He worked as a tanner in a factory just over the bridge. He was discovered after the neighbours became suspicious.'

'Where's the body?'

'Right here.'

And now they see why the officer hasn't moved. He is standing between them and the corpse.

'It really isn't pretty,' he says.

'So we've been told,' replies Duncan.

The scene-of-crime officer steps lightly to his right, leaving their view of the corpse unobscured.

Oh God. Oh dear Lord. Bile rises hot and fast in Red's throat.

Worse than the others have been. Worse than he's ever seen before.

Red feels Kate's hand clutching at his shoulder for support, and hears Duncan groan in disgust.

My God, thinks Red. When I die, make it anything other than this.

Bart Miller has been skinned alive.

44

Red puts his hands on his knees to stop himself from falling. He breathes deeply and the air he inhales is fetid with evil.

Worse than he's ever seen before. Ever.

Red stands upright again and forces himself to go closer. His feet don't want to move. His synapses are on strike as muscles refuse to respond to brain commands. One foot in front of the other at last, very slowly. His feet seem to be miles away.

Bart's body is propped up on a wooden chair with a high slatted back. Red looks at the corpse's front, then takes a couple of paces further forward and peers round at Bart's back.

No skin on either.

Bart's entire torso has been flayed. There is a neat line round the base of the neck where the killer – the monster – started cutting, and again round the waist, just above the line of the underpants. Two more lines run through each armpit and over the shoulders.

He hasn't cut the skin off the arms. Just the torso. A vest of skin.

And where the skin was once is now just a mass of areolae. Thousands and thousands of patches like tiny spiders' webs packed in tightly against each other, individually separate up close but blending into a formless sea of white from a few yards away.

This thing we hunt. What in God's name are we up against?

Not who. What. This is beyond human.

Absolute terror shows on Bart's eyes – not because they are wide and staring, but because they are clenched so tightly shut that clusters of lines have exploded on the skin nearby. And as with the others, a silver spoon protrudes from the bloody goo of his mouth like a swizzle stick atop a Bloody Mary.

At what stage does terror stop and yield to white incomprehension? When does evil become so acute that your brain simply refuses to accept it, and instead sends the shutdown order racing round your body? Red looks into Bart's lifeless face and sees what has been done to him, and reckons that he must have come as close as anyone to it.

Bart Miller's left hand is hanging limply below his thigh, with something in it. Jez squats down by the side of the chair to examine it.

The object in Bart's hand looks like a scrunched-up cloth.

Red follows Jez's gaze.

Not a cloth.

Skin.

Bart Miller is clutching his own skin.

45

The traffic on Tower Bridge is backed up bank to bank. They're in the squad cars, but they don't use the sirens. Red wants time to compose himself. He remembers what he said to Kate in the pub a couple of weeks back – *there's nothing I see that makes me stop and think, 'wow, that's way too fucked up for me'.*

There is now.

The lorries coming the other way bounce slightly as they cross over the middle of the bridge, the part which lifts when ships pass beneath. Red can feel gentle juddering around the squad car's shell. Tourists mill around on the pavements. A few miles east, the Canary Wharf tower glows deep gold in the sunshine.

It takes ten minutes to cross the bridge and then they are almost there. Under the railway tracks which branch out from London Bridge station, then first right and immediately left, past the skips at the gate and across the forecourt to the tanning factory.

They had called ahead to Ashley Lowe, Bart Miller's erstwhile employer, so he is waiting for them outside the factory door. Red and Duncan follow him upstairs. They have left Kate and Jez to supervise the house-to-house enquiries back in Wapping.

Lowe's office, perched above the factory floor, is hot and stuffy. The light slants through ragged partition blinds onto an old Pirelli calendar stuck at November 1985. Lowe sits in the swivel chair behind his desk. Red and Duncan take the hard chairs opposite him.

'This place, Tanner Street, used to be where the whole industry was based,' says Lowe. 'Like the leather version of Fleet Street, if you like. All of us in a row, right down to the leather market at the end of the road. Look at it now. Compound blocks for the bankers who work across the river, mostly. We're the only tanners left here, and I can't imagine it'll be too long before we go under as well. All that heavy industry and machinery will be the death of us. We're a small outfit. We just can't compete.'

Through the dust on the windows which give onto the factory floor, Red can see a couple of men hunched over long tables. There are three large machines, and all of them are standing idle. He turns to Lowe.

'Mr Lowe, what exactly is it that you do here?'

'Processing leather, really. Taking it in its natural form –'

'Off the animal's back?'

' – exactly, and processing and curing it into something that can be used for shoes and handbags and all that stuff. You can't just whip it off the cow and shove it on your feet, you know.' Lowe laughs his smoker's laugh, low and rasping as it tails off into a coughing fit.

'Pardon me,' he says, wiping away a globule of mucus from the side of his mouth. 'Not as fit as I used to be.'

Another chuckle, and another cough.

Red is making notes. *Leather*, he writes, and underlines it. *S&M?*

'So do you actually take the skin off the animals?' he asks.

'Oh no. That's done one step down the line, between the abattoir and here. We get the skins and then we work on them. But we don't take them off ourselves.'

'And what did Bart Miller do here?'

'Everything. Everyone does everything here. Like I said, we're a small outfit. We can't afford to have specialists. If something's got to be done, then everyone mucks in. You know what I mean?'

'Did Bart ever wear leather? Did he ever dress in leather clothes?'

Lowe snorts.

'He had a leather jacket, if that's what you mean, and occasionally he'd wear a pair of leather shoes, but that's all.'

'He didn't get all togged up in leather trousers and chains?'

'Bart? Do me a favour. He wasn't no faggot.'

'You're sure?'

'Sure? 'Course I'm sure. Bart was the straightest geezer I ever knew. He was beating women off with a shitty stick. Had about five or six on the go at any one time, he did. He'd always be boasting about it, how he screwed one bird one night and then her mate the next, and how none of them knew about the others, and then he'd meet some new sort and add her to the list. God alone knows how he did it.'

'Did you ever see any of these women?'

'A couple.'

'Where did you see them?'

'When they came here. Sometimes they'd pick him up at the end of the day, or maybe drop him off in the morning. Know what I mean?' Lowe winks conspiratorially. 'And there'd always be birds on the phone. I had to ban him from using the phone after a bit. Couldn't keep hauling him off the factory floor every time one of his floozies got her knickers in a twist.'

'So they definitely existed, then?'

'Who?'

'These women.'

'Oh yeah. Definitely.'

Red taps his pen thoughtfully on his pad.

So Bart wasn't gay. And no one in their right mind could have mistaken him for being gay.

The leather angle had been too good to be true. Unless . . . *unless* Bart was privately into leather with his girlfriends, and somehow Silver Tongue had found his S&M gear and mistaken this for homosexuality.

Check Bart's wardrobe, Red writes, though he knows the chance is pretty slim.

'One more thing, Mr Lowe. What did you pay Bart?'

'Five-fifty an hour.'

'So, over the course of a year, that worked out at . . . ?'

'About twelve grand.'

'Did he have any private income?'

'Not as far as I know. If he had, I doubt he'd have been working here.'

'So he wasn't exactly well off?'

'Oh, do me a favour, officer. You want to be a millionaire in this place, you'd better win the lottery. Know what I'm saying?'

'I certainly do, Mr Lowe.' Red gets up. 'Thank you for your time. If we need you to make a statement or to talk to any of Bart's colleagues, we'll let you know.'

Ashley Lowe watches them go down the stairs and walk out across the forecourt, putting on their dark glasses as they step into the sunlight. He realises that he hasn't made any of the grief-stricken platitudes which he imagines are usual in these circumstances. He didn't tell them what a good employee or upstanding citizen Bart had been. He hopes that the policemen didn't notice. Not that he isn't sad about Bart's death. But now he's got to advertise for a replacement and that's going to cost money. And Bart *had* been a good worker. Knew what he was doing, that's for sure. Those boys down on the factory floor right now, they're little more than apprentices.

He hears the police car drive away.

Funny how that one detective did all the talking. The other one, the big fat bloke, said nothing all the way through. Just sat there and never took his eyes off him, as if he was passing some sort of judgment on him.

46

The whiteboard is covered in photos again.

'This puts Silver Tongue into a totally different league,' says Lubezski. 'The three previous killings have demonstrated merely that he's strong and he's angry. But this one – this one required *skill*.'

He points to the photos of Bart's torso, front and back.

'This is only a preliminary finding, but it's enough to go on. Look here. Look at the cut marks. Round the neck, the upper arms and the waist. Just like a vest, or a sleeveless pullover. Now, my guess is that he started here.'

Lubezski jabs a finger against his own chest, right at the base of the neck, in the space between the inside edges of his collarbones.

'Then he would have cut all the way down here.'

He runs his finger straight down his chest to the waistline. 'Everyone with me?'

Red, Jez, Kate and Duncan nod.

'Next, he would have cut around the neck, all the way round. Then probably the shoulders, under the armpits, each side. Then two long cuts like this.'

He lifts up his right arm and traces a line from under the armpit down to his waist.

'Both sides. Then round the waistline. You see?'

They do. All too clearly.

'And then he would have taken the skin off.'

'Just like that?' Kate looks sceptical.

'Oh yes. You can peel skin back like Sellotape if you've done your cutting right. And our man obviously did. See, skin is not uniformly thick on the body. It's thickest on the soles of your feet, where the average is about 8 millimetres, and thinnest on your face – say 2 millimetres. Of course, he hasn't touched those parts of the body. The skin on the chest is slightly thicker than that of the face, but thinner than on the back. He knew that, and he adjusted for it.'

'How can you make such an accurate guess?' asks Jez.

'Because we found three separate pieces of skin in Bart Miller's hand. Two pieces were virtually identical and the third was larger and thicker than the other two. This last piece, the big piece, came from his back. The two smaller pieces came from his front. Silver Tongue peeled the skin away from the main incision down the front of the chest until it met the incision on each side, beneath the armpit. This gave him the two pieces off the front. Then he took off the back in one piece.'

'How long would it have taken him?' From Jez again.

'That depends on a lot of things.'

'Like what?'

'Partly on whether the victim was struggling, but also on Silver Tongue's own nerves and skill. But at a rough guess, probably about half an hour. Maybe less.'

Red steeples his fingers together.

'What about the tongue? Did he take that out before or after he did the flaying?'

'After. Definitely after.'

'Why?'

'Three things. Firstly, there's not enough blood on the flayed skin found in Bart's hand to suggest that Silver Tongue cut the tongue out before he did the flaying. If he *had* cut the tongue first, then there would have been blood everywhere. We've seen that from the other killings.

'Secondly, if he had done the tongue first, he'd either have had to wait until the bleeding had stopped – thus increasing the time he had to spend in the house and therefore the likelihood of him being caught – or else he'd have had to work under a spray of blood.

'And thirdly, I imagine that he had turned Bart upside down before starting work on him.'

'Upside down?' queries Red. 'Why?'

'Silver Tongue is a sadist. He enjoys inflicting pain. And if the victim is inverted, then blood pressure is maintained in the head, keeping the victim conscious for longer and thereby increasing his pain. Moreover, Bart Miller's underpants are relatively free from blood. That is consistent with their being above the line of flaying, which could only have happened if he was upside down.'

'And then he turned him back the right way up?'

'He must have done. That's what I think happened, at any rate. Because Bart Miller didn't die from massive blood loss.'

'He didn't?'

'No, though he would have done so eventually. He actually died of a heart attack, probably brought on by shock. His body could stand what was being done to it – just – but his mind couldn't.'

Lubezski's voice is as calm as if he is reading the football scores.

'I think,' he concludes, 'that Bart Miller died of fright.'

47

Died of fright. Lubezski's words rattle round Red's skull as he prowls through Bart Miller's flat. Outside, the warm evening is fading towards another sticky night.

He checks the wardrobe first. No whips or chains or leather chaps. Bart obviously liked his sex straight. Maybe working with leather all day puts you off the stuff when it comes to free time.

Red goes back into the living room. The chair where Bart's body was found is still there. There are gouge marks at the top corners of the chair's back, where Bart's ankles were tied.

Lashed to the chair by your ankles and your wrists, all the way down the high back on the opposite side to the seat, so you hang straight. The blood rushing to your head and keeping you conscious while someone goes to work on you with a knife.

Red tastes Bart Miller's pain. He rolls it around his tongue, up and over his gums and right down to the back of his throat. Bart Miller's excruciating pain and Silver Tongue's exquisite pleasure. A craftsman, a surgeon, teasing sharp shining metal into glistening flesh, peeling the skin back like taking the rind off an orange.

You don't rip the skin to shreds as you take it off. What you produce is a work of fucking art. And we thought you were just a violent little shit. Apologies for the underestimation.

But if you're not going to take the skin with you, why flay someone in the first place? People who flay their victims normally want the skin for their own purposes. But Silver Tongue didn't want the skin for himself. He'd left all the skin behind, forced into Bart Miller's left fist. The only thing he'd taken, as usual, was the tongue. Why?

Maybe he'd been disturbed as he worked and had to leave

quickly, scrunching the skin into Bart's hand rather than folding it neatly. But that doesn't make sense. He would just have dropped the skin on the floor if he was in that much of a hurry. And besides, Lubezski said that the tongue was cut out after the flaying. So, if he had to leave with the flaying just completed, then the tongue would still have been intact.

Come back to the *why*. Try the *who*.

Lowe said that none of his employees is responsible for taking skins off animals. That is done before the skins get to them. Between the abattoir and us, he said.

Who's between the abattoir and them? Could it be one of Lowe's suppliers?

Skinning animals would be good practice before graduating to humans. And they wouldn't necessarily have to be dead animals, either. The FBI has a theory of the 'homicidal triad': three childhood characteristics of which almost all serial killers demonstrate at least two. Bed-wetting is one, arson another.

Cruelty to animals is the third.

How big a step is it from pegging cats' cadavers out on the lawn to skinning a man alive?

Connections in Red's head. The homicidal triad. Arson.

Arsonists like to admire their handiwork. Police always check crowds at the scenes of fires. If the fire was caused deliberately, then it's a good bet that the firestarter will be among those watching. But Silver Tongue doesn't come back to watch. The only murder at which there was a crowd was the first one, that of Philip Rhodes, though of course there were all those journalists covering James Cunningham's murder the same day. There's been no one at any of the scenes since. No one at the scenes and no clues on the bodies.

Red slams his head into his palms. It's hopeless. Four people dead, and he can't do a damn thing for any of them.

Worse, he can't do a damn thing for those who don't yet know that they are being hunted.

48

It is past nine when Red gets home, and Susan isn't in. She must be working late.

Red leaves the car at home and starts walking towards Paddington Station. He crosses Sussex Gardens, the line which divides opulence and detritus as effectively as a fence of barbed wire. South of Sussex Gardens, down towards Hyde Park, the big houses stand proud on clean pavements. To the north, litter and drunks alike spill into the gutter. Two worlds separated by a set of traffic lights. Red wonders how long it will be before the have-nots take the short step across the road and trash the place.

He walks down the streets where Kevan Latimer took them on a wild goose chase last month. Shop fronts glide past Red's vision: the off-licence where the manager's armpits smell like goat's cheese, the whitewashed and revamped pub, the delicatessen on the corner which seems to change hands every few months.

The evening buzzes with the peculiar polyglot of summertime London: Dutch tourists, Bengali newsagents and Scottish labourers. On a street corner, a bunch of football supporters stand bare-chested and tattooed, their faces flushed red with heat and alcohol. They sing loudly and threateningly, and passers-by step into the road to give them a wide berth.

Red walks through the middle of it all, lost in his own forcefield, the world just a cardboard backdrop to the thoughts and fears jumping and crackling in his head. He turns left, walks past the 7-11 and ducks into the underground station. Red hasn't taken the Tube in more than a year and he isn't quite sure why he is doing it now.

The colours on the Tube map lie across each other like tangled intestines. The brown of the Bakerloo line between

Harrow and Charing Cross. The yellow ellipse of the Circle Line as it rings Zone 1, going round on itself in an endless loop. Red smiles. That makes two of them.

He can go west or east. West takes him through St James' Park, right next door to Scotland Yard. Back to work. Back to fruitless searches. He chooses east.

The first train comes within two minutes. Circle Line via Liverpool Street, spelt out in points of orange light on the dot matrix display. Some of the letters have holes in them where the dots haven't joined.

The doors hiss open onto a carriage that is almost empty. Red gets on board and sits down. A discarded section of the *Evening Standard* rests on the seat next to him, its salmon-pink pages splayed open on the fabric. The business section. He doesn't bother reading it.

The train heads into the tunnel and Red can see his reflection, wild and distorted, in the unyielding blackness of the curved window opposite. His forehead seems to disappear entirely into the roof of the carriage.

The train fills up at Edgware Road and then again at Baker Street, until virtually all the seats are taken. People on the move, going from one place to another in the confines of their small lives.

Is one of them Silver Tongue?

Red looks slowly round the carriage, searching for possible suspects. Take out women, children and pensioners and see what you've got left. There's a fat man directly opposite him, with a baseball cap and a green sweatshirt. He's wearing tracksuit bottoms tucked into gleaming white hightop trainers. All the gear, but too much of an overweight slob to make any use of it. What about the guy next to him, the one who looks a bit like Salman Rushdie? His scalp is showing through thinning dark hair, and there is the briefest brushstroke of a double chin. And next to *him*, a man in a pinstripe suit with a pink shirt and a yellow tie patterned with windmills. His blond hair is cut short at the sides and slicked back on top. Merchant banker. American psycho.

This is ridiculous. It's not any of them. You can't go round looking at every innocent person as if they're a mass murderer.

But that's what he's doing. That's exactly what he's doing.

Calculations tick over in Red's head: how many people use the Tube each day? Two or three million, he'd read somewhere. Most of those use it at least twice a day – for going to work and returning home again. And most of *those* will use it at rush hour. So now, at quarter-past eight on a summer's evening, how many people are somewhere on the Underground system. Half a million, say?

Half a million. Eight million people in central London. A one in sixteen chance that Silver Tongue is now, *right now*, either on a train or waiting for one. One in sixteen. Almost worth grinding the whole system to a halt and demanding alibis from everyone there.

Yeah. *Right.* Like *that's* practical.

And then the odds start lengthening dramatically. What are the odds of Silver Tongue being on this train, the very one Red is sitting on? Or the one after, or the one before? Or in any of the stations that they pass through, one of the faces flashing past the window in the brief stops of light between the tunnels? What about *really* stacking the dice? What price would you get on him and me *and* the next victim all being on this train? In this very carriage? You'd have more chance of winning the lottery, and that's 14 million to one.

Ashley Lowe said something about winning the lottery this afternoon.

Red sits there, formulating permutations and chalking up odds on the blackboard of his mind, until the numbers start running into each other and racing past his mind's eye too fast for him to count, and then he is slapping his face to wake himself up and he realises that people are looking at him askance, and the train pulls up at St James' Park, right back to work, and he has gone two-thirds of the way round the Circle Line without even realising it.

49

Susan is in when Red gets back. In, and spitting mad.

She is slumped in front of the TV, watching the commercial break in the middle of the Ten O'Clock News. The screen pulses with colour and sweat, images of a sporting endeavour. An advert for Nike.

'You'd better have a fucking good explanation,' she hisses.

He looks fast at her, surprised.

'*Explanation.* For what?'

The rage comes from her soul and out through her eyes. 'Kensington Place. Our wedding anniversary. *Remember?*'

The guilt and shame smack Red square in the gut.

'Oh Susan. Oh my God. I'm so sorry. I'm so so sorry. We had another –'

'You sent me a fax telling me that we were going out to dinner. A fax with a heart saying "Love missive", with lots of little hearts around the inside. *Remember?*'

She isn't shouting. Yet. Which makes it even worse. It would be easier for Red if she just lost it and started yelling. Then they could trade screamed insults, and be as much to blame as the other. But while she stays calm, she'll trowel the guilt onto him in thick layers until he is the one who breaks and lashes out, and then he will be doubly in the wrong: not only for screwing it up in the first place, but also for losing his temper with her. When she wants to, Susan can play Red better than anyone else in the world.

'Susan. *Honey.*'

Red takes a single step towards her, and no further. He knows better than to try to touch her when she is in this mood. Little spikes of anger stand up on her skin like a porcupine's prickles.

'I know nothing I say is going to make any difference, Susan,

188

but let me just explain what happened. We had another murder today. I got tied up in that. I've been working flat out since lunch time.'

Not quite true, but better than saying, *I've been slowly going mad on the Circle Line.*

'Do you have any idea, Red, *any* idea, of what you've done?'

'Susan, I –'

'No. Let me finish. Then you can have your say.'

She pauses as if trying to work out where to start, even though she must have practised this speech over and over in her head while waiting for him to come home.

'OK, Red. We try to patch things up. You come over all romantic, like we'd just started going out, not like we're trying to save our fucking marriage. You send me that fax, that really lovely fax. And there's me, feeling just a little bit warmer inside than I have done for a while, determined to do my bit to make tonight special, and I come home and put on a little bit of perfume just here and here –' she dabs at her wrists and neck, '– and I wait here until eight, and I figure you're probably coming straight from work, because you've been so busy lately, so I get a cab to Kensington Place to make sure I'm on time, and I sit there like a lemon for an hour, and I dial your mobile three times – *three times* – and each time I get that fucking digital voice telling me that the mobile phone I have dialled is switched off, and everyone in the restaurant is looking at me, little sideways glances, nothing too obvious, naturally, and they're thinking, "Poor sad bitch, she's been stood up", and eventually I give up waiting and I walk home, and all the way home I'm crying my eyes out and thinking how much I'd like to kill you, because if you're going to be a pig then that's one thing, but if you say you're going to make the effort and you *still* behave like a pig then you're fucking scum and I don't know why I bother with you.'

She gets up and stalks past him, out into the corridor and up the stairs to the bedroom. She doesn't shut the bedroom door. He's obviously not going to get his say, as she promised.

Red goes into the kitchen and flicks the kettle on to boil.

He puts a tea-bag into a mug, splashes some milk onto it and spoons some sugar out from the jar. White sugar, flecked with the dark brown of coffee grains. The spoon catches on the rim of the mug, knocking sugar all over the sideboard. Red swears and sweeps the granules up, using his right hand to brush them into his left.

I know friends whose marriages have failed, he thinks. I've listened to them talk about it and cry about it. But until now, I've never really appreciated what it's actually like. All those little parts which make up a marriage are slipping through my fingers like sand, and the more I scrabble to retrieve them, the more they skitter and slide out of my reach.

I also know people who deliberately manufacture arguments because the reconciliation sex is so good. Good enough, in fact, to make up for whatever else is missing. Relationships which can only be maintained by constantly pulling them this way and that, stretching them to their limits and then clinging onto the rush as they snap back into place, fearing that if you let them stay static for too long they will implode, deflate.

The kettle boils. He pours the water in, stirs and pokes at the tea-bag until the tea is dark enough for him, then drops the tea-bag into the bin and goes up to the bedroom. Susan is already in bed, her back turned to the door. Red sips at his tea and puts it down on the dressing table.

'Can I say my piece now?'

She doesn't move. He waits for a few seconds, and then decides to take her silence as assent. 'He struck again.'

'Who?'

'Silver Tongue.'

'When?'

'Today. Just after I faxed you. Literally. I was on my way back from the fax machine, just about to go and grab a sandwich with Jez when the phone rang.'

'I don't want to hear it, Red.' Her voice is muffled under the duvet.

'Number four, Susan. Number four! A man called Bart Miller.

And you know how Silver Tongue killed him? He skinned him, Susan. Skinned him alive and left the skin crumpled up in his hand. Quarter of an hour after faxing you, I was looking at a man with no skin on his torso. Do you understand now?'

The duvet unravels from around her head as she rolls over towards him.

'Red, we've been through this before. I couldn't care if Bart Miller was found in the Thames with his feet in a concrete bucket. He's not my fucking husband, he's not my fucking friend. I don't *care*. Don't you see?'

Red is rising fast. The lava bubbles in his throat.

'Bart Miller was held upside down so he would remain conscious for longer. He *knew* what was happening to him. Lubezski reckons it could have taken up to half an hour. All the way through, with the skin being sliced from his chest and his back, he could feel it all. Can you imagine that, Susan? *Can you?* Half an hour, where every pain-laden second feels like a century. Think of it, just for a moment, and then you might realise why I'm behaving the way I am.'

Susan rolls over again, away from him. Red dives on the bed and grabs her shoulders, shouting now with anger and frustration sparked by her refusal to listen.

And suddenly the impotence of his fury finally seems to get through to Susan. She turns onto her back and pulls him close to her, entwining her arms around the back of his shoulders and nuzzling her mouth in his hair. They are both talking gibberish now, his shouts subside into sobs, she makes little nonsensical soothing noises.

She pushes his face up and away from her, then her lips are on his, their tongues – *tongues* – touching like electric currents in the middle of their open mouths, and his hands are moving under her nightgown, finding the hem and pushing it up, over her thighs so that the darkness beneath her navel is exposed, up and over her breasts, and she lifts her head off the pillows so he can ease it over her head, and she is fumbling at his shirt and his trousers, and between them they kick the duvet away so that it lies half on and half off the bed, and they are both naked, and he is between her legs as she reaches down to guide him inside her, and he shuts his eyes . . .

Skinned alive.

He can feel the bones of Susan's hips shifting under the skin beneath his touch, and it is as if that touch is the only thing connecting him to reality. He is whirling away from this dimension. All he can see behind his eyelids is what he's seen too much of already: skin clenched into fists, bodies hanging from banisters, spoons wedged into mouths and pools and pools of blood where the tongues had been, on and on and on until he opens his eyes and the images are still there, fusing into Susan's face before they melt away into vapour trails.

Red looks down. His penis hangs limp and useless, mocking him. So much for the grand passion that reconciliation sex is supposed to be.

He pushes himself back off the bed, reaching down only to pick up his underpants and cover his shame. He takes the still-hot cup of tea off the dressing table and goes back down to the living room where he sits in front of the TV, seeing nothing and hating himself.

WEDNESDAY, JULY 14TH 1982

Eric lasted a week before confessing. Red has lasted three months and now he can't take any more.

Not a single day goes past that Red doesn't think about the boy and wonder what happened to him. Whether he's dead or alive, whether he ended up OK or as a vegetable. What his name was. Not a single day when Red doesn't relive those few seconds of skidding horror in his head, when the remorse and the anguish don't gnaw away at him.

He ducked the local news and papers for two weeks after the accident, too frightened to find out if – like his brother – he had stepped over the line marked KILLER. But every day, he walks past the spot where he hit the boy. The police have removed the yellow ACCIDENT: CAN YOU HELP? sign now, but they haven't managed to take away the guilt with it. Red knows what Eric went through now. He knows how it feels to suffocate under the pressure of this huge thing inside you, a secret so huge you fear your body isn't physically strong enough to deal with it. Most of the time the monster just pushes against the inside of his stomach, but sometimes it bubbles up in his throat, trying to get a look at the outside world, daring him to blurt out the truth.

He can't count the number of times he's reached for the phone to ring the police and claim responsibility. He's gone as far as lifting the receiver and dialling the number. But he's never held on long enough to hear someone answer, because if they answer then he might tell them everything. He has always hung up as the connection is made through the ether. He's never heard the phone ring at the other end.

Because what good would it do now? It wouldn't help

the boy. It wouldn't serve any purpose, because it was nothing but an accident, more of an accident – *much* more of an accident – than what happened with Eric and Charlotte Logan. Eric meant to harm her, if not actually to kill her. Red never even meant to hit the boy. He doesn't want to go to jail for an accident.

That's what he tells himself. That's what he's told himself for three months. But now he's not so sure that going to jail wouldn't be better. He can't carry his burden any more. He can't live his life consumed by rain-sodden guilt.

He's done his finals, got his degree and now is looking for a job. His life is in limbo as it is.

Just after lunch, as the sun squints through the clouds for the first time that day, Red takes the long walk down to the police station. He's done this walk before, of course, when he turned Eric in. This time, it's himself he's going to hand over.

WEDNESDAY, SEPTEMBER 9TH 1998

The Commissioner clasps Red's right hand in both of his.

'Red. Good to see you.' He ushers him to an armchair. 'Sit, please. Coffee? Tea?'

'I'm fine, thanks.'

Red sinks into the armchair and feels the white leather cushions spread under his weight. The Commissioner goes back to the other side of his desk and sits down. His head is a good two feet above Red's. Basic tactics of mild intimidation. From the depths of the armchair, Red has to look up at the Commissioner throughout the meeting. The Commissioner could easily sit in the other leather armchair a few feet away, or give Red an upright chair.

Why don't you go the whole hog and schedule the meeting for late afternoon, thinks Red, when the sun will be shining straight into my eyes, blinding me?

'How's the case going, Red?'

The case. Only one. They've been pulled off all other work since it started. Fat lot of good it's done them.

At least the Commissioner doesn't beat about the bush. Red decides to be equally direct.

'Not too well, I'm afraid. It's been going on for more than four months now, and we've got absolutely nothing.'

'Nothing?'

You know it's nothing, you fool. You would hardly have asked – sorry, summoned – me here if we had a suspect in custody and a watertight case for the Director of Public Prosecutions.

Red keeps his face neutral.

'Nothing. Our killer –' Red doesn't refer to him as Silver

Tongue, not in front of the Commissioner, '– leaves no physical clues on the bodies. The autopsies on all four victims have come up blank on that front. Friends, neighbours, passers-by, they all saw nothing. No sign of breaking and entering at any of the crime scenes. Either our man persuades the victims to open the door to him – and we don't know how – or he goes through open windows. The killings started in May, when it was already unseasonably hot, so people *do* leave their windows open at night. And the victims themselves have nothing in common apart from the fact that the killer singled them out. No mutual friends, no mutual interests. Every connection we make gets shot down sooner or later, as I'm sure you've heard.'

'Yes. I have heard that. But enlighten me anyway.'

You arsehole. This is the last thing I need.

'We thought there might be a homosexual connection. The first three victims all at least experimented with some form of homosexuality. But the most recent victim, Bart Miller, was by all accounts straight as a die, with a libido to match. We also considered that our man might be targeting males who live alone, but the third victim, James Buxton, disproves this. He lived with his brother. Incidentally, their flat was the only murder site so far which did not have ground-floor access. Again, looking for connections, we thought that the flaying of Bart Miller might have had something to do with his occupation as a tanner, but none of the others were killed in a way that had resonances with their jobs. Of course, if we get an account-ant who's been bored to death, then obviously we might have to revise this opinion.'

The Commissioner does not laugh. 'And so you're waiting for the break, Red?'

'Not at all.' Defensive. 'We're not "waiting" for anything. We're doing everything we can to make that break happen.'

'And is that likely?'

'I don't know. There's no sign of it yet, obviously. But it won't take much. A break is a break. It can come when you least expect it. If our man leaves a fingerprint or some fluid somewhere, or someone sees him, then suddenly we've got a whole lot more to work on.'

'But right now you're chasing shadows?'

Red sighs. 'Yes. Right now we're chasing shadows.'

A green glass paperweight turns in the Commissioner's hands.

'And you, Red? How are *you* bearing up?'

So this is what the summons is all about.

'Oh, as well as can be expected.'

'This isn't affecting your, ah, mental health in any way?'

My mental health? Oh no. I'm just quietly going insane. Don't worry about me.

'Well, obviously my team and I have all been working hard, and so we've all been tired and probably a bit run down . . .'

'Have you been to see any stress counsellors?'

'I spoke to one the other day, as part of the mandatory quarterly review.'

'Do you know what she said?'

'No, I don't. Though I presume she was satisfied.'

'Why do you presume that?'

'Because I haven't heard back from her.'

'But *I* have.'

The paperweight is back on the table and a thin manila folder is now in the Commissioner's hands.

'She was so worried about you that the report came straight to me. Would you like to know what it says?'

Not in the slightest, thinks Red. He flaps an assenting hand with a nonchalance he does not feel.

The Commissioner doesn't open the folder. He has obviously read the report carefully.

'It says that you have placed yourself under levels of stress which are, and I quote, "quite intolerable". It is the counsellor's opinion that your self-esteem is being eroded by your failure to make anything approaching decent headway towards solving this case. She concludes that you may suffer a nervous breakdown if you do not slacken off.'

'That's ridiculous.'

'Is it?'

'Yes, it is. I'm prepared to accept the first two findings, about stress levels and self-esteem. She's right about those. Not that she has to be a psychiatric genius to work them out, of course. But I'm not on the verge of a nervous breakdown. Any suggestion that I *am* is quite absurd.'

The Commissioner clears his throat. 'Would you be amenable to being moved onto other projects?'

'No, I would not.' Heartfelt and vehement.

'Why not?'

'It would be totally counter-productive.'

'It might save your health.'

'My health is fine. Good enough, anyway. More to the point, if you pull me off this case, then you drastically cut our chances of finding this man.'

'You haven't exactly covered yourself in glory so far.'

Ouch. Red actually winces.

'No, we haven't. But we've got a good team and we trust each other. The killer's good. He's very good. The best I've ever seen, to be honest with you. And I genuinely don't think that anyone else would have more success. My team and I are the best people available. Take me off it – take any of us off it, for that matter – and we'll be starting from scratch.'

Red looks at the green of the paperweight and the brown of the envelope in silence as the Commissioner ponders what to do. Green and brown. Nature's colours.

'All right, Red. I trust your judgement – against *my* better judgement, I should add. But I want you to agree to more frequent counselling than the quarterly programme you're currently on.'

'How frequent?'

'Monthly.'

Red bites back his objection. I hate counsellors. They can't speak to me for more than five minutes without mentioning my fucking brother. Four times a year is bad enough. Twelve times a year is going to be murder. Not that I have much choice. Knuckle under or lose the case.

'OK.'

'And if they recommend that you should be transferred, then I shall have no hesitation in acting on such a recommendation.'

Red doesn't say anything.

The Commissioner stands up, signalling that the interview is at an end. He escorts Red to the door and turns to him when his hand is already on the handle.

'I want this man found as much as you do, you know. I just don't want you driving yourself into the lunatic asylum in the process. Good-bye, Red. Keep me posted.'

52

The last time Red went to Parkside, he was almost preternaturally alert – details, sounds, images, all battered into his brain as he wrestled with his conscience. This time, it's as if he's on autopilot. He is vaguely aware of walking along the pavement, of turning right and left when he has to, but he sees and hears almost nothing. When he gets to the police station, he gives a little start, as if surprised to find himself there.

There is no one at the front desk. Red stands there for a moment, trying to get his brain back in gear. It's as if his decision to confess has robbed him of the power of thought. He's not thinking anything, feeling anything. He's not rehearsing the words he's going to use. He doesn't have butterflies in his stomach. Nothing.

He turns away from the desk and glances at the noticeboard on the far wall. The appeal for help from the accident is pinned in the centre, the only notice that isn't half-hidden by other ones. A simple CAN YOU HELP? with the time and place of the accident below. No names. No follow-up. It might as well have happened to someone else.

Any moment now, a policeman will appear and he'll confess everything, take his punishment like a man and start his life afresh. So why does he feel so flat?

'Yes, sir?'

The voice makes Red jump. He turns away from the noticeboard and looks at the man who's just materialised at the desk as if by magic. A young constable, not much older than Red. Early twenties. Young enough still to have traces of acne around his jaw. Fresh-faced and keen.

There's something about the way the constable stands, straight but not ramrod straight, which tells Red that this man loves his job, loves it because he truly believes that what he does is good and right.

Red walks towards the desk. He knows what he wants to say now. The flatness is gone.

'I'd like to join the police force, please,' he says.

53

Monday, September 21st 1998

Keith Thompson stands halfway up the ladder and makes lazy circling movements on the window with his sponge. He watches the sweeps of white suds arrange and rearrange themselves under his prompting and then, with a flick of his squeegee, they are gone, a swathe of perfect clean glass cutting through them like Moses parting the Red Sea.

The net curtains hanging on the inside of the window prevent Keith from seeing too far into the room. He clicks his tongue.

It isn't that Keith is a potential thief casing the joint or a pervert – though he has seen his fair share of naked women in more than fifteen years' window cleaning. The truth is more prosaic. Keith just likes seeing the way other people live. Even from a static view of an empty room, there is a lot you can tell from the magazines, books, pictures and ashtrays.

Keith imagines himself as a detective, taking a few scraps of evidence and building an entire life story around them. Families with kids squabbling, the parents shouting at them and at each other. Young couples in the first flush of cohabitation, when being together is still an adventure. Bachelor boys drinking beer and boasting about their sexual exploits. Thirtysomethings living alone and trying not to face up to the fact that marriage has maybe passed them by – or, if it hasn't, contemplating a contract of emotional and economic convenience as both parties settle for something rather than nothing. Keith Thompson, supersleuth. Of course, he often gets his diagnosis wrong, but he never knows and he doesn't care. Window cleaning is hardly the most cerebral of occupations and his mental meanderings stave off terminal boredom while he is up his ladder.

He finishes cleaning the window with the net curtains and climbs up to the top of the ladder to start on the window above. The building is divided into flats, so this new window belongs to someone else. Another vista on another life.

Damn. The curtains are drawn. Big thick curtains too, not flimsy net ones. Some lazy sod must be sleeping in. He dips his sponge in the bucket of soapy water and presses it against the window.

The curtains have not been pulled tight together after all. There is a crack between them, perhaps about a foot wide. Keith presses his face tight up against the glass and cups his hands round his eyes.

Dim light falls into the room from beyond its door. Not much, but enough for Keith to see by. On his left there is a sofa flanked by a TV on top of the mantelpiece. On the other side of the room, by the far wall, a figure is kneeling. A small statue, by the look of it. Something dark has been spilt next to it, staining the light carpet. Red wine, perhaps.

Keith's eyes roam. Not just one stain. Another there, and another, and another, until he sees the whole carpet is mottled dark and light.

He looks back at the figure by the wall.

Not a statue.

A man. A man with wounds striping his back. It's blood from the wounds that caused the stain.

Keith feels the balance going in the spirit level of his ears. He yanks his hands away from the glass and grips the top of the ladder. His right foot slides off the rung and into space. The ladder sways gently sideways.

Keith is twenty feet above the pavement. If he falls that far, onto hard unyielding stone, he will break at least one leg. Maybe two. Perhaps an arm too. In plaster for six weeks, unable to work. Not so handy for a one-man business. Keith knows someone who fell twenty feet out of a window once. Too shocked even to scream, she sat and flailed her own faeces onto the walls next to her for half an hour until someone found her.

He clings onto the ladder, willing it not to topple, knowing he is helpless. If the ladder falls, it will go in a parabola of agonising slowness, gradually picking up speed only as the weight revolves around its own centre of gravity. And he will be aware of every elongated second.

Go limp, he thinks. Just become floppy and you won't suffer half as much damage as you will if you hit the pavement with every muscle tensed in fear.

He waits and waits and waits, and then suddenly realises that the ladder has stabilised. Keith Thompson isn't going to fall. Not today.

He climbs down the ladder with exaggerated caution, feeling with his soles for the corrugated surface of each rung and putting both feet down before taking another step. He is so intent on getting down safely that he doesn't even realise when he has reached the pavement and tries to take another step down, a heavy juddering step, like descending stairs in the dark.

With trembling hands he unclips the mobile phone from his belt and dials 999.

54

Another Monday, another stiff. Bitter thoughts from a bitter man.

Red looks at his notes. Matthew Fox, thirty-five years old. A tax inspector, almost thirteen years in the Inland Revenue, currently working in the Blackheath section at the Lancaster House office in Newington Causeway. Hacked to death, probably by a machete. Not the calculated sadism of skinning Bart Miller, or the clean quickness of decapitating James Buxton. Just a whirlwind of rage finding its outlet through the head of a machete.

Matthew Fox has been hit more than two dozen times. The wounds are long and jagged, some so deep that flashes of white bone poke through the red pulp. Most of the blows were to his back and shoulders. Matthew's right arm has almost been severed – it hangs limply by his side, connected to his shoulder by a flimsy hinge of gristle and sinew.

High marks for technical merit. Very few for artistic impression.

The body has been left as Keith found it, on its knees, facing the wall as if in supplication. Silver Tongue must have placed it that way postmortem. Red can't imagine anybody being able to maintain that position under such a sustained attack. Even if Matthew was tied up, he would surely have been rolling around on the floor, trying to make himself as small as possible. If nothing else, the force of the blows would have battered him to the ground.

There are no obvious head wounds. Either Silver Tongue avoided the head altogether, or Matthew had his arms clamped over his head in self-protection. Which means that he couldn't have been tied up.

Red squats down so he can examine Matthew's face from

the underside. He knows what he will find, but he wants to be sure.

There it is, just like with all the others. A silver spoon wedged into the side of the mouth. Blood all down the body's bare torso, not from machete wounds but from the severed tongue.

There is blood everywhere. *Everywhere*. Not just on the carpet, but on the wall above Matthew's head and even on the ceiling. Red cranes his neck to look at the long spray marks above his head. He imagines the blood flying off the machete's blade as Silver Tongue rips it from the body and hoists it high, a back-swing to another murderous downwards crashing arc.

Silver Tongue must have got some of the blood on his clothes. *Must have*. This was one of the first problems Red thought of after Philip Rhodes' body was discovered, and still he hasn't got near to solving it.

How do you get away, my man? Do you walk the streets covered in blood? Do you get in a car and smear it all over the seats? Or do you change clothes and dump the soiled ones somewhere? Where? We've checked all the rubbish bins and skips near every crime site, and they've turned up precisely nothing.

Red goes to the window and looks out, down the hill towards Westcombe Park Station. He can hear the screeching of the train as it stops there. One of the old Southern Region trains, clanking through the grey squalor of Deptford and Bermondsey on its way into town. That's the problem with Blackheath. It's a nice place, but you have to go through some shitholes to get there.

He turns back into the room.

Five down. How many more to go?

55

When Red gets back to Scotland Yard, he does something he hasn't done in a long time. He locks the door of his office, unlocks one of his drawers and pulls out the folder full of the articles he won't put on the wall.

Sometimes he glances through all of them, but today he's looking for a specific one. A piece which appeared in a Sunday magazine just after Eric's conviction, when Red was still in his first year of being a policeman. Even now, he's still not sure whether he was being very honest or simply very stupid to have said what he did, when he tried to explain to a cute young journalist named Janine Bloom why he feared that the madness in Eric might be in him too.

He finds the article, folded twice on itself, and smears it flat on the table. The words leap out at him:

What I'm talking about is walking down the street and seeing a total stranger and thinking, 'I wonder what it would feel like to kill you. What would it be like to stab you in the heart or kick you till your head explodes? Maybe I could bite your nose off, or rip your ear clean away from the side of your skull. I wonder what your intestines would look like if I slashed your stomach open. Would your blood spurt miles in the air, or would it trickle pathetically onto the ground? What sounds would you make as life evaporated from you?'

Words he said because he meant them. And because he wanted to get across something of what it felt like to be the one who betrayed your brother.

Friday, 25th September 1998

Eric's application for parole has been denied, as he knew it would be.

He applied as soon as he could. Most criminals sentenced to life imprisonment are set a tariff of a certain number of years, after which their punishment is complete and they can be released as long as the parole board decides that they are no longer a threat to the public. When Eric was sentenced in 1983, his tariff was set at fifteen years – not including the time he had already spent at her Majesty's pleasure before and during the trial. And now that fifteen years is up and still they won't let him go.

There are some people who will never be eligible for parole. Until June 1993, the Home Secretary could secretly alter an individual's tariff without explanation, so that some prisoners didn't know that they would never be let out, and would appeal in vain year after year. But in June 1993, the House of Lords ruled that prisoners whose tariffs were extended by the Home Secretary should be informed and given a chance to appeal.

There does remain a 'hitlist' of criminals who will never be let out. Among them, Jeremy Bamber, who killed five members of his own family for money, and Myra Hindley, one half of the Moors Murderers. But Hindley's partner, Ian Brady, is not on the list, and nor is Peter Sutcliffe, the Yorkshire Ripper.

And nor is Eric Metcalfe. But they still won't let him go. Not the first time, at any rate. And he knows the reason why.

His brother, Red, Mr Fucking Supersleuth, who put him inside all those years ago and is now the reason they won't let him out, because they're so keen to avoid charges of favouritism. If he was anyone else, anyone else's brother, they'd have let him out long ago, but because he is who he is, he has to earn his stripes twice over.

The irony is that Eric could have been freed at any time during his incarceration without the slightest fear that he would turn bad. This is what he has kept trying to tell them. This is why he has been the model prisoner – fifteen years inside and the only report for bad behaviour is the time he tried to kill Red. Condemned to an existence behind bars for a moment of madness, a moment outside of life itself. He can hardly remember what Charlotte Logan looked like, it was so long ago. The image of her face has faded with the years. Sometimes he thinks he can catch it in his mind but then it goes, melting away like the Cheshire Cat.

At least he has a cell to himself. It's small and cold and spartan, but his own nevertheless. Sometimes Eric wonders what life would have been like if he had committed his crime elsewhere in the world. The States, for example. Well, he would have had to pick his state carefully. Washington DC doesn't have the death penalty, for example, but Florida does. That was Ted Bundy's big mistake: he was executed because he killed some of his victims in Florida. If Bundy had picked his sites more carefully, he would still be alive today.

But then again, Eric could have been in Bangkok or Bogotá or Baghdad. The cells like furnaces in the summer, your pores dripping with the stench of sweat and excrement and fear, where you never know when you will next be shoved up against the wall and fucked ruthlessly hard with the pain like a sword through your membranes.

So, all in all, Eric has it OK. He survives by funnelling all his rage and hatred into one bottleneck. He doesn't hate the warders, neither those who try to be matey nor those who treat him like dirt. They are nothing to him. He doesn't even hate the system that denies him his liberty because of his brother's position.

There is only one thing, one person, whom Eric hates. That brother: Red.

He hates Red now as much as he did when he tried to kill

him at Highpoint. Charlotte's face might have faded with time, but the enormity of Red's betrayal hasn't.

Eric counts the reasons he hates Red, and they come thick and fast. For putting other people's families above his own. For taking the fucking reward. For not *understanding*. Eric can accept that the public misunderstand him, but not his own brother. He is sorry for what he did to Charlotte, but would never have done it again. Whatever they have done and continue to do to Eric, they cannot bring Charlotte back.

He hears about Red, of course. He sees his name in the papers or on TV from time to time.

What Eric doesn't see is Red waking up every day teetering on the cliff face of his own sanity.

Brothers in arms. Who knows which one is more dangerous?

SUNDAY, SEPTEMBER 27TH 1998

Early autumn, but it's still hot in the city. Hotter still bumper to bumper on Stoke Newington High Street. Duncan and Sam sit in a silent car at the end of a weekend. Another forty-eight hours gone and another month until their next weekend together. Precious snatched time for Duncan, getting his son away from Helen's bitterness.

'Dad?'

'Yeah?'

'Can I ask you something?'

Duncan inches forward in the traffic, trying to nudge his car in front of a Ford Fiesta in the next lane. The Fiesta driver moves up to block Duncan off. Duncan glares at him, but the man looks straight ahead. His car doors are locked. Duncan turns away from the Fiesta driver and looks across at Sam.

'Sure.'

'In your . . . I mean, when you're at work, do you have to hurt people?'

'What do you mean, hurt?'

'You know. Hit them. Beat them up.'

'No. Not me. I'm a detective. I solve crimes.'

'But you arrest people, don't you?'

'Yes, sometimes.'

'And when you arrest them, do you hurt them?'

'No.'

'Not ever?'

'If they're resisting arrest, then we use the minimum amount of force necessary to subdue them.' Come on, thinks Duncan. How stupid can you sound, giving the party line to your nine-year-old son?

'That's not what Andy says, Dad.'

Andy. Duncan might have known.

It would be Andy, wouldn't it? Andy, a lecturer at the University of Westminster, moved Helen and Sam into his Stoke Newington house six months ago. Since when he has spent an inordinate amount of time trying to poison Sam's mind against the police force in general and Duncan in particular. Duncan met Andy only once, the first time he went to pick up Sam from Stoke Newington, when they predictably hated each other on sight – so much so, in fact, that Andy now makes himself scarce whenever Duncan comes to pick Sam up or drop him off.

Andy. Fucking trendy *Guardian*-reading wanker.

Typical Helen, too. You don't need to be Freud to see her logic in taking up with a man who is in every way the diametrical opposite of her ex-husband. Duncan is reactionary, abrasive, undemonstrative and pragmatic. Andy is progressive, conciliatory, effusive and principled. No wonder they hate each other.

Duncan forces himself to be reasonable. This isn't Sam's fault, after all. He is too young to appreciate the dynamics of the situation.

'What *does* Andy say?'

'He says that police brutality is on the rise and that most victims don't report it because they're too scared or think their cases will get lost in red tape.'

Said verbatim, without inflection, as if by rote. Andy's words transported into Sam's mind.

'What's red tape, Dad?' asks Sam, a puzzled nine-year-old again rather than a parrot.

'Um . . . it's bureaucracy.'

'What does bureaucracy mean?'

'It's . . . well, it's the system, really. You've got all the different government departments, like the ones that run the schools and the hospitals, and then you've got the emergency services, like the police and the fire brigade and the ambulances, and so on – basically everybody needed to keep the country running smoothly. But in this case, what Andy's probably talking about is police procedure. There are a lot of laws governing what we can and can't do, to make sure that everybody who's in trouble gets the help they're entitled to. And since there are so many laws, it can take a long time to get things done.'

'Oh.'

They lapse into silence again. The cars in front shuffle up as the lights ahead go green. Sam speaks again.

'Is that true, Dad? About the victims?'

'I don't know. If people want to complain against the police, there are ways in which they can do so, and those ways are well-known. We try to treat everybody as fairly as possible.'

Off the high street at last, and moving quickly through the side streets where whitewashed houses jostle for space alongside council estates. A decade ago, Stoke Newington was just another rundown inner-city area. Now it looks set to follow in the footsteps of Islington and Bayswater as the next battle-ground for gentrification.

Duncan turns left into Evering Road, where Helen and Andy live. He parks the car on the corner nearest their house and looks at Sam.

'I've really enjoyed our weekend, Sam.'

Sam doesn't answer. He is looking over and beyond Duncan's right shoulder.

'There's Mum,' says Sam.

Helen is standing outside the front door, arms folded. Probably been checking her watch to make sure Duncan doesn't break the forty-eight-hour rule: six to six, Friday to Sunday, with no exceptions. Once so much in love, Duncan and Helen are now punching the clock like factory shift workers. Six to six. And after that, an already empty Sunday night made lonelier by the hole which Sam fills so briefly. But Duncan sticks to the agreement, because he knows that not doing so would cause more trouble than it's worth.

Sam gets out of the car and hurries across the road to hug his Mum. Sam's parents will be civil in front of him. They always are.

Duncan steps out of the car and glances up at the house. The front door is open, but there is no sign of Andy.

Helen unwraps Sam from her grasp and looks down at him. No acknowledgement to Duncan, not even so much as a 'hi'.

'Have a good weekend?' she asks her son.

'Yes, thanks.'

'What did you do?'

'We went to that place on Queensway. The one where you can go ice skating and bowling and play video games. It was *great*.'

Duncan smiles. 'Yeah. He whipped me on the video Grand Prix. Looks like we've got ourselves a Damon Hill in the making.'

'Ourselves'. What a joke, thinks Duncan. If it wasn't for Sam, he and Helen would never see each other again, and even that would be too soon.

Helen looks at Sam, warmth in her face and love in her eyes. Then she transfers her gaze to Duncan and there is neither.

'Anyway, Duncan, thanks for bringing him back. I expect you want to be on your way now.'

That is, I want you out of here as soon as possible.

'Actually, Helen, there's a couple of things I'd like a word with you about.'

He knows she won't refuse, not in front of Sam. Helen shoots him a look of pure hatred for manoeuvring her into this position. She looks down at Sam again.

'Sam, Dad and I have got a few things to clear up. Do you want to run along inside and get yourself a Coke or something? I'll be right with you.'

They think they're sparing him, but Sam has been around his parents long enough to know when there's an argument coming, and that in itself is tragedy enough. He detaches himself from Helen and puts his arms awkwardly round Duncan's waist.

'Bye, Dad. See ya.'

'See ya yourself.'

A quick fatherly ruffle of Sam's hair as he runs up the steps

214

and through the front door. Helen is snapping almost before Sam is out of sight.

'What do you want?'

'What's Andy been saying to Sam?'

'About what?'

Duncan mimics a bleeding-heart liberal voice: 'Police brutality is on the rise, and most victims don't report it because they're too scared or they think their cases will get lost in red tape.'

'Police brutality?'

'Yes. Those are the exact words that Sam used. How many nine-year-olds do you know who use that phrase? What else has Andy been telling him?'

'It came up at dinner one night. Andy had brought home some survey or other which the university had commissioned. Sam asked what it was. Andy showed him. We discussed it for a bit. That's all.'

'You tell Andy to back off.'

'Oh, leave it, Duncan. Andy can do what he likes.'

'If Andy wants my fucking wife —'

'Ex-wife.'

'— then he's more than welcome to her. But he's not going to get my son. Do you understand?'

'Don't be a prick, Duncan. Andy's not trying to muscle in on Sam. He's not trying to be a surrogate father and he's not trying to poison Sam against you. Andy lives with me and Sam. He and Sam are friends. They talk about lots of things. You may be amazed to know that you don't head the conversational agenda every night.'

Duncan wags his finger in Helen's face. 'If I hear that Andy's been feeding Sam any more bullshit, then I'll show him what fucking police brutality is about.'

'Is that a threat?'

'Just tell him.'

Helen stalks up the steps and slams the front door behind her, a barrier between her old husband and her new life. Duncan gets back into his car and drives off slowly, determined not to give Helen the satisfaction of hearing a squeal of angry rubber.

He grits his teeth in frustration.

The wasteland of a marriage. The wasteland of a life.

58

Perhaps in other circumstances Red's parents would have approved of him going into the police force. It wasn't the job in accountancy or banking or law that his father might have expected, but it was a good solid career nevertheless. In other circumstances, perhaps.

With all that had come before, though, they saw Red's joining the police as the final insult to be added to the many injuries he had already inflicted. His father came to see him unannounced one day to tell him that they wouldn't be party to him trying to salve his conscience, and that as far as he and his mother were concerned, they no longer wanted to know him.

Red tried to reason with the old man and, when that didn't work, he tried to hit him. It was a mistake – he knew that even as he was drawing back his fist, and the only saving grace was the fact that he missed. His father walked out of the room and, as cliché would have it, out of his life.

Single, solitary and driven during his training and early in his job – volunteering for extra duty didn't lend itself well to relationships – Red had almost given up on women when he met Susan at Addenbrooke's Hospital in Cambridge, where she was a nurse and he was questioning a man who had been stabbed. They went out for a drink the next night and were married within three months. Fast – maybe too fast. Red swallowed his pride and invited his parents to the wedding, seeing an opportunity for reconciliation. They didn't even reply, let alone attend. From the moment he and Susan were married, he considered her the only family he had – his other half in every way, the person with whom he would build a future and who would enable him to forget the past.

That was before it all went wrong.

Even now, more than seven years on, Red doesn't really know how or why it went wrong. It was fine for the first couple of years, when marriage and each other were still new and fresh. Then the novelty wore off, and with it went the shine and the spark. Maybe it would have been different if they'd had children, something to distract them from each other while keeping them together. As it was, the distractions came from Red's work and his increasingly high media profile.

Most people would enjoy being married to a minor celebrity, thinks Red. There's a bit of reflected glory, a sense of pride in seeing your spouse in the papers. And Red's not a pop star or a footballer, not someone who's going to have tabloid reporters rummaging through his bins for evidence of mistresses or clandestine cocaine habits.

But Susan doesn't like it. Sometimes Red thinks that she actively resents the attention that Red gets, doesn't like the fact that her husband is successful. Sure, he can understand her not liking the fact that he works such long hours and that he can get called away at the drop of a hat. She wants attention from him, doesn't want to feel second best – but recently she doesn't show much of an interest even when he is around. She wants him to pay attention to her without having to give it back. That's what he thinks.

And so it goes round. He doesn't tell her about his work because he doesn't feel that she's interested in it. When he confronts her on this, she turns his words back on him and says that she doesn't ask because he doesn't tell her. She's being disingenuous, but then so is he. Sometimes he stays away on cases longer than he needs to because he can't face going home, because he'd rather put himself through sleepless nights and unspeakable horrors than try and batter down a blank wall of indifference.

And sometimes, like now, Red wants to make it better – if only to prove that he can. Loath as he is to admit it, the counsellor was right. He is working shorter hours now, and he's making up for their disastrous anniversary by taking her away for the weekend. Maybe it's sweeping the problems under the carpet rather than giving them a good airing, but it's better than nothing.

Or is it? Because it's all going to go pear-shaped when Silver Tongue comes out to play again, when Red's invisible puppet-master jerks his strings and tells him to dance.

SATURDAY, 17 OCTOBER 1998

'Oh *baby*,' says Susan, putting on a mock American accent. 'I can feel my arteries hardening just looking at that.'

Red grins at her and looks down at his plate. It's lunch time, but he's ordered the full English breakfast – sausages, bacon, baked beans, fried bread, eggs, mushrooms and black pudding. He shovels some of the black pudding onto his fork and pushes it into his mouth. Susan winces.

'How can you *eat* that? It's pig's blood, that's all it is. I'd have thought you'd have had enough of blood these past few months.'

Red takes another mouthful and sips at his pint. Susan is looking beyond him, a forkful of Caesar salad halfway to her mouth.

'Why does that guy look familiar?' she asks.

Red turns to follow her gaze.

'Which guy?'

'There, at the bar. Black T-shirt and suede jacket. Just being served now.'

'That's Nick Beckett. I was at university with him. He came to our wedding.'

Red shouts across the pub. 'Nick!'

Nick turns towards Red's voice and his face lights up in surprised recognition. He takes his change from the barmaid and comes over to them, one hand clasping a pint, the other outstretched in welcome.

'Red and Susan Metcalfe. Well I never.'

He shakes hands with Red, kisses Susan on both cheeks and sits down at their table.

'Long time no see. Must be three or four years since I last saw you two.'

'More like six or seven, I would imagine. I don't think we've seen you since we got married.'

'Bloody hell. That *is* a long time. Though obviously I still catch Mr Metcalfe here on TV every now and then. So how is the great detective?'

Red laughs.

'Oh, you know. Still trying to make the world a safer place. How about you? Still painting?'

'Not so much recently. I've opened up a gallery. Spend my time flogging other people's crap rather than my own.'

'A gallery? Where?'

'Just over there.' Nick points through the window. 'The street next door, literally. Just popped in here for a quick lunch-time sherbet.'

'So this is your local? The White Horse?'

'Yeah. Nice pub, shame about the clientele.'

'What do you mean?' asks Susan.

Nick looks at her. 'Chinless wonders and brainless Sloanes, almost without exception. It's the only pub I know which you can go to at half-past ten on a Saturday night straight from a wedding, pissed off your face on champagne, wearing tails and being thoroughly obnoxious, and no one bats an eyelid. In most places, you'd have the shit kicked out of you before you'd even got through the front door. When I come here with the staff from the gallery, we play Fantasy Sloanes. It's like Fantasy Football, but with Sloanes. You get ten points for a pair of red jeans or yellow cords, fifteen points for a rugby shirt, and a full fifty if you get both with a blazer on top.'

'And the girls?'

'Twinset and pearls, mandatory. Little penny loafers with pink socks are also a fave.'

'What happens if you get your fifty points?'

'Oh, this is the best bit. You get given the following scenario: Friday or Saturday night in the summer, everyone is standing outside in the courtyard, braying about how Oofy did this or Fofe did that. Then you get to choose one of three methods of killing everyone in the pub.'

'Which are?'

'Firstly, the nail bomb in the courtyard. Lots of maiming and flying glass. A touch impersonal, but undeniably effective. Next, the drive-by shooting. Just rake the fuckers with a sub-machine gun from a passing car. Very Cosa Nostra. And finally – this is my own favourite – you hire a top-floor room just across the road and start sniping. Take them out one at a time, just like that bit in *Lethal Weapon* when they think Mel Gibson's dead but he's lying in the desert shooting them one by one. Maximum panic, maximum satisfaction. Can't beat it.'

'Beckett, you really are a sick fuck.'

'I know. Got any spare jobs going? I'd be great at helping you catch the weirdos you deal with.'

They laugh. Nick drains his pint.

'Got to be off. No rest for the wicked.'

'Back to the gallery?'

'Yeah. Do you want to come and see it?'

Red looks at Susan, who nods.

'Why not?'

Nick waits for Red and Susan to finish their food, and then leads them across the road and down a side street.

'Most places on this road are garages, as you can see,' says Nick. 'There's one music company there,' he points to a green building on the corner, 'and my warehouse up ahead. That blue building on the right. Otherwise, it's just cars, cars, cars. I'm amazed they don't spend their whole time pranging each other. It's a bit off the beaten track, but the rent's low and the area's good.'

They walk through a pair of sliding glass doors and into a massive whitewashed room. The gallery.

'Jesus Christ, Nick,' says Red. 'It's like an aircraft hangar.'

Nick grins.

'Yeah. We call it an "art warehouse" rather than a gallery, but you'll probably dismiss that as Beckett pretension.'

'Nick, I dismiss *everything* you do as Beckett pretension.'

Nick goes off to serve a customer, while Red and Susan wander around. The paintings are hung in rows from shrouds which come cascading down from the ceiling like stalactites. Each painting has a piece of cardboard hung next to it on which the artist has written something about the work. The quality of both art and writing is varied – some good, some mediocre, some moving and some six miles up itself.

Susan likes to linger on paintings. Red doesn't. For him, you either see it at once or not at all. If you need a piece of paper to explain a painting to you, then it's not good enough in the first place. Can you imagine Van Gogh putting a note next to 'Sunflowers' saying, *Here's a little something I knocked up earlier?*

Red quickly gets bored of walking silently through the make-shift corridors of paintings. He goes back to the reception desk, where there is a coffee-maker with a sign saying PLEASE HELP YOURSELF. He does, and carries the steaming mug over to a fake leather sofa. There is a pile of art books on the low table next to the sofa. Red sits down and picks up the top book, turning it over so he can see the title: *Michelangelo: The Sistine Chapel.*

Red flicks idly through the pages. This is more like it. Not the offerings of the mediocre, but the works of a genius.

The first picture is a view of the entire chapel, dark red in the late-afternoon sun, with the figures clambering over the walls and ceiling as if stitched by a mad tattooist.

Red turns the pages on the dawn of man itself. Adam's hand limp against his musculature as he reaches out to God. The Creation of the Sun and the Moon, with God's bearded face furrowed deep in concentration and his arms stretched wide like a conductor. God again, stretching backwards and upwards, goalkeeper-style, as he gives Order to Chaos. David's cloak whirling round his waist as he stands astride a prostrate Goliath. A damned soul vainly clutching at himself as the demons drag him down to hell.

Images pass from the pages into Red's mind.

He has missed something. He flicks back a few pages and looks again.

The wall of the Last Judgment. Christ is at the bottom of the wall on the cross, and again at the top, his right arm raised as the Virgin turns demurely away. The Creator portrayed not simply as the bearded figure of folklore but an actual incarnation of the irresistible primeval force of the cosmos. There is the pink of well-defined bodies against the full blue of heaven behind. So much going on, and yet nothing happening. A bizarre combination of dramatic excitement and serene tranquillity.

Flicking through the pages. *There.*

The image he missed. Just below Christ, to his left.

An image there, and a close-up of it a few pages on. That is what he remembers. The close-up.

Red rifles frantically through the pages, almost tearing the paper as his fingers dance across it.

Got it.

A detail of Saint Bartholomew, wild eyes turned upwards towards the Messiah. He has a huge curly beard and a totally bald pate, as if his head has been inverted, and his massive thighs grip the rock which he sits astride.

Bartholomew brandishes a knife in his right hand, and in his left he carries his own skin.

Just like Bart Miller.

Time stands still.

Red knows what he is seeing, but he cannot unravel his mind far enough to wrap it around the enormity of his discovery.

Sensory overload.

Eyes staring at the picture until it fills his vision.

Ears roaring tonelessly like driving through a tunnel.

Fingers gripping white on the shiny hard cover of the book.

The taste of egg on his suddenly dry tongue.

The smell of coffee wisping from the cup next to him.

Red's gaze slides down from the picture to the black spiders of text beneath: *Plate 26. St Bartholomew. According to legend, the apostle Bartholomew was flayed alive. This figure – the most famous depiction of Bartholomew's fate – reveals the depths of Michelangelo's despair. The face on the flayed skin which the saint holds in his hand is that of Michelangelo himself.*

Red looks back to the picture and sees for the first time the face in the skin, hideously lopsided and distorted and with dark holes where the eyes and mouth should be.

St Bartholomew. Bart Miller. *Bartholomew* Miller.

Something in the names.

Jez said that on the way to interview Alison Bird in Reading. But he had been talking about the name James. He was on the right line all along, but they did not know it. So close back in Reading, and so many hours and weeks wasted since then. Until now, when they've come full circle, back to this point.

Red reads the text again, and the word he is looking for comes leaping off the page at him.

Apostle.

Something in the names.

Philip Rhodes. James Cunningham. James Buxton. Bart Miller. Matthew Fox.

Philip. James. James. Bartholomew. Matthew.

All apostles.

Not a gay killer. Not someone with a grudge against the rich.

Red finally knows what they are up against, and the knowledge scares him more, much more, than the uncertainty ever did. But he has found the link and right now he has the strength of ten men.

He puts the book down slowly on the sofa next to him and shuts his eyes.

A quote comes into his head. A quote from *The Silence of the Lambs*, which he keeps in a little frame on his desk at Scotland Yard.

Problem-solving is hunting. It is savage pleasure, and we are born to it.

Part Two

Part two

'I live in sin. I live dying within myself'
Michelangelo

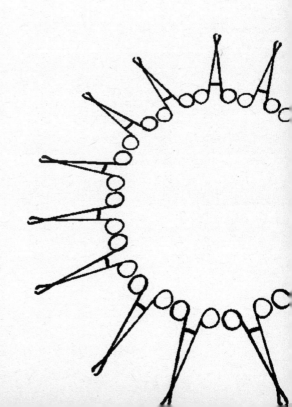

It's just the four of them now, sitting round the table in Red's kitchen. Susan has gone out to a dinner party, taking with her a bottle of white wine and Red's apologies. She knows better than to try to force him, not now that he seems alive for the first time since this whole thing started.

Kate has done the cooking, grumbling with good humour about male chauvinist pigs before announcing that it is probably just as well that she is on food duty, as anything *they* try to cook is bound to be inedible. She serves up steaks brushed lightly with mustard sauce and a massive bowl of cucumber, sweetcorn, lettuce and avocado. They eat quickly and ravenously, as if barely able to contain their excitement at Red's finally having cracked Silver Tongue's pattern.

Red is reading from the Bible. 'Here. Matthew, chapter 10, verse 2: "The names of the twelve apostles are these: first, Simon, who is called Peter, and Andrew his brother; James the son of Zebedee, and John his brother; Philip and Bartholomew; Thomas and Matthew the publican; James the son of Alphaeus, and Thaddeus; Simon the Canaanite, and Judas Iscariot, who betrayed him. These twelve Jesus sent out."'

His eyes gleam in the strip lighting.

'Now, I checked this list with the other gospels, and there are some variations. Not, I hasten to add, in the names of those who have already been killed, but in those still left.' He consults a piece of paper beside his plate. 'I can't find a full list in Mark, but there is one in Luke, where the name "Thaddeus" seems to have been changed to "Judas the brother of James".'

'So what happened to Judas Iscariot?' asks Jez.

'He's there, too. There are two Judases in Luke. And John refers to someone called Nathanael, though there isn't a full list in his gospel either.'

Red picks up a thick book with a dark gold dustcover.

'And I found a third list in here. Look at this. It's the best of the lot.'

'What is that book?' asks Duncan.

Red turns it round so the others can read the cover: *Brewer's Dictionary of Phrase and Fable, Centenary Edition*.

'It's a very old edition,' says Red, 'and I found it on a shelf when I was looking for some reference books here. I don't even know where it came from. I certainly don't remember buying it. It might be Susan's, or it might have belonged to my parents. Either way, it doesn't matter.'

He opens *Brewer's* to a page already marked with a yellow Post-It note and lays it flat on the table for the others to see.

Apostles. The badges or symbols of the fourteen apostles (i.e. the original twelve with Matthias and Paul) are as follows:

Andrew, *an X-shaped cross*, because he was crucified on one.

Bartholomew, *a knife*, because he was flayed with a knife.

James the Great, *a scallop shell, a pilgrim's staff* or *a gourd bottle*, because he is the patron saint of pilgrims.

James the Less, *a fuller's pole*, because he was killed by a blow on the head with a pole, dealt him by Simeon the fuller.

John, *a cup with a winged serpent flying out of it*, in allusion to the tradition about Aristodemos, priest of Diana, who challenged John to drink a cup of poison. John made the sign of a cross on the cup, Satan like a dragon flew from it, and John then drank the cup which was quite innocuous.

Judas Iscariot, *a bag*, because he 'had the bag and bare what was put therein' (John 12:6).

Jude, *a club*, because he was martyred with a club.

Matthew, *a hatchet* or *halberd,* because he was slain at Nadabar with a halberd.

Matthias, *a battle-axe*, because he was first stoned and then beheaded with a battle-axe.

Paul, *a sword*, because his head was cut off with a sword.

Peter, *a bunch of keys*, because Christ gave him 'the keys of the kingdom of heaven'. Also *a cock*, because he went out and wept bitterly when he heard the cock crow (Matthew 26:75).

Philip, *a long staff surmounted with a cross*, because he suffered death by being suspended by the neck from a tall pillar.

Simon, *a saw*, because he was sawn to death, according to tradition.

Thomas, *a lance*, because he was pierced through the body, at Meliapore, with a lance.

Red closes the book with a thump.

'Oh my God,' whispers Kate. 'Oh my *God*. He thinks he's Jesus Christ, doesn't he? He really thinks he's the Messiah. He's collecting apostles. He's killing them according to their symbols.'

Red nods.

'I've checked them back against the deaths we've already had. Listen.'

He skims the relevant passage, reading aloud: 'Philip suffered death by being suspended by the neck from a tall pillar; James the Less was killed by a blow on the head with a pole; James the Great's symbols are a scallop shell, a pilgrim's staff or a gourd bottle; Bartholomew was flayed with a knife; and Matthew's symbol is a hatchet or halberd because he was slain with a halberd. You see? They all fit, except for one. If you assume that the bishop is James the Less – the one who was beaten to death with the fuller's pole – then James Buxton must be James the Great. But James Buxton was beheaded. I've checked back on the case notes. There was no sign of a scallop shell, a pilgrim's staff or a gourd bottle anywhere in the house where he was murdered.'

Kate picks up the *Brewer's* off the table and looks through the list.

'So how's he picking them?' Duncan looks puzzled. 'Just according to their names?'

'It looks that way,' says Red. 'So far, at any rate.'

'Then how are we going to find him?' says Duncan. 'Warn every Londoner called Andrew or Simon or John or whatever they're called that they're in mortal danger from a lunatic who thinks he's the Messiah? I think I preferred it when we were looking at the gay angle.'

'As I recall, Duncan,' says Jez, 'you were the one who told us we were barking up the wrong tree when we were searching for a gay serial killer. Looks like you were right.'

Duncan has the grace not to gloat or look smug. Kate turns over a few pages in *Brewer's* and gasps at the text in front of her.

'What, Kate? What is it?' demands Red.

'Look at this separate entry.' She points at the text, and begins to read: '*Apostle spoons*. Silver spoons having the figure of one of the apostles at the top of the handle, formerly given at christenings.' She looks up. 'Except he's using just plain silver spoons, otherwise we'd have got the pattern straight away.'

'Right,' says Jez.

Kate continues reading: 'Sometimes twelve spoons, representing the twelve apostles; sometimes four, representing the four evangelists; and sometimes only one is presented. Occasionally a set occurs, containing in addition the "Master Spoon" and the "Lady Spoon". Silver spoons are given to children of the wealthier classes, hence the saying "born with a silver spoon in one's mouth".'

'Well, that solves the mystery of the spoons,' says Duncan.

'It probably solves another problem, too,' says Red.

'Which is?'

'Whether our man is going after all fourteen apostles mentioned in *Brewer's*, or just the original twelve – i.e. not including Matthias and Paul. Since he's using the spoons, then it's my guess that it's just the twelve. Twelve spoons, twelve apostles.'

'That's pretty flimsy logic,' says Jez.

'On its own, maybe,' says Red. 'But look at it in a wider context. Look at the tongues, too.'

'Why the tongues?'

'What do you use your tongue for?'

'We've had this question before,' says Duncan.

'Yes, that very first Saturday back in May, after the first two murders. *And we were right all along.* We just didn't know it then. The tongues and the names, both mentioned early on in the investigation. Little random things we've said, and we had to wait until now to find out what they mean. Anyway, come on. What do you use your tongue for?'

'Eating,' volunteers Kate.

'And speaking,' says Duncan.

'Exactly. Eating and speaking. Now, apply those to what you know about the apostles.'

'Well,' says Jez. 'I guess eating is probably the Last Supper.'

'Or the feeding of the five thousand,' says Kate.

'And speaking?'

They look blank.

Red opens the Bible again and flicks quickly through a couple of pages.

'Here. Matthew, chapter ten. Jesus sends the disciples out. Why? To spread the Word. "Go rather to the lost sheep of the house of Israel. And as ye go, preach, saying, The kingdom of heaven is at hand." You see? *Preach.* Spread the Word.'

Jez is nodding. 'I see. The Last Supper, the feeding of the five thousand, the sending out of the apostles – it was just the original twelve participating in all those things, wasn't it?'

'*Exactly.* He keeps the tongues because they're symbolic for him. They represent the cornerstone of what the apostles – *his* apostles, as he sees it – are about. He doesn't need to keep their bodies, only that little bit which lives on in him. All of their soul in one small piece of flesh. And that definitely rules out Paul and Matthias. They weren't *Jesus'* apostles. They both became apostles after he was crucified.'

233

Method in Silver Tongue's madness. Red sees it now. A mission from God, quite literally.

'And that explains the underpants, too,' says Jez.

Universal incomprehension. Jez smiles.

'Think about it. Who does our man think he is? Jesus Christ, right? Now, plenty of serial killers have thought they were Jesus at one time or another. You remember Larry Gene Bell? He killed two girls in the States back in the Eighties; he was executed a couple of years ago. He claimed that he was Jesus and said he wanted to die in the electric chair rather than by lethal injection because the chair was made of "true blue oak" – just like Christ's cross. But we've already seen that our guy, Silver Tongue, takes his calling very literally. And what's the most enduring image of Christianity? It's the crucifixion, isn't it? More than the birth in Bethlehem, more than the miracles, Jesus was famous because of his death. Think of that cross. Silver Tongue believes, *really believes*, that he's Jesus reincarnated. So when he kills his victims, he's also thinking of his own death on the cross – when all he was wearing was a loincloth. All his victims are basically wearing what Jesus had on when he died.'

Kate gestures at the remaining steaks.

'Come on, eat up. Food's getting cold. We can continue the discussion later. There's been altogether too much religion in one go for me.'

The only sound is the soft *chink chink* of cutlery on porcelain as they eat.

Problem-solving is hunting. It is savage pleasure, and we are born to it.

Red eats with the huge mouthfuls of success. He spears large pieces of steak with his fork and shovels salad high on top. He finishes long before everyone else and, still chewing his last mouthful, gets up to fetch some water. The others munch on at the table.

Red finds a glass jug in one of the cupboards above the sink and fills it with tap water. The meat is heavy in his mouth. Maybe he's eaten too much. He puts the jug on the sideboard and swallows. The lump of steak lodges in his windpipe. Red swallows again, harder. Nothing happens.

He opens his mouth to suck in some air, but the steak is stuck hard. His breath whistles as it tries to find a way around the blockage. Red tries to swallow for the third time and still nothing happens.

Panic rising.

He tries to shout. *Can't get any air in. Can't get any sound out.*

Red closes his eyes, and when he opens them again the world has gone monochrome. He looks at the little pots of herbs arranged side by side on the shelf in front of him. The usual red and green and brown have become various shades of grey. Funny, that. He remembers thinking only this afternoon how much better the pictures of the Sistine Chapel looked in colour. And now his whole world is black and white.

The sound has gone off, too. No clanking of cutlery on plates or clinking of glasses. Not even the low rumble of traffic which forms a permanent soundtrack to the urban existence.

Total silence.

And suddenly he doesn't care any more.

He feels himself turning round to face the others, but it is as if someone else is moving him. Red feels an absurd sense of freedom. The oxygen is draining from his brain but he doesn't care. It is like the best of all dreams, the dream you never want to end.

Red can see the others now. They move in slow motion. Duncan's mouth drops slowly open and shapes itself into a perfect 'O'. Kate's eyes widen until they seem to take up half her face.

And Jez, kicking back his chair so that it falls silently onto the floor behind him.

Jez covers the ground between them in two enormous strides, filling Red's vision and then disappearing again.

Red's world spins back towards the sink. He feels a dull sensation between his shoulder blades.

And suddenly the sound is on again and the colour comes flooding back into his watery eyes and everything is moving at the right speed and he is bending over the sink coughing his guts up. Long globules of spit drip slowly from his lips and the chewed grey chunk of meat which came flying out of his mouth sits in the bottom of the sink.

When he has finished coughing and has got some air back into his heaving chest, Red looks up. 'Thanks,' he says, and smiles weakly.

Jez looks like he's seen a ghost. 'Bloody hell, Red,' he gasps. 'Thought you were a goner there.'

'Looks like you're more shocked than I am.'

'Probably.' Jez doesn't smile. 'Seriously, man, you gave me a hell of a fright.'

Jez places his hand in the small of Red's back and they return to the table. Kate jumps up and kisses Jez full on the lips in relieved thanks. 'I didn't even realise what was going on,' she says. 'One minute you were getting water, and the next thing I knew, Jez was bending you over the sink and doing a karate chop on your back.'

They talk about the incident for a while, agreeing again and again how lucky Red has been, and drink a small toast to Jez for saving Red's life. Duncan clears the plates and makes some coffee, then they sit with their steaming mugs and try to work out what to do next.

Duncan gestures to the books on the table. 'All this is very well,' he says, 'but how does it really help us? OK, we know Silver Tongue's pattern now. We know that there's a finite number of future victims. We know what these victims' names are, their first names anyway, and we know roughly the manner in which they're going to be killed. But that's all. It sounds a lot, but it isn't. When it comes to predicting the next strike, we don't know where or when or who. And that's almost worse than knowing nothing at all. Our chances of catching him haven't actually been greatly increased.'

'But we know where to start looking,' says Red. 'I reckon religious fanatics are our best bet. The millennium's just around the corner, for God's sake. There are thousands of nutters around, predicting the end of the world and all that shit. First

236

thing Monday morning, we're going to start checking them out. I want cults seen and their leaders interviewed. I want the vicars of every church in London spoken to. Anything vaguely Christian, I want it put under a fucking microscope. Even the guys who stand around on street corners shouting about the Bible. In fact, we can do some of that tomorrow. Anyone fancy a trip to Speakers' Corner? There's always a heavy Bible-bashing contingent there.'

'I don't suppose you want to go public on this,' says Kate.

'No,' says Red. 'Definitely not.'

'But we're going to have to get some uniforms to do the legwork, aren't we? We can't carry this out between the four of us. We'll be doing it until kingdom come.'

'Granted, but we don't have to tell the uniforms *why* we're doing it. We don't have to tell them the pattern. We'll work the religious aspect until it's exhausted. We're bound to turn up something there. Silver Tongue thinks he's Jesus Christ – I mean, he *literally* thinks he's Jesus Christ. He *must* have some religious connection somewhere. All we've got to do is find it.'

'But now we know what his pattern is, surely we've got a duty to warn people?'

'How, Kate? How can we warn them? Put out a statement warning people with the following names to watch their backs until quote such time as the Metropolitan Police Force has apprehended a suspect unquote? It would cause mayhem. Absolute fucking mayhem. All we'd do is muddy the water and create thousands more hours of pointless work for ourselves.'

'Why?'

'Because we'd be deluged with false claimants, all of whom would take time to check out and dismiss. We'd probably get a few copycat crimes into the bargain and we'd only succeed in driving Silver Tongue even further underground than he is already. No. No way are we going public.'

'It might have the opposite effect.'

'What?'

'If we go public, it might bring him out. Make him determined to show everyone that he is the real Messiah.'

'Kate, he's already convinced that he's the real Messiah, in his own mind at least. He probably spends his evenings turning water into wine and walking across the fucking Thames. He's on a mission, in the truest sense of the word. He won't break cover just to assert himself.'

'But this could go on for years.'

'No,' says Jez. 'It won't.'

They all look at him.

'Why not?' says Kate.

'We've just mentioned it. The millennium. This is why he's doing it. What's next year? 1999. You read any prediction, any tract, whatever, they always say – or they can always be *interpreted* as saying – that big things are going to happen in 1999. The end of the world, World War Three, the four horsemen of the apocalypse, Armageddon, Judgment Day. You name it, it's going to happen. *That's* our man's timetable. Sometime next year, and probably earlier rather than later, to give himself time if anything goes wrong.'

They're almost with Jez, but not quite.

'He's got a master plan. He's not merely satisfying random urges to go out and kill people. He's preparing himself.'

'For what?'

A divine wind through the room as Jez spells out the unbearable truth.

'This is his Second Coming.'

Interlude

Red's euphoria is short-lived.

They search for a week, working round the clock, and find nothing.

There are five DIY preachers at Speakers' Corner on the Sunday of that week. Red and Kate go along, mingling with the crowds, listening to anyone and everyone get up and say their piece. It's grey overhead as the weather starts to turn colder, autumn sidling in on the tails of the long hot summer, and the men on upturned milk crates repeat themselves or embark on wild tangents which drift off as quickly as the crowds.

Red knows that Silver Tongue is not among the preachers. Silver Tongue is highly organised: not only does he have a defined mission, he has also killed five people without leaving so much as a speck of physical evidence. None of these sad losers wrapped in blue puffa waistcoats and haranguing the curious can hold a candle to him.

Red has the preachers taken in anyway, kicking and screaming about freedom of speech as a van-load of uniforms turn up and drag them off. They all have alibis for at least one of the murders: two of them are immigrants who didn't even arrive in Britain until June. They are out of police custody before nightfall, moaning about infringement of civil rights and threatening legal redress. And fuck you too, thinks Red.

First thing the next morning – Monday – Red assembles a team of fifty detectives and sends them out to all Christian denominational churches within strictly defined geographical sectors. They are back by Friday lunch time and between them have nothing to report other than the fact that church attendances are falling. Local vicars and priests have all been interviewed, not only to establish their credentials, but also to check on members of their congregations who are acting strangely. The clergymen are not told why they are being asked these questions. A few of them point hesitantly in the direction of 'weirdos' or people new to their church, but these come to nothing.

The number of religious sects in the Greater London area is fewer than Red thought. Red, Jez, Duncan and Kate manage most of the questioning between the four of them, and again turn up nothing. Jez dismisses all adherents to religious cults as 'happy bloody clappies' – a sentiment which Red is only too happy to endorse.

They check all outpatients from mental hospitals in the London area going back five years from May 1st. None of them seems to think he is Jesus Christ.

The stress counsellor comes round one lunch time and indulges in half an hour of verbal fencing with Red that he could have done without. He points out to her that, now they have identified the killer's pattern, he is very far from being on the verge of a nervous breakdown. Fuck the counsellor, and fuck the Commissioner if he is going to pay attention to her report. This is Red's case, and he will solve it if it kills him. The look on the counsellor's face suggests that he could have rephrased this last sentence to better advantage.

Patience. They need patience.

But Red isn't patient. He has got a foot in the door of Silver Tongue's mind and, though that door has not been slammed shut in his face, it hasn't opened an inch further either. He knows it is unreasonable of him to expect results so soon. He knows that cracking the code is only the start. Duncan is right that, in itself, it might not lead anywhere. In fact, the limited knowledge only increases Red's feeling of powerlessness. He is able to predict something about the next killings, but not able to stop them.

Names on a piece of paper. A chronicle of deaths foretold.

Like a spoilt child, Red is expecting concessions because he has been clever. He has conversations in his head with Silver Tongue: I make a move, you make a move. But you've got the dice so loaded in your favour it's a joke, my man. My moves are still way behind yours. You're wearing a mask *and* you can see my cards. In return, I've got nothing.

Still hunting blind. Still sifting haystack after haystack for a needle that might never come to light.

Even though they know his pattern now, they still refer to him as Silver Tongue. None of them feels comfortable calling him anything religious and besides, Silver Tongue is how they have grown to know him. It's how they think of him, relate to him.

Red worries about the case all through the following Saturday afternoon and into the evening. Susan goes out, comes back and goes out again on the hen night of one of the girls she works with. Red has hardly seen her in the past week. He climbs into the same bed as her when he gets home in the small hours and shares a cup of coffee with her in exhausted silence first thing in the morning. He knows he is driving her away again as he puts a wall up around himself. If she minds, she doesn't say anything, not to his face at any rate, in the few minutes each day that she sees it. Maybe she just accepts it. Maybe she's bottling it all up, ready to explode one day. Maybe he hasn't got time to wonder what she thinks.

He falls into a deep, dreamless sleep late on Saturday night and wakes on Sunday morning to find Susan sleeping off a hangover on the sofa. A copy of the *News of the World* is scattered on the floor. She must have bought an early edition from one of the late-night stores by the station on her way back.

Red sits on the floor and picks the paper up. He turns it over so he can see the front page.

The headline screams at him in bold two-inch-high letters.

The main story. Front-page lead and four more pages inside. Pages one to five inclusive.

APOSTLE KILLER ON THE LOOSE.

SUNDAY, OCTOBER 25TH 1998

'It has to be one of you three. *Has* to be.'

They are back in Red's kitchen. Last week, when they celebrated the cracking of the code, it was something shared. Now
it is something divisive. Somebody leaked that story to the
News of the World, but no one is admitting it. Trying to unearth
the mole. A mystery within a mystery.

Suspicion. Everyone watching what they say so as not to
incriminate themselves. Kate is the first to find her voice.

'Red, going round bandying accusations isn't going to help.
It doesn't *have* to be one of us. It could be anyone. It could be
Lubezski, or the Commissioner or any of the policemen who
went out to the churches in the last week and somehow found
out more than they were supposed to. Or maybe it could just
be a massively lucky break on the *News of the World*'s part,
putting the case together at the same time we did. Perhaps
they have been working on it and didn't ask us for comment
because they knew we'd have an injunction slapped on it.'

'Kate, after nearly six months of trying to find this fucker,
I'm beginning to lose my faith in lucky breaks. You know what
I'm saying? And no, it couldn't have been anyone else.' Red
jabs a finger at the inside pages of the newspaper. 'Look here.
Look at the *detail*. These articles contain things that only the
four of us know. The incident in Nick Beckett's art warehouse,
for example. No one else knows about that, unless one of you
talked. They've got the picture of Bartholomew from the Sistine
Chapel here. "Picture which unlocked murder riddle" it says.
They've got details of us going to the Coleherne and Substation. They've got pictures of the victims' houses and details
of how they were killed. They've even mentioned the arrest of

Kevan Latimer. This is detailed stuff. I could almost use it as a case resumé. Put it all together and it leaves us with only two possible explanations. One, the *News of the World* reporters have got ESP, in which case we should draft them onto this case without delay, because they'd almost certainly do a better job of finding Silver Tongue than us. Or two, one of you went running to them with the details.'

'They haven't mentioned the signatures,' says Duncan.

'Yeah, and that's the sole saving grace. I presume that even the *News of the World* isn't sufficiently irresponsible to publish that kind of detail, unless they didn't know about it in the first place. Because if they'd blabbed about the tongues and the spoons, or about the fact that we call him Silver Tongue, then we'd really be in deep shit. As it is, the restriction of that knowledge means that we can weed out ninety-nine per cent of the nuisance calls we're going to get, and we'll also be able to tell the real killer from any copycats. But that's not much compensation for having this thing blasted wide open in the media.'

Red looks at them each in turn. One of them has gone to Britain's biggest-selling tabloid with the crime story of the decade and shattered the very molecular structure of the little team which has worked on the case single-mindedly for the best part of six months. Which one? And *why*?

Kate angled for going public last week and was overruled. Did she take the law into her own hands?

Jez wanted to put out warnings to the gay community a few months ago. Is this his way of getting his own back?

Duncan had always argued that the gay angle was wrong. Did he want some belated recognition as to how clever he'd been?

Red looks at each of them, one by one, and in return he receives three stares which are rock-solid neutral. No defiance, no cowering, no challenge. The stares of people with nothing to prove and nothing to hide. Except one of them *does* have something to hide and is a good enough actor to mask it. Red clears his throat.

'We're obviously not going to find out right here. I don't expect the guilty party to confess, not in front of everyone else. I don't necessarily even expect you to tell me in private. Whatever you did, you did for your own reasons, and I'm sure those reasons don't extend to breaking down and confessing the moment someone starts asking questions.

'So I'm not going to bullshit you. I'm not going to say that if you decide to own up you will be treated leniently. Because you won't. At the very least, you'll be suspended without pay and I shall recommend instant dismissal. Because whichever one of you it is, you've destroyed – absolutely *destroyed* – the basis of mutual trust and co-operation on which this team worked. Until I catch you – and I *will* catch you, you can rest assured of that – until then, we will all be looking over our shoulders. Whenever you tell someone something, there will always be a little doubt in your mind. Because the person you trust to watch your back might just be the one to turn round and stab you in it.

'Secondly, the leak is going to bring about all the things we feared when we decided not to go public last week. Hoax calls, media panic, maybe even a few copycat crimes. And I will hold the guilty party entirely responsible for the thousands of police hours wasted dealing with crank callers and entirely responsible for any deaths suffered in copycat crimes.'

His anger floods through the room and breaks on their heads like waves on a beach.

'Whichever one of you it is, I hope it was worth it. Now get out.'

Monday, October 26th 1998

Three quick breaths forced in and out from above the diaphragm. Body tensed and untensed. Fingers waggling till the blood stings in the tips. Get the adrenaline going. Gird up the mental loins.

It's what athletes do before every race and politicians do before every speech. What Red is about to do is no less of a challenge. Quick body, quick mind.

Red can hear the clamour in the next room. It is the biggest press conference he can remember being held at Scotland Yard – ever. The press office has been deluged with calls since the *News of the World* story broke yesterday morning. So many calls, in fact, that they had to bring people in from their weekends to man the phones. Red shudders to think how many other calls reporters have made to their unofficial contacts in an effort to find out what's going on, though he can't imagine they'll get much more information than that already published. The *News of the World* has done a pretty comprehensive job. Give them credit for that.

Protect Silver Tongue's signature. At all costs, Red mustn't let any details of the spoons or the tongues get into the open. If nothing else, *they* must be kept secret, or he can kiss good-bye to his chances of solving the case. That knowledge is the sieve which lets them sift the real killer from the cranks.

The Commissioner comes through the door of the ante-room.

'How are you feeling, Red?'

'Rather like a Christian before the lions, actually.' The irony is lost on the Commissioner.

'You'll be fine. I'll leave the talking to you, and confine myself to expressions of support when necessary.'

'That's great. Thank you.'

The Commissioner checks his watch.

'Three o'clock on the dot. Shall we go in?'

Red opens the door to the main room. Lights like starbursts from the camera flashes make him squint. He deliberately stops himself from putting a hand up to shield his eyes. He knows how such a picture would look in tomorrow's papers, how many captions would start with the words 'blinded by the light'.

There is a long table with an outsize police emblem forming a backdrop behind it. Red makes his way to the table and sits down in the furthest of the two chairs. The Commissioner sits next to him. Just the two of them against more than 150 journalists packed into every nook and cranny of the room. The first ones to arrive have taken all the available seats and the others flow round them like liquid. Some stand at the back, others sit stretched-legged on the floor at the sides.

Microphones clipped to the table bristle up at Red's mouth. Red and white lights on the TV cameras glare at him. He clears his throat.

'Ladies and gentlemen, I'm Detective Superintendent Redfern Metcalfe. I am leading the investigation into the so-called "apostle killer", whose existence was revealed in one of yesterday's newspapers. I am here to answer any questions you may have about the case. You will understand that I cannot discuss operational details, but I will try to give you as much help as I can on any other issues. I would ask you please to state your name and the organisation you represent, and to keep your questions brief. Thank you. Who's first?'

An instant forest of hands. Red points to a man in the front row.

'Iain Wakefield, *Daily Telegraph*. These killings have been going on for six months. Why have you not released details of them before now?'

'We're up against a very clever killer. The connection has only recently become obvious.'

Wakefield again, fast, before anyone else can get a question in.

'Did you authorise the release of the material which appeared in the *News of the World*?'

'No, I did not. Lady to my left, in the red jacket.'

'Did the *News* . . . ?'

'Your name, please.'

'Sorry. Louise Farrington, *Daily Mail*. There was no official quote from any member of the police in the *News of the World* story. Did the *News of the World* contact you prior to publication?'

'No, they did not.'

She is quick too. 'Do you know why not?'

'I would imagine because they thought I would have stopped them publishing it.'

'So you object to the details of the killings being made public?'

'Yes, I do. It jeopardises the efforts we are making to bring this killer to justice.'

'Don't you think the people have a right to know?'

He glares at her. 'Ms Farrington, I'm not here to debate the rights and wrongs of press freedom with you or anyone else.'

He looks around again, and points. 'Lady at the back.' A woman raises her eyebrows questioningly. 'Yes, you.'

'Claire Stewart, BBC Radio Scotland. Have you arrested anybody for the murders yet?'

'We haven't charged anybody, no.'

'Do you anticipate an arrest soon?'

'We have the best people available on the case. We are confident that we will bring this killer to justice.'

Move quickly on. 'Man in the third row.'

'Guy Dunn, *Newcastle Evening Chronicle*. Has the killer made any contact with the police?'

'No. None at all.' Point.

'Alex Hayter, *Evening Standard*. Has anybody claimed responsibility yet?'

'Yes, 782 people by lunch time today, and rising.'

The room laughs.

'And they've all been cranks?'

'So far, yes.' Point.

'Roy Pembridge, *South London Press*. If you don't mind me saying so, Detective Superintendent, this whole case reeks of police incompetence.'

Red sighs. There's always one, some chippy journalist with a point to prove.

He smiles thinly back at Pembridge.

'No, Mr Pembridge, I don't mind you saying so, if you can back your statement up. If you can't, then I *do* mind you saying so.'

Pembridge goes for the opening Red has given him and gets to his feet, enjoying his moment.

'Look at the facts,' he says. 'You've been after this guy for ... what ... nearly six months now? You've got no serious suspects. The only person you've arrested turned out to be totally unconnected with the case. You haven't found anything worthwhile at the scenes.'

'As I said earlier, we're up against a very clever killer. He's not just going to jump into our arms.'

'You've got a very good record, Detective Superintendent –'

'Thank you,' interjects Red, not without sarcasm.

' – but six months without success is a long time. Have you considered stepping aside from the investigation?'

'No.'

'Do you think you should consider such a move?'

'No. No, I don't.'

'Why not?'

'Mr Pembridge, I don't have to defend my position to you –'

'It seems like you do, actually.'

There's something about Pembridge's smugness, the whiney tone to his voice, that makes Red want to break his neck. He snaps his head round to the two policemen waiting by the door, knowing even as he does so that he shouldn't.

'Adams. Morris. Get him out.'

They look blankly at him.

'GET HIM OUT!'

Pandemonium. Voices loud like the call of wild geese. Disbelief on the faces which gawp.

Adams and Morris breaststroke their way through the scrum to get to Pembridge. The crowd sways away from the policemen and then back, surging like water in a bath. And all of it recorded on the TV cameras which swivel away from Red to follow the fracas.

Adams is the first to get to Pembridge, who stupidly lashes out at him. Assaulting a police officer. They can arrest him now. Adams and Morris grab Pembridge in an armlock, push his head forward and barge their way out of the room.

Red, leaning forward onto the table, locks his arms straight to stop them from shaking.

I wonder what sounds *you* would make as I choked the life out of you, Mr Pembridge.

The Commissioner is saying something, but Red can't hear him above the din.

He snarls at the serried ranks of journalists and walks stiffly to the door, not trusting himself to look back as they call after him.

TUESDAY, OCTOBER 27TH 1998

Every single national newspaper carries the story the next morning, most of them on the front page. The *Guardian* runs a sermonising editorial about the public's right to know, but the *Independent* photographer is the only one to have caught Red's snarl at the end of the conference. The photo is large and above the front-page fold, a visual stunning enough to compare with the one of the police marksman silhouetted on the roof of the Conservative Party conference which appeared on the paper's very first front page back in the Eighties.

The snarl of a man with his soul stripped bare.

They let Pembridge off with a caution in the end, though they could have charged him for breach of the peace, affray or assaulting a police officer. Red suspects that the Commissioner personally intervened to secure Pembridge's release and ensure that charges were not pressed. Whatever Red thinks about Pembridge, he is smart enough to realise that letting him go is the quickest way to defuse the situation.

In any case, Red has a more pressing assignment with another member of the fourth estate. He finds a copy of Sunday's *News of the World* and checks the by-line on the apostle story, trumpeted as a 'World Exclusive' at the top of every page. The story has been written by a journalist named Roger Parkin, complete with mug shot. Red flicks through the newspaper until he comes to the editorial page. The phone number is on the masthead. He dials it.

'News International.'

'Roger Parkin, please.'

A brief pause, and then another ringing tone.

'Parkin.'

'Mr Parkin, it's Detective Superintendent Metcalfe from Scotland Yard.'

'Hello.' Cautious. Parkin knows who Red is, of course. He was almost certainly at the conference yesterday. Even if he wasn't, he will definitely have seen the coverage.

'I read your piece on Sunday with interest,' Red says.

'I'm sure you did.'

'I thought it was very good. Very comprehensive. There's just a couple of things I'd like to clear up with you, and I've got some more information that you might find useful. Perhaps you'd like to discuss it further?'

'Sure. Can we do it over the phone?'

'Actually, I'd like to show you some documents. It would be better if you came here, to Scotland Yard.'

'OK. When's convenient for you?'

'Any time. The sooner the better. In fact, I tried to get hold of you yesterday, but I forgot that you work Tuesdays through Saturdays, being a Sunday paper.'

'Let me see.'

Papers rustling and Parkin's gentle humming on the other end of the line. Trying to make it sound like he's got better things to do. As if. Unless he has just seen Elvis stacking shelves in the local supermarket, Parkin will be clearing the decks to keep his inside track on the apostle story. He just won't want to appear too keen.

'I'm supposed to be having lunch with someone, but I can cancel that. One o'clock suit you?'

'Fine. Come to Scotland Yard and ask for me at the main desk.'

'See you at one.'

'Right. See you then.'

Red hangs up and smiles to himself.

Hook, line and sinker.

65

Roger Parkin is balder and chubbier in the flesh than in his mug shot. Red, clutching an orange cardboard folder full of papers, meets him at reception and takes him up a couple of floors to an interview room. Anodyne and anonymous. They make small talk in the lift.

'You don't look much like your by-line photo,' says Red.

'No.' Parkin laughs. 'It was taken five years and a full head of hair ago. Journalistic vanity. You should see some of the others. How to make Quasimodo look like Robert Redford.'

Red leads him into the interview room. They sit down on either side of the table. Parkin takes the seat nearest the door. Red puts the folder down on the table. Parkin nods at it.

'Those the documents?'

'Yes. We'll go through them in a sec. I've got a few quick questions for you first.'

Parkin's eyes narrow. 'Fire away.'

'How did you get the story?'

'Come on, Superintendent. You know I can't tell you that.'

'Protecting your source?'

'Of course.'

'Mr Parkin, what your newspaper has done is massively irresponsible. That's not up for debate. This investigation is incredibly sensitive and time-consuming and your story has placed it in serious and possibly irreparable jeopardy. It's my job to minimise the damage. A large part of that involves finding out who leaked the story to you, why they did so and what they told you above and beyond what appeared in your newspaper. There's only a small number of people it can be.'

'Superintendent, you *know* I can't co-operate with you.'

'Why? You think your source has got some more information for you?'

Parkin shrugs. Red goes on.

'If need be, I can send twenty-five officers down to Wapping right now and have your files and notes impounded. I can have you up on a charge of obstruction of justice and put you behind bars quicker than you can say "freedom of speech".'

'Fine. I'll go.'

'To jail?'

'If I have to.'

'Mr Parkin, if you want to be a martyr to your profession, then go ahead. But I haven't spent six months twisting myself in knots on this case to have it pissed away by your newspaper.'

'Superintendent, if you have a problem with what we've published, then I suggest you take it up with my editor and stop bullying me.'

'Tea?'

Instant change in tone and angle of attack. Where Parkin expects more argument, he gets a perfectly civil request. The switch catches him off guard.

'What?'

'Tea. Would you like a cup of tea? Or coffee?'

'Tea would be fine, thanks. Milk and one.'

'I'll be right back.'

Red gets up and walks past Parkin as if to go to the door. Parkin doesn't turn to watch him go; he is busy writing something in his notepad.

Red has the plastic handcuffs out of his pocket in a second. He grabs Parkin's left arm and pulls it behind the chair back, snapping one cuff onto Parkin's wrist and already moving fast for the other arm.

Parkin is too slow. A line of ink glistens on the paper where his hand has been dragged away and the pen clatters on the linoleum floor.

Red yanks Parkin's right arm through the bars of the chair and snaps the second cuff on him. Parkin is pinioned to the chair, his hands attached to each other and his arms laced through the ribs of the chair back.

'What the fuck . . . ?'

Red leans over Parkin's left shoulder and feels inside the reporter's jacket. His hand goes straight for the left-hand inside pocket, rather than the right. Most people carry their wallet in the right-hand pocket, but Red is looking for something else.

He finds it first time. A small book with a red spine and a black cover, the pages tabbed by letters of the alphabet. Parkin's contacts book.

'You can't do that!' Parkin's voice is pompous with outrage.

'Save it, Mr Parkin. I can and I am. And don't think about shouting or screaming either. We get that all the time in here. Policemen ignore screams from interview rooms the way most people ignore car alarms.'

Red is flicking through the book. There are hundreds of names in Parkin's neat sloping script. Most written in black ink, but a few in green or red or blue when that had obviously been the pen closest to hand. Some names are followed by parentheses enclosing the name of the story they helped on. Other names are so well-known they needed no qualification. Ex-directory and mobile numbers of the rich and famous. It is a pretty impressive list.

Red starts looking for his mole.

Nothing under 'B'.

Nothing under 'C'.

He runs his thumb down the tabs until it reaches 'W' and flips open the page.

Too easy.

The last – and therefore the latest – entry in the 'W' column.

Duncan Warren. Home and mobile numbers only. Duncan must have told Parkin not to ring him at the Yard.

Duncan. Why?

So now you know who it is, Red. Does that make it better, knowing that you can stop suspecting two people who've done nothing wrong, or worse, because it removes the last scintilla of doubt that one of your team has sold you out? Someone you trusted and they betrayed you.

Eric. That's how Eric feels, isn't it?

Red walks round to the front of the chair and sits on the edge of the table, facing Parkin.

'Duncan Warren is your contact, yes?'

'I can't tell you that.'

'Mr Parkin, his name's in your book. It's a very recent addition to your list, too. Only two other people could have told you about the apostle case, and their names aren't in your book. So Duncan Warren is your source. Yes or no?'

'I can't reveal my sources.'

Red puts his foot on Parkin's chest. His leg is flexed.

'If I kick now, the chair on which you're sitting will go crashing backwards, trapping your arms underneath it. There's a pretty good chance that you'll break at least one arm and maybe both. Perhaps a couple of fingers, too. Or a wrist. I'm not asking you to *reveal* your source, Mr Parkin, but to *confirm* his identity. This,' he waves the contacts book, 'has already told me what I need to know. All I want you to do is put the issue beyond doubt. Be a second opinion for me, if you like.'

'If you hurt me in any way, I'll sue.'

'Do you think you could write with a broken arm? Or type?'

'I swear to God, I'll fucking sue.'

Parkin shifts in his seat, trying to untangle his arms. The fear behind Parkin's bluster gives Red a kick, quivering the skin of his perineum. Like a cat playing with a ball of wool.

'You know, Mr Parkin, you're really putting yourself through a lot of trouble for a very small thing.'

Red starts to push with his foot, straightening his leg. The chair tips onto its back legs. Red's foot holds man and chair in unsteady equilibrium. His decision. His power.

Parkin cracks.

'OK. It *is* Duncan Warren. He is my contact. Happy?'

Parkin looks down, ashamed of his cowardice. Red pulls his foot back, letting the chair rock forward onto all four legs again.

'Thank you. And now you've told me your source, you won't be shouting your head off about this little exchange, will you?

Because you won't get many more hot tips if people think you divulge the contents of your contacts book at the drop of a hat. So we've both got an interest in keeping this quiet, haven't we?'

Red unlocks the cuffs. Parkin brings his arms back round in front of him and stretches them, rubbing his wrists where the plastic has dug into the skin.

Red hands Parkin his contacts book. Parkin snatches it and shoves it roughly inside his jacket.

They take the lift down to the ground floor in silence and don't shake hands at the front door.

66

Duncan is alone in the incident room when Red walks in. He is eating lunch. A brown bap with a white wedge of Brie squeezing out of the side. He raises a hand in welcome.

'Where are Jez and Kate?' asks Red.

Duncan swallows his mouthful.

'Gone out to lunch.'

'Good. It's you I want to talk to, anyway.' Red sits down opposite him.

Duncan takes a sip of Coke. 'Shoot.'

One word. One word, seeking understanding.

'*Why?*'

'Why what?'

'Why did you do it, Duncan?'

'Why did I do what?'

'Talk to the *News of the World*.'

'I didn't.'

Red is on his feet, fist pounding the desk.

'Yes, you fucking *did*. I saw your name in Parkin's contacts book. He *told* me it was you. So why? Why did you have to go and fuck it up for all of us?'

Red's fury pricks a hole in Duncan and drains the defiance away like air from a balloon.

'For the money,' he says quietly.

'The money?' Red sits back down.

'Yes.'

'They *paid* you?'

'Yes.'

'How much?'

Duncan looks down at his desk.

'How much, Duncan?'

'Twenty grand.'

'*Twenty grand?*'

'I needed it. I needed the money. It's the alimony payments. They're crippling me. Not to mention Sam's school fees. Helen's moved in with that wanker Andy, but I still have to keep pouring money down her throat. I'm mortgaged up to the hilt and the building society have threatened repossession. I'm trying to do it all on a copper's salary and I just can't. I *can't.*'

'Who approached who?'

'Um ... That's hard to say. A bit of both, I guess. I was having a drink on Monday night with an old contact of mine who works at the *News of the World*, a crime reporter, and we were chatting about things, as you do. He asked me if we had any good cases on – not suspiciously, just by way of conversation. I said no, of course, but something must have given me away, because he kept pressing. Eventually he said, jokingly at first, how much would it cost to prise the information out of me? And I said, how high will you go? He said he'd get back to me. It was all a joke at first. We could have stopped at any time. But somewhere along the line it became serious. Anyway, I said I'd think about it, and we arranged to meet the following evening.'

'And?'

'The next night he introduced me to Parkin. We haggled a bit, then settled on twenty grand.'

'Presumably you'd told him a little bit about the case?'

'Not much. Just enough to get him excited.'

'Meaning how much?'

'Just that there was a serial killer who thought he was Jesus Christ and was going round collecting apostles.'

'You call that "just enough"? No wonder he was excited. So when did you sit down with Parkin and spill the beans?'

'Wednesday night and again on Friday. It was too much to do, all in one sitting.'

'Duncan, we were working round the clock last week. We didn't leave here until ten or eleven most nights. When the fuck did you find the time?'

'After we'd clocked off. Late at night.'

'And you told him everything?'

'Everything apart from the killer's signature.'

'Did he ask you about that?'

'Yes. He specifically asked if the killer left any kind of signature.'

'And you said . . . ?'

'I said no. I knew that if I told him about the tongues and the spoons, we might never catch Silver Tongue.'

'Not "we", Duncan. Not any more. As from now, you're suspended.'

Duncan doesn't move. Red stands up.

'Let's go. I'll escort you out of the building.'

'What about my things?'

'I'll make sure they're sent on. Let's go.'

'Can I say good-bye to Jez and Kate?'

A man who has sinned, and still expects forgiveness. Red grabs him.

'For fuck's sake, Duncan. Of all the people in the world, they're the two that want to see you least. Myself excluded, of course. Now *get up*.'

For the second time in half an hour, Red rides down in the lift with silent company. They walk across the reception area stride for stride, showing no sign of the conflict between them. At the main door, Red thinks of something.

'The other night at my house, when Kate wanted to go public and you argued in favour of keeping the details under wraps, did you have this in mind already? Were you seriously considering using our secrecy to your own advantage, even then?'

Duncan's silence speaks volumes.

Red takes Duncan's security pass off him. He watches Duncan walk across the street and into St James' Park Tube station. The mad old woman who was there that morning with her poster announcing a Jewish conspiracy is gone.

One backward glance from Duncan, still pleading for forgiveness.

Red thinks back to the very start of the case, when he tossed a coin to decide between Duncan and Pritchard for the last place on the team. The coin landed tails and he chose Duncan. A pretty expensive mistake, as it turns out.

There's no point trying to co-opt anyone else onto the team now. There is too much for a new person to learn, too much trust for them to have to build in too short a space of time. They will have to soldier on with just the three of them.

Three blind mice. That's what they are. Three blind mice, chasing their tails in the darkness.

Red turns and walks back towards the lifts.

67

The message counter on the answering machine is flashing once when Red gets home. He presses the PLAY button and goes into the kitchen to get himself a drink. Susan's voice, tearful and strained on the answerphone, brings him running back into the living room.

'Red, it's me. I'm . . . I'm in Rickmansworth. I'm staying with Shelley for a few days. Shelley from work, that is. Er . . . could you call me?'

She gives him the number twice, once fast and once slower. He scribbles it down on the pad by the phone while Susan's voice goes on. 'I need to talk to you, Red. *Soon.* Give me a ring. Bye.'

The briefest snatch of conversation with someone else before the connection cuts.

She's leaving him. She hasn't said so, but he knows it. She's leaving him. What a fucking awful day.

Bad things come in threes. Parkin, Duncan, and now this.

Red lifts the receiver and begins to dial Shelley's number. Halfway through, he puts the receiver back down and goes into the kitchen. Probably better to face this with a stiff drink. He finds a can of Heineken in the fridge and pours a large splash of whisky into a tumbler. Straight with chaser. That'll keep him going for a while.

Red goes back into the living room and dials the number for a second time. A female voice answers instantly. Not Susan. Must be Shelley.

'Is Susan Metcalfe there, please?'

'Hold on a sec.'

Footsteps on the other end of the line, clattering on a hard floor. A distant voice saying, 'It's Red.' More footsteps, getting louder this time as they approach the phone.

Susan's voice. 'Red?'

Tearful. She has been crying.

'Honey, are you all right?'

'I'm fine. Well . . . I'm OK. Not fine. Not at all. I just . . . I just need some time to think, I guess.'

'Why?'

'Oh Red, can't you *see*? This case. It's just taken over your life. I haven't existed for you, not for the past six months.'

'That's not true. You know that . . .'

'No, Red. Shut up and let me finish. This thing is dominating your life. You haven't left room for anyone or anything else. I can't live with that any more. I know you've tried to make time and I *do* appreciate that, but basically you're a slave to this case. I see you for a while and then something happens and you're gone for another week. Do you hear what I'm saying? I can't go on living somewhere where I'm either being ignored or where I feel like I'm walking on eggshells in case I say the wrong thing.'

Pause. Red holds his breath.

'And then I saw you on the news last night and in the paper today.'

Oh God. Susan always buys the *Independent*. She saw the snarl picture.

'It scared me, Red, it really did. I saw the footage of you, and I saw that picture of you snarling, and I read what that awful man Pembridge said and none of it was you. Except it *was* you. It was like suddenly . . . I don't know, like I'd been married to only half of you, and there's this whole other side of you that I'd never seen before. *Never.* The you I know is not the man on the front page of the paper looking like he's about to rip someone's lungs out. And that's what this case has done to you, Red. It's changed you.'

'No, Susan, it hasn't. I promise you.'

Not *I'm not like that*. Because I *am* like that. That face of monumental rage is mine.

'It *has* changed you. Or if it hasn't, then you've lied to me and deceived me all this time, and that's just as bad.'

262

'Susan . . . we shouldn't talk about this on the phone. Can't I see you somewhere?'

Silence down the phone as she lets her anger evaporate into sorrow.

'Red, I don't even know which way is up any more. I just want to be on my own for a while. That's all.'

'How long is "a while"?'

'I don't know.'

'Guess.'

'Red. I told you, I don't know. But at least until you catch Silver Tongue. Then we'll see.'

'Susan, that could be *months*. It could be years. Fuck, we might never get him.'

'Red, as long as you are obsessed with that case, then we have absolutely no chance of working things out. There's no point in us having a huge heart-to-heart when you're too tired to talk or when you might have to drop everything at any time to go to a murder scene. It's not fair on you, and it's certainly not fair on me. Concentrate on one thing at a time. Once you've got him, then we can talk about things properly and rationally.'

'Can't I come and see you at work? Take you out to lunch or something?'

'Only to cancel at the last minute? Red, *please*. Just back off. For the time being.'

He knows when to stop pushing. 'OK.'

'Thank you. Listen, I'm going to go now. I'll give you a ring . . .'

'When?'

An instinctive plea. Too desperate.

'When I'm ready.'

Pause.

'Take care of yourself.'

'You too.'

'Bye.'

'Bye.'

The receiver is almost back in its cradle when he hears her voice erupting from the earpiece, calling him back.

'Red?'

'Yes?'

'Your killer? I hate him as much as you do.'

The soft burr of the dialling tone sounds in his ear.

Red turns the lights off, puts his headphones on and lets *Messiah* fill what's left of his world.

68

The police say that I kill innocent people. But I don't. I don't kill them, I martyr them. That's the difference. When I martyr them, their souls come to me. That's why I keep their tongues. Have you read Proverbs? Chapter 21, verse 23: 'He who keeps his mouth and his tongue keeps himself out of trouble.' I take their tongues out as they lie dying, so that their souls come to me. And that's how they live on, spreading the Word through me. In death, they give themselves totally to me, something they wouldn't have done — couldn't have done — in life. Before I took them, they were nothing. When Jesus chose his twelve, they were all ordinary people. It was his presence, his influence, which made them exceptional. So it is with me. I take those men and make them into something. I change them. From life to death, the changing from this dimension to the next. But it works the other way round too. When they were alive, they were spiritually dead. But now they are dead, they have everlasting life through me . . .

WEDNESDAY, OCTOBER 28TH 1998

'Samaritans, can I help you?'

Janet 749 rubs the sleep from her eyes as she answers the phone. She squints at the clock on the wall. Half-past four in the morning. Beneath the clock, her fellow volunteer, Abigail 552, dozes fitfully on a camp bed. Two grey blankets are pulled tightly round the contours of her body.

For anonymity's sake, Samaritan volunteers use numbers rather than their surnames. Partially unknown to their colleagues, wholly unknown to the people who ring them up.

At the other end of the line there is just silence. Janet waits patiently. This is quite usual. People who call the Samaritans often need a few seconds to pluck up courage and start speaking. She uses the time to bring herself fully awake.

Still silence. Janet speaks again. 'I'm here if you want to talk.'

Nothing.

She knows never to hang up, never to cut the connection until they do.

And then a voice, muffled but unmistakably male.

'I have killed someone.'

Janet crooks the phone between her neck and shoulder, covers the mouthpiece with her left hand and clicks the fingers of her right hand. Abigail opens one weary eye, sees the urgency in Janet's expression, and swings her legs off the camp bed. The blankets fall to the floor. She pads across the room and picks up the extension handset. Janet takes her hand off the mouthpiece and speaks.

'Do you want to talk about it?'

'You know the apostle killer?'

'I'm sorry, I didn't catch that,' says Janet.

The man's voice is dull and opaque, as if he's speaking into a handkerchief.

'I said, do you know the apostle killer?'

'The one who's been in all the papers?'

'Yes.'

'Yes. I know who you're talking about.'

'That's me.'

Yeah, sure, thinks Janet. You and the thousands of nutbags who've rung the police already.

His voice again, slicing through Janet's scepticism.

'You don't believe me, do you?'

There's nothing in the Samaritans' training on this. They are taught to deal with people whose partners have just left them and with teenagers who think spots and bullying are the end of the world. They aren't taught what to say to someone claiming to be Britain's most wanted man. Janet says the first coherent thing which comes into her head.

'Do you want to talk about it?'

'The coppers know where I'm at now. But they can't stop me. I've killed more people than they know about.'

'You've killed more people?'

'That's right.'

'How many more?'

'Two tonight. Two in the last three hours. That's why I'm ringing.'

'Why?'

'To tell you where to find them. Well, where to find *one* of them. I figured you should know at least about this one.'

'Why?'

'Because he works with you.'

Janet swallows hard, trying to work some saliva into a mouth suddenly dry.

'Who is he?' she says. 'Who did you kill?'

'He's called Jude Hardcastle. Do you know him?'

'I'm afraid we can't discuss details of –'

'It doesn't matter to me whether you know him or not. He's

267

here with me, in his home, and I've killed him. Do you want the address?'

'Yes.'

'Westwick Gardens, London W12. Basement flat. Can't remember the number, but there's a red Toyota parked outside. You got that?'

'Yes.'

'Read it back to me.'

She does.

'Good. Jude will still be here when you come. But I won't.'

'What about the other one? The other one you killed?'

Too late. He's gone.

Janet is shaking. She runs her hand through her hair, and feels the pull on her scalp.

'Oh my God,' says Abigail.

'Right. I'm going to call Alex,' says Janet. Alex 192 is the head of their Samaritans Centre.

'You don't think we should go straight to the police?'

'Not without telling Alex. It'll only take a couple of minutes.'

Janet runs her finger down the duty rota sheet to find Alex's home number and punches it into the telephone. Three rings, four, five, as Alex struggles from the darkness of his sleep. While Janet is waiting for him to answer, she searches for Jude Hardcastle on the volunteer list. His name isn't there.

'Yes?' Alex's voice, sleepy and irritable.

'Alex, it's Janet 749. We've just had a very strange call.' She doesn't bother to apologise for waking him. Alex knows that none of the volunteers would ring at quarter to five in the morning without a good reason. 'We've just had a man who says that he's killed Jude Hardcastle.'

'Jude Hardcastle?'

'Yes. Apparently he works with us, but I can't find his name on the rota.'

'He does publicity and PR. He gave up doing the phones about six months ago. That's why he won't be on the volunteer rota.'

'Oh. Well, the man gave me an address. Do you want it?'

'Please.'

She reads it down the line.

'Right,' says Alex. 'That's not far from me. I'll go have a look.'

'Don't you think we should call the police?'

'No. Not yet. If this guy who called you is a crank, then the last thing we want is a fleet of squad cars turning up at Jude's house and turfing him and his neighbours out of bed for no reason. I'll go round there myself. It'll take me ten minutes. Thanks for calling.'

Red is already awake when the phone rings.

He has hardly slept. Confused thoughts bounce off the darkness and swirl around the emptiness in the bed that was once
Susan. Faces haunt him, painted on the shades of night: Parkin
crashing to the floor with his hands pinned to the chair; Duncan
fulminating against homosexuals; Eric, like Dorian Gray in his
prison cell, his face young as when Red last saw him, fifteen
years ago, while his portrait grows old and disfigured on the
photos that Red keeps hidden alongside the articles he doesn't
like. At some time Red must have ducked below the surface of
a shallow dreamless sleep, but for how long he does not know.

He grabs the phone before the opening chirp has finished,
his stomach already tight with apprehension. There is only one
thing that someone will be ringing about at this time in the
morning.

Five minutes later, he is speeding down the deserted A40
towards Shepherd's Bush.

71

Jude Hardcastle's skull has been so badly battered out of shape that his head is squashed and elliptical – the top of his cranium is now flat rather than rounded.

His corpse is found in exactly the same position as James Cunningham's: lying on one side with an arm across the face. Same killer, probably with the same weapon. If it wasn't for the fact that Jude had a full head of hair and was about three stone lighter than the bishop, Red would swear that he is looking at the same corpse, exhumed and presented for him all over again in some ghastly version of *Groundhog Day*.

The dull orange light from the petrol station across the road washes through the window.

Red doesn't need to look in Jude's mouth, but he does anyway.

No tongue. No surprise.

He remembers the entry in *Brewer's*: 'Jude, a club, because he was martyred with a club'.

Six down. Six to go.

72

'How did you find this man?' Red asks a shocked-looking Alex 192. 'How did you come to be in Jude Hardcastle's house at five in the morning?'

'I don't mean to be obstructive, but I'm afraid I can't tell you that.'

'You can't tell me why you came here?'

'That's right.'

'Well, did you hear something? A struggle, a scream?'

'No. I live ten minutes away.'

'Did Jude telephone you?'

'I . . . er, no. Not exactly.'

Red looks at Alex for a moment, then gets up and walks over to the telephone. He pulls his sleeves down over his hands, lifts up the receiver and hits the redial button. A female voice answers.

'Samaritans, how can I help?'

Red puts the phone down again and looks at Alex.

'You work for the Samaritans?'

Alex nods reluctantly.

'OK,' says Red. 'I know how you people operate. I know that you keep everything confidential and I respect that. But this is a murder enquiry, so I need to know whatever you know. Now, do you work for the Samaritans?'

Alex relents. 'I'm head of the local branch.'

'And where's that located?'

Alex tells him.

'Let's go,' says Red, pulling out his mobile to call Kate and Jez.

*   *   *

There are six of them crowded into the Samaritans reception area: the three detectives, Alex, Janet and Abigail. The operations room is bigger, but the police aren't allowed in there.

'How would you describe his voice?' asks Red.

'I think he was trying to disguise it,' says Janet. 'It sounded muffled, as if he was speaking into a handkerchief or something. What I could make out wasn't very distinctive. He didn't have a strong regional accent. Just a normal voice.'

For normal, read middle-class and middle England. White, male and well-educated. Things they know anyway.

'And how did he sound? I mean, emotionally?'

'Totally unemotional.'

'He didn't sound angry?'

'No.'

'Upset? Remorseful?'

'No. '

'Triumphant?'

'No. Not even that. He couldn't have sounded less concerned if he was ringing to tell me that he'd forgotten to put the cat out.'

Cool as a cucumber. But then he would be, wouldn't he?

For someone who's just taken a confession – of sorts – from the country's most wanted man, Janet is remarkably composed. Or maybe she's just too tired to take it all in.

'I don't suppose you have a recording of the phone call, do you?' asks Red.

Alex cuts in. 'We don't record any calls. It's a deliberate policy. We can't record calls and we can't trace them either.'

'Trace?' asks Jez.

'Yes. You know, hit 1471 and find out the last number called. We asked BT for that facility to be removed, for the same reason that we don't have phones which flash up the caller's number before you answer. The whole *raison d'être* of the Samaritans is that we offer help in confidence. We never know who the callers are unless they choose to tell us.'

'Anyway,' says Janet, 'he phoned from Jude's house, didn't he? That's what he said, anyway. Maybe he left fingerprints there.'

'Maybe,' says Red.

Not in a month of Sundays. Silver Tongue has already killed five people without leaving a trace of evidence. He's not going to suddenly get careless and start smearing his paw prints all over the phone.

'And he's not on any of your files?' adds Red.

'We don't have any files,' says Alex.

'Can I have a look?'

'The man had never called here before. I promise you that.'

'We can get a warrant,' says Jez.

'I'm sure you can,' says Alex. 'But you'd be wasting your time.'

Red gets up. 'I'm sure a warrant won't be necessary. Thank you all for your co-operation.'

They are almost at the door when Red turns back and looks at Janet.

'You know something?'

'What?'

'You're the only person in the world who has spoken to this man and lived to tell the tale.'

They leave before she can answer.

73

'Three large cappuccinos to go, please.'

It is only seven-thirty in the morning but Red already feels like he has been up half a lifetime.

The cafe gleams with metallic cleanliness. At the prices it charges, so it should.

The cappuccinos come in large cardboard cups with a small hole in the lid for drinking through. The hole apparently makes for the best mixture of froth and coffee in each mouthful. Seattle style, it says on the side of the cup.

'That stuff about mixing froth and coffee is bullshit,' says Jez. 'If you drink it through the hole, all the froth stays inside. Then you can open it and lick it up. *That's* the best bit.'

Their breath floats in lung-shaped plumes as they step out of the cafe and walk back towards Scotland Yard. The first trickle of commuters are coming out of the Tube station, most of them heading towards the Japanese bank on the other side of Victoria Street. This may be the heartland of the civil service, but no government department starts work this early.

'It's interesting, don't you think?' says Red.

'What?'

'That Silver Tongue makes some form of communication so soon after his pattern becomes public. He hasn't communicated at all before, but now he's ringing up the Samaritans.'

'Where he knows he can't be traced or recorded,' says Jez.

'True. But communication is communication. So why did he do it?'

'Maybe he's getting cocky,' says Kate.

'Or maybe he wants to stop,' says Jez.

'No.' Red is adamant. 'He doesn't want to stop. We know that. He's going to see this through to the end. So I think Kate might be right when she says that he's getting cocky.'

Red's mobile trills. The three of them stop walking instinctively. Red passes his cappuccino to Kate, unclips the phone from his belt and answers it.

'Metcalfe.'

Kate and Jez watch him as he speaks. Absolute flatness in Red's tone and posture. He is no longer scared or excited. He is just weary, wanting it all to be over. He looks at them while he is talking and nods slightly.

Another corpse. Two in one morning. Just like when it first started.

There is a sudden infusion of urgency in Red's voice.

'*Who?* . . . Yes, of course I know who he is . . . Yes, I know. Hard not to, isn't it? He's on the news virtually every bloody night . . . Where? . . . Yes, I know it. What number? . . . Right. We'll be there . . . I'm with them now . . . No, we'll walk, it'll be just as quick . . . It's just down the road . . . Look, what's the fucking hurry? He's dead, isn't he?'

He snaps the phone shut and says two words to them: 'Simon Barker.'

'The MP?' they say in unison.

'The very one.'

'Oh my God,' says Kate. 'Where is he?'

'Catherine Place.' Red points towards Victoria station. 'Five minutes that way.'

He takes his cappuccino from Kate's hand.

'Come on. We can drink while we walk.'

74

Simon, *a saw*, because he was sawn to death, according to tradition.

75

That Simon Barker was marked for death by Silver Tongue was an ironic end to his colourful life. Barker had made so many enemies over his twenty-five years in the Commons that only JFK and JR from *Dallas* could possibly boast a greater variety of potential assassins. Name a social group and Simon Barker had offended it. He referred to homosexuals as 'spawn of the devil'; single mothers as 'irresponsible sluts'; the IRA were 'bog-brained Murphys' or 'bloody scum'; women MPs were either 'dykes' or 'dead from the neck upwards'; the Palestinians were 'towelheads', the Africans 'jungle bunnies'. Juvenile, unimaginative and offensive epithets from a man who once described himself, only half in jest, as 'making Genghis Khan look like Ken Livingstone'.

In the world according to Simon Barker, a single European currency was the surest way to Britain's political and economic ruin, the police should have virtually infinite powers of stop and search, mandatory sentencing was right and proper and immigration should be halted altogether. And, since he had no desire whatsoever to hold high office, he expressed these opinions long and loud, secure in the knowledge that he was part of one of the largest Conservative majorities in the country. Simon Barker got airtime that most Cabinet ministers only dream of.

And now he is dead. Sawn in half.

Catherine Place is a quiet, elegant back street across the road from Buckingham Palace. The black lampposts date from Victorian times and the small number of companies based in the street announce their presence on understated brass plaques. Catherine Place lies almost exactly midway between the House of Commons to the east and the nearest fringes of Simon Barker's Kensington and Chelsea constituency to the west.

Simon was scheduled to appear on BBC's *Business Breakfast* shortly before six-thirty that morning to discuss the latest amendments to the Criminal Justice Bill. The BBC driver who came to pick him up at five-thirty found the black front door of his house hanging ajar. When no one answered the doorbell, the driver walked into the house to look for his fare. The contents of the driver's breakfast lie prominently on the carpet by the door of the living room.

Simon's body is in front of the fireplace. He has been severed at the waist and Silver Tongue moved the bottom half about a foot away from the top. Two halves of a body, divided by an ocean of blood.

Every time Red thinks that no murder scene could possibly produce more blood than the ones he has already seen, he is proved wrong. This is the worst of them all. Simon's blood has flowed and spurted and gushed out from where Silver Tongue has sawn, and it squelches under Red's feet as he walks over to the corpse and squats down next to it.

Simon's skin has torn where the saw's blade first broke through. Red inclines his head to one side and examines the bottom of his torso.

It's like a sandwich in cross-relief, with the skin like bread round the outside and all the organs squashed like the filling within. The organs glisten livid shades of red, light blue, purple, yellow and black; the ripe stench of bile hangs thickly in the air.

Red winces. All this stuff, all this mess, is also in me.

The bellybutton hovers an inch or so above the severance line. Silver Tongue chose the logical place to cut: the path of least resistance just above the hips, through the yielding warmth of the intestines, so that the only bone he came into contact with was the spinal column.

Red's eyes flick tiredly over the rest of Simon's body. The bloodstained underpants look incongruous, at the top of a stump rather than in the middle of the body.

Hands and ankles are both tied, so that Simon couldn't struggle effectively.

Red does not need to see the face, but he looks anyway.

Simon Barker's eyes aren't wide with terror; they are scrunched shut against the pain.

Imagine having a limb amputated without anaesthetic. Back before modern medicine, they used to tie you down and put a plank of wood between your teeth so that you wouldn't bite your tongue off as your mouth snapped shut with the agony. Silver Tongue hadn't needed that here. Just cut his tongue out first. Bet that stopped him screaming.

Red wonders how long it took Simon to die.

He stands up and looks round the room. It is impeccably tidy. Magazines arranged just so on the table by the sofa. Desktop closed. Pictures perfectly straight on the walls.

And the bright flash of a scarf on the floor by Simon's head.

Red takes a closer look. It is a red and white football scarf with the word SAINTS woven into the pattern. And it has been laid out flat on the ground. Not dropped there in a heap, but laid out deliberately.

It has been laid out like that so it would be found.

No communication for five months and then two messages in one day. 'Cocky' doesn't cover it.

Red looks over his shoulder. Jez and Kate are standing by the door.

'Jez – which football team is called the Saints?'

'The Saints? Southampton. Why?'

'Because there's a scarf here. Look.'

Kate and Jez walk over carefully.

'I wouldn't have thought Simon Barker was a football fan,' says Kate. 'He probably regarded it as frightfully common.'

'Oh, I don't know,' says Jez. 'Being a football supporter is very trendy now. MPs are queueing up to show that they're men of the people. Except for some reason they all seem to end up supporting Chelsea.'

'So why didn't Simon?' asks Red. 'If he was going to support any football team, then Chelsea would seem the logical choice. It was his constituency, after all.'

'Red, people support football teams for lots of reasons.

Maybe he was born in Southampton. Maybe his Dad was a lifelong fan. Who knows?'

'Hmm. Maybe.'

Red looks at the scarf again.

Not the team's name. Its nickname.

Saints. Not Southampton.

Saints.

Saint Bartholomew, with his skin in his hand.

Back at the art warehouse, one word had come screaming out of the text at him. The word 'apostle'. But there was another word there whose significance he missed.

Saint.

Red has it. The final piece of the jigsaw.

Problem-solving is hunting. It is savage pleasure, and we are born to it.

The veil of his weariness lifts once more. He turns to Kate and Jez.

'The fucker's taunting us. Look at this. Look at what it says.'

'Saints?'

'Exactly. And what were the apostles? They were all saints.'

'Judas wasn't,' says Kate. 'Quite the opposite, in fact.'

'Well, all apart from him. But that doesn't matter.'

'So they were saints. So what?' says Jez.

'Don't you see? They were apostles, but they were also saints. And what do saints have?'

Red answers his own question before they can speak. 'Saint's days, and occupations for which they're patron saints. And I bet Silver Tongue's working on those lines. Bet you anything you like that those criteria match the killings.'

He looks at his watch.

'What time do bookshops open?'

76

I got the highest mark ever in Religious Studies A-level. The official examiner wrote that I knew a quote astonishing unquote amount about Christianity. And at university I used to spend days at a time in the library, poring over book after book, anything about religion and belief and thought. The dons who taught me theology thought I was a pain in the arse. I was always questioning them about dogma and faith and this and that. I wouldn't let anything lie. I challenged every assumption they made. Some people thought I was just an arrogant little prick who was doing it for show, but of course I wasn't. I wanted to find out. It was important to me.

And after all this, I only scraped a low second-class degree in my finals. They told me I was lucky not to have got a Third. And I said to them: how come I got the highest A-level mark ever, and then three years down the line I'm a no-hoper? They said that I didn't answer the questions in the exam. Damn right I didn't. The questions were bullshit. The dons wanted us all to follow their arguments and flatter their egos and then they'd give us Firsts. It was the academic version of Faust's pact with Mephistopheles. You write what we want, and we'll give you a good degree. We know that what you write isn't necessarily what you think, because you're all intelligent people, so it's pretty dense of us to be flattered by the fact that you're slavishly rehashing our arguments without even the slightest pause for original thought, but sod it. It was a cosy little agreement to perpetuate the status quo and those dons' sinecures.

And so many people fell for it. There were these people, my contemporaries, all with good brains in their heads, and they just sold their souls. First to the exam board, and then mostly to the City or to law and accountancy. This was the late Eighties, remember, when you walked out of university and assumed that the world owed you a living. I was trying to challenge things and make people think, and they were all too far up their own arses to see.

I read the Bible again and again, trying to make some sense of it. And the more I read it, the more I saw so much of Jesus in myself. Except you can't say something like that in public, or people will just label you a nutter. Look how David Icke is treated. But it was true. All that stuff about a prophet being without honour in his own country. Jesus was more misunderstood by his contemporaries than anyone else in history. And that's how I felt. I didn't want to think it, at first. It's not the kind of thing you really want to admit. 'Oh, I'm the new Messiah.' Because it's an awesome responsibility. But eventually it became inescapable.

You want to know why I think I'm the Messiah, don't you? After all, anyone can say they are. Look at all those charlatans who set up cults and then order their followers to commit suicide. But I am. I know I am. I'll tell you why, when the time is right.

77

Red arranges his notes in order and looks across his desk.

'Right, quickly, before I tell you what I've found. Kate, did Lubezski say that there was anything unusual about the bodies?'

'Apart from the fact they're dead?'

Red chuckles. 'Yes. Apart from that.'

'No. He's found nothing as yet. As usual, it'll take a couple of days to fully forensic the bodies, but he doesn't expect anything helpful to turn up.'

'What kind of saw does he reckon was used on Simon Barker?'

'Any kind, as long as it was sharp. A small surgical one, perhaps, or maybe a larger handsaw. The only thing they've managed to establish so far from the cut marks is that the saw's teeth were closely serrated.'

'So Silver Tongue wouldn't have had to use a chainsaw?'

'Oh no. Lubezski says that anyone reasonably strong can cut through a human body in about ten or fifteen minutes. We know from the beatings that Silver Tongue dished out to James Cunningham and Matthew Fox that he's a lot more than just reasonably strong. And besides, he couldn't have used a chainsaw at that hour without waking the entire street.'

'I suppose not. Jez? Nothing from either set of neighbours, I presume?'

'You got it. Still looks like we're hunting a phantom.'

'Doesn't it just?' Red clears his throat. 'Right. Are you both ready for this?'

They nod.

'OK. I thought I'd turn literary. So I went to the bookshop down the road and bought these.' He gestures to a pile of books on the desk next to him. 'A Bible, a *Who's Who in the Bible*, and a *Dictionary of Saints*. I worked through all of them, right from the start. I cross-checked every victim and do you know what I found? He's got them perfectly. *Perfectly.*'

'So you were right about the saints?' says Jez.

'Largely. The occupations of the victims either match the professions of which the apostles are patron saints, or they're connected in some other significant way. And the saints' days are all spot on. Saints' days vary between Western and Eastern calendars, but Silver Tongue is naturally following the Western dates. They all fit exactly.'

He looks down at his notes.

'Jesus had twelve apostles and a further seventy disciples to help to spread his teachings. People often use the terms "apostle" and "disciple" as if they're interchangeable, but in fact they're not. They mean different things. "Apostle" comes from the Greek for "a person who is sent out", whereas "disciple" comes from a Latin word meaning "pupil". And, while we're at it, if our killer does think that he's the new Messiah, the word "Messiah" is Hebrew for "a person anointed", which may have some significance.

'But back to our victims. I began with the first body, with Philip. The biblical Philip was one of Jesus' earliest disciples, and was probably a follower of John the Baptist before that. Now, he's not a patron saint of anything that I can find, but, of all the apostles, he was one of those most closely connected with the feeding of the five thousand.'

'Hence the choice of a *caterer*,' breathes Kate.

'Exactly. There's a specific reference to Philip answering Jesus about how to feed the five thousand in John, chapter 6; and Philip's feast day is May 1st. You remember the envelopes of death which Lubezski and Slattery outlined for Philip Rhodes and James Cunningham that first night? They said that Philip was killed between midnight and two o'clock, and Cunningham between three and five in the morning – i.e. both since the start of a new day. That goes for all the victims. They're all killed early on their respective saint's day, in the small hours. Silver Tongue makes sure that they're alive at least until the new day has begun.

'And there's another thing I found, though this may be sheer coincidence: apart from the feeding of the five thousand, Philip also appears as the apostle who was approached by the Greeks when they wanted to meet Jesus. When Philip asked Jesus to show them the Father, you know what Jesus replied? "He that sees me, sees the father".'

'I don't understand,' says Jez.

'It's a theme for the whole series,' says Red. 'I was reminded by what I'd said to that woman in the Samaritans, the one who took the call about Jude Hardcastle. You know, about her being the only person to have spoken to the killer and lived to tell the tale. "He that sees me, sees the father". The only people who have *seen* Silver Tongue are the victims. In *his* mind, when they see him, they see their Redeemer. It's like what you said about the Second Coming, Jez.'

Kate opens her mouth to say something.

'Don't worry,' Red continues. 'It gets worse. The next victim was James Cunningham, the bishop. We identified him as James the Less on that *Brewer's* list because that fitted the method of killing – beaten to death with the fuller's club. Right. I looked up what I could find about James the Less, which isn't very much. Apparently very little is known about him, though he is often identified with any combination of the following people: first, the James whose mother stood by Christ on the cross; second, the author of the epistle of St James; and finally – and most importantly – James the "brother of the lord", who saw the risen Christ and *who is often called the first bishop of Jerusalem*.'

Kate whistles through her teeth. Jez is shaking his head in amazement. Red goes on.

'Either way, James the Less was beaten to death with a fuller's club after being sentenced to stoning by the Sanhedrin in AD 62. His feast day is – surprise, surprise – May 1st. You both with me so far?'

They nod.

'Good. The next one to be killed was James Buxton – by elimination, James the Great. Along with Peter and John, this

James was one of the inner triumvirate of apostles who were the only ones to witness Christ's Transfiguration and his agony in the garden at Gethsemane. He was also the first apostle to die for the Christian faith, and the only apostle whose death appears in the Bible.'

'But surely it was only Jesus who was killed in the Gospels?' says Jez.

'Yes. But James was killed in Acts. Here, Acts 12: "About that time –" AD 43, according to one of these books – "Herod the king laid violent hands upon some who belonged to the church. He killed James the brother of John with the sword." You remember how the emblems of a scallop's shell and a pilgrim's hat didn't seem to make sense? Well, they don't have to. James Buxton was beheaded, just as James the Great was. Apparently Herod thought that persecuting the Christians was the way to win popularity with the Jews.'

'And our killer's criteria fit here?' says Jez.

'Yes. James the Great is patron saint of several groups: pilgrims, rheumatism sufferers and soldiers – even fresh-faced ones straight out of Sandhurst. James was supposed to have been buried in Santiago de Compostela in Spain, and quite a cult grew around the pilgrimage to Compostela between the twelfth and the fifteenth centuries. In fact, only Jerusalem and Rome consistently attracted more pilgrims. Medieval pilgrims used to sew scallop shells into their clothes as good-luck talismans. Walter Raleigh's poem "The Pilgrimage", which he wrote the night before he was beheaded, begins with the words "give me my scallop-shell of quiet". And James' feast day is July 25th.'

'How does Silver Tongue *find* all these people?' says Kate.

'We'll come on to that in a second,' says Red. 'Next one to die was Bartholomew – or Nathanael, as St John called him. We know all about him already, of course. After Jesus' death, he was supposed to have gone to India and Armenia, where he was flayed alive at Derbend on the Caspian Sea. Because of the manner of his death, he has become patron saint of tanners and all who work with skins. Feast day, August 24th. Again, spot on.

287

'After him came Matthew, though he is called Levi by both Mark and Luke in their Gospels. Matthew was a publican – not a pub landlord, as we understand the word today, but a tax collector of Jewish race who worked for Herod Antipas, in Galilee. Tax collectors were very unpopular with the local population, who banned them from taking communion and shunned them socially. They were unpopular not only because they were seen as stooges of the hated Roman occupying forces, but also because they used to supplement their income by means of extortion. Matthew's calling appears in the first Gospel, from Jesus himself.'

'And Matthew Fox worked for the Inland Revenue,' says Jez.

'Exactly. That's why he fitted the pattern. St Matthew – patron saint of tax collectors, accountants and bookkeepers. Feast day, September 21st.'

'Is that Matthew the same one who wrote the first Gospel?' asks Kate.

'Possibly. Opinions among scholars vary.' Red looks up quickly to see if they have any more questions, and moves on. 'And then we come to today's haul. Jude and Simon, both sainted today, October 28th. Let's take Jude – or Thaddeus, as he's sometimes called – first. In modern times, Jude has acquired considerable popularity as the patron saint of hopeless causes. You know why? Because his name so closely resembles that of Judas, no one except the absolutely desperate ever call on him.'

'Hence the Samaritans,' says Kate. 'The last resort of the desperate. Nice touch.'

'Isn't it just?' says Red. 'He's got quite a sense of humour, has Silver Tongue. Actually, it comes through with Simon as well. In the last two centuries BC, Judaism was divided into sects, of which the most prominent were the Pharisees and the Sadducees. Simon belonged to a third group, the Zealots, which consisted of – check this out – the more inflexible and combative conservatives.'

Jez laughs out loud. 'That's Simon Barker down to a tee, I would say.'

'Why are they placed together?' says Kate.

'Seems they went to Persia together, where they were martyred at Sufian.'

Red bounces the papers on the desk to get them back in order. 'Those are the ones so far.'

'How does Silver Tongue get them so precise?' says Kate. 'If it was just a matter of finding people with the right names and killing them when he can, then OK, that wouldn't be too difficult. But if he's looking for the appropriate occupation too, *and* tying himself to specific dates, then he must have done a massive amount of research. What if one of his victims was on holiday or away on business or something? It would screw his pattern up totally. He'd have had to call the whole thing off – or wait until next year to get him, when the saint's day comes round again.'

'I think,' says Jez slowly, 'that he sees the fact that the victims *have* all been available as God's will.'

'I'm beginning to think he might have a point,' says Red. 'The good Lord hasn't exactly been on our side so far, has he? But I reckon our luck might be turning.'

'Why?' says Kate.

'We can use Silver Tongue's own strict guidelines against him. Remember when we were despairing because the potential catchment area was so wide, when we thought it was just *names* he was looking for? By giving us that clue about the saints, he's drastically narrowed the parameters of our search. We know *when* he's going to strike and we have a pretty good idea of the type of person he's going to go for.'

'But since he gave us the clue,' says Jez, 'he must be pretty confident that we're still not going to catch him.'

'Maybe. But perhaps he's getting too cocky for his own good. The more information we have, the more chance we have of getting him. He's already killed seven. That leaves five apostles, but only four saints.'

'Because Judas wasn't a saint,' says Kate.

'Exactly.'

'I don't think we should rule Judas out,' says Jez.

'Nor do I,' says Red. 'But we should concentrate on what we know for the time being.' He picks up another pile of paper. 'Here. These are the ones still left. Andrew, John, Peter and Thomas. I've had to do them in a bit of a hurry, but I'll tell you all that I've found out. Some or most of it may be irrelevant. It's the bits that *aren't* which we've got to identify. OK?'

They nod. Red goes on.

'Andrew first. He was a fisherman by trade and he and Peter were brothers, which may or may not mean something. I doubt that our man's going to go for actual brothers.'

'Why not?' says Kate.

'Two reasons. For a start, killing one brother would warn the other one off, and secondly, we've already had a case of brothers that came to nothing.'

'We have?'

'Yes. James the Great was the brother of John. But James Buxton only had one brother, Nick – the one who found his body. So we don't necessarily have to take the fraternal link too literally. But back to Andrew. He was the very first apostle to be called and, in the lists of the apostles which appear in the Gospels, he is always amongst the first four. Like Philip, he was a disciple of John the Baptist before becoming an apostle of Christ. When John the Baptist acknowledged that Jesus was the son of God, he was overheard by Andrew, who went to Peter and told him that they had found the Messiah. And, also like Philip, Andrew is specifically mentioned at the feeding of the five thousand. In fact, he was the one who found the boy with the original loaves and fishes.'

Red sips at his coffee.

'Andrew was martyred in Patras, on the northwest coast of Achania, where he was crucified on a saltire – an X-shaped cross. Legend has it that he preached to the people from the saltire for two days before he died. His relics were later taken from Patras to Scotland by the bishop of Patras, St Rule, who was told by an angel to travel northwest until ordered to stop. Eventually Rule stopped in Fife, where he buried Andrew's remains and built a church on top of the grave. That is where the town of St Andrew's was founded. Andrew is the patron saint of fishermen and of Scotland – the saltire features on the Scottish flag.'

'A white "X" against a blue background,' says Jez. 'Of course.'

'Next we've got John, the second member of the inner trium-virate which witnessed the Transfiguration and the agony in the garden. He's often called the "beloved disciple" and features strongly throughout the Gospels. John was the one whom Jesus asked to look after his mother Mary after the crucifixion, and he was also the first of the disciples to see the empty tomb after the Resurrection. John is supposed to have been the author of the Fourth Gospel and of the Book of Revelation, which was written on the Greek island of Patnos. The cave in which he received the vision of the Revelation is still visible near the monastery which bears his name. John is the patron saint of theologians, writers and all those who work in the production of books. But his death causes us a problem.'

'Why?' Kate again.

'Because, of all the apostles, he's the only one that wasn't martyred. He was persecuted under the Roman emperor Domi-tian – including a legendary escape from being dunked in a cauldron of boiling oil – but he survived and travelled to Ephesus, where he died of old age. His tomb lies just outside Ephesus, at what is now Selcuk. In the Middle Ages, dust from it was thought to cure all kinds of disease.'

'So if he died of old age, do you think Silver Tongue's just going to let him go? Not bother with him?' says Jez.

'No. I don't think that for a second. John's an integral part of the pattern. He's at least as important as any other apostle, and probably more important than most of them. Silver Tongue will find some way of doing it.'

Kate taps her pencil against her teeth. 'But how?'

'I don't *know* how. We've got to work it out. Anyway, let's get on with what we *do* know. Next up is Peter. He's the leader of the apostles. In every list, he's always the first to be mentioned. Like his brother Andrew, he was a fisherman by profession. In fact, Andrew was the one who introduced Peter to Christ. Peter was originally called Simon, but Christ renamed him Peter.'

'Why?'

'From the Greek word *petros*, meaning "stone". Jesus said that Peter was the rock on which his church would be built. Peter was also the one who would personally be given "the keys of the kingdom of heaven". He was the first apostle to do lots of things – the first to acknowledge that Jesus was the Messiah, the first to see Christ after the Resurrection, the first to work a miracle, and the one who was designated the successor to Judas. However, this prominence was double-edged. For example, Peter was the one who failed to walk with Jesus on the sea of Galilee, when Jesus lambasted him as "ye of little faith". He is also the only apostle to have a wife mentioned in the Bible, though again that may or may not be significant.'

'It has been so far,' says Kate. 'All our victims have been single.'

'Philip was engaged,' says Jez.

'Yes, but he wasn't *married*. That's the difference.'

'We can discuss this later,' says Red, anxious to press on. 'Peter suffered under Nero and was crucified in Rome in AD 64. He was crucified head downwards, because he didn't see himself as equal to Jesus and therefore didn't want to suffer exactly the same fate as Jesus. Peter's body was buried in Rome, in the cathedral named after him. Peter is the patron saint of popes and – like Andrew– of fishermen too. He's usually portrayed with a set of keys – to the kingdom of heaven, presumably – or a cockerel, after he denied Christ three times before the cock crew.'

'That's quite a selection,' says Jez. 'Silver Tongue could choose virtually anything from all that lot. Peter gives him loads of ammunition.'

'Right. Fortunately, the ones still left don't seem to have such an extensive range of symbols. Peter will be the hardest to nail down, but I'm sure it will still be possible.'

'Who *is* still left?' asks Kate.

'Just Thomas. Doubting Thomas, of course. He was the one

who refused to believe in the Resurrection unless he actually touched the wounds of the risen Christ. It's in John, chapter 20: ". . . the other disciples told him, 'We have seen the Lord.' But he said to them, 'Unless I see in his hands the print of the nails, and place my finger in the mark of the nails, and place my hand in his side, I will not believe.'" Of all the apostles, he went furthest afield after Jesus' death. He is supposed to have gone to southern India, even further than Bartholomew. He was killed by a lance and buried at Meliapore near Madras. While he was there, he was said to have built a palace for an Indian king – which is why he has become the patron saint of architects. On the west front of Exeter Cathedral, he is portrayed with both a lance and an architect's square.'

'Well, he should be easy, at any rate,' says Kate. 'An architect called Thomas who gets lanced through. All we need is the date.'

'Shit,' says Red. 'How stupid can you be? I've forgotten to check their saints' days.'

He picks up the *Dictionary of Saints*.

'Which one is that last one? Thomas.'

He thumbs through the pages.

'Thomas. December 21st.'

Looks down at his notes.

'And the other ones. Andrew, John and Peter.'

He turns to the front.

'Here we go. Andrew. November 30th.'

Flick flick.

'John. December 27th.'

Flick flick.

'And Peter. June 29th.'

'*June* 29th?' say Kate and Jez in perfect stereo.

'Yes. June 29th. That's what . . .'

Red's mouth drops open as he realises the significance.

'Oh my God,' he whispers. 'We've missed one.'

'We can't have,' insists Jez.

'We *have*,' says Red. 'We *must* have missed one.'

'Maybe Silver Tongue tried to kill him and couldn't make it,' says Kate. 'Maybe Peter moved house or something.'

Red shakes his head.

'No. I don't think so. Kate, you said it yourself just a moment ago – this whole thing needs an immense amount of planning. We know how meticulous Silver Tongue has been. He hasn't made even the inkling of a mistake so far. He won't have missed it. There'll be a victim called Peter out there somewhere. That's why he gave us the clue about the saints. He wants us to know. He's playing with us.'

'But we've found every victim within hours of their death,' says Jez. 'And yet, this Peter would have been killed,' he counts the months off on his hands, 'four months ago tomorrow. So if Peter is dead, then Silver Tongue must have hidden him. *Why?* Why would he hide this one?'

'I don't know,' says Red. He shuffles through his notes until he gets to Peter. 'Fucking typical. Peter's the one with the most possibilities, too. He'll be the hardest to find, because there are so many things that he could be.' Red scans the text impatiently, muttering to himself. 'Fisherman . . . leader of the apostles . . . keys to heaven . . . crucified upside down . . . only one with wife.'

Crucified upside down. Red's fist comes down hard on the desk.

'That's it. He was crucified upside down. If we'd found Peter right away, right after he was killed, we'd have worked out the pattern. Crucifixion always signifies something religious. And being crucified upside down is sufficiently rare to arouse suspicion in a moron. If we'd found Peter, the pattern would have been obvious.'

He checks the dates.

'Peter should have been the third victim. If we were on to Silver Tongue after just three victims, then he'd have had a lot of trouble keeping up the targets, wouldn't he? So he hides Peter, and we spend our time buggering about in the fleshpots of Gay City. He chooses what to tell us and when to tell us. He gave us the clue about the saints and yet he withholds Peter from us.'

'There must be some record, though, mustn't there?' says Kate. 'I mean, you can't kill someone in June and expect no one to notice that he's gone until October, can you?'

'Unless Peter was someone like a tramp, whose disappearance wouldn't have been noticed,' says Jez, half to himself.

'Maybe,' says Red, 'but more likely, Peter would have had a job. All the victims have been employed, up until now.' He turns to Kate. 'Get onto Missing Persons. Get all records of people reported missing from June 29th onwards. Give it, say, a month from that date. Anyone reported missing from the end of June to the start of August. That'll cover any allowances people would have made for thinking that he was on holiday or ill or something. Tell them to search for men called Peter in London first. If that doesn't show up anything, then expand the search criteria. Stay with them while they do it, and don't leave until you've got something.'

'What about occupations?' says Jez. 'What does Peter represent?'

Red looks at his notes again.

'Locksmiths, fishermen and popes.' He smiles. 'I think we can rule out the last of those. Even the Vatican would have trouble covering that one up.' He looks at Kate. 'Don't worry about the occupations too much. Look for the missing man first, then check if he fits the occupation. He'll probably be a locksmith or something to do with fish, but don't tie yourself down to those. Peter was lots of things. The rock of God, for example. He could be something like a stonemason too. But like I said, make the missing man fit the occupation, not vice versa.'

'Got it.' Kate scribbles the instructions down and gets up. 'There is one other thing,' she says.

'What's that?'

'If he had a wife, like Peter did in the Bible, how on earth would she not have known that he'd disappeared?'

'Maybe she was the one who reported him missing in the first place. Maybe they're separated. Maybe Silver Tongue killed her too. Who knows?'

'No,' says Jez. 'He wouldn't have killed her too. It wouldn't fit his pattern. He'd think it . . . ugly, I guess. Killing anyone other than the chosen ones would sully the purity of his masterpiece.'

79

Kate is back exactly an hour later.

'Jesus, I had to use a bit of female charm on the boys down in Missing Persons. They weren't keen on anyone jumping the queue, especially when they found out that the person we're looking for has been dead for the best part of four months. Still, I had my wicked way with them in the end. And guess what I found.'

'What?'

'Sixteen people called Peter went missing between late June and early August. We can rule out twelve immediately, because they weren't from London. That leaves four. Two of those have been found, both very much alive and kicking. And of the remaining two, one is a boy aged eight.'

'Wasn't that what's-his-face?' says Jez. 'The one who went missing from that council estate in Tower Hamlets? You know, the kid that was in the papers. Peter Stokes. That's his name.'

'Yes, that's the one. No one knows what happened to him, though the local cop shop reckon he's dead by now. Anyway, he's too young for our purposes. So that leaves just one, and I reckon he's our man.'

She hands them copies of the printout.

'There. Peter Simpson. Hilldrop Road, Holloway. Locksmith. Fits to a tee.'

'Damn right it does,' says Red. 'Let's go to Holloway.'

Kate clears her throat. 'There is just one thing that's strange.'

'What's that?'

'Peter Simpson's name didn't come up on the original search. We only found him when we expanded the criteria.'

'What do you mean?'

'The original parameters you gave me were June 29th to August 1st. But we only found him when I asked them to extend the start date. Peter Simpson was reported missing on June 25th – four days *before* he would have been killed.'

Red and Jez look blankly at her.

'He was reported missing *before* he was killed?' says Jez.

'Yes.'

'Perhaps the Missing Persons people got it wrong. Maybe they keyed in the wrong date or something.'

'No. They checked back in the computer system to find the start time on that file. It was created at 4:03 pm on June 25th.'

'Who reported him missing?' asks Red.

'The woman who lives in the flat upstairs. She's called Sandra Moore.'

'Well, we'll talk to her as well. Come on.'

80

'Stephen, will you please stop it?'

Sandra Moore reaches over to disentangle her four-year-old son from Kate's leg, which he is using as an impromptu climbing frame.

Kate smiles at her. 'It's OK. Really.'

Sandra grabs Stephen and pulls him back across the room. She whispers something sharp and urgent in his ear and wraps her arm around his little neck in a gesture that is half maternal affection and half restraining measure.

'I'm sorry, officers.'

'You were saying,' prompts Red.

'Oh yes. It was one of Pete's clients who first alerted me to it. Apparently Pete was supposed to do a job for him, and he didn't turn up, so this guy rang Pete and there was no answer, so eventually he came round to see Pete. Now I was here, minding my own business – '

Like hell, thinks Red, bet you were twitching the net curtains like there was no tomorrow.

' – when this bloke turns up, and he's buzzing on the intercom over and over again, and you can hear it through the whole block, the walls are so thin, and then he starts buzzing every-one, every flat I mean, and I answer my bell and he says he wants to find Pete, and I remember thinking that *I* hadn't seen Pete for a few days, so I let this man in and we knock on Pete's door and there's no answer. And the man says, this is very unlike Pete – Pete had done a lot of work for him, I think, so he knows him quite well, and Pete's always been very reliable – so we call the police, and this young constable, in uniform and everything, turns up and opens the door with one of those skeleton keys you people have. I always tell Pete that he should give me a key, in case something goes wrong when he is out or away or something, and he always promises, but he never has.'

'And what did you find?'

'Well, Pete's gone, hasn't he? There's a note on the kitchen table saying he couldn't take it any more, after Karen's death . . .'

'Who's Karen?'

'His wife.'

'His wife died?'

'Oh yes. Start of this year, it was. In a car crash. Oh, it was terrible. *Terrible*. She was such a sweet woman. They'd only been married a few months, too. Not even any time to start a family. I don't think Pete ever really got over her death. I mean, obviously he didn't, otherwise he wouldn't have left, would he? That's what his note said. That he wanted to be alone and have time to think, and that he was going to disappear for a while and we shouldn't try to contact him, he'd be back in his own good time and he'd be OK and he's not going to kill himself or anything, and sorry for the inconvenience to all the people he's booked in to do jobs for.'

'And you saw this note?'

'Oh yes. The constable read it and then showed it to me.'

'And you're sure it was Peter's writing?'

'Oh yes. He has very nice writing, Pete. Probably something to do with him being good with his hands and all.'

'Would you say that Peter was – *is* – the kind of person just to up and off?'

Sandra Moore doesn't notice Red's slip.

'No. Not at all. As I said, he's very reliable. But he wasn't thinking straight after Karen passed away. Who knows what was going on inside his head? People react in strange ways to things like that, don't they? Live and let live, that's what I say.'

'And you haven't heard from Peter since?'

'Oh no. Not a word. I remember saying to the constable, well that's that then, we know what's happened. And he says, no, we have to report him missing anyway, since we don't know where he is. That's the law, apparently.'

300

'Yes, it is. Do you remember the constable's name?'

Sandra furrows her brow and shakes her head slowly.

'No. It was a long time ago, mind.'

'Not to worry. Do you know what's happened to Peter's flat?'

'Nothing, I don't think. I mean, he still lives there, doesn't he? It's still his place, isn't it? He's just gone away for a while.'

'So it hasn't been sold or rented?'

'Oh no. No one's been in or out of there at all, not as far as I know.'

'Right.'

Red stands up, and Jez and Kate follow suit.

'Mrs Moore, you've been very helpful. Thank you.'

'My pleasure, officers. If you need anything else . . .'

'That's very kind. Thank you.'

She shuts the door behind them, leaving them in darkness on the landing. Jez feels around for the wide smoothness of the communal light switch, and presses it hard. The lights come on. There is a low humming as the timer in the switch begins its countback to zero.

Red is musing.

'So there was no one in the house the day the policeman came round and they found the note. But that would have been on June 25th, the day Peter was reported missing.'

'Assuming that the officer reported it that day,' says Kate.

'Yes, of course. But even if he didn't, that would only be taking the timing further away from the killing. I mean, if he left it a couple of days before reporting Peter missing, then that puts the date of finding the note at around the 24th or the 23rd.'

'You know what's puzzling me,' says Jez, 'all the victims have been killed in their houses, and that's where their bodies have been found. They haven't been left on rubbish tips or dumped in the river or anything. But there's nothing in Peter's home.'

'We don't know that,' says Kate. 'We haven't been in there yet.'

Red turns round and knocks hard on Sandra Moore's door.

She opens it instantly, so fast that she must have been standing just the other side of it, listening to them speaking.

'Mrs Moore, you did say that, to the best of your knowledge, no one has been into Peter's flat since he was reported missing, didn't you?'

'Yes. That's right.'

'Thank you.'

She closes the door reluctantly. They walk down the stairs, so she won't be able to hear them any more. The lights go off as they reach the landing on the level below. There is a switch on every landing; Jez presses the nearest one and the lights come on again.

'What I'm thinking,' says Red, 'is this: Silver Tongue doesn't want us to discover Peter's body too soon, right? But equally he knows that, once he kills him, we'll find the body. Because the body will be at home and someone will notice that he hasn't turned up for something or other. Now, he could go and hide the body somewhere, but that spoils the tidiness of his whole pattern, doesn't it? They've all been killed at home. His own criteria drastically narrow his field of action. So he must kill Peter in his house on June 29th. They're imperative: the date and the location.

'So this is what he does. He breaks into Peter's house about a week before the 29th, makes him write the note, and then kidnaps him and holds him somewhere. A week is long enough for someone – in this case, the bloke he was supposed to do a job for – to notice, call the police, check the flat, find the note and report Peter missing. File closed. People go missing every day, it's no big deal. And then, on June 29th, he comes back to the flat with Peter and kills him. Right there. Everyone thinks Peter's walking the earth trying to get over Karen's death. So there's been no reason for anyone to go into Peter's flat since then. And since no one *has* been in, no one's found the body.'

'You're saying the body will be in his flat?' says Jez.

'Bet you anything you like it will. It's the only solution that fits.'

'In that case,' says Kate, 'it's been in there for four months. That place is going to *stink*.'

Red looks at them.

'Tough shit. That's what we're paid for.'

81

They go down Hilldrop Road, looking for an off-licence.

Across the road from Peter Simpson's flat is the Holloway Community Education Centre. Through the glass front, they can see the local gospel choir at practice. Sweet soul music, which fails to soothe the troubled souls of the police officers on the pavement outside.

They find an off-licence at the end of the road, buy a quarter-litre of whisky, and head back to Peter's flat. Outside his front door Red opens the bottle and says, 'Splash it on thick. Around your mouths, right up into your nostrils. Put on as much as you can. It won't do an awful lot, but it's better than nothing.'

The whisky smarts on their nasal hairs, harsh and pungent. Honey in comparison to the swamping smell of death.

'Just as well we didn't have time to shave this morning, eh?' says Jez, stuffing the whisky into his pocket. 'This would sting like nobody's business if we had.'

'Speak for yourself,' says Kate. 'I managed to shave this morning.'

'The famous bearded woman,' replies Jez. 'We'll put you in a circus and make a fortune out of you.'

She smiles weakly at him, and he curls his arms around her, holding her close to him, nuzzling his mouth against her forehead. Red feels momentarily like an outsider. He sees how well Kate and Jez's bodies fit together, even in something as asexual as a reassuring hug, and knows that they have something special. Maybe they don't know it, maybe they've done nothing about it, but it's there.

Jez unwinds himself from around Kate.

'You all right?' he asks, and she gives him a small quick nod.

Red takes a deep breath.

'Right. Let's do it.'

304

He jangles a small bunch of skeleton keys and inserts the first one in the lock. It slides smoothly up to the hilt, then wiggles a fraction each way. The tumblers don't turn.

'Damn.'

The second one fits perfectly. Red twists it hard to the right, feeling the click through his fingers as the mechanism catches, and pushes at the door. It doesn't move. Red pushes harder, and still the door won't budge.

'Maybe you haven't turned it far enough,' says Jez.

'Uh-uh. The key's over as far as it'll go. And there aren't any other locks on the door. There must be something jamming it on the other side.'

Red leans his shoulder against the door and shoves. The door peels open a fraction at the top.

'There's something on the floor that's causing the obstruction,' says Red. He turns to Jez. 'Come on, Mr Triathlete. Use those muscular thighs of yours.'

Jez kicks at the door three times, hard, and it flies open. Splintering wood, cracking loudly around the frame. The warm fermenting stench of death eases through the whisky. Jez winces in disgust and clamps a hand to his mouth. His eyes are wide above his fingers.

Red looks at him and Kate.

'All right?'

Kate nods. Jez takes his hand away from his mouth.

'Ah *shit*. I've wiped most of the whisky off. Hold on a mo'.'

He pulls the bottle out of his pocket, unscrews the top, clamps his hand over the mouth of the bottle, tips it upside down, then runs his hand all round his nose and mouth.

'That's better. Thanks.'

They go in slowly and cautiously, like deep-sea divers moving in an unknown world. Pointing rather than speaking, whispering rather than shouting. There is no need for them to be quiet, but instinctively they are, here in a flat which has not generated a single sound for four months.

The air hangs low, heavy and asphyxiating; it's very dark, for the curtains have been pulled tightly shut.

Red reaches for the light switch by the door and presses it. No light.

'Electricity's been cut off, I should think,' whispers Kate.

Red nods at her.

Jez edges past them into the hall. He peers round the other side of the door and points. Red and Kate peer round him to see the piles and piles of envelopes, scattered in an ungainly pyramid of brown and white. That is what has been blocking the door. The accumulated mail of a corpse which no one knows is there.

Jez steps back without looking, bumping into Kate and throwing her off-balance. She puts her hand on the edge of the door to steady herself and gasps in surprise.

'What?' hisses Red.

'Look. A layer of rubber, all round the door.'

Black rubber, like a bicycle's inner tube, stretched out and held on with brown swathes of masking tape.

'Hermetically sealing the place, so that the smell doesn't escape and alert people,' says Jez.

'Clever boy,' says Red.

'Me, or Silver Tongue?' asks Jez.

'Him, you berk. Most people wouldn't have thought of that.'

They start searching the flat, quickly and efficiently. Rubber strips are around all the windows as well. There's nothing out of the ordinary in the living room. Nothing in the kitchen. Nothing in the bathroom.

They finally find Peter's body in the bedroom, the furthest room from the front door and the last place they look. A makeshift cross is leaning against the far wall, and a hideously decomposed body is hanging upside down on it, like a mangy bat. The skin on the body patches dark green and black, with white splashes where the maggots crawl. The face is bloated and bubbly, like a balloon. There are only black ovals for eye sockets. Hard, dark brown blood is solidified in trenches on the inverted corpse, coming from the holes in the crossed feet and the outstretched hands where the nails have skewered the body to the wood behind.

There's black linoleum on the floor, between the door and the corpse. Red starts to walk across it and feels it slide beneath his feet.

Not linoleum.

Congealed blood which has formed a skin on top, like hot chocolate.

Monday, June 29th 1998

Silver Tongue pulls hard at the rope which lashes the two pieces of wood together at right angles. It doesn't give an inch. Good.

Peter Simpson watches him, his eyes saucer-large and white above the strip of masking tape across his mouth. Peter must know that Silver Tongue is going to kill him. He has shown Peter his face right from the start: every night when he comes back from work, and every morning when he sets off again. Twice a day, for an entire week.

No one has seen this face, known his true identity, and lived. If you see this face, even once, then you know you are going to die. If Silver Tongue was going to let Peter go, then he wouldn't have shown him his face. But since he has shown Peter his face, he isn't going to let Peter go. Not alive, anyway.

Maybe the week of confinement has knocked the fight out of Peter. A week spent splayed on a bed, in Silver Tongue's house, the house of the holy. Cuffs on Peter's wrists and irons on his ankles. He wrapped the chains in rubber, of course, so that Peter couldn't possibly rouse the neighbours or anyone else by rattling them and making a noise.

A week of confinement, and a week of silence. Silver Tongue hasn't said a single word to Peter since he made him write the note saying he'd gone away, and then he wafted the ether under his nose.

Peter let him in, of course. They all do. The pretext he uses works every time, as indeed it should. After all, it's true.

Silver Tongue wishes there was an easier way to deal with this. Having to hold Peter captive for a week wasn't ideal. But that's the way the dates have fallen. That's the way it has been ordained.

It's not too bad. With luck, he will be able to get through at least half of them before anyone works it out. And even then, even once they know, they still won't catch him. It is God's will that they won't.

And now they are back in Peter's grotty flat in Holloway, under cover of night, with the rubber taped round the windows and the front door.

If he was Peter, and he was the one lying there bound and gagged while someone makes a cross for him, he would be trying everything he knew to get out of it. Martyrs shouldn't just lie down and die. They should go out in a blaze of glory. That's why they're martyrs.

That old boy Cunningham had tried. Caught him by surprise when he threw the nightshirt at him and hotfooted it out of the bedroom. He had a good go at escaping. More than this spineless piece of shit, anyway. It was almost a pity to kill Cunningham.

But it is God's will. God has chosen them for him, and if some of them are less worthy than others, then so be it. That's the point, isn't it? Ordinary people made extraordinary through the very act of martyrdom. The first Messiah's apostles were all ordinary. Only Jesus' calling changed them.

Just like he is changing his chosen ones now. The changing. From man to martyr.

Silver Tongue gets up off the floor where the cross lies and speaks to Peter for the first time.

'Now Peter was sitting outside in the courtyard. And a maid came up to him, and said, "You also were with Jesus the Galilean." But he denied it before them all, saying, "I do not know what you mean." And when he went out to the porch, another maid saw him, and she said to the bystanders, "This man was with Jesus of Nazareth." And

again he denied it with an oath, "I do not know the man."
After a little while the bystanders came up and said to
Peter, "Certainly you are also one of them, for your accent
betrays you." Then he began to invoke a curse on himself
and to swear, "I do not know the man." And immediately
the cock crowed. And Peter remembered the saying of Jesus,
"Before the cock crows, you will deny me three times." And
he went out and wept bitterly.'

Silver Tongue kneels down and puts his face close to
Peter's. The smell from the adhesive on the masking tape
which binds Peter's mouth is like stale fish.

'Do you know Jesus?'

No reaction. Peter is beyond terror, in some distant hyp-
erspace where fear ceases to have real meaning because
everything is fear and everything will always be fear.

'Answer me. Nod your head if you know Him. Shake your
head if you don't. And don't even think about lying, because
I'll know if you are. Now, let's try it again. Do you know
Jesus?'

Peter moves his head slightly from side to side.

'Is that a no?'

Nod.

'Yes, that's a no, or no, that's a yes?'

Confusion mingles with the terror on Peter's face. Silver
Tongue laughs.

'Oh, of course. You can't answer that question. You're
gagged. I'm sorry. My fault for being ambiguous. Right.
We'll start again. Make sure that it's either a clear nod or
a clear shake. Do you know Jesus?'

Shake.

'Do you know Jesus?'

Shake.

'Do you know Jesus?'

Shake.

'And Peter remembered the saying of Jesus, "Before the
cock crows, you will deny me three times." And he went
out and wept bitterly.'

The denial has been done. Silver Tongue moves fast now.

Drag Peter across the floor and onto the cross, still lying flat on the floor.

Roll Peter onto his stomach. Put the key in the handcuffs, flick them off Peter's wrists.

Throw Peter's arms out wide, while he's still trying to move muscles stiff from a week's immobility.

Lash one of Peter's wrists to the cross, keeping the other wrist pinned underfoot. Lash the other wrist to the cross.

Leg irons off. Feet crossed. Ankles lashed to the cross.

Peter's hands and feet form a triangle where he is bound to the cross. Peter has to be lashed, otherwise the weight of his body will tear the flesh of his hands away from the nails.

Take the end of the cross by Peter's feet and lift.

Man and cross are heavy, but Silver Tongue is strong.

Lean the cross up against the wall.

The blood is running to Peter's head, turning his face red. There are tears in Peter's eyes.

'And he went out and wept bitterly.'

Silver Tongue goes over to the kitchen table and picks up the hammer, bouncing it gently in the heel of his hand.

Then he picks up the nails. Three of them, each six inches long.

He sees Peter's chest spasm, and rips the masking tape off his mouth just in time. Peter turns his head sideways and the vomit splashes down his cheek and gurgles onto the floor. When the retching has stopped, Silver Tongue puts the masking tape back on.

'He that sitteth at the right hand of God, from whence he shall come to judge the quick and the dead.'

He rests the tip of the first nail on the skin of Peter's right palm.

Peter looks once, and turns away in impotent horror.

Four quick strikes of the hammer, to pierce skin and bone and wood and come out the other side. Peter's fingers clenching tight round the nail, the tendons in his forearm standing out like violin strings.

Four more strikes on the left palm. Six to get through the crossed feet.

The blood runs freely onto the floor. Silver Tongue has some of it on him. No matter. It will wash off easily. The police can hunt for the soiled clothes all they like, on this and every other murder, and they will never find them. He could wave the clothes under their noses and they still wouldn't know. He is so clever, and they are so stupid.

And he is the Messiah.

He goes back to the kitchen table, puts the hammer down, and picks the surgical knife up.

Back to Peter. Masking tape off the mouth and knife into the mouth, two parts of one fluid movement. Cut under the tongue, down both sides and then round the back.

'Scream all you like, boy, because you can't speak any more. Can't speak, and can't eat. Except with me.'

83

FRIDAY, OCTOBER 30TH 1998

Jez flicks through Lubezski's autopsy report on Peter Simpson.

Peter was killed too long ago for a precise date of death to be determined, but that does not matter. They know the date as surely as if Peter was killed before their very eyes.

The report makes for familiar and depressing reading. No stray fibres. No hair. No semen. No blood, other than that of the deceased. No saliva.

Eight bodies, and not a single piece of useful forensic evidence on any of them. Jez wonders idly if that constitutes some kind of record.

At least they've managed to keep these last three discoveries secret. The media have been told that Simon Barker suffered a heart attack – it was hard enough to get the Samaritans to speak anyway – and Sandra Moore still believes that Peter Simpson has gone away and will be coming back any day now.

Kate comes into the incident room with three cups of tea. She sets the mugs down on the nearest table and blows on her fingers.

'Ow, that's hot.' She looks around the room. 'Where's Red?'

'Counselling.'

'Oh, that'll put him in a *great* mood. I thought he'd had it rescheduled.'

'He had. Twice. Even he couldn't get away with postponing it a third time. The counsellor's staying late just to make sure that he attends.'

'Oh well. Guess his tea will get cold, then.'

Kate walks over to Jez's desk and leans over his shoulder.

'Is that Simpson's autopsy report?'

'Uh-huh.'

'Found anything useful?'

'Absolutely nothing. Silver Tongue doesn't seem to have left us any helpful clues.'

Kate makes a raspberry sound from between her teeth and returns to her desk.

Red's phone is ringing. Still reading the autopsy report, Jez picks up his receiver and punches the code to divert the call to his own phone.

'Clifton.'

'Could I speak to Detective Superintendent Metcalfe, please?'

Male voice. Slight flattening of the vowels. Hard to place.

'I'm afraid he's in conference. Can I help at all?'

'Are you working on the investigation into the apostle killer?'

'Yes, I am.'

'I . . . I know someone who might be the killer.'

'Who's speaking, please?'

'I'd rather not give my name. But I'll tell you who I think might be your killer, if you want.'

Fifty quid says it's another dead-end lead, thinks Jez. Eight bodies without a trace, and suddenly an anonymous tip-off leads us straight to Silver Tongue. As if.

'Sure.'

'He's called Israel.'

Jez raises his eyebrows. *Israel*. Ten out of ten for originality. They'll have fun with this one.

'Israel what?'

'No, just Israel. That's the only name he uses.'

'Just one name?'

'Yeah. Like Pelé or Cher.'

Jez almost laughs.

'And what does Israel do?'

'He is the head of the Church.'

'What's the church called?'

'The Church of the New Millennium.'

'Hold on a second, please.'

Jez hits the hold button, checks that the phone's red secrecy light is on, and turns to Kate.

'We didn't come across any outfit calling itself the Church of the New Millennium when we trawled those cults, did we? Run by a guy called Israel.'

Kate shakes her head.

'Uh-uh. I'm sure we would have remembered.'

'That's what I thought.'

Jez hits the hold button again. The secrecy light goes off.

'Where's this church based?'

'Kensington. Just off the High Street.'

'Sir, I don't want to sound sceptical, but we've already checked a substantial number of churches and none of them match this description.'

'That's because this one's very secretive. We don't advertise our presence.'

'*We?* Are *you* a member of the church, sir?'

'Yes. Yes, I am.'

'So why are you ringing?'

'I'm ringing because I'm afraid. I listen to what Israel says, and all he talks about is the wrath of God and how he's preparing for the Second Coming. *His* Second Coming. He used to be much calmer, but recently he's become really ... *violent*. In his speeches, I mean. I don't know about anything else. Not physically. Not that I know of.'

'Do you live communally?'

'No, but we're not allowed to tell anyone that we're members. Not everyone is as ready for the true word as we are. That's why I'm ringing you anonymously. We attend Bible study and share meals at the Church on certain days of the week, but we don't live there.'

'Do you have the address of the church?'

'Yes.'

'Could I have it, please?'

'Oh, yes. Sorry. Phillimore Terrace. Number 32. It's on the left as you come down from the High Street. Big red house. You can't miss it.'

'I thought you said it was a church.'

'Well, it is, sort of.'

'How do you mean?'

'There's a church there, in the house.'

'*In* the house?'

'Yes.'

Jez whistles through his teeth.

'And which days of the week do you attend Bible study?'

'Tuesday, Friday and Sunday.'

'*Friday?* But that's today.'

'Yes. It starts at seven-thirty.'

'Seven-thirty in the evening?'

'Yes.'

'In about,' Jez checks his watch, 'an hour's time, then.'

'Yes.'

'Will you be there?'

Pause.

'I'd rather not answer that.'

'Sir, it would be very helpful if you would agree to meet –'

'I *can't*. You don't understand. We're not allowed to talk about the Church outside its four walls. We're not allowed to say we're members. We're not even allowed to reveal the Church's existence. Israel would kill me if he found out that I'd done this.'

Kill me.

'Do you mean that literally? That he'd kill you?'

'Um . . . Yes, I think so.'

'What would he kill you for? Mentioning the church, or suggesting that he's a murderer?'

The voice ducks the question.

'You know what Israel's favourite saying is?'

'What?'

'That Jesus Christ was betrayed by one of his own apostles.'

84

Red is still in his counselling session, so Kate and Jez go to Phillimore Terrace alone.

There is faded grandeur on one side of the street, where big houses have been allowed to become run down; on the other side stands the bright stonework of new developments which haven't yet become sullied by age and city fumes. Jez and Kate walk between worlds of old and new, past the pale brownstone of the Kensington United Reform Church and up the steps to number 32.

Jez presses the doorbell. They hear heavy footsteps inside.

A voice is already booming as the door swings open. A massive voice, starting way down in the stomach and deepening as it rises up towards the mouth.

'Come in, my children.'

He is huge. *Huge.* At least six-foot-eight. His massive head is topped by a pad of hair peroxided dark yellow above black roots. Forearms like oak banisters where his shirtsleeves have been rolled up, and hands like hams at the ends of his albatross armspan.

He fills almost the entire doorway. There is a glowing aura around him where the light from the hall fuzzes the edges of his body. Consternation and hostility sit in the pouches of his face. His baritone rumbles with malice.

'I was expecting someone else. Who are you?'

'Is your name Israel?' asks Kate.

'I asked who *you* were. Kindly do me the courtesy of replying.'

Kate flips her badge out, holding it somewhere between her chest and his waist.

'Detective Inspectors Jez Clifton and Kate Beauchamp.'

He is more than a foot taller than Kate, and probably twice her weight, but she does not flinch.

'Yes, I'm Israel. What do you want?'

'We'd like to ask you a few questions.'

'I'm afraid that won't be possible right now.'

'Well, I'm afraid it'll have to be.'

'You'll have to come back some other time.'

'No. Now will be fine. But if you want, we'll listen to your Bible study before we talk to you.'

A shift in the light behind Israel as he starts. He didn't know they knew about the Bible study.

For a second Israel seems to shrink before their eyes, before they realise it is just because he has stepped back from the door to allow them in.

The door clicks shut behind them and they follow him up the stairs. The dark green carpet is flanked by dark red walls and framed pictures run up the wall by the stairs, following the line of ascent like advertisements above the escalators in the Underground. They are small, stylised etchings of men with beards and robes, individually different but part of the same group. The dim picture lights throw shadows on the edges of the steps.

It is not until the fifth painting up, a portrait of a man holding a large knife in his right hand, that Jez realises what the pictures represent.

The apostles.

Peter with a large key. Thomas with an architect's square. Simon with a saw. Others not so immediately recognisable.

Jez nudges Kate and inclines his head towards the paintings. She raises her eyebrows at him. At the top of the stairs, Israel turns left into a very modern and white room, totally out of character with the rest of the house. Like walking out of a gentleman's club and straight into an operating theatre. Israel's office, obviously. A massive glass desk sits in the middle of the room, two sofas meet at right angles in the far corner and there is a wall-mounted television above the door and to the left. Strip lighting glares harshly from the ceiling.

318

Israel pulls up two chairs for Jez and Kate and goes round to the far side of his desk. He lowers his considerable bulk into a black leather swivel chair, which lists slightly before stabilising.

'What can I do for you?'

He asks the question to Jez, but it is Kate who answers.

'As I said, we'd like to ask you some questions.'

'Concerning what?'

'In general terms, the –'

The doorbell rings, cutting Kate off. She exhales loudly in frustration.

'Excuse me,' says Israel. 'I would imagine that the people for whom I mistook you have arrived. I shan't be a second.'

Punctilious with his grammar and courteous now, but still not welcoming, Israel heaves himself back onto his feet and walks out of the room.

Jez looks over the contents of Israel's desk: a computer, with the monitor resting on the hard disc and the printer on a separate table; a three-tiered black fibreglass letter rack with writing paper, envelopes and postcards; a leather blotter, with blotting paper of the same dark red as the walls outside. All perfectly arranged.

They hear the front door open downstairs and the new arrivals come in. Three voices exchange greetings – Israel's distinctive boom joined by the softer tones of two women.

Kate gets up from her chair and creeps out of the office to the top of the stairs. She peers down into the hall, where all she can see are the tops of their heads. Even from directly above, Israel's peroxide is obviously higher than the two grey buns of the women he is talking to. Kate goes back into Israel's office.

'Who are they?' says Jez.

She shrugs her shoulders.

The stairs creak as Israel comes back up. He starts speaking before he enters the room.

'My apologies for the interruption. Those were the last two people who have come for Bible study. It's supposed to start in five minutes and I'd really rather not be late. Perhaps you'd like to come and sit at the back. It usually takes about twenty minutes. I like to keep them short.'

For the first time, Kate is slightly fazed.

'Um . . . Thank you, but that offer wasn't made seriously. We're quite happy to wait here until you've finished.'

'Oh no. You're quite welcome.'

Israel smiles, but it does not reach his eyes. 'I've got nothing to hide, officers. You never know. You might even want to join up once you've heard what I have to say.'

They follow Israel back down the stairs, past the paintings of the apostles again. A small door is set into the wall opposite the front door, painted the same dark red as the walls so you have to look hard to see that it's there at all.

Israel pushes the door open and steps through it. He has to duck his head and bend his knees simultaneously in order to fit. Kate and Jez follow him through the door, along a passage panelled with wood varnished a deep brown and down another flight of stairs. There is a row of pegs at the bottom, with coats hanging on most of them. Their shoes clatter loudly when the carpet runs out and the floor turns to stone.

'Here we are,' Israel says, without turning round. 'The chapel is in the basement.'

Flickering light from the candles placed on the altar and in wall brackets all around the room dimly show walls painted in swathes of red, blue and purple and fabric drapes with gold borders hanging between mirrors shaped like church windows. Above the altar is a massive picture of Israel himself, arms stretched wide like Christ on the cross, a halo dancing above his peroxide crop.

It is all that Jez can do not to laugh. The chapel looks like it has been designed along the lines of what a teenager would regard as magical and mystical. Jez half-expects to see luminous stickers of stars and planets on the ceiling. It is . . . well, *kitsch*, he reckons, for lack of a better word.

320

There are about twenty people in the room. They are all facing the altar, with their backs to Jez and Kate, and they are all wearing identical indigo robes with hoods. There are no pews, no chairs in this room. The devotees sit on the floor, the better to feel even smaller in front of their outsized God.

Israel walks slowly round to the altar.

'My children, we have with us two guests.' He gestures towards Kate and Jez. 'They will be attending our Bible study tonight.'

Blank faces as the congregation, uniform in their bovine docility, turn to look at the police officers. Israel doesn't elaborate on why Jez and Kate are there and no one asks.

Jez scans the faces under the hoods. Men and women in roughly equal numbers. He wonders if the mysterious telephone voice is here, and, if so, which one he is. He looks for a signal, however cryptic, from the informer. Something – anything – to identify him, put a face to the voice.

Nothing.

Jez leans over to Kate and whispers in her ear. His lips brush the tip of her lobe as he speaks.

'Israel hasn't asked why we're here yet, or asked how we know about his Bible study. He doesn't seem overly curious to know what we're doing. So either we're wasting our time, or else – if he *is* Silver Tongue – he's so supremely confident that he's prepared to put on a show for us.'

'He's certainly big and strong enough to have killed those men,' she whispers back. 'But could he have gone unnoticed at eight separate murder scenes? People don't forget someone as big as him.'

'True. But Silver Tongue is playing with us, and so is Israel. Proclaiming yourself the son of God is no crime. Look what he's saying to us: you can come and watch, but you can't do anything to me. Your laws mean nothing. You can mock me or pity me or despise me or fear me, but you can't touch me.'

Israel's voice sounds loudly through their whispers. The congregation turn their heads back towards him.

'And I saw in the right hand of him who was seated on the

throne a scroll written within and on the back, sealed with seven seals; and I saw a strong angel proclaiming with a loud voice, "Who is worthy to open the scroll and break its seals?" '

Jez bends his head and presses his mouth up close against Kate's ear again.

'Revelation, chapter 5.'

'I'm impressed. Been doing your research?'

'Damn right. But so's he. He's doing this from memory.'

'You're right.'

Israel's voice is immensely powerful as he speaks, like James Earl Jones and Luciano Pavarotti rolled into one.

'I have seven eyes and seven horns. My name is the Word of God. I am the Word, and the Word is me. I am the Lamb whom St John saw in the Revelation. I am humanity itself.

'And I will loose the seven seals, and when I do, the only ones who will be saved are those here today. You, all of you, who every day step into the den of iniquity that is what we call society, which accepts sloth and envy and gluttony and pride and avarice and anger and lust as things to be praised rather than reviled. You, who walk through the fires of hell, but who are unscathed because you have *faith*. Jesus Christ did not lock his apostles up behind the walls of a monastery.'

Israel glances towards Jez and Kate for the first time since the study began.

'No, Jesus Christ did not lock his apostles up. Rather, he sent them out into the world to do his work. He sent them among the unbelievers, so that they would believe. The Gospel according to St Matthew, chapter 10. You remember? "Go rather to the lost sheep of the house of Israel. And preach as you go, saying, 'The kingdom of heaven is at hand. Heal the sick, raise the dead, cleanse the lepers, cast out demons. You received without paying, give without pay . . . Behold, I send you out as sheep in the midst of wolves; so be wise as serpents and innocent as doves.'"'

Israel bends down towards the front row, and every head in the room drops slightly in response, mimicking him even in the smallest things.

'*You* are my apostles.'

A longer look at the two detectives this time. There is palpable tension as Jez bites on his anger. Kate puts a hand on his arm, partly as a warning and partly for reassurance. Give and take, in a single gesture.

Israel again, talking to his flock as if they are the only things in his world.

'*You* are my apostles. All of you. You are the ones who are doing my good work. You are the ones who go out into the world and spread the Word. You might not know it yet. Right now, I ask you to keep our very existence secret. That will change. Soon, when the time is right, everyone will know. But you are the ones who will be saved, because you obey the Prophet. And you know what happens to those who do not obey the Prophet. You remember what happened to Korah, who disobeyed Moses? The earth opened up underneath him and buried him alive. And you know what happens to unbelievers. Let me remind you of the one hundred men who mocked the prophet Elijah. He called the fire down from heaven, and it consumed them in its rage. That is what happens. That is why there are two types of people I will not have in the Church – troublemakers and unbelievers.'

That's us disqualified on both counts, thinks Jez.

'The unbelievers and the troublemakers, they say that I'm brainwashing you. And you know something? They're right. I *am*. When you come here, you have your mind filled with all kinds of thoughts and opinions. You learn the Revelation of Jesus Christ. You learn it because I am the only one – *the only one* – who has been shown its true and entire meaning. I have been chosen to see the Word, and I have been chosen to pass it on. The words I speak cleanse your mind and your opinions. They wash out the filth that you are exposed to every day, and with the cleansing water comes the truth. Your brains are clean and pure. You are brainwashed. You are *cleansed*. And because you are cleansed, you will be saved when I loose the seven seals.'

Israel is not looking at the congregation any more. His face is tilted slightly upwards and his hands are lightly clenched by his side. He looks like he is going into some sort of trance.

'It is not long now. Not long until the four spectres come out of the night. Four horsemen gliding across the earth. They have no substance. Nothing can stop them.

'The first horseman rides a white horse, shining against the blackness of night eternal. He wears a crown of solid gold and in his hands he wields a bow. He fires again and again, his arrows piercing flesh and bone. He never misses. He conquers, and no one dares oppose him.

'Behind him comes the horse of blood-red. The rider cradles a gleaming sword, which he swings and slashes in arcs that are as wide as they are deadly. Where he passes, slaughter follows and peace flees the earth. Men slay one another, pitting brother against brother and father against son in mortal combat.

'Over the mound of dead and dying comes the rider on the black horse. His weapon is famine, the merciless, biting spectre of hunger. Those whom the sword has spared, hunger takes, long and agonising in its killing. The people's stomachs shrink and then swell in pain, and they die slowly, by degrees, praying for their end long before it comes.

'In the fourth seal, the terrible one comes. Silence is his shroud. He is pale, and his followers are riders from Hell. Where he passes, no hope remains. His name is Death, and he must claim his own. Plague goes before him, and a fourth of the world's inhabitants fall.

'In the fifth seal, the headless bodies cry out for justice. "How long?" they ask. "How long must this go on?" And they receive no answer, for there is no answer they can receive.

'Then the earth trembles. The sun darkens, and the moon appears as blood. Those who are left from the bow, the sword, the famine and the plague cry out in despair. He comes from the east, shining like the sun. A sharp sword appears from his mouth. Humanity cries to the rocks and mountains to cover them. Islands disappear, mountains tumble like trees in the wind.

'The seventh seal. The final one, in every way. Nothing but

silence, covering the devastated landscape. No life remains, not in the cities and the countryside, not in the highest mountains nor the deepest oceans. Even the wind is dead. A world without life of any sort, and from no life can no life spring. This, truly, is the end.'

Israel unclenches his hands and slowly opens his eyes.

'That is all. Children, go and prepare yourselves for the evening meal. We eat in fifteen minutes.'

The congregation stand up and begin to file out. Their heads are bowed under the hoods, so they don't look at Kate and Jez. As they go through the door, one of the followers catches his foot in the bottom of his robe. He stumbles forward and begins to fall, instinctively reaching out to the nearest person.

Jez.

The man grabs at the lapel of Jez's jacket. His momentum carries them both down towards the floor. Jez, twisting so as not to land on his back, puts out a hand to break his fall. He feels a sharp pain under his skin as his palm scrapes along the stone floor.

A crowd of indigo around them, jostling like cattle in a corral as they help Jez and the other man to their feet. Many hands are on Jez, brushing the grey patches of dust off his suit.

The crowd moves on, taking with it the man who fell.

Jez turns to Kate.

'Did you get a look at . . . ?'

Israel's voice and presence beside him.

'I'm very sorry about that. Just an accident, I'm sure. Are you all right?'

'Yes, I'm fine, thank you.' Jez examines his palm. 'Just a bit of blood where I grazed the skin. It looks worse than it is. I think I'll live.'

He smiles.

Israel is not smiling. He is staring at Jez's hand. A bead of sweat wells at the end of his nose.

'What's wrong?' asks Kate.

Israel is backing away from Jez.

'Blood. Can't stand the sight of . . . blood. Cover it up. *Please.*'

Jez and Kate look at him in astonishment.

'Seriously . . . I'm not joking . . . I'm a haemophiliac . . . I can't stand the sight of it . . . It makes me . . .'

Israel crashes to the floor in a dead faint.

85

Jez and Kate are hunched close over a corner table in a crowded pub, getting progressively drunker.

The barman reaches up above his head and rings a bell. 'Last orders at the bar, per-leeease!'

Kate gestures at the dregs of Jez's pint. 'One more?'

'Yeah. Why not? Might as well make tomorrow's hangover even worse.'

'Same again?'

'Please.'

'Beer's fattening, Jez.'

'So they say. But it's also carbohydrates and liquid. Perfect for athletes like myself.'

Kate wrinkles her nose at him as she gets up. She sways slightly as she stands, and has to put her hand on the back of the man at the next table to steady herself.

'Sorry,' she says. 'Bit pissed.' She goes to the bar, concentrating on every step.

They're in a small pub off Kensington Church Street. An oasis of sanity, less than quarter of a mile from the weirdness of the Church of the New Millennium and its thought control, up close and personal. The power of a leader like Israel, cradling in his hands the hearts and minds of people who are so convinced of his deity that they would do anything for him. The power of life and death. Just like Silver Tongue.

Except of course Israel isn't Silver Tongue. There wasn't much point continuing the interview after he fainted in front of them. The cut on Jez's hand was no more than an inch long and stopped bleeding within minutes. But Israel reacted as if Jez had slashed his wrists in front of him.

Blood at the murder scenes. Reservoirs of blood.

Anyone with that strong a reaction to a tiny cut can't possibly be the man they are looking for. And if Israel really *is* a haemo-philiac, like he claims, then that's another reason he can't be Silver Tongue. He couldn't take the chance that one of his victims would injure him as they struggled, no matter how slightly.

Once Israel came round, they went through the motions anyway. Do you know what you were doing on the nights in question, sir? Israel would have to check his diary for most of the nights, but he knows that he was in the States for the first two murders. Do you have proof, sir? Of course. Right here, in my passport. Entry stamp at JFK, dated 18 April 1998. Exit stamp through O'Hare, 9 May 1998. Saturday through Saturday, three weeks. Thank you very much, sir. Sorry to have troubled you. Israel wasn't even late for dinner with his flock. They did consider whether one of the congregation was carrying out the murders by proxy, but all of Israel's followers seemed so docile as to make the idea laughable. Still, they'd check it out on Monday morning.

And ever since the failed interview Jez and Kate have sat in the Elephant and Castle pub, isolated in their corner as the Friday-night crowd ebbs and flows around them. Their conversation flitting away from the case but always staying close by, always ready to make the short journey back to the topic that has obsessed them both for six months now. They talk about Red's mental state and his counselling, and from there to discussing therapy and how the British antipathy towards psychiatrists leaves the troubled with no one to talk to, and that leads on to the role of the Samaritans, and from there back to Jude's murder, and on again to general questions of privacy and anonymity.

Kate comes back with the drinks. Lager for him, vodka and tonic for her. The lager splashes over the rim of the glass as she sits down.

'Red said something funny to me the other day,' she says.

'What?'

'Well, by the other day, I mean a few months ago. Back in the summer.'

'What did he say?'

'He asked if we were having an affair.'

'Who's "we"?'

'You and me.'

'And what did you say?'

Kate looks for the answer in her glass. The clarity of the vodka oiled by the lemon.

'I can't remember. It doesn't matter.'

She plucked up the courage to say it while she was at the bar, and now she's bottling it.

'No, come on, Kate. You can't back out now. What did you say?'

'I denied it.'

'And did he believe you?'

'I don't know.'

Jez sips at his pint. He watches her from above the rim of the glass.

'I presume he knows you've got a boyfriend?'

'Of course he does. But still . . .'

'But still what?'

'Well, it's hardly unknown, is it?'

'What?'

'Affairs at work.'

'True.'

'It's not as if we would be the first people in the history of the Yard to be . . . taking interdepartmental communications seriously, is it?'

'Intra, Kate. Not inter.'

She laughs.

A Rubicon to cross. The cards are on the table, but they're still face down. They can both retire at this stage with their pride intact. They watch each other through the pause.

Kate takes the plunge.

'Anyway,' she says, 'I know it's the beer talking now . . .'

'Vodka.'

'Oh yes.' She giggles. 'Vodka. I know it's the vodka talking, but I just want to say that I think you're really attractive. I . . .

really want to kiss you. Oh God. You make me feel like a teenager again.'

'You've got a boyfriend,' he says, not without kindness.

'I know. But it's gone stale, Jez.'

'And so what am I to you? An easy lay?'

'Jez, don't say that. You don't know – you *can't* know – how much I think about you. You're you, and David's David, and what I think about you has got nothing to do with what I think about him. But what you just said . . . it insults both of us.'

Jez stands up. 'I can't think with a full bladder,' he says. 'I'm going for a slash. Back in a sec.'

He runs his hand across the back of her shoulders as he squeezes past her, and she puts her hand up to touch his. Her fingertips are on the back of his knuckles, just for a second.

The slightest touch, she thinks, and I go crazy with desire.

The three places at the metal trough urinal are full, so Jez goes into the flush toilet at the end. Tight, small writing on the wall above the cistern. Jez reads it as he urinates.

Builders are dead good in bed there was one in here the other day short dark hair big muscles under his T-shirt and we got chatting he said his name was Steve and he bought me a beer we couldn't keep our hands off each other and then we went back to his flat and fucked each other all night he was a dynamite shag.

Written in the *men's* toilets. Shades of the Coleherne.

By the time Jez finishes, the three men at the urinal have gone. He runs his hands under the cold water tap, looking at himself in the mirror above the basin. Red lines in the whites of his eyes, where the alcohol cracks into his brain.

He knew this was coming, and he ignored it. A problem at least partly of his own making. He must let her down gently.

Back into the pub, sitting down opposite her. She leans forward.

'I've told you what I think, Jez. Your turn.'

'Kate. Kate Kate Kate.'

Her silence pushes him forward.

'I don't think it's a good idea, Kate.'

She says nothing.

'Whether it's going wrong or not, you've got a boyfriend, and –'

'That's my problem, Jez. You don't know him, so it's not like you'd be cheating on a friend or anything. What I do without David's knowledge is my decision and my problem.'

Jez holds up his hands, and starts again.

'OK. OK. That aside, I still don't think it would be a good idea. We still haven't found Silver Tongue, and we shouldn't get involved with each other while that's going on. We've got to work together, Kate. We don't need any more tension than we've already got. And besides, it wouldn't be fair on Red. Now Duncan's gone, there's only three of us. Imagine how Red'll feel if he finds out the other two-thirds of his team are screwing each other.'

'Oh, come on. He wouldn't mind.'

'No. He *would*.'

'Why? Because Susan's left him?'

'No, not at all. Just because we all get on really well and I don't want to do anything to upset the balance. I don't want Red to feel excluded.'

'Jez, you're clutching at straws and you know it. What's wrong? Are you gay or something?'

He laughs. 'Don't be stupid.'

'Well, you never know. The man who solved the Colin Ireland case. Wouldn't it be a great irony if you turned out to be "one of them" after all? No wonder you were so good at finding Ireland. Takes one to know one, and all that.'

'Colin Ireland wasn't gay, Kate, and neither am I.'

'Methinks he doth protest too much.'

'Kate . . .'

'Bet all the boys down at the Coleherne *love* you, Mr Muscleman,' she spits, suddenly spiteful and cutting in her drunken rejection.

Jez gets up. 'I don't have to listen to this. You believe what you want, Kate.'

'Oh, I will. Don't you worry about that.'

'I'm going. If you want me to see you safely into a taxi, I will.'

'No thanks, Jez. I'd rather be protected by a *real* man.'

Jez is out fast through the door, buttoning his coat against the autumn chill, and heads down the road without looking back.

Kate's boyfriend. Upsetting the balance of the team. Jeopardising the investigation. They are all plausible, but they aren't the real reasons, and Kate knows it as well as he does.

86

The world needs a new Messiah. I know the Germans said that at the end of the Weimar Republic and they got Hitler, but that's too parochial and too secular a comparison. The world needs a Messiah now like the world needed Jesus Christ 2,000 years ago. The world needs a saviour. It needs someone to take on all the suffering and pain and wipe the slate clean, so that mankind can start again. Look around you. Look at everything you see in the world today, and tell me that it's not rotten. Because it is. It's rotten to the core.

We've got no morals any more. We've got no sense of value. We had the spirit of the Eighties – unabashed materialism, greed is good – but when the recession came, it all went out the window. We were left with nothing. No leadership of any kind. Just a moral vacuum. Don't you see? We elect politicians to rule us, and they line their pockets with backhanders and bicker about petty party squabbles. Western multinationals have become more powerful and more wealthy than half the countries in the world, and they answer to no one bar a tiny clique of the rich and powerful. They rape the Third World for their own profits, and they imbue this rampant capitalism into all those whose lives they touch and destroy, so that those countries in turn have to ape our worst habits simply to survive. Look at Russia, China, or Brazil – all going the same way as the West, where the rich get richer and the poor get poorer.

And that's why you get crime. Because this shitty world makes us aspire to things we can't possibly have, and then wonders why we turn violent. That's why communism was a good idea. The things that people aspired to under communism – being a good farmer or a good worker – were attainable. The Soviet Union was based on the hammer and sickle. Our world is based on flash cars and plastic blondes. Be better. Be richer. Be more successful. And people can't live up to that. So they try and do it the quick way, by taking other people's possessions. Crime and violence and drugs, for one beaten generation after another.

The world produces enough food to feed its entire population. But a third of that population goes hungry. And you know what? Nobody cares. The small minority who do care – who campaign against environmental degradation or go to church or help the poor – are mocked as freaks or cranks. The rest of the world just sits in apathy and draws its horizons in closer. Well, that's no longer enough.

So I'm the one who's doing something about it. I'm the one who's making the difference.

87

MONDAY, NOVEMBER 2ND 1998

The only parking space they can find is at the far end of the lot. Six in the morning, and Billingsgate car park is already almost full. A few acres of activity in the middle of a sleeping city.

The external temperature gauge on Red's dashboard reads two degrees centigrade, not counting the chill from the gusting wind. The first of the winter's cold snaps.

'Come on,' says Jez from the back seat. 'Let's go catch some bad guys.'

Kate gets out of the car without looking at him. She and Jez haven't exchanged a word so far today. If Red has noticed, he hasn't said anything.

Bowed against the wind, they set off across the parking lot towards Billingsgate fish market. High above them, the aircraft light at the peak of Canary Wharf's pyramid roof flashes blue and regular. A flight of stone steps leads up from the car park to the market, and down these steps come an endless procession of people clutching brown cardboard boxes. They come down the steps in perfect sync, and when they reach the bottom they fan out like a starburst towards their cars.

Red, Kate and Jez squeeze through this human conveyor belt and go into the market. So much light and movement at a time when most people are still lying stock still in the darkness. White-coated porters bustle behind trolleys loaded with boxes of silver pomfret and red snapper. The floor is wet underfoot, and the tang of fish is as strong as if it is being pumped through the ventilation system itself.

They go up one of the staircases which lead off the market-place to the first-floor gallery which looks down into the market and whose outside is dotted with fishmongers' offices. Most of the telephone numbers on the office doors are still prefixed 01, the London code which went out of commission eight years previously.

They find the City of London Superintendent's office on the last side of the gallery. A coat-of-arms in relief jostles for door space with a combination lock. The door is ajar. Red pushes it open and they walk in. There is only one person in there, a short man with oily hair and fingers stained ochre from nicotine. A burning cigarette see-saws on the edge of the glass ashtray next to him.

'Can I help you?'

'I'm looking for the Superintendent.'

'You've found him.'

'I'm Detective Superintendent Metcalfe, and these are Detective Inspectors Clifton and Beauchamp.'

'Derek Welch. Hello.'

'We're looking for anyone called Andrew.'

Welch squints at him.

'Huh?'

'We'd like to talk to anyone in this building whose name is Andrew.'

'Do you know his surname?'

Red sighs.

'I don't think you understand. We're not looking for anyone specific. We want to talk to every person in this place who goes by the name of Andrew. Do you have a public address system here?'

'Yes.'

'Well then, could you please ask all people called Andrew to come to this office as soon as possible?'

'Is it urgent?'

'Mr Welch, if it wasn't, I would hardly have come down here at this ungodly hour with two of my colleagues, would I?'

Welch shrugs himself to his feet and crosses the office. He picks up the receiver of a yellow wall-mounted intercom phone and presses a button.

'Could everybody called Andrew please come to the Superintendent's office immediately? I repeat, everybody called Andrew to the Superintendent's office immediately.'

Jez walks out of the office and across the gallery, so he can see down into the marketplace itself. A few faces are turned quizzically towards each other or up at the Tannoy speakers. Two people – no, three – are walking towards the various exits off the market. The vast majority haven't paid the slightest attention to the announcement. It would take the four-minute warning to bring this place to a halt.

Within five minutes, they have four Andrews in Welch's office. One young, Andrew Turner. Two middle-aged, Andrew Marshall and Andrew Guildford. One old, Andrew Routledge. All unremarkable. All prime targets. The smell of fish wafts from their clothes.

Red introduces himself, Jez and Kate.

'What I am going to say to you may sound strange or like some kind of bad joke. I can assure you that it is very far from a joke. You have probably all heard about the so-called apostle killer, yes?'

All four Andrews nod.

'Since the story first came to light, we have uncovered certain . . . details, which allow us to pinpoint the killer's future targets with greater accuracy. We now know that he is choosing his victims according not only to their names, but also to certain specific aspects of their sainthood – particularly their saint's day, and the occupation with which they are traditionally connected. As you may be aware, St Andrew is the patron saint of fishermen, which is why we're here. We believe that the person the killer targets will be in some way connected with the fish industry. St Andrew's chosen day is November 30th – just under a month from now.'

The four Andrews gawp like guppy fish.

'I cannot emphasise strongly enough that the odds on any of you being singled out are extremely slim. I'm sure there are hundreds more men named Andrew working in fishmongers and supermarkets throughout London, and we will be speaking to all these people over the next two weeks. You are no more at risk than any of them. As such, this is nothing more than a precautionary measure. Are any of you married?'

The two middle-aged ones, Marshall and Guildford, raise their hands.

Red turns to Andrew Turner. 'You, sir?'

'No. Not yet.' He smiles sheepishly through his teenage acne.

'And you, sir?' Red asks Andrew Routledge.

'My wife has passed away.'

'I'm sorry.'

Andrew Routledge shrugs. 'It was a long time ago.'

'The reason I ask,' says Red, 'is that so far the killer has targeted single men.'

'So there's no need for me and Marshy here to get worried?' asks Andrew Guildford.

'I wouldn't go quite that far. The targeting of single men has been his pattern *so far*. He may change it at any time.'

'Will we get police protection?' asks Andrew Turner.

'As I said, the risks are very slight. You'll appreciate that we haven't got the manpower to protect hundreds of potential victims simultaneously, on the off-chance that one of them is singled out. What I *would* ask is that you take extra precautions up to and around the date of November 30th. If possible, make sure that you are with someone else at all times. Don't go round alone. Check that all your window and door locks are secure. Don't answer the door to strangers. And please don't hesitate to ring us if need be.'

Red reaches into his breast pocket and pulls out four business cards. He fans them out in his hand like a croupier, and holds them out to the four Andrews.

'Should we arm ourselves?' asks Andrew Marshall.

'Officially, I could not condone that,' says Red. 'This is not America: there is no constitutional right to bear arms. In fact, if you are stopped in the street with a knife in your pocket, you could well be hauled up on an offensive weapons charge. If you choose to keep a baseball bat by your bed, however . . . that would probably be a sensible precaution.'

338

He hurries on before anyone else can ask a question. 'Anyway, gentlemen, I don't want to keep you from your work any more than I have to. As I said, these risks are very slight. I know it's easier said than done, but please don't let the prospect hang over you in the next few weeks and ruin your life. You're more likely to win the lottery than find this person coming after you. And please keep this quiet. We don't want any of this getting into the media, because that might enrage the killer, and then who knows what he could do.'

The Andrews file silently back to market. Red gives Welch a card too, and thanks him for the use of his office. Welch, already on another cigarette, waves a smoke trail in acknowledgement. 'Any time.'

They walk out to the car. Still another hour of darkness left. Kate turns to Red as they walk.

'What you said about the lottery. You don't really believe that, do you?'

'Of course not. But we've got a few hundred people to see. If I told every single one of those exactly what they – and we – are up against, we'd have to build a fucking asylum.'

'I wonder what odds you would get on one of the people we warn being the next victim,' says Jez.

Red looks at him.

'Better than even, I would imagine.'

88

Kate waits until Red is out of the room before saying her piece.

'Jez,' she says uncertainly.

He looks up from his desk. Raises his eyebrows but says nothing, giving her no help.

'I'm really sorry about the other night,' she says. 'I was out of order. I shouldn't have said what I did. It was . . . childish, I guess. Childish and stupid.'

Jez shrugs.

'It's OK. You were drunk. I was drunk. Let's just forget about it.'

'It's not that easy, Jez. You led me on, you know.'

'You've got a boyfriend, Kate. I didn't think you were serious.'

'Well, now you know that I am. So are you going to tell me why, when push comes to shove, you're not interested?'

'I told you. I told you in the pub.'

'No, you made up some bullshit in the pub.'

'Kate, I'm not going to argue with you. You know I think you're wonderful, but I don't think it's fair to –'

'That's what you said on –'

'And that's what I *mean*. Even if you don't believe it. Look, you've said your bit, and I've said mine. Friends?'

'Jez, we haven't talked about it –'

She breaks off as Red walks back in the room.

'Friends?' says Jez again.

Red looks quizzically at him and then at Kate.

Kate sighs. She knows she's not going to get anything out of Jez, not when he's determined to close himself up like this.

'Yeah. OK. Friends.'

Interlude

For two weeks, they trawl – an apposite enough word, given the circumstances – every fishmonger and supermarket in central London. It is thankless and tedious work, explaining twenty to thirty times a day what the dangers are, what precautions people should take, what numbers to call. They feel like travelling salesman, repeating the same phrases over and over again. More chance of winning the lottery. Just a precautionary measure. Don't answer the door to strangers.

Red impresses the need for secrecy on everyone he talks to. Don't tell everyone, certainly don't tell the fucking media, because if you enrage or taunt this guy there's no telling what he might do. He appeals to their sense of self-preservation, and it works. Every day, Red scans the newspapers in trepidation, fearing a 'Something Fishy' exclusive, but no one goes blabbing to the press.

Red doesn't want Silver Tongue to know what they are doing. He wants him to guess nothing and suspect everything.

And every day that comes and goes is another day closer to St Andrew's Day. It is the first time in the case that they know when Silver Tongue is next going to strike, and the knowledge sits uncomfortably on Red. He doesn't know what will be worse: to warn someone and find that they are still killed, or to discover that the victim is someone they didn't think of. Will it be more painful to be outsmarted once more, or to find that, even within shrinking parameters, Silver Tongue still has the advantage?

At first Red thinks that any clues, no matter how slight, are better than stumbling around in the dark, like they have been for almost six months. Now they know the pattern of killings.

They know *what* is coming. They know *when*, they know roughly *who*, they know roughly *where*.

But they still can't do a thing about it.

It is that impotence which so frustrates Red. To have knowledge, but to know that it is marginally too limited to help him accomplish anything.

It's like building a bridge across a river. You start on either side of the river and you build and you build, and the two parts of the bridge reach towards each other like Leander and Hero across the Hellespont. And then you find that you haven't got enough material to finish, but there's still a gap in the middle and it's fractionally too wide to jump over. The whole edifice is perfect, except for the gap – and it is that gap which makes it useless, which undoes and nullifies everything else.

Sometimes, at odd moments, Red will stop and wonder what Silver Tongue is doing. He likes to think that perhaps they lead strangely parallel lives, not so much in the routines that break up every day – eating, sleeping, washing – but in ways altogether more personal and intimate. When Red wakes up in an empty bed at four in the morning with the image of a tongueless corpse in front of his eyes, is Silver Tongue envisaging the same picture at that same moment? When Red goes through the list of Andrews, stopping on each one in turn, which one is Silver Tongue thinking about?

Red and Silver Tongue. Two sides of a coin. Black and white. Positive and negative. Christ and Satan.

November 30th. D-Day. Or rather, A-Day.

A Monday. Start of the week. End of a life.

They have two calendars side by side in the incident room, each with a day to a page. One is already torn off down to the next saint's day. The other does the regular countdown, day after day.

Red ticks the dates off on the second calendar. Every Monday represents the start of another week, and another week gone. Going down in multiples of seven, like the deadly sins.

November 9th. Three weeks to go. Three weeks, a nice, safe distance. Longer than a summer holiday or the Olympic Games.

November 16th. A fortnight. Still breathing space. Still time to find something. Someone.

November 23rd. A week. Close now. A long time in politics. Not so long in the context of a murder hunt now well into its seventh month.

But it only takes a moment to get a break.

And suddenly the weeks become days, and the days become hours, and the hours minutes and the minutes seconds. It is as if time is simultaneously rushing and crawling.

Friday, November 27th comes and goes. Red looks out of the window at half-past five in the afternoon and watches London rushing off for its weekend. Two days off, to sleep late and watch the football and endure Sunday lunch with the relatives, and then back to the treadmill on Monday morning, grumbling good-naturedly about this and that, grateful for the routine that underpins the mundaneness of life.

No two days off for Red. Rather two days prowling an empty house or sitting in an office going over things for the hundredth time. Exercises in pure futility.

The ambulance and police units are placed on highest alert.

Red lies on his bed on Sunday night and watches the LED display on his digital clock slide silently from 11.59 to 12.00, transforming Sunday into Monday.

It is time.

MONDAY, NOVEMBER 30TH 1998

Anticipation of a ringing phone is perhaps the most effective antidote to sleep ever devised.

Red lies wide awake in the darkness for two hours before finally giving up the unequal struggle against insomnia. Fatigue is in every part of him apart from his mind. At two o'clock in the morning, he gets out of bed, pads to the kitchen and puts the kettle on.

What can I do?

Go somewhere.

But where? Where is the most likely place?

The yellow roof of Billingsgate is in his mind.

That is where they started their search, because it seemed the most logical place to start. And if it was the most logical place to start, it must also be the most logical place to finish.

They found four Andrews at Billingsgate but no more than two in any other single establishment. Billingsgate it is, then.

Red goes back into the bedroom and pulls on the clothes he was wearing yesterday.

Yesterday.

Days are basically time spans divided by sleep, not by cycles of night and day. So when you don't sleep, the days just become longer.

He makes sure his mobile phone is clipped to his belt, and drinks a quick cup of coffee. The liquid scalds his tongue.

The Vauxhall moves like a wraith through the deserted streets. Red turns on the radio. Channel-hopping on the pale green electronic display, from Capital to Radio 1 to Virgin and back again.

The disc jockey on Capital introduces a record by Joan

Osborne which Red recognises. He hums along with the melody and starts singing along to words he wasn't even aware that he knew. He listens to the words as he sings, and wonders why he's never noticed them before.

If God had a face
What would it look like?
And would you want to see it?
If seeing meant that you would have to believe
In things like heaven and in Jesus and the saints and all the prophets?

His voice rises with hers towards the chorus.

What if God was one of us?
Just a slob like one of us.
Just a stranger on the bus,
Trying to make his way home
Back up to heaven all alone
Nobody calling on the phone
'Cept for the Pope maybe in Rome.

The DJ, who seems capable of only talking in superlatives, starts speaking long before the end of the record. Red stabs at the OFF button in fury at the man's drivelling idiocy, and drives the rest of the way to Billingsgate with only an awful sense of foreboding for company.

91

Welch doesn't look in the least bit surprised to see Red again. He offers him a chair (accepted) and a coffee (refused), and says, 'I suppose this is the day, isn't it?'

'Certainly is. No one's been reported missing?'

'No, not at all.'

'Have you checked personally that all the men we interviewed are here?'

'Me? Not personally, no. You can go down and check with them, if you like.'

'Do you know which stalls they work on?'

'Sure.'

Welch leads him out of the room and across the gallery, so they can see down into the market.

'Right. Andrew Marshall's a porter. He'll be wandering around, not tied to any specific stall. Andrew Routledge works over there, beyond the clock. I can see him from here.'

Welch points. Red follows his finger, and sees the old widower packing fish into a white crate.

'Yup. I've got him.'

'Andrew Guildford works on the stall next door, the one with a banner saying EXOTIC SEAFOODS. All kinds of weird crap, they have there. I can't see him just at the . . . No, there he is. There. With his back to us. Bending down. Straightening up . . . *now*. He's got a box in his hands. Do you see him?'

'Yes.'

'Who's the other one?'

'Andrew Turner. The young lad.'

'Oh yes. He works . . . let me see . . . over in that corner, the stall next to the cafe. Can't see him right now. But there's Andrew Marshall, walking past it right now. The porter with the empty trolley. See?'

'Yup.'

'So there's only the young lad who's missing.'

Missing.

'Of course,' Welch continues, 'he could be anywhere. Getting some stuff from the storeroom, or gone to the toilet, or having a cup of tea. It's probably . . .'

He breaks off. Red is already halfway down the corridor.

The industrial-sized tea urn in the cafe hisses loudly as Red talks to Andrew Turner's colleague.

'Andy? Yeah, he works here. Hasn't shown up yet, though. Lazy bugger. Probably overslept.'

'What time was he supposed to be here?'

'Two o'clock. Like I say, probably overslept.'

Red looks at his watch. It is a quarter to three.

Two o'clock. Forty-five minutes ago. Jesus Christ.

'Do you have Andrew's address?'

'What?'

'His address.'

'Not me, mate. I just pitch up here and do my stuff. You wanna try the Superintendent, up on the first floor. Andy'll be registered on the files up there, like we all are.'

Red sprints back up the stairs to Welch's office and bursts through the door just as Welch lights another cigarette.

'Andrew Turner's address? Where is it?'

Red knows he should have taken it there and then, when he interviewed him. Because now he's wasting minutes that he doesn't have.

'I've got it here,' says Welch. 'Why? Hasn't he turned up?'

'No. He hasn't. Now give me his fucking address.'

Welch looks at Red with growing understanding.

'Oh my *God*.'

Welch reaches behind him and opens the second drawer of an old grey filing cabinet. He flicks through the files with his cigarette clamped between his teeth. 'Targett . . . Tucker . . . Turner. Here we go.'

Welch pulls out a slim brown paper folder, and passes it to Red. His hands are shaking.

Andrew Turner's address is on the first page. Donbey House, Flat 53, Wolesley Street, SE1. Just the other side of the Thames, off Jamaica Road.

Then Red is gone, his feet slipping on the wet stone floor of the market, knees high and breath spurting in the freezing air as he sprints across the parking lot, and he lays fifteen feet of rubber on his way out through the main gate.

92

Last time Red came south across Tower Bridge, he was on his way from seeing Bart Miller's body and the traffic had been gridlocked. This time, he is almost certainly on his way to *finding* a body and he takes the bridge at sixty-five mph.

Donbey House is a council block and Andrew Turner lives on the top floor. Red sprints up the stairs until he can go no higher, and then turns right. Doors flash past the periphery of his vision and his feet clatter loudly on the concrete causeway. No one yells in protest. Inner-city housing estates are about the most perfect environment imaginable in which to kill someone. No one would come to the aid of a man screaming in mortal agony for fear that they would be next on the list. See no evil, speak no evil, hear no evil. Someone else's problem, not theirs.

Andrew's flat is right at the end. A blue door. No point in ringing the bell.

The lock is flimsy. Red kicks the door in first time.

Andrew is there, *right there*, as if waiting for Red. The saltire is leaning against the far wall and Andrew is splayed across it, one limb nailed to each of the four arms of the 'X'.

A conventional cross follows the lines of the body, but a saltire leaves no support for the torso or the head. With nothing to rest against, Andrew's head and torso have slumped forward, putting too much weight on the hands and tearing them to shreds.

Red goes closer.

Silver Tongue has taken no chances. Two nails in each foot and each hand. Just to keep Andrew firmly attached, and to bleed him to death a little quicker. Blood has pooled on the floor under the wounds.

Why? Why has Andrew let this happen to him?

Red plants his feet on unbloodied patches of floor, squats down, and looks up at Andrew's face. The angle at which Andrew's head is resting makes his cheeks look puffy and his eyes bug-like. Drops of blood on Andrew's mouth from his severed tongue bubble slightly as they slide off his lower lip and onto the floor.

Bubble slightly.

Red is back on his feet so fast that he almost bashes his head against Andrew's.

He reaches out a hand towards Andrew's neck. Reaches, and touches. Two fingers on skin.

There. Underneath his fingertips. Faint, but unmistakably there.

A pulse.

93

Red dials 999 and asks for an ambulance.

Get Andrew down. Get him breathing properly again.

If Red can get Andrew off the cross, he might be able to reverse or stall the agony of asphyxiation. It's asphyxiation rather than blood loss which usually kills in crucifixions. Nailing someone's arms to a cross restricts the flow of air to their lungs by tightening their chest and diaphragm. The more difficult it is to breathe, the less oxygen reaches the muscles, preventing the arms from taking their share of the weight and allowing the torso and head to slump. This in turn places an even greater burden on the already weakened respiratory system. It is a vicious circle which only has one ending.

Unless someone gets there first.

Red grabs one of the nails in Andrew's right palm and tries to pull it out. He can't. Andrew's blood has made the nail too slippery for Red to get a decent grip, and the nail has been hammered in so hard that the sharp end protrudes from the back of the saltire.

Red looks round the room. He needs something to grip with. A pair of pliers.

No pliers anywhere in view. Not on the tables or the shelves or the chairs. As if there would be. Pliers are hardly an item which you always have ready to hand.

There must be some pliers somewhere. But if Red ransacks Andrew's flat looking for them, then he'll be wrecking the integrity of the crime scene. He could destroy the very clue which would give them their breakthrough.

Make the choice. Make it fast.

There is no contest. Eight murders already and not a shred of evidence at any one of them. Why should this be any different? And, if Andrew lives, he will be the only person to have seen Silver Tongue and survived. What he could tell them might be priceless.

Except he couldn't *tell* them anything, because he can't speak any more.

For a second Red wonders whether he should just let Andrew die. No one would know, except for Red himself. Andrew is unconscious. He doesn't even know that Red is in the room. If Andrew lives, he will be traumatised for life, alone in silence where all he can remember is experiencing more pain than most people will ever know.

People put animals down, when they are in agony beyond repair.

But isn't that the point? Andrew *isn't* an animal. He still has reason and intelligence and feeling.

It's not Red's choice to make. He has to try everything to keep this man alive.

Don't play God. There's already one person out there doing that.

Red rips through the tiny flat like a tornado as he looks for the pliers. He tears drawers clean off their runners and tips their contents on the floor, sifting through them fast and urgently with hands and feet. Fingers in cupboards, moving over baked bean tins and torches and tomato ketchup bottles and light bulbs, all the while using up precious seconds.

He finds some pliers finally, under the kitchen sink. A medium-sized pair, with handles sheathed in dimpled red rubber. Good enough.

Do Andrew's hands first. The right hand.

Red closes the pliers around the first nail, just below the head so that they won't slide off. He adjusts his grip, and pulls as hard as he can.

The nail doesn't move at first, and then suddenly Red feels it give and it comes sliding out through Andrew's palm with a slight slippery *pock* sound.

Andrew's body sags slightly, and Red sees the flesh tear around the remaining nail in that hand.

Fuck. Fuck fuck fuck. How could he have been so stupid?

Should have put the saltire flat on the floor first, to take the weight off Andrew's arms.

Red bends down, clasps the two ends of the 'X' by Andrew's feet and pulls hard at them. Noisy scraping as the saltire leaves jagged trails of brown on the wall and crashes to the floor.

Andrew is now on his back and Red quickly turns his head to the side so he won't choke on his own blood. It will be harder getting the nails out now, because Red will have to pull upwards, against gravity. But he'll be able to get greater leverage.

He plants his feet square, bends down, places the pliers round the one remaining nail in Andrew's right hand, and yanks.

Nothing.

He yanks again, and this time it yields.

He hears a distant chorus of sirens outside, rising and falling in their wailing. The ambulance on its way.

Red works fast now.

Grip, yank. Grip, yank. Grip, yank. Grip, yank.

Andrew's hands are free.

Red places Andrew's arms down by his side and listens at his mouth.

Nothing. No puffs of air on Red's cheek.

Andrew has stopped breathing.

Mouth-to-mouth. It will have to be.

Mouth-to-mouth on a man with no tongue.

Red puts his fingers in Andrew's mouth and clears out as much blood as he can. One of his fingers brushes against the spoon. He pulls that out too, and turns Andrew's face upwards.

He can't do this. He simply can't put his mouth there, onto the bloody pulp of Andrew's face.

Do it.

Red pinches Andrew's nose, and lowers his face to what is left of Andrew's mouth.

Breathe. Breathe. Breathe.

Hands on Andrew's chest, one on top of the other.

Press. Press. Press.

Back to the face.

Breathe. Breathe. Breathe.

Running footsteps on the causeway outside.

Press. Press. Press.

A voice over Red's shoulder.

'We'll do that, sir.'

The ambulance crew take over, fast and efficiently, like they are trained. Oxygen masks and plasma drips around the body. The stretcher down on the floor next to the saltire.

One of the crew takes the pliers off the floor and makes short work of the nails still skewering Andrew's feet to the saltire. They can't put him on the stretcher otherwise.

Red leans against the door, spent.

The paramedic doing mouth-to-mouth on Andrew looks up at Red, and speaks through the blood round his own mouth.

'He's gone.'

Red is down at his side in a flash. 'He can't have,' he says stupidly. 'He had a pulse.'

'I'm sorry, sir. This man's dead.'

94

Lubezski is insistent.

'Red, don't blame yourself. There is nothing you could have done.'

'No, that's not true. I could have lain him flat on the floor first. I could have tried mouth-to-mouth earlier. I could have –'

'Red!' Lubezski's voice is harsh enough to make them all jump. 'Listen to me. Andrew Turner had been on that cross for about three hours when you found him. It's only because he was young and quite fit that he survived as long as he did. Lots of people would have only lasted an hour or so. If Silver Tongue had picked that old man at Billingsgate instead . . .'

'Andrew Routledge.'

'Yes, him. If he'd picked Andrew Routledge, he'd have been dead long before you got there. There is no way – *no way* – that you could have done anything more for Andrew Turner. By the time you got there, he was already dead.'

'No, he wasn't. He had a pulse.'

'You misunderstand me, Red. When I say that Andrew was already dead, I mean that he was in an irreversible process of dying. We're talking brain damage, coma, persistent vegetative state. He wouldn't have been conscious of what you were doing to him – *for* him, I should say. There is no doctor on earth that could have stopped him from dying at that stage. It was simply a matter of time.'

'He's right, Red,' says Jez. 'You can't flagellate yourself in this way.'

'But I *knew* it was going to be at Billingsgate,' says Red. 'I *knew*. I should have gone down there earlier. I should have checked that all the Andrews had arrived at the start of their shifts. Andrew Turner had been missing for forty-five minutes before I found out. They should have been on alert after forty-five *seconds*.'

'Those forty-five minutes would have made no difference,' says Lubezski softly. 'If you want to blame someone, Red, blame the monster who does these things. The responsibility for these deaths is his and his alone. Don't take any of it on yourself.' Lubezski stands up. 'I mean it, Red. Go and catch this . . . lunatic.'

'That's the thing, though,' says Red. 'He's not a lunatic. If he was, we would have caught him by now. Don't make the mistake of dismissing him as insane. He knows exactly what he's doing.'

Lubezski shrugs. 'Whatever. Pathology I can do. Part-time counselling too, if need be. But not psychiatry. I have to go. I'll send through a full autopsy report later, and obviously we'll run the microscope over Andrew's body – though I doubt we'll get anything. And yes,' he says, anticipating what Red is going to say, 'you did exactly the right thing. Jeopardising possible evidence in a bid to save Andrew. I would have done just the same.'

'Except I *didn't* save him, and I probably destroyed vital evidence into the bargain. Parts one and two, both fucked up. If I'd left him, you might have got something.'

'And you'd have had sleepless nights for the rest of your life. Now forget about it.'

Lubezski places a hand of awkward affection on Red's shoulder, and shambles out of the room. Red sighs.

'Well, let's get on with it,' he says to no one in particular.

'I've got a theory,' Kate says, tapping her pencil against her teeth.

'Go on,' says Red.

'I think Silver Tongue is a policeman.'

Red nods slowly. Jez rubs his hand across his chin.

'You don't sound surprised,' she says.

'No,' says Red. 'I'm not. I've been thinking along similar lines myself. But you tell me what makes you think so.'

'It's not a sudden revelation or anything. It's a combination of things that have accumulated over some time, but three reasons mainly. Firstly, what we've just been discussing – the lack of evidence on any of the bodies. Two, maybe three murders without evidence could be passed off as luck, but we've had – what? – nine now, including today's, and we've found nothing on any of them. Whoever's doing the killings knows what we look for, and therefore knows what to avoid. It's *totally* unfeasible that anybody without a working knowledge of police and forensic procedures could have got away with this for so long. If we'd found some evidence and been unable to match it with anybody on file, then fair enough – although even that would mean we were probably dealing with a first-time offender, which I find unlikely. But, like I say, we haven't even got that.'

'Mind you,' says Jez, 'it's not hard to come by that kind of information if you know where to look. You can find it in libraries and on the Internet. There's a whole load of weirdos out there who track police investigations, listen into restricted radio channels and get tips from episodes of *NYPD Blue*. And that's not to mention all the ex-policemen, former soldiers, security consultants, doctors, nurses and so on who pick up that knowledge as a matter of course in their job.'

'Sure,' says Kate. 'I agree with all of that. My point isn't conclusive in itself. It's only when you look at it as part of a wider picture that it has some credence.'

'Kate, I'm not disagreeing with you. I'm just playing devil's advocate. We've been down so many blind alleys already on this case that we don't want to screw it up again.'

'Fair enough,' says Red. 'Go on, Kate.'

'My second point,' continues Kate, 'is that we've had virtually no communication with Silver Tongue whatsoever. The occasions on which he *has* communicated, through Jude Hard-castle and Simon Barker, haven't left him exposed to being traced. He's made no effort to contact *us*. That's quite unusual. Many serial killers communicate with the police, either directly or indirectly. Ireland rang up. Berkowitz wrote letters. Heirens scrawled on walls. Of course, not all serial killers communicate.

But in this case, where there's a clearly defined religious mission, I would have thought we'd have got something: quotes from the Bible, perhaps, or a drawing of a cross. *Something*. Like all religions, Christianity is very big on symbols and sayings.

'But we've got nothing. This seems odd – unless Silver Tongue is a policeman. For a start, he'll be afraid that any communication would give him away, that someone would recognise his writing or his turn of phrase or whatever. That's not a problem if you work in a factory and no one you know is ever going to see evidence from the case. But if you work in the cop shop, you up the stakes enormously if you start leaving messages. Better just to shut up. And while we're on that point, remember too that some killers leave notes purely or largely to taunt the police. They see the police as their enemy: it's them against the establishment, cocking a snook at authority. But if Silver Tongue is a policeman, this may not apply. He may not want to get caught, but equally he may not polarise his actions and those of law enforcement as much as he would otherwise. Am I making sense?'

'Perfectly,' says Red.

'Right. The third point is possibly the most important – especially after today. You know we were wondering how Silver Tongue gains access to his victims' homes? Well, what better way than to be a policeman? If you want to kill someone, then doing it in their own home is the best way to do it. Behind closed doors, you're much less likely to be seen or disturbed than you are out in the open. But you have to get into their houses first. It's easy for a policeman to turn up and say, "I'm terribly sorry to disturb you, sir, but we've had a report of this or that, and we'd just like to check a few things out." And he's in. We're talking about late at night here. People don't open their doors to just anyone, not at that time of night and certainly not in a city. They'll open it to someone they know, or to the law; either through trust or fear.'

'You said especially after today,' says Jez. 'Why?'

'Because Andrew Turner knew someone might be after him. He was the first victim to have been specifically warned, and still Silver Tongue got him. Put yourself in his shoes last night. He knows he's got to be careful. So he's sitting there, probably about to turn in for a few hours' kip before going to Billingsgate. The doorbell rings. Lubezski said he was on the cross since about midnight – not too late, granted, but late enough, especially on a council estate. He's going to be jumpy. He opens the door on the chain, and he sees a policeman there. "Sorry to bother you, sir, just seeing if you're OK. Can I come in and check that everything's secure here?" Andrew relaxes, lets the policeman in. And that's the last person he sees.'

Red wipes his hand across his face, pinching the bridge of his nose between his fingers. A killer within the force. That's all he needs.

'Makes sense to me,' he says. 'I buy it. Jez?'

'Yeah. Definitely. I think it's the best idea any of us have had for ages.'

'Thank you,' says Kate, and means it.

'Here comes the boring bit,' says Red. 'We're going to have to go through the records of every policeman stationed in London. We'll start in central London first, and spread outwards if we don't get any joy. Begin with the duty rotas. I want details from every station as to who was on evening and night shifts when the murders happened – i.e. 30th April/1st May, 28th/29th June, 24th/25th July, 23rd/24th August, 20th/21st September, 27th/28th October and last night. You can rule out anyone who was on duty on any of those nights. Even if they've just done one night of those seven, then eliminate them. Once you've done that, take out anyone who's married.'

'Why?' says Jez.

'This guy cuts out tongues and keeps them. He comes home covered in blood. It's highly unlikely that someone could live with him and *not* realise what was going on. And remember that he thinks he's the Messiah, and he's taking it literally. Jesus wasn't married either. Our man probably thinks no woman's good enough for him.'

'Those aren't exactly foolproof theories,' says Jez. 'Peter Sutcliffe was married.'

'Yes, and he was also a long-distance lorry driver. He killed on the road, far away from home, and he didn't keep souvenirs. I accept that my theories aren't foolproof. But we've only got a limited time span and I don't want to have to draft extra people on this. We're going to handle it between the three of us. We can always go back and include married men if we don't get anywhere first time round. But right now we want to cut our search area as far as is reasonably possible.'

'OK,' says Jez. 'That makes sense.'

'Those who've fallen through both the above sieves – being on duty, and married – we go and interview. Get alibis off them for the nights in question. Most of them will have some. Any that don't, you haul them in here for further questioning. Clear?'

Jez and Kate nod.

'Meanwhile, let's see if we have better luck with architects named Thomas than we did with fishermen called Andrew. I'll go through the Yellow Pages myself to find architects' firms, and then I'll go and see them. It'll be the same procedure as before, though there should be a lot fewer people to see. I can't imagine London has as many architects as it does fishermen.'

'You'd be surprised,' says Kate. 'I went out with an architect once.'

'If I can do the architects all by myself, I will,' says Red. 'I'll do the architects, and you two pretend you're Internal Affairs.'

'Are you going to tell the architects to watch out for policemen?' asks Kate.

Red pauses.

'I . . . no, I don't think so.'

'Why not?' she says.

'Because I can't go around telling ordinary citizens not to obey the law.'

'That's not what you'd be doing. You'd be saying to those architects that, on a given night, they shouldn't open their door to anyone.'

'But I'd have to specify that that included the police.'

'No you wouldn't. Just emphasise the word *anyone*.'

'Kate, anyone in their right mind will open the door to a policeman who's come to check they're OK. They won't think that the concept of *anyone* includes policemen. We're talking about architects, for God's sake, not crack dealers. Most of them have probably never even broken the speed limit.'

'So you've just defeated your own argument, Red. If they're so innocent, you have to protect them this way. You have to tell them – or at least imply – that our prime suspect is a policeman unknown.'

'No.'

'Why on earth not?'

'Because . . .' Red holds up his hands. 'If I go round telling people that, then somewhere along the line it's going to get out. One of them will speak to his wife, and she'll tell her next-door neighbour over the garden fence, and she'll mention it to her cousin who works for the *Evening Standard*, and before you know it it'll be splashed across all the papers. "You, the general public, have *carte blanche* to ignore any officer of the law." It'll make the police a laughing stock.'

'I –'

'Kate, if you want to go argue the point with the Commissioner, then be my guest. He'll tell you just the same as I have.'

'Red, I can't believe you're reacting like this. We know the killer's got to be a police officer, and here you are –'

'No, Kate. That's where you're wrong. We don't *know* anything. We *think* that Silver Tongue's a police officer, but we don't know for sure. And I will not jeopardise the work of police officers throughout the capital on the basis of a theory which, however plausible, remains unproven.'

'Don't preach at me, Red.'

'Then don't try to force me to do something which you know I can't do.'

Red stands up.

'I'm sorry. We're fucked if we do and we're fucked if we don't.'

'So what do we do?' asks Jez.

'Very simple. Find him before he finds them.'

95

I realise that I can't lambast society without trying to change it. That's why I chose to enter my profession and do what I do. I help in a very very small way, doing one of the few jobs in this whole stinking mess that's vaguely worthwhile. We help skim off a tiny part of the slag that is choking the life out of society. We get the worst offenders — no, we get the most obvious offenders, and there's a big difference — and we take them off the streets. But that's all we do, and it's not very much. We don't rehabilitate these offenders or make them better. We just provide a temporary respite. We prevent for a while, but we don't cure. And that's what I mean by helping in a very very small way.

I joined the police because I thought that I could make a difference. For the first year or so on the force, you really believe that. It's a big triumph when you catch a criminal or save someone's life. But gradually it gets on top of you. When you come up against the shit we have to deal with, day after day, then you realise that what we do means nothing in the greater scheme of things. So either you accept that it's always going to be like that, or you try to change the way we work so that it will mean something. That's what I've done.

Because people no longer listen, unless you turn the volume up loud and shove it in their face. The world at large isn't going to stir itself from stupor for some bloke wandering around with a small posse of men preaching the Word. People don't give a toss. Look at Koresh and the Solar Temple and the Hale-Bopp merchants. Nobodies, all of them. If people regard them at all, they look on them with amused pity. I don't want to be pitied. Reviled, maybe, but not pitied. Look at the papers. I'm the most wanted man in the country. I could break wind and I'd be lead item on the Nine O'Clock News. Because what I've done has made people sit up and take notice. They'll remember me. They'll remember, and they'll think, and eventually they'll see that I'm right. I've got their attention. That's the important thing. The rest is the easy bit.

96

Twenty-five days until Christmas. Twenty-one days until Silver Tongue is due to strike again.

December, and the annual homage to festive consumerism glitters with bright lights and excited children. At times, when he needs to clear his head, Red walks across the road from Scotland Yard to the Army & Navy department store and amuses himself by watching men trying to find presents for their wives or girlfriends. He is surprised that no one has made a spoof movie about it. *Assault on Perfume Counter 13*, perhaps.

Of all the shops on Victoria Street, it seems that only The Body Shop has actually taken pity on floundering men. Red doesn't know what the official marketing term is for the items in question, but he has always thought of them as 'stuff in a basket' – a hotchpotch of all those lotions and creams and soaps and perfumes that men reckon women like, jammed into a cheap basket and available in three or four different price ranges. Walk in, decide how much you want to spend, grab a stuff-filled basket in said category, pay and leave. One-stop shopping, done and dusted in ninety seconds flat.

Red spends a lot of time trying to buy something suitable for Susan. He hasn't seen her since she left, though they have spoken on the phone quite frequently. She moved out of Shelley's and is renting a place somewhere near Potter's Bar, out beyond the M25. They have tentatively arranged to go for a drink before Christmas, but have yet to fix a date for it. Red knows that he is better off keeping the arrangement fluid than committing himself to a time and place which Sod's Law dictates he will have to cancel at the last minute. All of which probably means that they won't manage to see each other at all. Like he said earlier – fucked if he does, and fucked if he doesn't.

The Yard is full of rumours about a Christmas spectacular from one of the fringe Islamic movements. Bomb hoaxes are a common occurrence: single phone calls capable of locking large chunks of the southeast's transport system down at a moment's notice. But for all the hoaxes, there will be one call that is real, so they can never ever afford just to go through the motions.

It is like that with what Red, Jez and Kate are doing. Hours and hours looking for things that will almost certainly amount to nothing, and little to sustain their interest other than the fear that the tiniest detail they discount will turn out to be the crucial factor. Red rings round every architect's firm he can find in the Yellow Pages and on the national association's database. He goes through the same speech over and over again to each Thomas in turn, until he can do the whole thing word perfect. He begins to think he is turning into a fucking parrot.

But whenever he is tempted just to call it a day and not bother with this firm or that firm, because they are a two-man outfit and so they won't have anybody called Thomas on their staff, he thinks about how he will feel if there *is* a Thomas there and it is that Thomas who is killed. Not telling them the whole story – however good his reasons are – is one thing. Missing them out altogether is something else entirely. Red also puts every police station in the capital on alert for the night of December 20th.

Kate and Jez plough on, compiling huge computerised databases of every policeman in central London and then slowly whittling the lists down. They spend the first week in the office in front of their screens, and then they start to get out and about, interviewing people, establishing alibis, checking and cross-checking. By the third week, they are bringing people into the Yard. Red interviews every one of those himself, but he knows it is a waste of time. Whether they are the picture of co-operation or whether they moan about how they have given twenty-five years' valuable service to the force, they are all innocent. Red just has to look at them to know that.

When he sees him, Red thinks – Red *hopes* – he'll know. Instantly. He'll know the way people who meet their future spouses at a party know from the first moment that they are going to spend the rest of their lives with that person.

Red knows Silver Tongue now. He knows what he thinks, what he hopes and what he fears. He knows him in broad brushstrokes. What Red does not know is the details. He does not know where Silver Tongue lives, or what he likes to do at weekends.

Most of all, Red does not know what he looks like.

97

Friday, December 18th 1998

Red goes to the pub, just to get away from an empty house. There's something ineffably pathetic about getting drunk on your own in front of the TV, he thinks. Better to go to the pub, even if you just sit at the bar and don't talk to anyone.

The place is crowded, full of young people clustered around tables and talking loudly. The pool players are in the far corner, making the balls go *clack clack* as they chase each other across the baize. Red finds a spare stool at the bar and orders a double whisky and a pint of lager.

The whisky is gone and he is halfway through the pint when his arm is knocked by someone sitting heavily on the stool next to him. He looks up.

'Do you mind, mate?'

The new arrival swivels round to face him. He is wearing a donkey jacket, and his eyes are bloodshot. Drink or drugs.

He peers at Red for a few seconds, and then plonks a plastic bag on the bar.

'Got a skinned rabbit in here,' he says, pointing to the bag. 'I'll fight you for it.'

The barman, pouring a Guinness a couple of taps away, stiffens.

'Fight you for it,' repeats the man.

Red shouldn't react, he knows that. But what are you supposed to do? Can't ignore it, not when it's happening right in your face. Can't get up and walk away, because that shows weakness, and then he'll come after you anyway. Can't try and talk your way out of it, not when you're dealing with someone blitzed out of their mind.

Red stands up and punches the man in the face. He hits him

so hard that the man bounces back against the bar and then to the floor, clutching at the bag which opens on the way down. The rabbit spills out onto the carpet. Red feels mildly surprised that there really was a rabbit in there, and then he kicks the man once in the groin and once in the head, feeling through the leather of his shoe the crack of the man's nose as it breaks.

The barman vaults over the bar and grabs Red by the shoulders. Red swivels round so he can pick up his jacket from the bar stool, but other than that he doesn't resist. He lets the man take him to the door and push him roughly into the street, and he walks home without looking back, not hyped-up or shaking or scared, just thinking how good it felt to break someone's face.

98

SUNDAY, DECEMBER 20TH 1998

The drawing on the table in front of Thomas Fairweather is covered with red lines. His red lines.

The firm of architects for whom Thomas works is designing a cinema complex in Riyadh, and Thomas is heading up the project team. He has let one of the office juniors have a go at doing the outline drawings, just by way of experience, and now he has to correct all the mistakes at home. Hence the red lines.

Behind him, Thomas' computer is making a three-dimensional model of the cinema complex. The program is taking several hours to run.

He looks at the clock. Quarter to midnight. Cold coffee sloshes as he picks up a mug and goes to the window, where he gazes out across the streets of Hampstead.

In a city made up of villages, Hampstead is the one that has best kept its character. Everything about it is at odds with the rest of London. The little triangles of grass at crossroads suggest wide open countryside rather than city streets. The way the hills undulate through high roads and low is the very antithesis of gridiron urban planning. Even the street signs are determinedly different: white letters on black signs, rather than vice versa.

Light mist curls damply around the glass bulb cases of the Victorian lampposts. That's something else about Hampstead: it's one of the few areas of London that is at its best in the cold and the dank. Bright sunshine works in wide open spaces, but the Hampstead streets wind close through dark houses and low trees. Intimate or claustrophobic, it doesn't matter what you call it, but Hampstead is best when human breath billows and the leaves on the trees weep raindrops.

The rasping buzz of the doorbell makes Thomas jump.

He pads to the door in shoeless feet and peers through the spyhole. A policeman, his face distorted wide in the fish-eye lens. Thomas opens the door on the chain.

'Mr Fairweather?'

'Yes.'

'Just come to check that you're OK.'

'OK? Why shouldn't I be?'

'Didn't you receive a visit from Detective Superintendent Metcalfe a couple of weeks ago? About the apostle killer?'

'Huh? Oh, yes. I remember. He came round one afternoon. Made me late for a meeting.'

'Did he tell you that you were in danger?'

'He said there's some nutcase running around who thinks he's Jesus, but that I had more chance of winning the lottery than being killed by him.'

'That's good. Nevertheless, we're still checking on everyone Mr Metcalfe visited, just to make sure they're taking sensible precautions. Would you mind if I just gave your house a quick once-over? I'm sorry to bother you at this late hour, but you know . . . better safe than sorry.'

'I couldn't agree more, officer. Please.' Fairweather unlatches the chain and opens the door. 'Be my guest.'

The policeman walks into the house. He is carrying a long black sausage bag over one shoulder.

'Late night?' says Thomas, gesturing at the bag.

'Yeah. My shift ends in a couple of hours, and then I'm going straight to my girlfriend's. Got a change of clothes in there. Trying to make my armpits my charmpits.'

Thomas laughs.

'Would you like me to show you round?'

'Please.'

Thomas takes the policeman round the ground floor of the house. The policeman examines all the locks on the doors and windows, but he does not touch any of them.

They stop in the kitchen, where the policeman puts his bag on the floor and reaches inside it.

'There's also upstairs,' says Thomas. 'But we must be careful not to wake –'

Pain, sharp and spiky from the blow to the skull behind his ear, and then oblivion.

99

The transition back to consciousness is so seamless that for a few seconds Thomas isn't even sure if he has come round at all. He opens his eyes and he's still in darkness.

Except that this darkness isn't as relentlessly black as the one behind his eyelids. He can make out a patch of grey where the window must be.

The window in his bedroom. Thomas is lying on his bed. There's a chill on the skin of his legs and chest, and the press of elastic round his waist. His underpants. The only thing he has on. Except for the ropes which lash his ankles and his left wrist to the bed.

Other senses crowd in on him. The throb of his head where he has been hit. The sound of his breathing.

Except it's coming from a few feet away, so it can't be his breathing.

Thomas holds his breath, and the breathing continues. Inhale, exhale. Steady as you like.

There is someone else in the room.

The policeman come to check the locks.

Thomas crooks his right elbow on the bed and tries to push himself upwards. A hand pressed quickly on his chest eases him back down again.

Thomas forces himself to say something. Anything. The first thing that comes into his head.

'Who's there?'

Silence.

'Are you the policeman?'

Silence.

'What happened to me?'

An answer at last.

'You hit your head.'

'What time is it?'

The flash of luminous hands on a moving watch.

'Ten past midnight.' Monday already.

'Can you see, Thomas?'

'Yes.'

'Keep your eyes open. Look around you a bit. Make sure your night vision is working.'

The policeman's voice in the dark.

Thomas looking around, shapes appearing and sharpening into familiar objects. The chair by the window, the chest of drawers under the mirror. Uniform black resolved into shades of grey.

Silver Tongue is sitting on the side of Thomas' bed. He is barechested, and his weight drags the sheet into lines which disappear under him. He has rubber gloves on his hands.

A long dark shape on the bed next to him. The sausage bag.

Silver Tongue rummages in the bag, and brings out something square and shiny. A sheet of plastic. He gets up off the bed, puts the plastic down, and sits on it.

'What are you doing?'

No answer.

Silver Tongue is looking in the bag again.

A glint of metal in the half-light.

A knife.

Oh God no. Oh please God no.

Thomas shuts his eyes.

Not a knife. Anything but a knife.

'Thomas. Look at me.'

Thomas opens one eye.

Silver Tongue is cutting himself.

He runs the knife along his right flank, just below the ribcage. On the white skin, a dark line of blood holds perfect straight and then drips down like raindrops on a window pane.

Silver Tongue wipes the blade of the knife on his arm, and puts it back in the bag. He doesn't seem to have felt any pain.

The whites of his eyes as they swivel towards Thomas.

'Except I shall thrust my hand into his side, I will not believe.'

He reaches out and feels for Thomas' right hand.

'Give me your hand, Thomas.'

Thomas feels his hand being guided across a vast expanse of space and time.

Silver Tongue runs Thomas' fingers back and forth along his wound. Lightly over the edges of the gash, and deep into the sticky warm wetness of the blood.

'Be not faithless, but believing. Thomas, because thou hast seen me, thou hast believed: blessed are they that have not seen, and yet have believed.'

Air on Thomas' fingertips again, and then plastic.

Silver Tongue puts Thomas' hand down on the plastic sheet, and shifts his weight so that he is sitting directly on the hand.

'Does that hurt?'

Thomas shakes his head.

'Good. I'm sorry, but I'm sure you understand that I have to do this.'

Thomas doesn't understand. Not at all.

Still sitting on Thomas' hand, Silver Tongue puts the knife back in the bag and pulls something else out. Thomas can't see what it is.

Silver Tongue leans forward.

'Open wide, Thomas.'

The wash of headlights as a car passes by outside, illuminating the object in his hand.

A scalpel.

Thomas clamps his mouth shut.

'Open your mouth, please, Thomas.'

No response.

'Thomas. Open your fucking mouth.'

No no NO.

The punch comes so fast that Thomas doesn't even see it, let alone have time to block it or roll away. Silver Tongue's left arm straightens whiplash-quick into Thomas' chest, just below the solar plexus. The air whistles out of Thomas' lungs like an express train, forcing his jaws open as he gasps for breath.

The scalpel is in Thomas' mouth, flicking through the frenum and along the edges of his tongue. Blood spurts across the tiny space to the roof of his mouth. Cutting in the back of his throat now.

Thomas tries to scream, but there is nothing to scream with.

Thomas' tongue in Silver Tongue's hand.

Silver Tongue pulls a jar half-full of liquid from his bag, unscrews the top, drops Thomas' tongue in, and screws the top back on. The jar is put back in the bag, and something else pulled out.

Still with his weight hard on the bed, so that Thomas can't move his right hand, Silver Tongue speaks to Thomas for the last time.

'Thomas, a lance, because he was pierced through the body with a lance.'

Silver Tongue is holding the lance with his hand on top of the shaft, like a snooker cue. As he raises the lance above his head, he switches to a javelin-style grip, with his hand under the shaft.

The lance comes down *whooooosh* through the air and into Thomas' stomach.

A dull impact while the pain has yet to come, like when you stub your toe and you know that in two seconds' time all your nerve endings will be on fire, but you still have to endure those two seconds in dreadful anticipatory limbo.

Silver Tongue tears the lance out of Thomas' body and then plunges it in again, so that each strike blends into the one before and the one after, bouncing in each other's shockwaves. His arterial blood is like a spurting fountain. Thomas moans as the lance rips him into a thousand pieces of all-consuming pain, pure and beyond dimension. Through the agony comes the shadow of Death offering sleep eternal, and Thomas reaches out to it in an embrace of welcoming desperation.

100

'Uncle Thomas?'

A small voice, coming from outside Thomas' room. A child's voice.

Silver Tongue turns his head. Light spills pale yellow through the crack where the door has been pushed slightly ajar.

He leaves the lance embedded in Thomas' body and gets up off the bed. His side is still bleeding from where he cut it, so he pulls his top back up, feeling the warmth where the blood sticks his skin to the fabric.

There will be none of his blood left here tonight. That is good.

A shadow bisects the oblong of light. He crosses the bedroom in three quick strides.

The child is opening the door.

'Uncle Thomas?'

Silver Tongue stands in the doorway. The child looks up at him.

A boy. Six or seven years old, perhaps, wearing a pair of brown pyjamas patterned with train engines. His eyes are flat and narrow from sleep and his hair stands up in wispy blond tufts.

Suffer little children, and forbid them not to come unto me: for of such is the kingdom of heaven.

Silver Tongue squats down on his haunches, so that his face is level with the child's.

'Your uncle's ill. I've given him some medicine. He'll be fine.'

The boy looks at him with curiosity rather than suspicion. An apparition all in black with yellow rubber gloves on his hands, like a giant bumblebee.

Silver Tongue stands up straight again and reaches out for the boy's hand.

375

'Come on. I'll take you back to bed.'

The child shrinks away, and Silver Tongue realises why. Thomas' blood has splashed bright red on his gloves. It doesn't show up on his black clothing, but it does on the yellow rubber.

'It's your uncle's blood. He was hurt, but I've made him better. He'll be fine. You should go to bed. I'll tuck you in.'

Silver Tongue lets the child lead him down the corridor, a step ahead so he doesn't have to hold hands with his uncle's blood. The boy takes two and a half strides for every one of his.

They go into the last room on the right. A small room, sparsely furnished and unlived-in. A spare room. The boy climbs back into bed and pulls the duvet up around his neck.

'Don't you worry about Uncle Thomas,' Silver Tongue says. 'He'll be fine.'

The child nods and then rolls away from him, ready for sleep.

Silver Tongue turns the bedside light out, closes the door, and goes back to Thomas' room.

Thomas now a lifeless lump on the bed, with the lance sticking straight up from the body like a radio mast. He pulls the lance out of Thomas' body and tucks it in the black bag.

Out of the bag comes a silver spoon. Number ten. He tucks it in Thomas' mouth.

His police uniform lies neatly folded on the chair in the corner of the room. He will put it back on when he has finished. But he has not finished yet. There is one more thing he has to do.

The only deviation he has allowed himself. The only sully on his masterpiece.

Thomas' right hand still rests on the plastic sheet.

His blood, the blood of Christ, on that sheet and on Thomas' fingers. Nowhere else.

All the evidence must come with him.

Silver Tongue takes the knife out of the bag and severs Thomas' right hand at the wrist.

101

Red doesn't recognise Thomas Fairweather's face, but he knows he warned him. The date and time of the meeting are faithfully recorded on the database.

If only he'd warned him about policemen.

Red shakes his head. He'd taken his decision to keep the police angle quiet, and he'd taken it for the best reasons. Those reasons are as good now as they were then. Besides, they still have no proof that Silver Tongue is actually a police officer. Kate's theory makes sense, but they have been checking the Met records solidly for three weeks and have so far got absolutely nothing to show for it.

Thomas Fairweather's body was found by his sister Camilla Weekes shortly after eight o'clock that morning. It was her son Tim – Thomas' nephew – who had all but walked in on the carnage. Tim was staying with Thomas for the weekend, so that Camilla and her merchant banker husband could enjoy a weekend in the Cotswolds alone. Camilla arrived early so that she could pick up Tim before Thomas left for work.

Mother and son are now downstairs together in the kitchen, and it is hard to tell which one of them is more traumatised. A constable is with them.

Lubezski comes into the bedroom, blowing on his hands. 'Merciful Father,' he says. 'It's absolutely freezing outside.'

He takes one look at Thomas' body and asks the obvious question.

'Why has his right hand been cut off?'

Red glances wearily at him.

'The story of Doubting Thomas, I would imagine.'

Lubezski looks blank.

'Thomas wouldn't believe in the Resurrection until he had seen Jesus in the flesh, and – more importantly – until he

377

had *touched* him,' says Red. 'He only believed after he touched Jesus' hands, where the nails which pinned him to the cross had been driven in, and his side, where the Roman soldier had slashed him.' Red looks down at the corpse. 'I reckon that's what happened last night.'

'He made Thomas *touch* him?'

'Yes. Probably inflicted the wound on himself, either in his hands or his side. His side is more likely, since a wound there is easy to cover up under his clothes. If he cuts his hands, he has to bandage them, and that would draw attention to himself.'

'Unless he wears gloves over the bandages.'

'But he'd have to take them off sometime, wouldn't he? When he's indoors. Or else he'd just look odd, same as with the bandages. So I reckon he slashed himself in the side, and then he made Thomas touch him, so that Thomas believed.'

Lubezski picks up Red's train of thought.

'But now Thomas has got Silver Tongue's blood on his hands, and he can't afford for us to find that blood. So Silver Tongue chops Thomas' hand off and takes it with him.'

'Exactly.'

'However,' says Lubezski, 'if he cut himself, then he might have left some blood somewhere here.'

Red gestures at the bloody mess on the bed.

'If you can find a few rogue drops of blood among all that lot, Professor, you're a fucking genius. Personally, I don't think he's left any traces.'

'Well, he's very lucky if he's cut himself and still left nothing behind.'

'Luck doesn't come into it. We know that by now. Whatever he chooses to do by way of fulfilling his mission, it doesn't involve giving himself away. This is the tenth murder, and the other nine have all been perfect.'

Red runs his hands through his hair.

'I'm going down to the kitchen to see how little Tim's doing.'

'Who?'

'Thomas' nephew. He was staying here last night.'

'Oh *God*. Did he see any of it?'

'That's what I'm going to find out. If Kate or Jez arrive in the next ten minutes, tell them where I am.'

He goes downstairs into the kitchen, where Camilla looks incongruously casual in her jeans and thick blue sweater. She is sitting on a folding canvas director's chair, balancing Tim on her knees and clasping his blond head close to her chest. A green train engine on the collar of Tim's pyjama top sticks out from under the tartan blanket round his body. Camilla looks up at Red through eyes puffed pink with tears.

'Mrs Weekes. How are you doing?' he asks, and feels totally inadequate.

She doesn't answer.

The constable is standing by the sideboard. Red turns to him.

'Why don't you get yourself a cup of tea?'

'Yes, sir.'

He reaches out and turns the kettle on. Red looks pained.

'No, you berk. I meant make yourself scarce.'

'Oh. I'm sorry. I thought . . .'

'That's OK. Now beat it.'

The constable ducks his head and hurries out of the kitchen. Red pulls up a chair opposite Camilla and leans forward, elbows on his knees and fingers latticed under his chin.

He asks the first question quietly, easing her into it. 'What was Thomas like?'

She gulps back a sob. 'He was a good man. He worked hard. He was never going to set the world on fire, but he worked hard and people liked him. He . . . he didn't deserve this.'

'No one does.'

'I know.'

Camilla's hands make little rubbing motions on Tim's head.

'How's Tim?' says Red.

'Bad.'

'Did he see . . . ?'

Red points to the roof. Upstairs. Thomas' bedroom. The body.

Camilla nods.

'The body, or the killer?' says Red.

'Definitely the body. I found him in Thomas' room when I arrived this morning.'

'How did you get in?'

'I let myself in when there was no answer from inside. I've got my own key.'

'And you found Tim in Thomas' room?'

'Yes.'

'What was he doing?'

'Standing there. Looking at the body.'

'But you don't know if he saw the killer?'

'Superintendent, he hasn't said a word since I found him.'

Red leans forward still further, but he doesn't reach out to touch.

'Hey, Tim,' he says softly.

Tim turns his head slightly on his mother's chest. One eye, wide and scared, peers out at Red.

'It'll be OK,' says Red, and feels even more inadequate than before.

Tim's eye is still looking at Red, and then his little head turns so that Red can see both his eyes widening in alarm and surprise at something beyond. Camilla has seen it too. Red hears her gasp.

Red swings round.

There are two people standing in the doorway. Jez, just arrived, with his fleece jacket still zipped tight around his throat, and Lubezski, the one they are looking at.

Lubezski is covered in blood. *Covered.* His white shirt is stained dark red and clings in patches to his stomach where the wetness has seeped through to his skin. Blood on the left side of his face and on his hands. He looks like an abattoir worker.

'What the . . . ?' says Red.

'I just came to tell you that I'm going home to change,' says Lubezski.

'What the bloody hell happened to you?'

'I'm sorry. I was kneeling on the bed examining the body,

380

and I just lost my balance.' He looks helplessly at Camilla. 'I landed right in the middle of all the blood.'

Tim screams.

Screams.

High-pitched and primal, as if the scream comes from another soundwave altogether. There are crow-feet on the skin around Tim's tight-shut eyes, and his tonsils wobble livid red at the back of his throat.

Camilla's hands scrabble on her son's head as she tries to smother his grief. Lubezski stands stock still, bloody and stammering in his embarrassment. Red pushes him out of the kitchen.

'Jesus Christ, Lubezski. Get the fuck out.'

He has to raise his voice to make himself heard over Tim's screaming.

'I –'

'Are you out of your fucking mind? Look what the sight of you has done to that poor kid. Go on. Fuck off. And use your fucking brain next time.'

'I'm sorry. I didn't know that the child was there. I just wanted to tell you –'

'Save it. I don't want to hear it. I'll see you back at the Yard. Go on. Go home and get changed.'

Lubezski turns tail and goes out of the front door.

'Bloody *hell*,' says Jez.

'The body's upstairs.' Red is shaking. 'Go take a look.'

Jez goes upstairs. Red returns to the kitchen.

'I don't know what to say, Mrs Weekes. I'm so, *so* sorry about that.'

Camilla's eyes flash with fury. 'So am I.'

Tim's head is buried in her chest, and his little arms are wrapped tightly round her neck. He is perfectly still.

Whatever Tim did or didn't see last night has just become immaterial because he's not going to tell them now. Not soon enough to make a difference, at any rate.

Tim has gone catatonic.

102

It's not hard to select your victims, if you know where to look. Police databases, electoral rolls, mailing lists, whatever. It's amazing how much information you can find on people when you want to. I knew what I was looking for, and I checked and I checked until I found them. First I had to identify them, and then I had to watch them, make sure they lived alone, see what their movements were, all that. Some of my original choices — three, I think — weren't suitable. I had to bin them and start again.

And the ones who are chosen? Technically, they might not be available for martyrdom on their appointed days. They could be on holiday or something. If so, then it wouldn't be God's will that they are to be martyred. But they are all there, so it is God's will.

When I go to their houses, I wear the police uniform, just to be sure that they let me in. It might be easier to go in plainclothes with ID on me, but it's riskier. Anyone can say they're plainclothes. People check when plainclothes come to visit. They make you wait on the doorstep while they ring the station. But not if you're in uniform.

I don't wear the uniform during the actual act of martyrdom, of course. The jersey and the trousers could leave fibres on the bodies. And I make sure that I don't pick up fibres from home before I go. You've never been to my house, have you? There are no loose fibres there. The floors are bare hardwood. I don't have any carpets or any rugs. I've got blinds rather than curtains, duvets rather than blankets. There's nothing that I can take from home to the scenes of the changing. Before every martyrdom, I go home and make sure that I'm clean, so there's no evidence from anywhere else that I might have been. And if I take fibres from one scene to another, on the nights when I have to do two, then so be it. The police know that the same person has been at both scenes.

They just don't know who that person is yet. That's all.

103

Red stands in the middle of the incident room and barks orders like a sergeant-major.

'Go through the lists of policemen again. Check with every station who was on duty last night and take them off the list. Then see who we've got left. We must have missed someone. And get onto Hampstead cop shop. I want a list of all calls logged last night and all responses to them. We need to make sure they match up.'

'Maybe I was wrong,' says Kate. 'Maybe it's not a policeman after all.'

'Maybe not. But your theory made sense when you first said it. Just because Silver Tongue hasn't walked into our arms doesn't suddenly render it a crock of shit. And right now we don't have many other ideas. So we keep looking.'

Jez turns back to his computer and clicks open the database he and Kate have been using. There are two lists: one of every officer in the Metropolitan police, and one of those who have survived both Red's cuts. He prints out the small list.

'Has anyone got a hole puncher?' he says. 'I want to put this little lot in a ring binder.'

Red shakes his head.

'Duncan had one,' says Kate. 'It's probably still in his drawer.'

'Haven't we cleared it out yet?' says Red.

'No,' says Jez. 'I took a shit in it the other day, by way of expressing my feelings for Duncan.'

'You *didn't*,' says Kate, wide-eyed.

Jez looks at her like she's an idiot.

'No. Of course I didn't. Though I must say, I have thought about it.'

Duncan's desk has three drawers, plus a flat stationery tray.

Jez opens the top drawer and starts rummaging through the contents.

'Shouldn't we give all this stuff back to him?'

'Suppose so,' says Red. 'It hasn't exactly been high on my list of priorities.'

'But just *look* at all this shit,' says Jez. 'Shoe polish, nail clippers, a tape – *The Planets* by Holst – those little cottonbud things for cleaning your ears out, a Swiss army knife, some sachets of Lemsip –'

'Jez,' says Kate. 'This isn't *The Generation Game*, you know. Shut up.'

'– a paperback, *Where Love Has Gone* by Harold Robbins – who'd have guessed that, eh? – a couple of postcards, a letter from . . .'

His voice tails off. Red and Kate look up.

'What?' says Red. 'What have you found?'

Jez has unfolded the letter. His eyes dart jerkily across the text.

'Oh my *God*,' he says, double spacing the words.

Kate comes over to Duncan's desk. Jez hands the letter to her.

She recognises the name on the letterhead. The Church of the New Millennium, 32 Phillimore Terrace, London W8. The letter is dated February 12, 1998.

Red's voice from the other side of the room. 'What is it? What does it say?'

'It's from that mad cult Jez and I visited back in October,' says Kate. 'The one where that huge bloke banged on about the seven seals and then fainted because Jez cut his hand.'

Snatches of words drop from Kate's lips as she reads.

'Dear Mr Warren . . . Thank you for your enquiry . . . Bible study meetings three days a week, Tuesday, Friday, Sunday . . . blah blah blah . . . attendance is not compulsory, but of course it is encouraged . . . donations according to what you can afford . . . devotees from all walks of life . . . blah de blah . . . Yours sincerely.'

The signature is one word, written with a flourish. Israel.

Kate looks at Jez.

'I don't understand. Why would Duncan keep the letter here? He wouldn't have been so careless, surely?'

'Is it genuine?' asks Red.

'Oh yes,' says Jez. 'I saw some writing paper just like this on Israel's desk when we were interviewing him. This is definitely his. Written to Duncan here, at the Yard's PO Box number. Maybe he didn't want Israel to know his home address.'

'I don't suppose that he could have been doing this undercover?' says Kate. 'You know, posing as a genuine cult member to get information.'

Red shakes his head. 'That's not our turf. That would probably come under MI5's remit. Internal surveillance of possible subversives, I would imagine.'

'I thought MI5 was supposed to be purely political,' says Kate.

'Exactly. "Supposed" is the right word. But basically anyone who's in any way potentially subversive gets listed. You don't have to be a dab hand with the Semtex to have your name in there. Those boys we arrested at Speakers' Corner that day – they'll all be on MI5 files, I guarantee it.'

'But if Duncan *is* a member of the Church of the New Millennium,' says Jez, 'then why wasn't he there when we turned up?'

Kate shrugs. 'Maybe he couldn't make it that day. Maybe it was one of his weekends with Sam. It was a Friday when we visited, after all. Maybe . . . Jez, you don't think that Duncan was the one who tipped us off, do you?'

'No. It wasn't his voice on the phone. Not unless he was using some kind of distorter, and it didn't sound like it. I'm sure I would have recognised him.'

'Either way,' says Red, 'it seems that Duncan is – or at least considered becoming – a member of some sort of apocalyptic cult. But that in itself proves nothing. We can't just go and arrest him on the basis of that. It doesn't mean he was involved with the murders. He sold the story to the papers, yes, but joining a cult is not a crime. We need solid evidence.'

'Like what?' says Kate.

They're all silent for a moment as they accept the implications of what they are thinking.

'Got it!' shouts Jez suddenly.

'What?'

'The credit card list.'

'What credit card list?'

'You know. The details of those who bought the silver spoons. Let's see if he's on that.'

Jez searches through the files piled on Duncan's desk, which they have been using as a spare table ever since he was sacked.

'Here.' He holds up a folder of orange cardboard. 'This is it.'

'But he *can't* be on that list,' says Kate. 'We checked every person on that.'

'Not we. *He*. Duncan. Duncan was in charge of compiling information about the spoons, if you remember.'

Kate claps a hand to her mouth.

'But surely he'd just have deleted his name when he saw it?'

'Probably. But names were coming in thick and fast. He might have entered it into the database without thinking. If it came up as just a surname and an initial, he might not have spotted it. Warren's quite a common name, after all. In that case, he would have crossed it out as checked when he came to it.'

Jez flicks through the pages.

'Why don't you start at the back?' says Red. 'That's where you'll find names beginning with "W", isn't it?'

'The names aren't in alphabetical order,' says Jez. 'They're just here any old how, as they came in from the retailers.'

He runs his finger down the pages.

'Come on,' he mutters. 'Come *on*.'

The names are typed in a grid system, printed straight from the computer, and have been crossed out as they were eliminated. The list is fourteen pages long.

Jez has reached the penultimate page when he sees it.

About a third of the way down, one of the names has been struck through in thick black marker pen. Not so much crossed out as totally obliterated.

Jez turns the sheet of paper round, so that he is looking at the back of it, and holds it up to the light.

'Well, I'll be damned,' he says.

They crowd round him.

From the back they can just make out what Duncan has been at pains to hide.

Warren, Mr D. Credit card number and details of purchase attached.

'Transaction dated Thursday 1 May 1997,' says Red. 'Exactly one year before this all started. The *bastard*.'

'But why?' says Kate. 'Again, why would Duncan put this information down? Why not just leave it out altogether?'

'Who knows?' says Red. 'If it wasn't a mistake, perhaps it was the vicarious thrill of tapping in something that incriminating when his colleagues were sitting just feet away. You talked about taunting the police, Kate. How much more in your face than this can you get?'

He snorts through his nose in disgust.

'Let's bring him in.'

They have him.

'Wait a sec,' says Jez. 'If we pitch up at Duncan's house with the cavalry, there's no knowing what he'll do. If he's even there, that is. And if he isn't there, we risk alerting him to the fact that we know. His neighbours will talk, if nothing else. The last thing we want to do is start him running or force him into doing something stupid. We want to take him in nice and easy. We don't want to get into some big long siege and find after twelve hours that he's popped himself.'

'So what do you suggest?' says Red.

'A bit of surveillance. See how the land lies. Something subtle and unobtrusive.'

'Are you volunteering?'

'Yeah. I know where he lives. I'll go up there and check things out. If he's at home, then I'll radio in and we can take it from there. If he's not there, then we'll station watchers round the clock until he comes back.'

'You're not going on your own.'

'Why not?'

'Jez, if Duncan *is* Silver Tongue, then remember that he's killed ten people. I'm not letting you go up against him alone.'

'I'm not going to "go up against him", Red. I'm going to stay well out of his way. He's not even going to know that I'm there.'

'I'm coming with you.'

'Don't be stupid, Red. The more of us there are, the more likely we are to blow it. He's twice as likely to spot two of us as one. And remember that you're the one who sacked him. He's liable to go nuts if he sees you. I'll go on my own. I'm younger and fitter and uglier than either of you.'

'OK. You can go and see if he's there. Once you've done that, radio in for instructions. But you are *not* to do anything other than watch. You are not to enter his house. I don't want him to know you're even there. I don't want any fucking heroics. Is that clear?'

'Crystal.'

104

Duncan's house is empty. Jez waits ten minutes at the end of the road, just to make sure.

Duncan lives in a cul-de-sac off the North Pole Road and when Jez arrives there are children playing football in the street. A woman in a combat jacket watches them from her doorway. She has dyed blonde hair and a pinched face and she doesn't look at Jez. When the children finish their game and the woman goes back inside, Jez gets out of the car and walks up to Duncan's house.

There is a brass 21 on the brown door and a hanging basket above the front window. Jez presses his face against this window and peers inside.

No sign of life. No lights, no sound, no nothing. Totally empty.

Jez steps back from the window and looks around him. What a depressing place to live, he thinks. Estate agents describe this area as North Kensington, because the word 'Kensington' is supposed to connote automatic visions of opulence and good taste. The fact that Kensington High Street is at least three miles south of here is apparently irrelevant. Other people call the area East Acton, which doesn't sound quite so posh but is slightly less economical with the truth. But the reality is that this street is slap bang in the middle of White City, notable for the presence of the BBC Television Centre and not much else.

Duncan's house is right at the end of the street. A narrow passageway leads down the side of the house and through to a small paved garden. Jez walks down the passageway, turning sideways to avoid a pair of dustbins.

He examines the house from the back. One set of glass patio doors, locked. Two first-floor windows, shut. One drainpipe, plastic. He tugs at the drainpipe, and it flexes in his hand. It won't support his weight.

He needs Red's skeleton keys, but of course he couldn't have asked Red for them. He isn't allowed into Duncan's house. That's part of the deal.

By rights, he should ring Red and tell him to send a surveillance team up. But if they wait for Duncan to come back, they could be here for days. Maybe he's gone away for Christmas.

Jez looks at the patio doors.

Fuck it, he thinks. Bend some rules. Get the results. Then the end justifies the means.

The patio doors are easy to open. The locks are built into the handles, so they can be locked from the inside without a key. Twisting the handle up once the door is shut is all that is needed. So Jez has only to break the glass and push the handle down, and he's in.

He wants to finish it.

Jez goes back to the car and opens the boot. He pulls up the carpeting, opens the compartment housing the spare wheel, unscrews the wheelbrace which is resting in the middle of the wheel and closes the boot.

Back down the passageway and into Duncan's garden.

Two quick taps with the wheelbrace and faultlines radiate in the glass around the door lock. Jez pulls his sleeve down over his hand and knocks out a hole big enough for his arm. The glass tinkles onto the linoleum inside.

Jez reaches inside the door and pushes the handle down. He slides the door across. It moves smoothly on well-oiled runners.

He steps carefully over the broken glass on the floor and walks softly through the kitchen.

The house is not big so it takes Jez less than ten minutes to go through all the rooms.

No mess anywhere in the house. Everything neat and tidy. Duncan must have gone away.

It's like being a burglar. Rifling through someone's life without their knowledge. Scanning bookshelves and opening cupboards. The power to choose what you take and what you leave.

Jez never stops listening for the sounds which tell him that Duncan has suddenly come back. He now knows why burglars shit themselves so often.

Fear and loathing in White City.

Jez has been through all the rooms and seen what he wanted to see. He stands in the kitchen, by the broken pane on the patio door, and dials Red's number on his mobile.

'Metcalfe.'

'It's me.'

'Where are you?'

'In Duncan's house.'

'*In* his house? How the fuck did you get in?'

'Through the patio doors.'

'Were they open?'

'They are now.'

'Jez, you stupid fucking idiot. I told you not to go in there.'

'Red. Don't worry. We've got him.'

'*What?*'

'We've got him. This place is crawling with evidence. Absolutely crawling. It's definitely him. Duncan's Silver Tongue.'

105

They work quickly and quietly. From the street outside Duncan's house, there is absolutely no sign of the frenzied activity going on within. No police cars striped in orange and blue. No radios crackling with urgent voices. No helicopters whirring overhead. Nothing to alert Duncan that anything is amiss, if he is to come back. He will walk right in the front door and then they will have him.

A police repairman has come to fix the glass in the patio door and Kate has gone to get a backdated search warrant.

They find the murder weapons in the cupboard under the stairs, each wrapped in its own plastic bag and hidden behind a stack of fruit boxes overflowing with bits and bobs. There are seven separate weapons – the wooden pole with which James Cunningham was beaten to death, the sword which beheaded James Buxton, the knife which was used on Bart Miller, the machete which brutalised Matthew Fox, the surgical saw which severed Simon Barker in half, the baseball bat which beat the life out of Jude Hardcastle and finally the lance which just the previous night skewered Thomas Fairweather to his bed. Each weapon has been cleaned, though the wooden implements have proved at least partially resistant to scrubbing – flecks of blood are still lodged between the wood grain on the pole and the baseball bat.

On the shelves in the living room, they find two books with passages marked. The first is a copy of the Bible, with ruler-straight red biro lines running under certain passages in the Gospels pertaining to the calling of the apostles, the denial of Peter or the doubting of Thomas. The other is a *Dictionary of Saints*, just like the copy that Red bought after they had found the bodies of Simon Barker and Jude Hardcastle. Eleven entries are marked down the side of the page in the same red biro. Only one of these entries – that of St John – is yet to be completed.

In one of the drawers in Duncan's bedroom, they find a copy of the *Sunday Times* magazine. The pages are splashed with holes where letters or words have been cut from the text.

The only things they can't find are the tongues of the dead men, the remaining silver spoons, or any implement small and sharp enough to cut tongues from mouths.

'He must have taken them with him,' says Jez. 'Which suggests that he's not coming back here at least until after he's killed John, on the 27th. That's just six days away.'

Red nods. He is far away in his own thoughts.

Eight months. Eight months of feeling almost unremittingly like a failure because he couldn't stop the crimes. Eight months in which his neglected marriage has pulled at the seams and then broken apart. And all because of a man he trusted. A man he chose – *personally* chose – to be on his team. A man who not only threw that trust back in Red's face, but then turned it on its head and used it for his own ends. Duncan was part of the investigation from the beginning. He knew all along where their enquiries were headed. At any time, if they were getting too close, he was able to knock them off line or nudge them away from the truth.

And then, when Red discovered the pattern anyway, Duncan went in pique to the *News of the World* and sold them the story. *His* story.

Except he'd left out the best bit, hadn't he? That the one who spilled was also the one who killed. A man who was above suspicion, and who consequently regarded himself as above the law.

Red wants an afternoon alone with Duncan, in a windowless room with no one watching. He wants to know not so much *why* Duncan has done this, but *how* he managed to hold down such a devastating double life without anybody knowing. A team of four, and one buries a secret so fundamental to its entire existence that it almost defies belief.

What kind of person are you, Duncan, that you watch us scrabbling around in the dark and show us no mercy?

And when he has found that out, Red will handcuff Duncan to the chair and kick the living shit out of him. This will not be for understanding or enlightenment. This will be for revenge, pure and primal simple.

Red wakes up every morning teetering on the cliff face of his own sanity.

But Red won't get a minute alone with Duncan, let alone an afternoon. He might get the answers to his questions, but he won't get the satisfaction of physical release. There will always be someone else in the room with him, just to make sure.

Red turns on his heel and walks out onto the patio.

106

'We are *not* going public, and that's final.'

'But this is different,' says Jez. 'We didn't have a *name* before. When we were looking simply for a police officer, name and face unknown, then what you said about not putting the police's good name in jeopardy made perfect sense. I understand that you couldn't go round saying, "If a policeman comes to your door, don't trust him." But it's different now. We'll be putting out a specific photo of a specific person. The fact that he used to be a policeman is immaterial. It doesn't reflect one iota on the reputation of the Met. It's a straight murder hunt now. "This is Duncan Warren, wanted for murder. If you know where he is or see him, please call the police. On no account approach him yourself." All the usual stuff. We've got no reason to cover it up any more, Red.'

'Yes, we have.'

'What, then? Give me a reason.'

'Because I want Duncan. I want him alive and I want him in custody. I don't want to do anything that jeopardises that. *Anything.* I don't want him to know that we even suspect him. The first time he knows that he's been rumbled is the moment when he's face down on the ground and I'm reading him his fucking rights.'

'Red, you're making this personal,' says Kate.

'Damn right I am. I'm surprised you two aren't. He hasn't exactly made your lives fun the past eight months, has he?'

'That's not the point.'

'No. That *is* the point. That's very much the fucking point.'

'What about the next victim? John's date is less than a week away and we haven't even started warning people yet.'

'And we're not going to, either.'

'What?'

'Look at it this way, Kate. We spend weeks and weeks warning fishermen called Andrew and architects called Thomas that on such-and-such a night they might be in danger. And still he got them. Twice, he got them. It could have been fifteen or twenty times, and he'd still have got them. We had limited parameters on those two, with Andrew and Thomas. But you know what the criteria are this time? Someone called John who is involved in writing or the production of books. Do you have any idea how wide *those* parameters are? We're talking authors, journalists, publishers, literary agents, book-binders, even paper manufacturers. We're talking bonkbuster novelists who sell millions and professors who write obscure technical manuals. We're talking about the editor of *The Times* and freelance correspondents on *Hot Dip Galvanising* magazine. Is that enough for you?'

'I –'

'And we don't even know *how* he's going to do it this time. St John died of old age, remember? He was the only one of the apostles that wasn't martyred. So I, for one, have no idea how our friendly fucking Messiah is going to get round *that* little logistical problem. We can warn and warn all we like, and it will have as much effect as it's done before – i.e. zero. The only thing that going public will achieve is to make it harder for us to catch Duncan. If you want him to go to ground completely, then you put his picture on *Crimewatch* and see what happens. As it stands, we don't even know where he *is* right now. Jez, did you manage to get hold of Helen?'

'Left a message on her answering machine.'

'Try her again.'

'I just did.'

'Then try again. Now.'

Jez picks up his phone and dials Helen's number.

'Answerphone again,' he says, putting the phone down. Kate resumes her argument with Red.

'I can't believe you're saying this, Red. You're effectively letting Duncan *have* John for free.'

'No, I'm not. I'm making a choice based on the best of two bad options.'

'You're saying that one more killing doesn't matter.'

'No, I'm not. Of course we're not just going to let the murder go. You think I want another notch added to his belt? He's outwitted us long enough. But we can't afford to tip Duncan off. No public manhunt. *That's* what I'm saying.'

'I don't think that argument is valid.'

'Kate, I couldn't give a shit what you think. That's the way we're going to do it. If you want your objections noted –'

'Damn right I do.'

'– then consider them noted. Remember where the buck stops, Kate. If I fuck it up, then I'm happy to take the blame. But I'm not taking responsibility for a course of action unless I'm satisfied with it.'

'Jez doesn't agree with you either. What if we vote on it?'

'This isn't a fucking democracy, Kate. Even if you two out-vote me, we're still going with what I say.'

'So you're not going to listen to us?'

'I always listen to you, Kate. There's not been a single moment on this investigation when I haven't listened to you or Jez. But just because I listen to you doesn't mean that I have to agree with you.'

'He's right, Kate,' says Jez.

'He's *not*.'

'No, he is. We've got to finish this. We've got to get Duncan. Whatever it takes.'

'I can't believe you, Jez. Two minutes ago, you were arguing that we should go public.'

Jez's phone rings. He holds up a hand to stop Kate talking and picks up the receiver.

'Clifton . . . Oh hi, Helen, thank you for phoning back . . . No, not at all . . . I was just wondering if you know where Duncan is . . . No, I need to talk to him about something . . . Yes, yes, exactly, boring old police business, that's all it is . . . He has? You don't know *where* he's gone? . . . No details at all? . . . No, I don't suppose he *would* give them to you, would he?

. . . Do you have any idea when he'll be back? . . . Of course he will . . . New Year's Day, you say? . . . Thank you very much . . . Listen, would it be OK if my colleagues and I came to visit you this evening? It'll only take a few minutes . . . I'd rather explain when we get there . . . We can leave now if that would be easiest . . . No, no, that's fine . . . What's the address? . . . Right. See you in about half an hour. Bye now.'

He puts the receiver down.

'Helen says that Duncan has gone away over Christmas. She doesn't know where, not even what part of the country he's gone to, let alone anything like contact details. There's not a great deal of love lost between them, as you know. She doesn't know exactly when he intends to come back, but she knows it'll be by New Year's Day.'

'Why?'

'Because he's got Sam that weekend. He's coming to pick him up on the evening of New Year's Day. It's a Friday.'

'He's picking Sam up from Helen's house?' says Red.

'Yup.'

'Definitely?'

'Definitely.'

Red smacks his fist into his palm.

'Got him. We can take him there.'

'I said we'd go and see Helen now.'

Red is already shrugging on his coat.

'Great. Let's go.'

'Hold on,' says Kate. 'Duncan's not expected back until New Year's Day? John is scheduled to be killed on the 27th of this month. That's virtually a full week before Duncan comes back. You're just going to let that murder go?'

Red pulls the collar of his coat up round his neck, and tucks his scarf down his front.

'Kate, we've discussed this. We've got a time and a place where we *know* Duncan is going to be. We all know him well enough to be sure that the one thing he's not going to miss is his weekend with Sam. He'll be there, sure as eggs are eggs. That's where we'll get him, if necessary. And I just hope to

God that we won't have to sacrifice another person to his mission in the meantime. Satisfied? If you have a problem with that . . .'

'So be it,' says Jez, finishing Red's sentence for him.

107

Red has had enough of kitchens. His day started in Thomas Fairweather's kitchen, with little Tim screaming his head off at the sight of Lubezski covered in blood, and it's ending here, him, Jez and Kate drinking tea with Helen while he plots the downfall of her ex-husband.

'Duncan never comes inside the house when he comes to pick Sam up,' says Helen. 'He arrives at six o'clock on the dot, and Sam and I wait outside in the street for him.'

'He *never* comes inside?' says Red. 'Not even for a cup of tea, or to use the toilet?'

'Never. I don't want him inside here, and I don't think he particularly wants to come in either. It's Andy's house, you see. He and Duncan don't get on. Rather like Duncan and I don't get on. If it wasn't for Sam, we wouldn't see each other at all.'

'Does Duncan get out of the car when he comes?'

'Oh yes. He and I exchange a few words on the pavement.'

'Mainly for Sam's sake?'

'No. *Entirely* for Sam's sake.'

'So if you and Sam weren't waiting outside for Duncan when he arrived, he would think it strange?'

'Yes. I would imagine so.'

'Right. That complicates things a bit.'

'Why?'

'Because it means we're going to have to take Duncan down outside.'

'Take him down? I thought you wanted to talk to him about "boring police business".'

Damn. Red has forgotten that Jez used the 'boring police business' line to fob Helen off on the phone. Too late now. He'll have to brazen it out.

'Er . . . not exactly. I suppose I'd better tell you the truth,

Helen. You'll find out soon enough anyway. You've read about the "apostle killer" in the papers, I presume?'

'Of course. Who hasn't?'

'Well, we think Duncan is the killer.'

Helen's mouth drops open. It can't be much fun being told that your ex-husband is prime suspect for the country's most wanted man, even if you do hate his guts.

'You *think*?' she says.

'No. We're sure. Ninety-nine per cent sure, anyway.'

'How?'

'I know this is very difficult for you to hear, Helen, but we found the murder weapons at his house, and we've got proof that he bought sil . . . certain items which were found with the corpses.'

'Jesus Christ.'

'That's rather what he thinks, I imagine.'

Helen gets up from the table and goes over to the sink, where she splashes her face with water from the tap. They let her compose herself. She takes a few deep breaths and returns to the table.

'And you want to get Duncan when he comes here to pick up Sam?' she says.

'We don't know where else he is. We're searching for him, but this is the one place we can be sure of getting him.'

'But . . . he's not going to try and harm me, is he? Or Sam?'

Or Sam? A hasty afterthought. Two words that tell them more about Helen Rowntree than she would want them to know. Me first. My child second.

'No. Not at all. In fact – and I'm not telling you this bit, you understand, we never had this conversation – there was a child at the scene of one of the murders and Duncan didn't touch him. There've been a couple of other near misses, too. Fiancées and brothers, who could easily have been there when Duncan went round. He only kills the people that fit in with his grand plan. He only kills the apostles, as it were. We think that anything else would . . . what were your words, Jez?'

'Sully his masterpiece.'

'Exactly.'

'How many people has he killed?' says Helen.

Red debates whether to tell her the whole truth, then decides that he has to.

'Ten, so far.'

'*Ten*? I thought it was just seven.'

'I know. We've managed to keep the details of the last three secret. The media coverage really wasn't helping us. We've had a lot more luck since we got them off our backs.'

'Three more murders doesn't sound like a lot more luck to me.'

'Maybe. But at least we know who it is now – though it's absolutely crucial that Duncan doesn't know that we know. So if he calls you, or attempts to contact –'

'Superintendent, Duncan would no more attempt to contact me than fly to the moon. As I said, we wouldn't see each other at all if it wasn't for Sam. The only time he ever rings up is to check the arrangements for Sam. Since we've got New Year's Day sorted out, he won't need to ring.'

Red holds up his hands.

'OK. But it's imperative that you don't tell a soul about this.'

'You think I want that man roaming the streets a minute longer than necessary?'

'Sure. But by "not a soul", I mean just that. Not a soul. Not even Andy, and especially not Sam.'

'I've *got* to tell them. If you're using Andy's house, then I've got to tell him.'

'Please, Helen. The fewer people that know, the less chance this whole thing has of going wrong. It's not about how much you trust this person or that person. We're just trying to mini-mise the risks.'

'So what do you intend to do?'

'On New Year's Day at six pm, I want you and Sam to be waiting for Duncan as normal. We're going to have the area covered with plainclothes officers and police marksmen. They'll all be in disguise or out of sight. You won't see any of them, and nor will Duncan. Duncan will arrive to pick Sam up. Once

402

he's out of his car and walking towards you, about a dozen armed officers will materialise from the woodwork.'

'And that's it?'

'Yes, that's it.'

'What if he grabs Sam or me? He could try to use us as . . . what do you call them, like in the Gulf War?'

'Human shields,' inserts Jez.

'Exactly. Human shields. He could take us hostage and put *us* in the firing line.'

'Helen, the team we're going to use on this is the best in the country, perhaps the best in Europe. They train for this kind of situation day in, day out.'

'I don't much fancy being a hostage, I can tell you.'

'It's not going to come to that. If Duncan makes a move towards either you or Sam, he'll be taken down, with a shot to the leg. A shot to wound, not to kill.'

'Is your team trained in hostage situations?'

'Yes, of course it is. But like I said, it won't come to that. I *promise* you that. He'll be massively outnumbered, and he'll also be taken completely by surprise. He'll have no chance.'

'Isn't there any other way you can do it?'

'No. Not if we don't find him first. If there was, we wouldn't have had to drag you into this.'

'Why don't you go looking for him?'

'Because we don't want to take even the slightest chance that he find out we're onto him. This is the best chance we've got, Helen. We've got a time and a place.'

'What about the risk to me and Sam?'

'If I thought for a second that the risk to either of you was anything more than infinitesimal, then I wouldn't sanction this operation.'

'You're sure?'

'In all honesty, you're in more danger of being hurt crossing the road.'

Just like Andrew Turner and Thomas Fairweather had more chance of winning the lottery than being killed by Silver Tongue.

Helen looks levelly at Red.
'This is the only way?'
'Yes.'
'And you're sure it's Duncan?'
'Yes.'
'OK. I'll do it.'

108

CHRISTMAS DAY 1998

Red sits at the end of a pew near the front of the church.

Next to him is a family, a traditional unit on this most traditional of days. The parents look like they're in their mid-thirties, and the children – one boy, one girl – are both still in single figures. The children are whispering excitedly to each other. The mother leans over to shut them up, and smiles at Red in apology. He smiles back, and gestures that he doesn't mind.

But he *does* mind. Not the children themselves, of course, but the fact that they remind him of Thomas Fairweather's nephew Tim. Young Tim, who hasn't said a word to anyone since he screamed in primal fear at the sight of Lubezski four days ago. Tim and his parents are away for Christmas, but Red has arranged for Tim to be seen by the finest child psychiatrist on Scotland Yard's books once they get back.

It's cold in the church. Red still has his overcoat on, but he could do with cuddling up to someone. Preferably Susan. They never managed to get together for their tentatively-arranged drink, and she turned down his offer to come and spend Christmas with him. He can hear the conversation in his head now: him romantic, her practical.

'It's only one day, Susan. Remember what a nice time we had last year, just the two of us? Opening presents and getting pissed and giggling like schoolchildren.'

'That's the whole point, Red. It's the one day of the year which has nothing to do with reality. It's when the world stops its headlong rush, and we can forget the trials and tribulations of the rest of our lives. And all we'll do is wallow in nostalgia about how wonderful last year was, and we'll end up convincing ourselves that everything is all right, and as soon as we put it to the test then it'll all fall apart and we'll be worse off than before.'

So he woke up this morning with the dull ache which afflicts all those left alone at Christmas, and lay in a steaming hot bath watching his tears mingle seamlessly with the bath water. All he had to do was put his head under the surface and open his mouth, and he could have ended it all, right there, right then.

Red hasn't told Susan about Duncan, because he doesn't want to put the knockers on the operation. She said she'd come back and talk about things when they'd found the killer. If the pay-off for waiting until they have that killer in custody is that she comes back to him, then he can last another week.

The priest's voice slices through his thoughts.

'Let us pray.'

Red leans forward, but he does not kneel. Kneeling makes his legs go numb.

What are you doing right now, Duncan, today of all days? What does someone who believes he is the Messiah do on the day when the Christian world celebrates his predecessor's birth? Have you gone to church, anonymous in an innocent congregation who are totally unaware that there sits a man who has killed ten times in the name of the religion they espouse? Or are you all alone, preparing to take the last of your saints?

All alone, just like Red.

A melodic lilt as the priest reads from the prayer book.

'Accept our praises, heavenly Father, through your Son our Saviour Jesus Christ; and as we follow his example and obey his command, grant that by the power of your Holy Spirit these gifts of bread and wine may be to us his body and his blood; who in the same night that he was betrayed, took bread and gave you thanks; he broke it and gave it to his disciples, saying, Take, eat; this is my body which is given for you; do this in remembrance of me. In the same way, after supper he took the cup and gave you thanks; he gave it to them, saying, Drink this, all of you; this is my blood of the new covenant, which is shed for you and for many for the forgiveness of sins. Do this, as often as you drink it, in remembrance of me.'

The congregation mumbles through the response.

Red isn't paying attention. He is reading the previous passage again.

Grant that by the power of your Holy Spirit these gifts of bread and wine may be to us his body and his blood. Do this in remembrance of me.

It is suddenly very important to Red that he take communion. He has never been a particularly religious person, but now things are different. There is a false Messiah out there.

The choir takes communion first, so that they can sing anthems during the general distribution. Then the congregation goes up, starting with those sitting at the front. The line shuffles wonkily forwards, fanning out at the altar like a river flowing into an estuary. The clergymen move back and forth, pressing wafers into cupped hands and the chalice to mouth after mouth, wiping it at every turn.

Red finds a spot right in the middle of the altar rail and holds out his hands. The priest comes past, pressing the host into Red's upturned palms.

'The body of Christ.'

Red takes the wafer, puts it in his mouth and begins to chew. It is tasteless at first, and then suddenly he feels the flavour on his tongue. A few people have saved their wafers to dip in the communion wine, so that they don't have to drink straight from the chalice. The priest comes past again.

'The blood of Christ.'

Red reaches out a hand to steady the chalice and takes a sip. He lingers at the altar for a few seconds, his eyes closed in prayer.

Please God, he thinks. Please let us catch him.

109

MONDAY, DECEMBER 28TH 1998

Red stretches his arms behind his head and drops the news casually.

'He got the last one.'

'Who?' says Kate.

'Where?' says Jez.

'John Macdonald, author and journalist. Found yesterday afternoon, at about four-thirty. All the usual traits: tongue severed, silver spoon wedged in his mouth, stripped to his underpants.'

'Why didn't you call us?' says Jez.

'No point.'

'What do you mean, "no point"? Come on, Red. We could at least have circulated Duncan's picture with a notice saying –'

'Kate. It wouldn't have done any good.'

' – watch out for this man. Then this John Macdonald might have had a chance.'

'No, he wouldn't.'

'It's easy for you to say that. You seem to have this image of Duncan as some sort of invincible super-psycho, immune to everything we say and do. But he *isn't*, Red. He simply isn't.'

'Kate. There's nothing we could have done on this one.'

'How can you be so sure?'

'Because John Macdonald died two years ago.'

'Two *years* ago? I thought you said he was killed yesterday.'

'No. I said his body was discovered yesterday. He *died* on December 27th 1996. Died, that is, not "was killed". Died aged seventy-eight, of natural causes. Yesterday, on the second anniversary of his death, his body was found lying on top of a mausoleum in Highgate cemetery.'

'Duncan pulled the body from its grave?'

'It was a mausoleum. He just had to roll the stone away.'

After ten murders, some things still have the power to shock. Uprooting bodies long dead and desecrating them is one of those things.

'Who found the body?' asks Jez.

'One of the gravediggers, apparently. He was coming back from a funeral when he saw it.'

'And no one saw anything or anybody there?'

'No.'

Jez creases his brow.

'But surely if John had been dead for two years, he would be just a skeleton now?'

'Normally, yes. But he was embalmed.'

'My *God*.'

'Some of his vital organs were taken out by the embalmer, but the tongue was still there.'

'Until yesterday.'

'Yes. Until yesterday.'

'So that's all eleven saints accounted for?'

'Yup. Unless we've missed something.'

'And that's it? He's just going to stop now?'

'What else is he going to do? He's got all his saints.'

The postboy comes into the incident room, pushing his trolley. He pulls out a stack of letters held together with an elastic band, puts it on Red's desk and goes out of the door.

Red flicks the elastic band off the bundle and picks up his letter opener. The postboy comes back in, holding a brown jiffy bag.

'Sorry, sir. I forgot this. Couldn't get the rubber band round it.'

Red takes the bag. It is heavy in his hand. His name and address are spelt out in letters cut from magazines and stuck down with Sellotape. He immediately thinks of the copy of the *Sunday Times* magazine in Duncan's bedroom, the pages splashed with holes where letters have been removed from the text.

Red looks up at the postboy.

'Hold on. Has this been checked?'

'Yes, sir. X-rayed and checked. The Bomb Squad says it's safe.'

'Right. Thank you.'

The postboy leaves. Red turns the jiffy bag over in his hands. No stray wires protruding. No grease marks where explosives might have sweated. Red puts the bag close to his nose and sniffs. No smell of almonds or marzipan.

If the Bomb Squad says it's OK, then he guesses it's OK. Red turns the bag back over and looks at the postmark. LONDON, SW1, 23 DEC 1998. SW1 is Westminster. Westminster includes Scotland Yard.

Duncan must have come within a mile of here to post it, and they never even knew.

Red runs his fingers over the bag's surface. Beneath the squish of the bubblefoam layer inside the bag, he can feel three hard cylinders. Each is a couple of inches long.

Kate and Jez are watching him intently.

'What is it?' says Jez.

'No idea. Only one way to find out, though.'

Red takes the letter opener and slits the end of the jiffy bag open. He reaches inside and his fingertips meet rough paper, and a hardness beneath that. One of the cylinders. It must be wrapped in paper.

He feels the cylinder. It is not smooth, but ridged at regular intervals. Curiouser and curiouser.

His fingers delve deeper, and find the other two cylinders. He pulls all three out at once.

Coins.

Three rolls of ten coins each, wrapped in bank paper. Three rolls of differing shapes and sizes.

Red rips open the paper on each roll. The coins clatter onto his desk.

Ten 10p pieces. Ten 20p pieces. Ten 50p pieces.

Thirty pieces of silver.

110

Red stares at the coins on the desk in front of him.

'Then one of the twelve, called Judas Iscariot, went unto the chief priests. And said unto them, What will ye give me, and I will deliver him unto you? And they covenanted him with thirty pieces of silver.'

A pounding in his head.

Red shuts his eyes and presses his fists hard against his temples. He wants to throw up.

He opens his eyes again. The coins are still there.

Eleven saints, and one other. The most notorious traitor in the history of mankind.

Yes, I took Richard Logan's money. But that wasn't why I turned Eric in. I turned Eric in because I thought it was right. I won the battle with my conscience and lost a brother. I took Logan's money, but it wasn't blood money. I gave it away.

Philip hanged and James beaten and Peter crucified and James beheaded and Bart flayed and Matthew hacked and Simon sawn and Jude clubbed and Andrew crucified and Thomas lanced and John desecrated.

And I'm next.

Red has never felt white fear before. He stands at murder scenes and imagines what it was like for the victims in the moments when they knew they were going to die. He wonders how they coped with the knowledge, or even *if* they coped with the knowledge. But he has never felt that sheerness of terror himself. Until now.

Motion on the edge of his vision. Someone coming into the room.

Duncan, bursting out of the blackness of his own soul and into their presence.

411

Not Duncan. One of the counsellors. Female and small, not male and Duncan-sized. Of all the times to pick.

Red feels rather than sees Jez intercept her at the door, but hears Jez's voice.

'Out.'

'I want to talk to Red. It'll only take –'

'OUT!'

The counsellor scurries out, confused and hurt. Kate curls her arm around Red's shoulders.

'Red, we'll get you protection. We'll get you to a safe house. Everyone here knows what Duncan looks like. He won't get within a mile of you, I promise. We'll get him. We'll take him down.'

The hunter hunted. The coins are still on the table, lying there just as he spilt them.

'I . . . I need some water.'

'I'll get it,' says Kate.

'I'll go and organise some . . .' says Jez.

'No.'

Pleading in Red's voice.

'No. He was in Highgate yesterday. He could be here now. Please . . . please don't leave me alone.'

Red has never pleaded before, not to anyone, not that he can remember.

'You get the water, Kate,' says Jez. 'I'll stay here.'

Red slumps down. Kate and Jez look at each other over the top of his head.

Red's phone rings harshly in the silence. Jez picks it up.

'Hello?'

'Is Detective Superintendent Metcalfe there, please?'

'I'm afraid he's in a meeting right now.'

'Well, could you please get him out of there?'

'I'm afraid he can't be disturbed.'

'This is very urgent.'

'I told you, he can't be disturbed.'

'He has to be. *Please*. This is absolutely crucial.'

Jez covers the mouthpiece with his hand and looks at Red.

'Someone who says they must talk to you now. Says it's absolutely crucial.' He sees the expression on Red's face, and quickly adds, 'It's not Duncan.'

Red shrugs.

'I'll take it.'

Jez hands him the receiver.

'Metcalfe.'

'Detective Superintendent Metcalfe?'

'Yes, speaking.'

'This . . . This is your brother Eric.'

III

When Red last saw Eric, he was behind the forbidding razor wire and control towers of Highpoint. Now he is in Pentonville, which is positively cheery in comparison. Its elegant white buildings fit easily into their north London surroundings, and the community around Pentonville pays the prison little attention as it gets on with its collective life. Highpoint dominates; Pentonville blends.

Red puts his watch, keys and small change on a white plastic tray and passes through the arch of the metal detector. It bleeps shrilly at him. One of the prison guards moves a step sideways to block his way.

'Go back through, sir, and try again, please.'

Red does so, and still the arch bleeps.

Then he realises why. His police badge. He takes the badge from his inside pocket, puts it in the tray and goes through the arch for a third time. There is no bleep this time.

Red reclaims his possessions from the tray and holds his arms out sideways while the guard frisks him. No exceptions made, even for an officer of the law.

'Thank you, sir. If you'd like to go through that door there and close it behind you. The second door will open only when the first one is shut. You'll be escorted from there.'

Red steps through the door and closes it behind him. It is like being in an airlock.

A slight buzzing as the inner door opens. Another prison officer is standing on the other side. He walks with Red down the corridor.

'I'm sure you know the rules, sir. Don't try to pass the prisoner anything. There'll be someone just the other side of the door at all times. If you need anything, just shout.'

'Last time I came to see my brother in prison, he tried to

kill me. I don't really fancy being left alone with him again.'

'We know that, sir. His ankles and wrists will be shackled.'

'But there won't be anyone else in there with us?'

'No, sir. Your brother specifically requested a meeting with you alone.'

'Did he tell you why?'

'He said he had some confidential information for your ears only.'

'That's what he told me on the phone as well. Fuck it. If he's shackled, I'm sure it'll be fine. Thank you.'

The interview room is small and sparse, just like those in Scotland Yard. The prison officer shows Red inside and then leaves him there, alone with his thoughts.

Red walks over to the window and looks out through the bars. A dreary vista of rooftops, as grey as the day. He walks back to the table and sits down.

He doesn't feel as nervous as he probably should, principally because everything is happening so fast. John's body, the thirty pieces of silver and then Eric's call, piling on top of each other and washing Red along with the flow of their momentum.

Some information that you need to know right now. That's what Eric said on the phone.

Not a trap. Too obvious to be a trap.

Then *what*?

The door opens and a man dressed in jeans and a jumper walks in. He has an envelope in his hand, and the shackles on his wrists and ankles clink as he moves.

Eric.

He is recognisably Eric, but he is no longer Red's brother. It is like finally meeting someone you have previously seen only in photographs, making flesh and blood from images on a page – or, in this case, from memories nurtured and fretted over year after year.

The door closes behind Eric and the Metcalfe brothers are in the same room for the first time in more than seven million minutes.

Eric sits down opposite Red. He doesn't say hello or offer

to shake hands. In his eyes are measureless depths of hatred.

He asked you to come here, thinks Red, not the other way round. Let him say what he wants to say.

Eric slides the envelope across the table. Slides it rather than hands it over, so their fingers won't touch, even momentarily.

'This came this morning.'

A plain white envelope, already opened, with magazine letters stuck on for the address. Posted London SW1, 23 Dec 1998. Just like the jiffy bag with the coins.

Inside the envelope, Red finds a sheet of paper folded three times. He unfolds it. More magazine letters in different sizes and typefaces for a scatter-gun effect. Red reads what they spell.

'Have I not chosen you twelve, and one of you is a devil?' (John 6:70). You know who the devil is, Eric. Your own flesh and blood, who betrayed you. He's the evil one, not you. I know the truth, and I know what he's thinking. He wants to be one of us, but he doesn't dare. So he betrays not only you and me, but even himself. A devil who pretends to be on the side of the angels. By the time you read this, I'll have eleven of the twelve. I need just one more. Your brother. Your Judas.

It doesn't address Eric by name, and it isn't signed.

Such control in the letter. Communications from killers are often rambling, demented and incoherent. But not this one. This one knows exactly what he is doing.

Red feels in his pocket and takes a cigarette out of the packet. He gestures towards Eric with it.

'You want one?'

Eric shakes his head.

'You smoke?'

'Sometimes.'

Red lights his cigarette and points at the letter.

'What do you want to do with this?'

Eric shrugs.

'You take it. It's about you. Got nothing to do with me.'

'Of course it's got something to do with you, Eric. It's addressed to you. It mentions you.'

'It's about me inasmuch as it's about what *you* did to me. It was sent to me as a way to get to you. I don't want it.'

Red scans the uneven letters again.

Fuck Duncan. Fuck him.

Red flicks the wheel on his lighter and holds one corner of the letter in the blue flame. Licks of orange climb in the air as the black line of charring sweeps across the paper. Red holds the paper until he feels the heat on his fingers and then drops it into the metal ashtray on the table. They watch the paper shrivel and die.

'Isn't that vital evidence?' says Eric.

'I know who sent it anyway.'

'OK.'

Silence settles on them.

'That's all I wanted you to see,' says Eric eventually. 'You've probably got things to do.'

So many things Red wants to say, and all of them useless. Words by themselves can't heal or undo.

The paper smoulders in the ashtray. Red points at it again.

'Don't tell anyone about this, OK? You're right. It *is* evidence. I . . . I shouldn't have burnt it.'

Another shrug.

'Whatever you say.'

Red gets up and walks to the door. He knocks twice and the prison officer opens it.

Red and Eric don't say good-bye.

Red tries not to look back as he leaves, just to prove he is strong enough. But he can't do it. Just like he did in Highpoint all those years ago, he weakens at the last. As he starts down the corridor, he glances back into the interview room. Eric is just staring straight ahead at the empty chair opposite him.

Red walks fast down the corridor. He wants to get out of the prison, the city, the country. He wants to fly far away to a world where he is twenty-one years old again and where a moment of madness in Cambridge never happened to his brother. He wants his life back.

It is only in the car on the way back to Scotland Yard that Red realises he didn't ask Eric whether or not he agreed with what Duncan had said in his letter. But he knows that he didn't ask because he didn't want to hear the answer.

TUESDAY, DECEMBER 29TH 1998

Red stands at the edge of the small lake and looks around. He can see a couple of houses in the distance towards the west and another over towards the northeastern horizon. Three houses marooned in a vast flatness of fields. It feels more like the deserted highlands of Scotland than the Essex countryside. The only road visible is the one which runs past the end of the drive on its meandering way between the villages of Kelvedon and Silver End. You can see someone coming a mile off.

Which is precisely why they have brought Red here.

Police safe houses all share a commitment to the three 'S's – safety, secrecy and security – but there the similarities end. Some safe houses are slap bang in the middle of cities, where the benefits of anonymity in a busy and transient community outweigh the risks of intrusion or detection. Other safe houses are in the country, where the neighbours are more likely to notice the coming or going of strangers, but where you can find a degree of isolation unknown in the urban environment.

Home Farm falls into the second category. To the casual observer, nothing appears unusual. Set in about three and a half acres of land, including an orchard and the lake which Red is currently standing next to, the farmhouse is inhabited by a charming retired couple called Henry and Penny Sparrow, who are well-known in Kelvedon village and keep an eclectic collection of maritime memorabilia in the barn halfway down the drive.

But look closer and you might notice a few things: the ten-foot ditch which runs all the way round Home Farm's perimeter; the security lights which stud the ground by the fence at regular intervals; the two video cameras which point

419

in each direction down the road outside. And when Home Farm plays host to someone who needs protective custody, then you might see the men who hold police-trained Alsatians tightly on their leads as they patrol the grounds, and hear the crackle of static on secured radio frequencies as the bodyguards keep their charge safe from harm.

Home Farm is larger than it appears from the outside and has five bedrooms, all but one of which can sleep two people comfortably, and four bathrooms. All nine beds are currently accounted for. Apart from Red and the Sparrows, there are the six men who form Target Protection Team Three. Whenever Home Farm is used as a safe house there is always an unholy rush for volunteers to help guard it – largely because Penny Sparrow was once a professional caterer and the fame of her cooking has spread far and wide in the force. The men who are looking after Red take turns sitting at the kitchen table with plates piled high and pissing themselves laughing at the thought of their colleagues in TPT2, who are currently on a diet of doner kebab and takeaway curry as they baby-sit a drugs informer in Streatham.

They brought Red down to Home Farm at lunch time the previous day, a few hours after he visited Eric in Pentonville. He didn't want to come, but he knew he had no choice. He is the stated target of a serial killer still at large, and as such the Commissioner has arranged for him to be placed under police protection until Duncan is apprehended. Red managed to wring only one concession from the Commissioner: permission to go to Helen Rowntree's house on New Year's Day and be present at the moment when Duncan is taken into custody. Even at that, the Commissioner was reluctant. Red eventually swayed him by pointing out that there would be even more armed policemen in Stoke Newington for the take-down than there currently are in Kelvedon.

In any case, there isn't an awful lot that Red can do back in London. He has no option but to sit tight and wait for New Year's Day. Then they can question Duncan, formally charge him on ten counts of murder and hand the whole thing over to the DPP. The case will be closed, Susan will come back and they can start rebuilding their lives safe in the knowledge that Duncan never got his Judas.

Before leaving London, Red went to two libraries – one on the first floor of Westminster City Hall on Victoria Street and the other down by the coach station on Buckingham Palace Road – and took out every book he could find with the word 'Judas' or 'apostle' in the title. He had to go in a bullet-proof vest accompanied by two men cradling Heckler & Koch sub-machine guns, which caused something of a stir among the library users.

Now, with one last look at the small lake as the sun fades on the crisp December afternoon and the Alsatians' breath billows in the cold air, Red steps back inside Home Farm and reads everything he can about the man whose treachery he is supposed to have emulated.

As in the art warehouse where he first broke Silver Tongue's pattern, it is the paintings that Red is drawn to most. Among the books Red has borrowed is one detailing the depiction of Christ and his apostles in art throughout the ages, with the longest chapters unsurprisingly devoted to the events surrounding Judas' betrayal – the Last Supper and Jesus' arrest in Gethsemane. Red turns the pages of the book slowly, seeing how different artists tackled the same subjects. A multitude of divergent interpretations, from the stiff formulaic representation of early Byzantine art to the impassioned emotion of the Renaissance.

As he studies the pictures, Red realises that he is lingering longest not on the most famous paintings, but on those which in some way challenge the conventional views of Judas' action. He is left unmoved by Leonardo da Vinci's masterpiece of the apostles recoiling in shock at the moment Jesus announces that one of them will betray him, because Leonardo's Judas is greedy and lascivious as he clasps the moneybag on the table in front of him. A few pages on, Judas again appears as the stereotypical mercenary without soul or scruples, this time through Signorelli's depiction of his shifty eyes and bony skull as he surreptitiously places the Host in the moneybag. Again, Red passes over it with barely a second glance.

Instead, Red is drawn to artists like Rubens and dei Roberti and Holbein, who painted Judas in shades of moral grey rather than the unremitting black of evil incarnate. Rubens has all the apostles crowding each other in their efforts to get nearer Jesus, with their glowing faces reflected in the aura dancing round the Messiah's head. Only Judas, wrapped in his huge golden cloak, turns his back to the light and averts his face from Christ – not in shame, but in confusion at his role as the man whose actions will ensure his Messiah's immortality and his own eternal condemnation. Rubens' Judas is all brooding strength and burning passion, a man made noble by the terror of his own thoughts.

So too is the Judas painted by dei Roberti. Placed on the near end of a three-sided table, where the apostles and master chat in small groups, Judas is the only one looking away from everyone else, a tortured and bearded figure face to face with the nightmare of his destiny. And Holbein sees his Judas seizing the supper table as if to overthrow it in revolt against the betrayal, a rebel angel in uproar against his fate.

A few pages on, Red finds another Holbein, this one portraying Jesus' agony in the Garden of Gethsemane. Holbein's Christ is the spitting image of his Judas at the Last Supper: they look so alike that they could be brothers, twins even. Where one goes to heaven, the other goes to hell.

Red notes one more thing: Judas is popularly supposed to have had red hair.

Red reads everything he can about Judas Iscariot.

Painting pictures round these bare words.

This is what he finds.

113

Thursday, April 7th AD 30
Jerusalem

'One of you shall betray me.'

The chatter round the table freezes instantly into silence. Light from the candles glows shifting orange on the faces of the men who sit on rattan divans round the low table, and the shockwaves from those fatal words rumble though the heavy beams embedded in the walls and ceiling.

Simon is half-crouched, as if he expects the traitor to strike right away. Thomas shakes his head slowly from side to side in disbelief. The other apostles look at each other in consternation and alarm.

Jesus sits in the middle of them all, and looks as if he is already of another world. His eyes do not flick from one man to another. He looks straight ahead and slightly upwards, his vision fixed on something that they can never see.

Peter sits on Jesus' right and John on his left. Physically, they could not be more different: Peter the wise, bearded old man whose features are fiercely set even when in repose; and John, the fresh-faced baby of the group, who slumps against Jesus' chest.

Peter leans across Jesus and hisses at John.

'Who is it? Of whom does he speak?'

John looks back in languor. Of all twelve, he seems the least concerned. He is Jesus' favourite apostle, the beloved one. He cannot possibly be the one charged to betray his Messiah.

John shrugs his shoulders. Peter hisses again.

423

'Well, *ask* our Lord.'

John turns liquid eyes up towards Jesus' face.

'Lord, who is it?'

Jesus does not look at him. It is as if he has not heard the question.

And then, just as John is about to repeat the question, he speaks.

'He who has dipped his hand in the dish with me, will betray me.'

Every man in the room stares at Jesus. He keeps looking straight ahead, oblivious.

It is traditional that the host at the Passover supper offers his guests a piece of bread dipped in *hazareth*, a red spicy sauce. The tradition goes back to the first Passover, when Joshua celebrated the arrival of the chosen people in Canaan and used the sop to express gratitude and friendship to all those who had survived the Exodus with him.

Again, it is Peter who breaks the silence. He turns to Philip, on his right, and murmurs something. Thomas, sitting on Philip's other side, says something else. From these seeds sprouts conversation, rippling first one way and then the other, until all the apostles are talking earnestly among themselves in groups of two or three.

What does he mean? Who will be the one to betray him? To whom will they betray him?

Their words ebb and flow and break over the man in the middle, but he appears to hear nothing.

He waits a few minutes, until they are all thoroughly engrossed in their chatter, then he brings his gaze down and fastens it on the man sitting directly opposite him.

Judas Iscariot looks back at his Master, and he knows.

It is as if Jesus and Judas are connected by a tunnel of light which excludes everyone else. The tunnel does not fade out towards the edges and the ends, it simply stops. It is there and then it isn't, an entity suspended in limbo from the rest of existence and entire in itself.

Jesus dips his sop in the *hazareth*, and holds it out to Judas.

He doesn't slide it across the table or put it down for Judas to pick up. He holds it out between his thumb and forefinger, so that Judas has to take it from him.

Judas reaches out for it. His sop. His destiny.

Their fingers brush fleetingly as the sop changes hands, and with that sparest of physical contacts comes the final transfer of responsibility onto Judas' mortal shoulders.

The tunnel of light disappears abruptly, and with it dies the babble of conversation.

Jesus speaks to Judas.

'That thou doest, doest quickly.'

Judas feels himself rising from his divan. It is as if he is being led by a higher power.

The others are watching him. He can see their faces turned towards him in surprise, but he can't make out individual features. Only the Messiah's face remains clear.

Someone's voice, Andrew's perhaps, asking if Judas is going to make provisions for the poor.

Of course. Everyone at the Passover meal has to drink four cups of wine: the first with the sanctification (*kiddush*), the second during the celebration of the lamb (*haggadsh*), the third after the prayers of thanks and the fourth with the closing prayers. Moreover, they must drink each cup from a different goblet, symbolising the four kingdoms which the Book of Daniel identified as the oppressors of the Jews: the Chaldaeans, the Medes, the Babylonians and the Romans. Even the poorest of the poor have to receive their four cups. If they cannot afford it, then they receive alms. But no one goes without.

Judas is the treasurer of the Twelve. He is the man with the bag of money. If anyone is to be sent out to give alms to the poor, it will be him.

Let the others think that that's where he's going. Only he and the Messiah really understand. This is their own private covenant.

But at this moment, Judas Iscariot has never felt so alone.

The house they are using for the Passover feast belongs to one of Joseph of Arimathea's servants. They have agreed to leave him the hide of the slaughtered lamb by way of thanks.

Judas hurries out of the gate and into the tumult that is Zion on the night of Passover. Zion, the oldest part of Jerusalem, is a maze of casbahs and souks, roof terraces and sunken courtyards. The district is off-limits to Roman soldiers: the passages which run between the houses are too narrow for them to negotiate in full armour, and only those Romans tired of life venture down here unarmed.

It feels like the whole world has descended on Jerusalem. More than 100,000 pilgrims have crammed into the city, outnumbering the residents by more than three to one. They huddle together in any shelter they can find – they bulge out of tents, perch on rooftops like rows of birds, or simply sit on the pavements. All the pilgrims have to be within the city limits this night, for they can only eat the Paschal lamb in the confines of Jerusalem itself. Every meal identical, as laid down in the Book of Exodus.

Judas sets off through the narrow streets and the power leads him on. The fires on which the lambs are being roasted crackle and spit in the cold night air and he can smell the distinctive odour of locusts being boiled in brine. The noise of the city is in his ears, an orchestral tumult of pedlars, town-criers, herders, tradesmen, singers and animals. He moves as swiftly as possible through the crowd, clutching the moneybag tight in his hand.

Eventually he reaches the Temple Court, where even at this hour the lambs are still being sacrificed in front of thick expectant crowds. The ground is ankle-deep in blood and the butchers are hard at work. Judas watches as they hold the lambs down and slit their throats, sawing away at the windpipes until the red fountains spurt and the animals jerk their last moments away.

The blood of the Lamb, that takest away the sins of the world, have mercy upon me.

Judas skirts round the outside of the main court and heads towards the Temple refectory, where the chief priests are eating. No one bars his way.

He reaches the refectory's large wooden door and pushes it open. The refectory is a massive vaulted hall, crowded now with diners on either side of three long tables which run parallel down the hall. Beyond these tables, set at right angles on a raised dais, is the High Table, reserved for the most senior of the high priests.

Judas walks towards the High Table. It seems like every single person is watching him as he goes past.

He climbs the small step towards the priests. There are chairs only along the far side, so that no one at the High Table has to sit with their back to those on the level below. Judas walks along the near side.

He stops in the middle, opposite the high priest Caiaphas. Behind Caiaphas stands Jonathan, the captain of the Temple guard. The chatter in the hall bubbles low and then vaporises altogether.

Caiaphas looks at Judas, but says nothing.

Judas it is, who speaks into the silence.

'I come to hand over the Lord Jesus Christ.'

Jonathan has assembled a force of 500 men to go to the Garden of Gethsemane.

It is still dark when he leads them out of the Temple, weighed down with lanterns and weapons. At the Golden Gate they meet a *centuria* of Roman soldiers, specially released by the tetrarch Herod Antipas himself. This *centuria* is formally put under Jonathan's command.

Six hundred men now, moving at a trot into the Kidron Valley. They pick their way past the tombstones of the

Jehosaphat cemetery and then wade knee-deep through the sluggish stream of blood and animal entrails that flows from the Temple altar. It's slippery underfoot and there's the stench of rotting intestines in their nostrils.

They divide forces at the tomb of Absalom. The *centuria* go down the valley towards the bridge which links the city of Jerusalem to the olive groves. They will close this bridge once the apostles have gone through. Jonathan takes his men up the hill towards the olive trees, and from there Judas leads them to the cavern where he knows Jesus will be.

Jesus has not told Judas that he is going to be there, but Judas knows anyway. He is a presence that only Judas can sense. The presence is close enough to feel but never close enough to touch. The presence pulls him towards his inexorable fate.

The moneybag is heavy in his hand, weighed down with the thirty pieces of silver they have paid him for brokering this meeting. The payment makes the agreement binding and gives it legitimacy. Without it, Judas could walk away at any time. Not that he would, of course. What he is doing is not of his own will. He never thought twice about taking the money. It is in the bag, along with the rest of the apostles' communal fund.

Jesus is waiting for them near the cavern, in the lee of a small copse. Behind him stand the most trusted three of the apostles: Peter, glowering through his beard, with James and John, the sons of thunder. Their accusations bore into Judas like the sharpest of spear points.

The Messiah is serene after his Agony.

'Whom seek ye?' says Jesus.

A voice from behind Judas: Jonathan.

'Jesus of Nazareth.'

'I am he.'

No wavering. No hiding.

Ranks break away to Judas' left and there are flashes of steel in the crepuscular cold. Peter's sword arcs through the air towards a guard's head and the man's ear spirals end over end as it drops to earth.

The other apostles come running through the trees. Simon is in the lead.

Peter stands with his sword held out in front of him, snarling at the guardsmen.

The Messiah is now in the dead ground between the apostles and the Temple guard. The umpire, and also the prize.

He turns to Peter and his voice is stern but measured.

'Put your sword back into its place; for all who take the sword will perish by the sword.'

And now Judas understands.

Jesus stands among his captors and with him stands the power of heaven, so majestic that it dwarfs and mocks the puny aspirations of the mortals who surround him. And yet he chooses not to use this power. He knows all things which must come on him. He submits himself to the will of men who are as dust in comparison with him.

Jesus gestures towards the apostles, but it is Jonathan whom he addresses.

'I have told ye I am he. If therefore ye seek me, let them go their way.'

The guardsmen come forward slowly and cautiously, as if expecting a trap. They lay trembling hands on Jesus. When he does not resist, they bind his hands and feet and lead him away.

Judas watches them go. When he turns round, the other apostles have gone.

The whole garden is now empty except for one man, face to face with the enormity of his deed.

Judas takes the thirty pieces of silver back to the Temple.

Caiaphas is in his office, along with Annas and some of the other Sadducee priests. They regard Judas with indifference. He has played his part – he is nothing to them now.

Judas places the moneybag on the desk, and looks at Caiaphas.

'I have sinned, in that I have betrayed the innocent blood.'

Caiaphas picks up the moneybag and turns it over in his fingers. Then he hands it back to Judas.

'What is that to us? See thou to that.'

Caiaphas is washing his hands of the affair. It is not his fate. Not his awesome responsibility.

Judas leaves the office quickly and heads past the altar in the Court of Priests, where he opens the bag and hurls the silver pieces down. He hurries, bewildered, through the Temple complex and out through the Mourner's Gate, through the lower city at dawn and straight to the Golden Gate, where the Temple guard met Herod's *centuria* only hours before.

Judas finally reaches an outcrop of rock above the Hinnom Valley and only then does he stop. Smouldering piles of refuse dot the ground around him.

He never meant for it to end like this.

He didn't know how it would end, of course. He was given his role and he played it. And he will continue to play it, right up to the end and beyond.

There is only one course of action open to him now.

Jesus knew all along what would happen to him. He knows that, since the chief priests mediate between the Romans and the rest of the populace, they will hand him over to the Romans as soon as possible. The Romans hold the priests responsible for outbreaks of civil unrest. They will not allow Jesus to become the focus for such unrest, not in the tinderbox that is Jerusalem at Passover.

Jesus knows that he must die in order that mankind might be saved. Only by distilling the sins of the world into his suffering can salvation be achieved. He could have stopped it all there in Gethsemane, but he didn't.

They all played their parts.

And what of Judas' part?

He has committed one of the most heinous of all crimes under Jewish law – the betrayal of innocent blood. The Messiah whom he handed over has committed no crime. Yet Judas delivered him straight into the hands of his murderers. No matter that any of the Twelve could have been chosen as the agent of betrayal. He was marked and he must atone.

He walks towards a tree right on the edge of the outcrop. He takes the girdle from his robe and fashions it into a noose. He loops the girdle over the bough which hangs out into space, ties it tight and pulls on it to check its strength.

It holds fast. He places the noose around his neck.

With the extinction of life comes valour in death. A man can prove his worth with the ultimate act of his life. A man whose soul flies to Calvary to beg forgiveness from the Messiah he has betrayed.

Judas Iscariot steps off the ledge and hangs himself.

114

FRIDAY, JANUARY 1ST 1999

The city is quiet. It always is, on New Year's Day. Not just because of the collective hangover after the celebrations of the previous night, but also because of the collective realisation in the cold light of day that the world is just the same as it was twelve hours before. The New Year is toasted in with the blind optimism that the coming twelve months will be better than those that have just passed, but deep down there is the knowledge that the arbitrary moment which marks the start of a new year is no kind of threshold at all. It is just a point in time like any other, with no special significance. The split second in which you say 'I do', or in which your first-born child appears into the world, or in which a loved one draws their last breath – those are the moments which change lives, not the chime of midnight at the start of the millennium's last year.

Red sits in Helen's kitchen and turns these thoughts slowly over in his mind, like clothes rotating lazily in a tumble-dryer. He has been here since two o'clock this afternoon, making sure that all the arrangements for the takedown are in place. Red has been careful to stay out of sight inside the house, just in case Duncan turns up early or decides to scout the area first. As a result, Red has been co-ordinating the operation blind, listening to the chatter on the radio sets lying on the kitchen table. Two armed policemen sit with him. Red might be technically in charge of the operation, but he is also prime target – a dual role which sits uneasily on his shoulders.

The house is on the north side of Evering Road, just at the corner with Maury Road. As Maury Road is a one-way street to the north, there are four ways in, but only three out.

They have left nothing to chance.

An unmarked white van parked three doors down from the house contains three officers from the Met's armed response unit, all dressed in bullet-proof vests and chequered police baseball caps and all armed with Heckler & Kochs. They will cut off any escape route to the west, down towards Rectory Road station.

A dark blue Ford Sierra is parked ten yards east of the Evering and Maury intersection and a grey Vauxhall points south down the one-way section of Maury Road. Each car contains two officers, also armed. They will cut off the east and north routes respectively.

Two snipers wait upstairs in Helen and Andy's bedroom, with two more in a public stairwell of the housing estate opposite. The stairwell has been sealed off with a local authority sign spelling out in big yellow letters DO NOT ENTER: HAZARDOUS.

On the street is the only female officer on the team, and the only one currently visible. Rose Buckley is wrapped in five layers against the cold and she pushes a pram up and down in front of the housing estate. There is a Heckler & Koch in the pram.

Twelve people covering every angle, all in radio contact with each other. The snipers and the men in the van listen in on headsets with mouth mikes that they can flip away from their faces if necessary. The four men in the cars tune in on their police radios. Rose's radio is on her lapel, so she can talk into it without moving her head. Anyone seeing her speaking will assume that she's talking to a baby in her pram. They won't know that her baby is made entirely of metal and can drop a charging bull at forty metres.

Duncan usually approaches from the south, on Maury Road. That is the only route they have left without vehicle protection, in case somehow he gets wind of what is up.

For the operation to be a success, Duncan has to come to the house unsuspecting. He has to get out of the car and walk towards Helen and Sam, who will be waiting for him. The last thing they want is for him to stay in his car and take them off on a wild chase through Stoke Newington.

Helen comes into the kitchen, her hand clasped tightly around Sam's. Red looks at his watch.

Quarter to six. Fifteen minutes to go.

'You'd better go out,' he says. 'In case Duncan's early. It's brass monkeys out there. He won't want you to freeze.'

'Don't count on it.'

'OK. He won't want *Sam* to freeze.'

A shadow of a smile on Helen's face.

'Probably.'

Red glances at Sam. The boy looks bewildered rather than frightened. The radios have been crackling intermittently all afternoon and he caught a glimpse of the two snipers in his mother's bedroom when he went to the toilet earlier.

Red gets up from his chair and squats down in front of Sam – just like he did for young Tim Weekes ten days ago. Another kitchen, another era.

Young Tim, who might well have seen this boy's father murder another man in cold blood, and who hasn't said a word since.

Red snaps his mind back to the present.

'Do you know why all these people are here, Sam?'

'Yes.'

'Why?'

'They've come to take my dad away.'

'We only want to ask your dad some questions, that's all. When he left the police, he left a few things unfinished. We just want to clear them up. We have to come here because this is the only place we know where we can find him.'

How lame can you make it sound, Red? The child's not a moron. He's seen enough TV to know you don't send in a dozen armed officers to 'ask your dad some questions'.

'Now, you know not to say anything when your dad arrives?'

Sam nods.

'Your mum's told you all this?'

Another nod.

'It's really important. Just do what she does, and you'll be fine. No one's going to get hurt.'

Red puts his face closer to Sam's.

'You trust your mum, don't you?'

Nod.

'Good lad.'

One of the radios on the table hisses. It's Rose's voice.

'Suspect vehicle westbound on Evering Road.'

Red stands up. 'Quick,' he says. 'Go.'

Helen squeezes Sam's hand white-tight as they hurry from the kitchen. Red picks up the radio.

'Describe the suspect vehicle, Rose.'

'Dark blue Fiat, registration number Golf seven four six Tango Oscar Bravo. Sole male occupant.'

'What does he look like?'

'He's wearing a hat. Face partially obscured. Can't get a clear visual.'

Duncan doesn't drive a dark blue Fiat, but you can never be too careful.

'Don't think he's our man. But keep watching.'

Ten seconds of silence, and then Rose's voice again.

'Fiat going away from house, towards Rectory Road. Not our man.'

'Roger.'

'Would he mind hurrying up? I'm freezing my tits off out here.'

The second hand on Red's watch ticks round in lethargic circles.

So many things that could go wrong. Helen might lose her nerve. Sam might try and warn Duncan. A neighbour might walk past at the wrong moment. Duncan might get spooked and not turn up. What if he knows?

How can he know? He can't. But then again, he murdered ten people without *us* even knowing.

Nerves bunch in Red's stomach. Let's get it over with.

Dead silence on the radio. No one is to speak unless they see a vehicle.

Six o'clock.

Come on.

Helen blows smoke rings with her breath. Sam's teeth chatter. Red fingers the megaphone which will shatter the evening silence and rebuild his broken life. He is supposed to stay inside until this is all over. But no one other than him is going to read Duncan his rights.

One minute past.

Helen says that Duncan is never late. Never ever.

He is now.

He knows.

Please God don't let him know. Please let something go right for a change.

Three minutes past six.

Rose's voice on the radio again.

'Dark grey Volvo saloon. Coming up Maury Road now.'

'Which direction?'

'Coming from the south.'

Like Duncan always does.

'Give me the registration number, Rose.'

'Hold on a sec . . . Hotel nine three eight Whisky Uniform Papa.'

'That's him.'

It's on.

Red pushes back his chair and grabs the megaphone. He speaks into the radio again.

'Have you got him all the way, Rose?'

'Damn right I have.'

'OK. You do the talking. You say when we go.'

Rose's voice is distorted through the static and the excitement in her breathing.

'Volvo pausing at junction with Evering Road . . . indicating left . . . turning left into Evering Road now . . . Sam's waving . . . Vehicle slowing down opposite Helen and Sam . . . Vehicle has stopped, double-parked . . . Engine off . . . Driver's door is opening . . . Suspect is getting out . . . Suspect is now fully out . . . GO!'

Everything happens at once.

Rose rips the carbine from the pram. The rear doors of the

white van are kicked open hard and three men jump into the street. The other men are out of the cars and down behind their doors. In the bedroom and the stairwell, the snipers train their crosshairs on Duncan's temples.

Red stands framed in the front door like an avenging angel. He presses the megaphone to his mouth.

'Place your hands on your head and lie down on the pavement. Do not attempt to resist in any way. You are surrounded.'

Duncan looks around him and sees the unwavering eyes of the gun barrels tracing lines to his head and his heart.

He turns to the two people standing in front of him. Helen's expression is unreadable, but in Sam's face there is only pure desperation.

Red's voice through the megaphone again.

'Get down on the ground. Do not attempt to resist, or you will be fired upon.'

Duncan laces his fingers round the back of his head and sinks slowly to the pavement.

115

'I didn't do it. I didn't fucking do it.' Duncan rubs his face. 'I don't believe this.'

Red leans forward across the table.

'Let's go through it again.'

No good cop/bad cop routine. No white lights shining in the suspect's face. No two-way mirrors with experts lining up to watch and listen from the other side of the wall. Just Red and Duncan, and, in the non-speaking parts, the two constables who stand impassively on either side of the door. The ashtray splutters with stubs of Marlboros.

They have been through Duncan's story twice already. The tape recorder on the table between them spools inexorably onwards, ready to record any inconsistencies. Speak now and pick over it later.

The odds are stacked against getting a confession out of Duncan. He knows all the interrogation techniques that the police use, because he's used them himself countless times in the past. He's killed ten people without a soul knowing that he did it, so he's hardly going to break down and tell all the moment someone's nasty to him. And he hasn't finished his masterpiece yet. He hasn't got his Judas. If he stalls them enough, and somehow they are forced to let him go, then he still has that chance.

'We'll go through it point by point, from the start.'

Duncan shrugs.

'I've told you everything already.'

'Where have you been for the past ten days?'

'I told you. Staying in a cottage in the Lake District.'

'Staying with who?'

'By myself.'

'Whose cottage is it?'

'I rented it.'

'Where from?'

'An agency.'

'With the money you got from the *News of the World*?'

Duncan says nothing. Red continues.

'And you've got evidence of this?'

'Yes, of course. You can check with the agency which hired it to me.' He points to a business card sitting on the table. 'There. I've already given you their number.'

'You could have checked in and then gone anywhere.'

'I could have done. But I didn't.'

'And did anyone see you while you were there?'

'I presume so.'

'Like who?'

'Pub landlords, for a start. I drank in a few pubs while I was there. Mainly in Ullswater. You can check with them.'

'Anyone else?'

'People I saw.'

'Like who?'

'Other walkers, mainly.'

'Do these walkers have names?'

'Not that I know of.'

'How convenient.'

'For God's *sake*. They were people I met on the hillside. I didn't ask their names. You chat about this or that for a few minutes, and then you go on your way.'

'So the walkers are untraceable. That's not much help.'

'Why don't you put out a notice asking for people who saw me to come forward? Put my picture out. That'll get you something.'

'You saw these walkers during the day?'

'Yes.'

'So no one can corroborate where you were on any given *night*?'

'Publicans. I told you.'

'And do you remember what nights you went where?'

'Not exactly. Apart from Christmas Day itself. I went to the Blue Boar in Ullswater that night.'

'Nothing apart from that?'

'I was on holiday. I just went where the fancy took me. I didn't keep track of days. I lost my job, in case you've forgotten. I wanted to get away for a while.'

Red changes tack.

'The silver spoons come from a set. You bought one of those sets.'

'No.'

'Yes. You bought it with your American Express on May the 1st 1997. We have the transaction records.'

'I told you before. My credit card was stolen. Whoever stole it must have bought the spoons with it. I reported the card missing. You know that.'

'Yes. We checked with American Express. The card was reported missing on May the 2nd. The day *after* you bought the spoons.'

'That was the first time I realised that the card had gone.'

'The last recorded transaction on that card before May 1st was on Saturday April 26th. You bought £23.76 worth of petrol from a Texaco garage on Wood Lane. You admit to that purchase?'

'Yes, of course. It's the nearest garage to my house.'

'So you say that the card went missing between that day – April 26th – and May the 1st?'

'Yes.'

'And you didn't notice until May the 2nd?'

'No.'

'I'd say that was a bit strange.'

'I wouldn't. I just didn't use my American Express that week. Do you check your credit cards every day, Red?'

'And it was just that credit card that was stolen?'

'Yes.'

'One piece of green plastic saying American Express? Nothing else?'

'No.'

'Now *that* I would call strange. You say that you had your credit card stolen, but the person who *supposedly* stole it didn't take any cash, any other credit cards, or anything else.'

'Exactly.'

'Because that's how thieves usually operate, isn't it, Duncan? Instead of whipping your wallet and getting the fuck out, they take the time to extract one single card. Do me a favour.'

'I'd say that made perfect sense.'

'Why?'

'Because that way I wouldn't notice so fast. If the whole wallet's gone, then obviously I'm going to realise, aren't I? And then I'm going to report the card stolen and it won't be valid by the time the mystery man comes to buy the silver spoons.'

'So who do you reckon stole your credit card?'

'It could have been anyone. I went to a police conference for two days that week. It was hot. I had my jacket hanging on the back of my chair most of the time. Someone could have swiped it then.'

'Did you check with the conference organisers when you realised the card had gone?'

'Yes.'

'And what did they say?'

'They said they hadn't got it.'

'And when you found your own name on the credit card list, you fucking obliterated it. Tell me that's the act of an innocent man. Tell me. Because I don't believe it.'

'I saw my name. I didn't know what it was doing there. I just scrubbed it out, instinctively. I knew I was innocent, but I knew it would be hard to explain what it was doing there.'

'If you were innocent, didn't you think it would be better to take your chances and come clean? Say, "this is my card, which was stolen, and I have no idea who nicked it, but it's turned up here"?'

'Yes. Of course. If I had my time again, that's what I would do. But I didn't. I was confused. I made a snap decision and had to keep running with it.'

'Even if that's true, it still doesn't account for everything else.'

'You're determined to find me guilty, aren't you, Red? You come in here with it all sorted out in your head, and nothing I do or say is going to change your mind one iota, is it?'

He begins to get out of his chair.

'Sit down, Duncan.'

Duncan, his body and voice rising together: 'I didn't do it. I've been framed. It's an elaborate set-up, so the police can get their man.'

'Sit the fuck down.'

'Why don't you *listen?*'

Red is out of his seat too.

'Down! Sit the fuck down! Now!'

The constables step forward. Duncan looks at them and then at Red, and he subsides back into his chair. The constables step back.

Red's voice is tight with control.

'Listen, sunshine. You sold the fucking story to the *News of the Screws* for twenty grand. You took the trust that we had in you and spat it in our faces. So forgive me if I don't see the funny side when *I* start getting notes from you addressed to Judas.'

'I didn't send those notes.'

'The fuck you didn't. We found a *Sunday Times* magazine with letters cut out of it at your house. Those letters correspond exactly to the ones on the jiffy bag full of coins that you sent me.'

Don't mention the letter to Eric, thinks Red. Act like you never got it. Don't undermine your case by admitting that you destroyed vital evidence.

'I don't know what you're talking about. I didn't send you any notes or any coins.'

Red moves on.

'There is also a letter to you, from the Church of the New

Millennium, 32 Phillimore Terrace, London W8. Dated February 12 1998.'

'I've told you. I never received any letter. I don't even know what the Church of the New Millennium is.'

'You know damn well what it is. It's a bunch of frigging nutters led by some bloke who calls himself Israel – the bloke who wrote the letter to you – who keeps preaching about the seventh seal and how the Lamb of God will come again. He also bangs on about how his congregation are his apostles. Just the kind of place for someone who thinks he's the Messiah, wouldn't you say?'

'I've never been there. I've never heard of them. I don't know what else you want me to say.'

'What about the weapons we found in the cupboard under your stairs?'

'Not mine.'

'None of them?'

'No.'

'Not the wooden pole?'

'No.'

'The sword?'

'No.'

'The knife? The machete? The saw? The baseball bat? The lance?' Red is almost shouting now. He struggles to regain some control.

'No, no and no.'

'Oh, so they just appeared there, did they?'

'I told you. They're not mine.'

'Duncan, if you were me – if you were on this side of the table – would *you* believe someone who'd told me what you have? You haven't given me a single alibi for any of the nights on which the killings took place. The only possible alibis you have are the weekends you spend with Sam. But the only murder which took place between Friday six pm and Sunday six pm – the period for which you have Sam, once every month – was that of James Buxton. And you didn't have Sam that weekend.'

'Red, half those killings were done on Sunday nights –'

'No. They were done – you did them – in the small hours of Monday morning. So on the weekends when you *did* have Sam, you had more than six hours after you'd dropped him back at Helen's house before you carried out the killings.'

'I –'

'No. Listen to me. We found the weapons for seven murders at your house. We found indisputable evidence of your payment for the silver spoons. We found a letter detailing your involvement with a religious cult whose leader's ideology is consistent with the mindset of the man who carried out all these murders. Bang bang bang. Three major points, all incontrovertible. You were on the inside, Duncan. You knew what we were thinking and when we were thinking it. You could get away with it because you were above suspicion. Which is why you got careless. Like leaving the murder weapons at your house, rather than getting rid of them – though I daresay you probably wanted to keep them as mementoes of your work anyway. Right now, you haven't given me a single reason, let alone a piece of concrete evidence, which would even begin to clear you. You fit this suspect like a glove, Duncan. And that's aside from anything I feel about what you've done to my life and my marriage. I'd willingly see you rot in hell for that, if nothing else.'

'Red, I know it suits you to have your victim – especially to have it be *me* – but I didn't do it. You say you found all this stuff at my house. But where are the tongues? Where's the scalpel? Where's the last silver spoon?'

'You tell me. You're the one that knows.'

'They're not in my house because Silver Tongue still needs them. And I'm not Silver Tongue.'

'The only reason you're holding out is so you can get at me. But you won't.'

Red has suddenly had enough. He gets up.

'Duncan Warren, I am going to recommend to the Director of Public Prosecutions that you be charged on ten counts of murder and that you be remanded in custody until your case comes to trial.'

Then Red does what he never managed to do with his brother Eric: walk out of the room without looking back.

Part Three

'I know the truth, and I know what
you're thinking'
The Stone Roses, Fools Gold

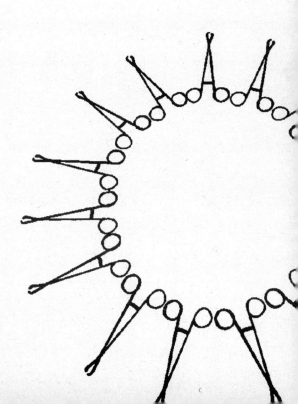

116

THURSDAY, APRIL IST 1999

Life as usual down at Scotland Yard. Three prostitutes have been found sliced open in London over the past two months and the media are all but exploding with excitement at the prospect of a new Jack the Ripper.

It is past eight when Red calls it a day. He wanders down the corridor and into Jez's office.

'Fancy a beer?'

Jez is leafing through the photos of the latest victim of the prostitute killer. They make gory viewing.

'Yeah. I think I need one.'

They go to the pub round the corner and settle themselves at a table with two pints of lager.

'Got anything nice planned for the Easter weekend?' asks Jez.

'Susan and I are off to stay with some friends in the New Forest. She's gone down there already. I said I'd join her tomorrow. Get away from our friendly whore-slasher for a couple of days.'

'She's cool about you coming down late?'

'Yeah. I think so, at any rate. She's been much more relaxed about the whole thing ever since Duncan was arrested and she came back. It took us a week or so to hammer things out totally, as you know, but it's worked pretty well since then.'

'You really thought you'd lost her at one stage, didn't you?'

Red blows air out through puffed cheeks.

'I suppose so. I didn't really think about it in those terms at the time, because I was so obsessed with the apostle case. But if I'd stopped to think about it properly, then yes, I probably would have said that.'

'You definitely took all that stuff with Duncan personally.'

'Fucking right. You guys saw what it was doing to me. I virtually had a breakdown with all the stress. It's difficult *not* to hate someone who's done that to you. You and Kate seemed to handle it so much better.'

'No, I think we just hid it better. And remember that Duncan didn't aim it at Kate and me personally, like he did you. Sending the coins to you and that letter to Eric . . . that was really low. Anyway, it's over now. Here's to a successful prosecution and ten life sentences for Duncan.'

They clink glasses and drink.

'When's the case coming to trial?' says Jez.

'November, I think. God only knows why it's taking so long. I'd have thought you'd be hard pushed to find a more open and shut case.'

'Except for the fact that Duncan keeps maintaining his innocence.'

'Well, he has to, doesn't he? If he pleads not guilty, then he gets the whole trial to tell the world what he did. He'll have it spelled out in all its grisly detail. Think of the publicity he'll get, all the acres of newsprint and the hours of airtime. The whole fucking planet wants to know about it. It's the Rose West trial magnified 100 times. But if he just cops a guilty plea, then the whole thing's over in hours and he never gets to say his piece.'

'Lucky we had that window mended, then.'

'Which window?'

'The one I broke to get into his house.'

Red laughs.

'Oh, *yeah*. That one.'

'Would have been a bit of a sickener to see him get off on inadmissible evidence. It's not as if we had a search warrant or anything. Not until Kate got that one backdated, at least.'

Red waves his pint glass at Jez jokingly.

'Don't do it again, young man. Mind you, you did the right thing. The wrong thing, but the right thing. As your superior, I should officially admonish you for breaking and entering. As your colleague, I think you did damn well. Finding all that stuff really clinched it. Duncan could try to twist his way round the stolen Amex card and the letter from the cult, but he can't get away from seven murder weapons stacked under his stairs.'

'Yeah. But let's not talk about him any more. That's ancient history.'

They talk shop for another ten minutes or so, and then Red stretches his arms behind his head and yawns.

'I've got to go, pal. I'm dead on my feet.'

'OK. When are you next in?'

'Hopefully not until after Easter. I'm not scheduled to come back until Tuesday, though I daresay events will conspire to drag me back sooner.'

'Well, I'll be around. So I'll see you when I see you.'

They walk back to Scotland Yard together in companionable silence and part company at the entrance to the car park.

'I'm going to get changed and get on my lil' ole bike,' says Jez. 'You just get in your big car and pollute the atmosphere a bit more on your way home.'

'Jez, I guarantee you that the stuff which comes out of my exhaust is less noxious than the stuff which comes out of your armpits.'

Jez laughs.

'Fuck you.'

'Fuck you too. Have a good weekend. See you next week.'

Red steps through the door into the car park and is gone.

117

Empty house, empty fridge. Shit. He'll have to go out for food now.

Red walks out into the corridor and nearly trips over the picture leaning against the skirting board. He's been meaning to put it up for days now. There's a pencil cross on the wall and a hammer and nails on the floor next to the picture, but for some reason he hasn't quite got around to putting hammer to nail to wall and finishing the whole process off. He'll do it later.

He slumps down on the sofa and yawns.

Must sleep. Must eat first. Random thoughts wander through his head.

He has the taste of lager in his mouth. Lager from the pub, where he was drinking with Jez. He's a good lad, Jez. Closed the case for us with his spot of illegal entry.

Jez, the coolest of them all under pressure. When Red was cracking, Jez was still rock solid.

What did Jez say in the pub? Something about taking it personally.

Remember that Duncan didn't aim it at Kate and me personally, like he did you. Sending the coins to you and that letter to Eric . . . that was really low.

The crackle of electrical charges in Red's brain.

Sending the coins to you and that letter to Eric.

That letter to Eric.

Red is on his feet in a second.

How the fuck does Jez know about the letter to Eric?

Red has never mentioned that letter to anyone. It was evidence and he burnt it when he shouldn't have. He didn't mention it to anyone at the Yard, or to any of TPT3 who were detailed to guard him down at Home Farm.

So how does Jez know about it?

Jez was in the incident room when Eric rang up that morning. Shit, Jez was the one who answered the phone in the first place.

So maybe I told Jez then.

But I didn't *know* then. I didn't know what Eric wanted until I arrived at Pentonville.

And I certainly didn't tell anyone afterwards. I didn't even mention it when I was interrogating Duncan, because I didn't want him to know that I'd seen it.

Red grabs the phone and dials 192.

'Directory Enquiries, what name please?'

'Pentonville Prison, London N1.'

A computerised female voice gives Red the number twice. He scribbles it down on the pad by the phone and rings it immediately.

Ring ring. Ring ring. Ring ring.

Nine o'clock on the eve of Good Friday. No wonder they're not rushing to the phone.

Come on.

A man's voice comes on, obviously bored.

'HMP Pentonville.'

'I'd like to speak to the Governor, please.'

'I'm afraid the Governor is unavailable until –'

'This is Detective Superintendent Metcalfe from Scotland Yard. I need to speak to the Governor as a matter of extreme urgency. I don't care what he's doing. You *have* to interrupt him.'

'How do I know that you are who you say you are?'

'You want me to send a vanload of uniforms round to prove it?'

'OK, OK. I'll just connect you.'

'Greensleeves' plays on the line.

Another man's voice now, this time irritable.

'Hello?'

'Is that the Governor?'

'Yes.'

'This is Detective Superintendent Metcalfe, and –'

'Your brother is an inmate of this prison.'

'Yes. Yes, he is. And I need to talk to him urgently.'

'Superintendent, the prisoners are all locked up until morning. I can't get him for you until then.'

'No. You must. It's absolutely vital that I speak with him tonight. Within the next ten minutes.'

'How vital is vital?'

'Let's put it this way. He might be able to tell me something that will totally change the course of a nine-month investigation.'

'And you need this information tonight?'

'Yes. Tomorrow may be too late.'

'Right. Give me your number. I'll get the warders to bring Eric out and ring you.'

'Thank you. Thank you very much.' He reads out his number.

'Stay by your phone.'

The line goes dead.

Red looks at the wall. Fear clutches at his gut like an octopus.

He turns on the TV and flicks through the channels. Nothing worth watching.

The shrill sound of the phone. He snatches it up.

'Hello?'

'Hi, honey. How are you?' Susan's voice.

'Susan. I'm fine. Listen, can I call you back? I'm waiting for a very important call.'

'Sure. I was just phoning to see when you're coming down.'

'Tomorrow. Morning, hopefully. Listen, I'll call you back in fifteen minutes.'

'Red, are you OK?'

'Yes. I'm fine. But I mustn't miss this call.'

'OK. Speak to you later.'

He cuts the connection. His heart hammers in his chest.

How long will it take them to get Eric? Five minutes, maybe ten? If they've got to go to his cell, get him out, bring him to a phone . . .

The unbearable agony of waiting.

454

He keeps his hand on the receiver.

Come on. COME ON.

The phone rings.

'Hello?'

'Superintendent Metcalfe, I have your brother here.'

'Put him on. Please.'

Shuffling in the background.

'This is Eric.'

'How are you?'

'What do you want?'

'You remember that letter you were sent?'

'The one you burnt?'

'Yes. That one.'

'Of course I remember it.'

'You didn't tell anyone about it, did you?'

'No.'

'Definitely not?'

'Definitely. You asked me not to, so I didn't.'

'Not a soul?'

'Which bit of the word "no" don't you understand? I didn't tell anyone. All right?'

'Yes. Thank you.'

'Anything else?'

'No. That's all I wanted to know. Thanks.'

Red puts the phone down.

Neither he nor Eric has told anyone about the letter. Which means that only three people in the world know that it even existed. The two of them, and the person who sent it.

So, if Jez knows about the letter, there's only one possible explanation.

Jez is the one who sent it.

118

The main door downstairs opens and closes.

Red leans against the wall and tries to work out what to do.

He should leave. Throw some things in a suitcase and get the fuck out.

Shali's front door opens then shuts with a slam.

Think. Think fast.

His mind is blank.

Red goes to the bathroom, runs cold water into his hands and splashes his face.

Shali's music comes thumping through the floor, unfeasibly loud.

Not now. Of all the times, not now.

Red presses his hands to his ears and tries to blot the music out so he can think clearly.

The bassline pounds into his brain.

Shali. Fucking inconsiderate bastard.

Red can't think above this racket.

Right. He's going to have words with Shali.

He stalks to his door and flings it open.

There's a figure standing right outside his door, dressed in cotton trousers and a denim shirt buttoned to the neck.

Jez.

119

Jez is holding a white cloth in his hand.

Red tries to speak, but no sound comes out.

Jez takes one step towards him. The white cloth rushes up to Red's face.

There's the sharp pungent smell of chloroform as Jez clamps the cloth around Red's nose and mouth.

Then there's only woozy blackness.

120

I never thought I'd get caught, except once – that time in the kitchen at Thomas Fairweather's house, with Camilla and little Tim. When I came in with Lubezski, and he was covered in blood. Remember? Remember Tim screaming? That wasn't because he saw Lubezski covered in blood. That was because he saw me. He came down the corridor when I was martyring Thomas. I took him by the hand and led him back to bed. And then he saw me again, the next day, by which time he knew what had happened to his uncle.

You might think I'm lucky that Tim still doesn't speak about that night. I choose to think of it as God's will that he doesn't. Just like it is God's will that I have come this far undisturbed. Because there's three reasons why I know that I'm the new Messiah, and two of them have been there for everyone to see since this whole thing started.

First: my name. My initials. Jez Clifton. J.C. Jesus Christ.

And if you look in my personnel file at the Yard, you'll see when I was born. December 25, 1966. That makes me thirty-two now. Just about the same age Christ was when he died on the cross.

These two pointers have been there for everyone to see. But, like I said, they're just pointers. The third reason is more than that, much more. The third reason is proof positive.

But the third reason can only be shared with my Judas.

121

When Red comes round, he is in his kitchen slumped against the wall. The only light comes from the candles flickering on the table, so it takes a few moments for his eyes to adjust.

He looks at the clock on the wall. Just past eleven. He has been out for over two hours.

The kitchen table has been laid for thirteen people. No place has been set at the end nearest the door, but there are six settings down each side and one at the far end.

There are jars on the table to mark each place, except for the place at the far end and the one immediately to the right of that, which have plates of meat instead.

They are small glass jars, with something suspended in each.

Red gets to his feet and peers more closely at the jar nearest to him and he sees what is inside.

A tongue.

Eleven jars with eleven tongues.

Jez suddenly appears in the doorway.

With some people, there comes a moment when they reach extremes of emotion so unexpected that your view of them is changed for ever. The first time you see someone mild-mannered become angry, *really* angry, that is, or the first time you see someone unexpressive break down and cry. After that, you can never look at them in the same way again. Something has changed and it cannot be undone.

When Red turns to look at Jez, it is like looking at a stranger. The face that stares back at him has Jez's features, but the expression into which they are arranged does not belong to the Jez that Red knows. He has seen Jez's face distorted in anger and laughter and pain, but he has never seen him looking so . . . so *blank*. An expression which isn't even an expression. Just blankness.

Not Duncan. Not Duncan at all. Jez.

Jez is wearing his wet suit. It takes Red a second to work out why, then he mentally tips his hat to Jez: blood doesn't show up on the black material and rubber doesn't shed fibres. It's the perfect attire for killing people.

Jez comes forward.

'I'll sit at the head of the table. You sit at my right hand. The front door is locked, and I'm bigger and stronger than you. I'm sure you know better than to try anything stupid.'

Red goes round the table and lowers himself queasily into the chair which Jez has indicated. Just keep calm, he tells himself. Keep him talking.

The tongues in their jars mock Red in their parody of a domestic table setting.

Don't look at the tongues. Concentrate on Jez.

Jez's black sausage bag is on the floor by his chair.

Big bag. Big enough to have brought all this food and the jars too. And whatever else he needs for tonight.

Jez bends down and picks something out of the bag. A piece of purple material, folded four times. He shakes it open and pulls it over his head.

A purple robe. Just like Christ wore on the way to Calvary.

There are two bottles of red wine on the table in front of them, uncorked. Jez sits down and pours them each a glass. 'The first of four,' he says. 'Passover ritual dictates that everyone, even the poorest of the poor, must have four cups of wine.'

Red sips at his wine. The acidic warmth runs over his teeth and onto his tongue.

His tongue. God no.

In the middle of the table are four small bowls of herbs. Jez reaches for them.

'The bitter herbs to go with the lamb,' he says. 'Crushed bay leaves, marjoram, basil and horseradish. Eaten as a reminder of the Jews' past as slaves in Egypt.' He sprinkles some herbs onto the meat on Red's plate and then onto his own. 'Go on. Eat.'

They eat in silence. The lamb is dry and difficult to swallow, so Red has to use the wine to wash it down.

Red only feels blankness through the silence; no coherent plan of action forms in his head. He tries to relax and hope that a plan comes to him; then he tenses and tries to force one into existence. Neither method works. His mind has shut down in self-defence, because it can't possibly accept the enormity of what is happening to him without imploding.

Slices of bread are arranged on a plate beyond the herb bowls. Jez picks up one of the slices, tears it in two, and offers one half to Red.

'And as they did eat, Jesus took bread, and blessed, and broke it, and gave it to them, and said: "Take, eat, this is my body".'

Red looks at the bread in his hand, and then at Jez.

It's only a piece of bread.

Jez stares unwaveringly at him.

Swallow your pride, Red. Swallow the bread.

Red puts the bread in his mouth and starts chewing. It tastes sour. Unleavened. He washes the taste away with some more wine. Jez refills his glass.

'And he took the cup, and when he had given thanks, he gave it to them, saying: "This is my blood of the new testament, which is shed for many".'

He looks at Red.

'Drink it.'

'This is not your –'

'Drink it.'

Red nuzzles the edge of the glass, letting the wine wet his lips.

Jez finishes his lamb. Red doesn't hurry to finish his. Jez watches him as he eats. He doesn't seem to be in a hurry either. When Red finally, reluctantly, places his knife and fork together, Jez speaks.

'Take off your shoes.'

'What?'

'Take off your shoes.'

Red pushes his chair back so that his legs are clear of the table, and slips his shoes off his feet.

461

'Now your socks.'

Red takes off his socks, and places them on top of his shoes. One of the socks falls onto the floor.

Jez reaches down and picks up a plastic washing-up bowl full of soapy water. He kneels down in front of Red and puts the bowl on the floor by Red's feet. The water slops from side to side in the bowl, but does not go over the top.

Jez reaches behind him and picks up a small hand towel, which he drapes over his left shoulder. Then he dips both hands in the water and reaches out for Red's right foot.

'Try anything, and I'll break your legs. Understand?'

Red nods.

Jez takes Red's foot in his hands, and begins to wash it. He washes the top of the foot, where the tendons spread out like struts of a fan towards the five toes, then he washes the sole of the foot, and then he washes the webbing between the toes. When he finishes the right foot, he takes the left foot and repeats the procedure. Jez washes gently and with tenderness, and he speaks in a low monotone as he does so.

'He rose from supper, laid aside his garments, and girded himself with a towel. Then he poured water into a basin, and began to wash the disciples' feet, and to wipe them with the towel with which he was girded . . . Jesus said, "He who has bathed does not need to wash, except for his feet, but he is clean all over; and you are clean, but not every one of you." For he knew who was to betray him; that was why he said, "You are not all clean."'

Jez dries Red's feet with the towel. When he has finished, he pushes himself to his feet and sits back down on his chair.

'Why?' asks Red.

One question. A lifetime of answers.

'Why what?'

'Why this? What makes you the Messiah?'

Jez smiles, and Red knows that he was meant to ask this question.

'I died, and then I was born again.'

'*What?*'

462

'I was resurrected.'

'Jez, what are you talking about?'

'I died on Good Friday, and on the third day I rose again.'

'Good Friday's tomorrow.' Red looks at the clock. Twenty to twelve. 'Virtually today.'

'Not tomorrow. Good Friday a long time ago. Good Friday 1982, to be precise.'

Jez raises his eyebrows, as if the date is supposed to mean something to Red.

'You don't remember?' says Jez.

'Remember what?'

Jez doesn't answer directly. He looks into the inner blue flame of the nearest candle.

'I was in an accident on Good Friday. I was in a coma for three days. On a life-support machine. All that time, I couldn't breathe by myself, couldn't eat, couldn't see, couldn't hear. I was trapped beneath the surface of life. The doctors thought it was just a matter of time before I died. They were preparing to tell my parents to switch the machines off.'

He looks back up.

'They wanted to flatline me, Red.'

Red says nothing.

'But then, on Easter Sunday, I came round. Just like that. One moment I was in a coma and then suddenly I was alive again, like nothing had happened. The first doctor to see me thought I was a ghost. I nearly gave him a coronary.'

'And you were OK?'

'Yes. I was fine. More than fine. In fact, the hospital staff couldn't believe I had suffered no ill-effects. They thought that, at the very least, I would have severe brain damage, but I didn't. None at all. They made me undergo every test they could think of, and I came through each one with flying colours. I wasn't brain damaged in the slightest.'

I wouldn't be so sure, thinks Red.

'The doctors said it was like a miracle. No. They said it *was* a miracle.'

Red is beginning to understand.

Jez is silent for a few seconds, and then he speaks again.

'Don't you want to know what kind of accident it was?'

'Oh. Yes. Of course.'

'I was hit by a car.'

Something clutches at the tendrils of Red's memory. Something trying to fight its way out.

Jez goes on.

'I was hit by a car, but the driver didn't stop. He just drove on.'

Something is coming fast to the surface of Red's memory.

'He just drove on, Red. A hit-and-run. On Good Friday. In Cambridge.'

Something bursts through into Red's consciousness.

Red knows. In the split second before Jez speaks again, he knows.

'You were driving that car, Red. You were the one who hit me.'

Jez leans forward.

'You were the one who left me for dead.'

122

Red remembers it as if it were yesterday.

The boy on the pavement, in tracksuit bottoms and a baggy sweatshirt, with his hair flattened by the rain on his scalp. Crossing the road and slipping on the football, sprawling face first onto the tarmac. Red stamping on the brakes, wheels locking, panicking, the car spinning round on itself. Two bumps under the car. The body in the rearview mirror.

And Red, checking that nobody was looking before driving on, round the corner and on with his life.

Jez was that boy.

'Oh God, Jez, I'm so sorry. I . . . I wasn't thinking straight. I'd just been to see Eric in prison. He tried to kill me. I wasn't concentrating properly. I saw you too late. I was all fucked up. And then, after I'd hit you, I saw the body in the road and just panicked.'

'Don't apologise, Red. If you hadn't hit me, I wouldn't have died and come to life again. I wouldn't have known that I am the Messiah.'

'But I didn't even stop to help you when you were lying on the road. That was unforgivable. I could have stopped. I *should* have stopped.'

Jez shrugs.

'The Lord moves in mysterious ways.'

'How did you know it was me driving the car?'

Jez doesn't answer directly.

'Like I said, that three-day period in a coma, when I was technically dead, was the irrefutable evidence that led to the realisation that I was the Messiah. Whenever I tried to deny my true identity to myself – and I *did* try – I kept coming back to that. I was dead for those three days, from Good Friday to Easter Sunday, and then I rose again. And the only way that

465

the incident made sense was as my resurrection, allowing me to live again to carry out the work chosen for me. It was a *sign*. You see?'

Red nods. Jez goes on.

'It was a sign of divine will, which meant there had to be an *agent* to carry out that divine will. I figured that, if the incident was important, then everything about it was important – including the people involved. The person driving the car that hit me was the agent of divine will. It wasn't just any old person who happened to be driving that car. It was *someone*. That person had been chosen, just like I had. I had to find out who that person was. The reason you didn't stop to help me was because you were trying to fight your destiny. You were scared of your fate.'

'I was scared of going to jail. That's what I was scared of.'

'No, Red. You misunderstand. The earthly consequences were immaterial. By fate, I mean your role in the divine plan. You were scared, so you ran away and hid, hoping that by doing so your role would be taken by someone else. But, just like me, you couldn't escape your fate. I had to find you. So, soon after I joined the police, I subjected myself to hypnosis, to retrieve the memories from the place in my mind where they had been buried.'

'And what happened?'

'Under hypnosis, I remembered the incident perfectly. I'd had flashes of it before, but most of it had been lost in the coma. Until I agreed to be hypnotised, that is. Under hypnosis, I could see your face as the car came towards me. Your face looked familiar – of course it did, you and your brother had been all over the papers for months – but I couldn't immediately place it. It was like having a film in my head, which I could run whenever I pleased. When I paused that film, I got a clear picture of the number plate. I told the number to the hypnotist, who wrote it down. And later I ran a check through DVLC in Swansea.'

'When was this?'

'Soon after I'd joined the force: 1990, I think.'

'But I'd sold the car by then.'

'Of course you had. That's why I also asked DVLC to give me the car's full ownership history for the previous ten years. There were three owners over that period – you, the person you bought it off, and the person you sold it to. But at the time of the accident, *you* were registered as owning it. I saw your name, and I remembered where I had seen your face before, and it all made sense.'

'What do you mean, it all made sense? *What* all made sense?'

'In the Gospels, Judas Iscariot was the agent of divine will. By his actions, however reprehensible they have seemed to Christians through the ages, he ensured that mankind was saved. And, 2,000 years on, you have been chosen to do exactly the same. It was *your* actions which made me realise that I was the Messiah. You are so like Judas, Red. Don't you see? Turning your brother over to the police and pocketing the reward. Thirty grand, wasn't it? Thirty. Even that was symbolic. It was perfect. *Perfect*. It was the final proof that you, like me, had been chosen – me to save mankind, and you to be the agent of that change.'

'But I haven't betrayed you, Jez. If anything –'

'No. You haven't betrayed me. Not yet. But you will.'

'How do you know?'

'Because you *can*. You betrayed your brother. By doing so, you demonstrated that you have the capacity and the willingness to do it again.'

'I didn't betray Eric. He committed a crime. He had to be punished.'

'You *did* betray him. You listened to the confession of your own flesh and blood, and you took that and went behind his back to the police.'

'I was placed in an impossible position.'

'Exactly. *Exactly*. As was Judas Iscariot. You know the story of Judas backwards, Red, I know you do. You read it when you were in the safe house at Kelvedon. You told me so. You're right. You *were* placed in an impossible position. Whatever you did was going to be wrong in some way. You did what you thought was best. You did what you thought was the lesser of the evils. Keep my brother's secret to myself and deny Charlotte Logan the justice that is rightfully hers, or hand him over and betray my own blood? I sympathise, Red, I honestly do. I would hate to have faced that choice. But that is not the role that God has chosen for me.'

Red opens his mouth to speak, but Jez cuts him off.

'You've missed something else, Red. Two other things, in fact. Firstly, you took the money. You took the reward that Charlotte Logan's father had offered. Like Judas, you took the money. It was an all too human thing to do. You turned your brother in and you took the money – you did that just like you do other things, for a combination of reasons both honourable and base. You gave the money to your father, just like Judas tried to give his reward back to Caiaphas. But you still took it in the first place.

'And the second thing is something that I am sure you know. When you handed Eric over, you were betraying not just him, but yourself. You know what I'm saying?'

Red knows. All too well.

'I know you, Red. I know what you show and what you hide. And I know that the wrong brother is in prison. Eric is not a bad person. He made a mistake. He had an accident. With you, however, it's different. That spectre lurks inside you, Red. That's what makes you so good at what you do. And that's equally what makes you so vulnerable. I've seen you at the murder scenes, visualising what happened. When I was in the middle of my work with the apostles, completely consumed in it, I would step outside myself for a second, and I saw you. You would have enjoyed doing what I have done.'

Red can't think of a reply, so he asks something else.

'Why did you choose Duncan as a scapegoat?'

'His bad luck, really. Nothing else. I needed a credit card to buy the silver spoons. His was the first I found. I just walked into his office one day when he wasn't there and took it out of his jacket pocket.'

'Why didn't you just use cash?'

'Too suspicious. Who walks in and buys a set of silver spoons with cash? And besides, I couldn't afford it.'

'And Duncan could?'

'Of course he couldn't. But he didn't have to pay for it, did he? American Express reimbursed him for that, and *they* can afford it. They always reimburse customers when purchases have been made on stolen cards. It's no skin off their nose, and they get loyal customers that way.'

'But you didn't know I'd choose Duncan to be on the team.'

'No, I didn't. That was my good luck. It made him easier to frame. But I *did* know that, when he saw his name on the list, he'd react the way he did. It's what I would have done, if I'd been him. He panicked. He thought it was much better just to suppress the details than try to explain it away. He probably never thought it would come to light again. He told you all that himself, when you interrogated him.'

'And I didn't believe him.'

A slim smile curves on Jez's mouth.

'You do now.'

'Yes. I do now.'

'Anyway, after that, the rest was easy. The letter from the Church of the New Millennium – well, obviously I forged that. I took the paper and the envelope from Israel's desk when Kate and I went to visit him. Israel had gone downstairs to let some people in and Kate went out onto the landing to check who they were. I was alone in the room for ten, maybe fifteen seconds, tops. I took the stuff then. It was just a spur of the moment thing. I saw Israel's signature on a fax that was lying on his desk and it was so illegible I knew it would be easy to copy. Just a scrawl, really. As it was, you didn't even check if the letter was genuine, you were so desperate to find Duncan guilty.'

'And you dumped all the murder weapons at Duncan's house when you went round there?'

'Yes.'

'No wonder you insisted on going alone.'

'Precisely. I thought for a second you were going to come

with me, or make Kate, which would have ruined everything. I drove back home, got the stuff, and went on to Duncan's. Prima-facie evidence, once you'd got there. You'd have killed Duncan at that moment if he'd walked in the door, Red.'

'Yeah, I know. Just as well for him that he was miles away.'

Red pauses.

'Don't you feel guilty, Jez?'

'About what?'

'Framing Duncan.'

'No. I never really liked him much anyway. Well, he never really liked me either, that was for sure. Maybe he saw the real me without even realising it. But I certainly didn't feel guilty after he sold us out to *News of the Screws*. Whatever else he did or didn't do, that was unforgivable. Two Judases in one team. I was spoilt for choice.'

'So it doesn't weigh on your conscience?'

'What?'

'The fact that Duncan's spent three months in jail for something he didn't do.'

'Conscience is just a polite word for superstition, Red, and superstition is just a polite word for fear. No, it doesn't weigh on me. Anyway, Duncan will be released soon enough, when the truth comes out.'

When the truth comes out.

'How are you going to do that, Jez? How are you going to make sure that the truth comes out?'

Jez looks deep into his friend's eyes, and tells him.

123

'When Judas, his betrayer, saw that he was condemned, he repented and brought back the thirty pieces of silver to the chief priests and the elders, saying, "I have sinned in betraying innocent blood." They said, "What is that to us? See to it yourself." And throwing down the pieces of silver in the temple, he departed; and he went and hanged himself.'

It is past midnight now. Good Friday at last.

Red is dressed in only his underpants and his hands are tied behind his back. He is sitting on top of the wooden railing which runs round the edge of the upstairs landing. A thick hangman's rope curls round his neck and down his back to the railing. Jez has secured the rope tightly to the railing, which feels sturdy and strong. The only thing that will break on the way down is Red's neck.

Jez stands next to him. He has squeezed a makeshift crown of thorns onto his head, and a few trickles of blood are winding gently down his forehead towards his eyebrows. He doesn't seem to notice. On the floor beside him is a plate of food.

Red steels himself against the terror. Don't show fear. Don't give Jez that satisfaction.

Jez has his mobile phone in his right hand and the scalpel in his left. The silver spoon – the last of the twelve – is on the floor by his feet.

He unties Red's hands and gives him the mobile phone.

'You know, don't you? You know that you have to betray me?'

Red nods.

'Say it.'

'Yes,' says Red. 'I know that I have to betray you.'

Jez picks up a slice of bread, tears off a small corner section, and dips it in a small bowl of red sauce. 'He who has dipped his hand in the dish with me, will betray me.'

Jez presses the sop into Red's hand, using his own hands to close Red's fingers over it. He puts his head close to Red's ear.

'That thou doest, doest quickly. Your last betrayal, Red. Do it. Betray me to the authorities. Ring the police. Ring *Kate*. Yes, ring Kate. Tell her what I've done. Hand me over to the police. They'll come once you're dead, and they'll put me on trial like the Romans tried Jesus. Then the whole world will know. Go on. Ring the police.'

'And then you're going to hang me?'

'No. You're going to hang yourself.'

'And if I refuse?'

'You can't. You won't. It is your destiny.'

The quicksand of Jez's mission, dragging Red down. Except struggling doesn't make you go down faster in this particular quicksand. Struggle, and you might stay alive. Let yourself go, and you are doomed.

Red takes the phone and dials Kate's number.

'Kate Beauchamp.'

'Kate, it's Red.'

'Hi, Red. How are you?'

Her voice, so fucking normal it might as well be coming from another planet.

'Kate . . . It's not Duncan. It's Jez.'

'What? What's not Duncan?'

'The killer. The apostle killer. It's Jez. He's the one.'

'Red, what on earth are you talking about?'

'He's here right now. He's about to hang me. Oh God, Kate . . . you've got to help.'

'Where are you?'

'I'm at – '

Jez grabs the phone from Red's hand and snaps it shut.

'Now. Hang yourself.'

I'm at . . . Kate will know I'm at home. He's done all the other victims in their houses.

Random thoughts float through Red's mind.

Philip Rhodes, hanging from his landing in Fulham last year. As it started, so will it end, with a body dangling lifeless off a landing.

Maybe Kate won't believe him. She and Jez . . . maybe she'll be the last person who'll believe it.

It's common knowledge that you can't hang someone against their will. They simply won't do it. They won't launch themselves off into the sweet hereafter of their own accord. You have to bludgeon them into submission or trick them.

No trickery here, and no bludgeoning.

Red won't hang himself. He won't play the part of Judas. If Jez wants him to hang, he'll have to do it himself.

Red looks at Jez.

'Fuck you.'

He sees Jez down a tunnel of light through which their respective wills rage. The force of Jez's convictions slams into Red's chest and whirls around his head, a divine wind which strains to push him off the railing and into oblivion. Red stands bent against the hurricane.

Don't break. Don't surrender.

Red clings onto the railing as if to life itself.

It is the moment when Jez realises that his Judas will not play out his allotted role. The moment when Red knows that he has won the battle of wills.

And then Jez's hands are rough on Red's shoulders as he pushes him forwards and Red slowly overbalances as his torso topples towards the horizontal. There is a pain in his arms as they twist, trying to support his falling body, and Red's fingers prise themselves free from the wood. He gathers speed as he begins to drop and his hands fly up to his neck faster than thought itself, grasping the noose before it tightens. The pain is excruciating on the inside of his knuckles and his fingertips as the rope locks at the end of its reach and the noose slams tight.

Only eight fingers and two thumbs, curled around a rope. A flimsy barrier between life and death.

Red kicks uselessly in the air, trying somehow to jerk the

rope free of the railing. The rope digs into his neck, forcing his head backwards and upwards. He opens his mouth to breathe.

Jez leans down over the banisters. The scalpel glints in his hand.

Red's mouth is defenceless as he gasps for air.

There is total concentration on Jez's face beneath the crown of thorns, his head so close to Red's they could kiss.

The scalpel is in Red's mouth.

There is a sharp taste of blood as the cutting edge nicks his tongue, just as Red imagined it when he went alone to Philip Rhodes' house.

Last chance.

Red uncurls the fingers of his right hand from around the noose and clenches them into a fist. The noose suddenly tightens in the places where he no longer holds it, and he twists his head the other way to ease the pressure.

Red swings his right fist round and up in blind desperate hope. He feels the crack of knuckles on bone and cartilage. Jez yelps in surprised pain, lets go of the scalpel and presses his hands to his bloodied face. The scalpel slides down towards the back of Red's throat and panic swells up to meet it.

I'm going to swallow the blade oh my God I'm going to swallow it and it's going to rip every part of my insides to shreds.

Red tips his head forward against the strain of the rope and uses his tongue to push the scalpel back towards the front of his mouth. The blade nestles against the inside of his teeth.

Red reaches inside his mouth and pulls the scalpel out.

Jez takes his hands away from his face and blows blood out of his nostrils. He leans down again and grabs hold of Red's left hand, trying to prise his fingers off the noose.

If Red doesn't keep that hand inside the rope, then he's going to die.

The scalpel is still in Red's right hand. He slashes out at Jez. The blade cuts through the rubber of the wet suit and tears along Jez's right flank, exactly where Jez cut himself while sitting on Thomas Fairweather's bed last December.

Jez screams as the scar tissue is ripped open. He lets go of Red's fingers and clamps both hands to his own side as he falls backwards against the wall.

Red reaches above his head and tries to cut through the rope with the scalpel. The rope jerks wildly with his own motion. He can't get enough purchase to cut through it.

Need to pull the rope tight. Then I can cut it. But I can't hold the rope tight and cut it with just one hand. I need my left hand to steady it while my right hand cuts. And my left hand is the only thing preventing the noose from choking the life out of me.

Jez is still slumped against the wall, trying to stop the blood pouring out of his side.

No choice.

Red lets go of the noose with his left hand. There is instant pressure, hard, all the way round his neck. Nothing to stop him being throttled now.

Work fast.

Red reaches above his head with his left hand and grabs hold of the rope. He presses the scalpel against a point on the rope just below his little finger, where it is at its most taut, and begins to cut through it.

There is no air in his lungs as his windpipe begins to close under the pressure of the noose. Specks of black dance behind his eyes.

Come on.

He is going to pass out before he can save himself. And if he passes out, then he dies.

COME ON.

There is motion on the edge of Red's vision. Jez is pushing himself up, leaning over the banisters again. The blood is shiny on his wet suit.

Jez reaches out for Red's right hand, the one with the scalpel.

There is intense pain in Red's fingers as Jez tries to peel them off the blade.

Red is about to black out. Oblivion beckons, dark and eternal.

Then the last threads of the hangman's rope give way and send Red crashing to the floor, six feet below.

124

Two men, bloodied but unbowed.

Red lies crumpled on the floor and works the noose loose with trembling hands. Jez stumbles down the stairs towards him, leaving blood trails of uneven crimson where he bounces against the wall.

Red pulls the noose over his head and drops it on the floor.

Jez is on the bottom step, almost at him now.

Red pushes himself to his feet and waves the scalpel loosely in front of him.

'Back off, Jez.'

'Can't.'

'I'm not yours, Jez. I'm not coming with you.'

'You can't fight it, Red. You can't fight what you must be.'

Can't fight what you must be. The agent of divine will.

Can't fight what you are.

Jez wants to be one of us, but he doesn't dare. A devil who pretends to be on the side of the angels.

I wonder what it would feel like to kill you bite your nose off rip your ear clean away from your skull blood spurting miles in the air sounds as the life evaporates from you.

The snarl on Red's face flattens his words as he speaks.

'You . . . you have the fucking nerve to call *me* Judas.'

A momentum of rage is building in Red. It starts like a tidal wave way out at sea, invisible while it gathers pace and power, and then it rears up and pounds down on the breakwaters of Red's self-control.

His muscles are powered by the fury.

Can't hold it any more it's flooding through can't fucking hold it.

Jez is clutching his side again. He sucks air through teeth gritted against the pain.

Red hurls the scalpel across the floor and sets about Jez with his bare hands. His vengeance swarms through punching fists and kicking feet, like the fight in the pub but for real this time; for more than real, Jez is down on the floor now with explosions of light in his skull from blows to his head. There are dull thuds on his ribs and kidneys as he tries to roll into a ball, gasping in pain as a foot kicks hard in his testicles. The thorns prick on his forehead – pain pain so much pain through the blood leaking from his side woozy now light-headed spinning can't see anything . . .

The battering stops as abruptly as it started.

Jez lies on the ground and listens to Red's footsteps recede.

Silence.

Jez tries to move, but can't. Too weak. Broken bones somewhere in his body.

The carpet is soft against his cheek.

Footsteps – louder as they return.

Red hauls Jez roughly to his feet and pushes him back against the wall. Breathless agony as the broken bones protest.

One word in Jez's ear.

'Strip.'

Jez tries to reply through mushy lips.

'Can't. Can't . . . move. Broken.'

Jez sags against the wall as Red lets go of him and walks away.

Jez tries to open his eyes. His left eye is closed completely and the vision in his right is blurred through the pain and the blood.

But he can see what's on the floor a few feet away. What Red went upstairs to get.

A hammer and some nails. Alarm sounds through the wool in Jez's mind and pricks on his scalp and cheek, where the crown of thorns rests lopsidedly.

Red comes back. He has the scalpel in his hand.

Slash slash slash through the wet suit, until it lies in tatters on the floor around Jez's legs.

Jez is dressed just in his underpants now, like all his victims.

Red presses his face close to Jez's.

'You think you're the Messiah?'

Jez nods.

Red speaks again, flecking spittle onto Jez's face.

'Fine. Then you can fucking die like the Messiah.'

Red drags Jez over to the double doors which open from the kitchen into the living room. He pulls the doors shut. Then he grabs Jez's left arm and pulls it out to the side until it is parallel with the floor. Jez's hand touches the side of the door frame.

Nails won't go easily into plaster walls, but they will go into wooden door frames.

Red feels the tension on the skin of Jez's outstretched palm as he rests the head of a nail against it. He keeps the nail in place between the second and third fingers of his left hand, and draws the hammer back with his right.

He smacks the nail as hard as he can, and keeps on hitting all the way through Jez's hand, not stopping until the head of the nail has almost disappeared into the flesh of the palm.

Jez is screaming and screaming and screaming.

Red is silent as the grave, ruthless as he kills at last.

Two nails in the right palm. Left arm up until the left hand rests against the other side of the door frame. Two more nails in the left palm.

Cross Jez's ankles and hammer two more nails through them, splintering his Achilles tendons on their way through to the wood of the doors behind.

A man crucified with a crown of thorns on his head.

Words come brokenly through Jez's screams, hard to decipher at first but then becoming clearer.

'Eli, Eli, la'ma sabach-tha'ni? My God, my God, why hast thou forsaken me?'

Jez's chest strains tight with the effort of breathing. He looks up at his killer and gasps his last words.

'But all this has taken place, that the scriptures of the prophets might be fulfilled.'

Red is impassive as he leans forward and speaks.

'Then two robbers were crucified with him, one on the right and one on the left.'

He eases the crown of thorns off Jez's head.

'You're not the Son of Man, Jez. You're the piece of shit who died alongside him.'

The intercom squawks through the silence. Red walks across and picks it up.

'Hello?'

Kate's voice sounds loud and breathless in his ear.

'Red. It's Kate. What's going on?'

'Come on up,' he says, and pushes the button to let her in. She comes running up the stairs and stops dead when she sees him standing at the door.

'Jesus Christ, Red. You're covered in blood. What on earth happened? Where's Jez?'

He steps aside to let her through, and gives her a few minutes alone with the corpse of a man he knows she once loved. When he goes back inside, he finds her slumped against the kitchen wall. He slides down onto the floor next to her. She doesn't move, doesn't try to get away from him. She knows he must have done this to Jez, but equally she has seen what Jez has done; she can imagine what Red must have gone through in the agonising lifetime of these past few hours.

'I'm sorry, Kate,' he says. 'I didn't know it was him. I didn't *want* it to be him.'

She buries her head against his shoulder. He can feel her mouth move as she speaks.

'What happened?' she says.

He puts his arm around her and rests his cheek against the top of her head. It takes him a long time to answer.

'I'll tell you down at the station,' he says.

Friday, April 21st 2000

The watermark by the window of Red's prison cell is getting bigger.

He lies on his bed with his hands laced behind his head. Distant voices echo across the cavernous gangways outside, mingling with the thoughts which amble through his mind.

Good Friday today. More than a year since he walked into Paddington Green with Kate and turned himself in for the murder of Detective Inspector Jeremy Clifton, asking only that Kate should be allowed to sit in on his confession.

When the full story came out, he was visited by a raft of people, all of whom told him the same thing: you were acting in self-defence; you were dealing with a psychopath; you've done the public a massive service. Susan, Lubezski and even the Commissioner all came to see him, and they all left empty-handed. It made no difference whether they pleaded or cajoled or tried to bully him. Every single word they said fell on deaf ears.

Red's lawyer wanted him to plead not guilty, period. Red insisted on entering a plea of guilty, period. The lawyer changed tack again and again, looking at the options of pleas of temporary insanity or diminished responsibility. Red remained unmoved. Whichever angle his lawyer took, Red's stance remained the same: I wasn't temporarily insane, and my responsibility wasn't diminished. I killed in cold blood, and I knew exactly what I was doing.

The first cut is the deepest. The first killing is the hardest. After the first blood, it becomes easier and easier. Red has interviewed enough killers to know that.

He has done the hard part now, and he enjoyed it. This is

why he welcomes his life sentence. Because he *enjoyed* killing Jez. He runs the reel of his memories through his head again and again, and each time the sensation comes back with the same surging orgasmic intensity.

The power of life or death. Once given, never taken away. Once used, never reversible.

Red enjoyed it, and he knows it is evil. He has become what he despised.

The power of reason, the ability to distinguish between right and wrong, is what sets man apart from other primates. Red uses this reason while he still has it. He has faced the reality of himself, and it has faced him down. So he has ensured that he is somewhere where the madness can be confined.

It will destroy him, but he will not be able to destroy anyone else.

It is better that way.

Storm

Boris Starling

A storm-tossed crossing on the North Sea; a catastrophic ferry accident; hundreds dead. DCI Kate Beauchamp is one of the survivors but her ferocious fight to stay alive brings with it a high cost: a burden of guilt that she should live while some of her friends died; a terror of water; a frozen inner core that never seems to melt.

Hoping to exorcize her demons, Kate insists on leading the hunt for a brutal murderer who has left a unique calling card on his victim's body: a poisonous snake.

Into this emotional cauldron steps the last man on earth Kate wants to see – her estranged father, Frank, in Aberdeen to conduct the marine inquiry into the sinking.

In a sweltering heatwave, Kate and Frank conduct their highly pressured investigations. But for both of them, danger is approaching fast - a vortex of violence which will sweep them up and endanger their very lives.

Elemental rage, bloody Greek myth, man's capacity for cruelty, the insane imaginings of a killer, all intermingle in *Storm* to create a novel of stunning ferocity.

'A furious, compelling and enjoyable read.' *Maxim*

0 00 651205 4